A mad
attacked her from all sides. . . .

Not only hadn't she imagined such a sensation, she hadn't even thought about it. The scent of him, the feel of his body molded against her own, the moist fullness of his mouth claiming hers, and his warm breath caressing her cheek made her heart lurch in her chest and her blood pound through her veins.

If this was heaven, she wanted to die right then. . . .

Praise for DEFY THE THUNDER:

"A richly moving novel . . . A captivating tale that is thoroughly entertaining. This is a top-notch read!"

—Sylvie Sommerfield,
bestselling author of
Passion's Raging Storm

Jove titles by Kay McMahon

BETRAY THE NIGHT
DEFY THE THUNDER

BETRAY THE NIGHT

KAY McMAHON

J

JOVE BOOKS, NEW YORK

BETRAY THE NIGHT

A Jove Book / published by arrangement with
the author

PRINTING HISTORY
Jove edition / November 1991

For information address: The Berkley Publishing Group,
200 Madison Avenue, New York, New York 10016.

ISBN: 0-515-10727-1

Jove Books are published by The Berkley Publishing Group,
200 Madison Avenue, New York, New York 10016.

PRINTED IN THE UNITED STATES OF AMERICA

10 9 8 7 6 5 4 3 2 1

For you, Karen Litscher

CHAPTER 1

January 1845
London, England

"Satan, get down from there," Catherine Chase ordered, once she had glanced up from the book she was reading to find the huge black tomcat strolling across her cluttered desk. When the command went unheeded, she clutched the volume against her chest, rose halfway out of her chair and leaned over a stack of papers to give the cat a shove. "It's hard enough for me to concentrate without you walking all over my notes."

The flick of his long, silky tail so much as told her that he was either immune to the scolding he'd received or that he was beyond fear of any physical retribution she might bestow upon him. He'd been a member of the household for more than six years now, and the young woman, who fed him table scraps and showered him with affection, had yet to strike him out of anger. The day Satan had sought refuge from the rain and had perched himself on the window ledge outside Catherine's bedroom had been the luckiest day of his life, for not only had he found himself a warm place to sleep, but the guarantee he would never go hungry again. All he had to do in return was tolerate a hug now and then. And right now, he wasn't in the mood as he swished his tail and sauntered from the room.

Warm blue eyes watched the regal exit of the feline from

over the top of gold wire-rimmed spectacles, and a hint of a smile curved Catherine's mouth before she settled herself back down with her book. Since her father's death eight weeks ago, she had busied herself with her detective work, accepting one case right after another in the hope that missing him wouldn't take over her life. She had succeeded for the most part, except at night when she'd retire and sleep wouldn't come as easily as she wanted. She'd lie awake for hours staring up at the ceiling and asking herself how she would go on without him. Then she'd remember his smile, his laughter, and his lectures.

"There isn't enough time in your life to allow one second of it to be wasted feeling sorry for yourself," he would tell her whenever he found her sulking over something that hadn't gone her way. "Put that energy to good use."

Catherine had never really understood what that meant until the accident, which claimed his life and left her all alone, forced her to think about it. He had been trying to tell her that drowning herself in her sorrow was unproductive and that the only way she could overcome her grief was to keep busy. After all, wasn't that what he had done after her mother died?

The slap of the shutters against the house startled Catherine and drew her attention to the window. The sun had disappeared shortly after breakfast, and a windy rainstorm threatened to erupt at any second. But it wasn't the distant thunder or even the wind that had so abruptly changed her frame of mind and made her body tremble. It had been the loud crack of wood against stone that shook the steel-nerved Catherine. It had sounded like gunfire, an explosive noise that hurled her back in time to when she was a child of six.

Catherine's memory of her mother was limited, but the one thing that always came to mind was Vivian's loving nature and how she doted on her only child. She always called Catherine her "little angel," and even though Vivian did everything for her daughter, Catherine wasn't spoiled. When her mother died, Catherine's world had shattered.

Although she was married to the renowned Professor Sterling Lloyd Chase of Oxford University, Vivian had her own identity. She was personable, polite, well mannered, highly respected for her honesty and unwavering loyalty, and extremely friendly to anyone with whom she came in contact. And many said young Catherine got her beauty from her mother, for Vivian was a tall, shapely woman with pale blond hair and bright blue eyes. Many of those same people claimed Vivian's devotion to her friends was what got her killed. Sterling never agreed. And Catherine blamed herself.

Although the Chases had a second home in London, they lived most of the year in Oxford so that Sterling could be close to the university and to his work. Their neighbors to the left of them were an English professor and his wife, who were quite a bit older than Sterling and Vivian, with grown children of their own. To their right lived a childless couple, whose days seemed filled with bitterness and anger. Alice and Jimmy fought constantly, and Catherine could remember all the times Alice had come crying to her mother and how Vivian would comfort her and tell her everything would be all right. And it usually was, except for one particularly bleak January morning.

Catherine's father had already left for the university and she and her mother were preparing to go for their morning walk, when Alice came bursting into the house screaming at the top of her lungs. Frightened, Catherine had hidden herself beside the credenza in the foyer, while her mother gathered Alice in her arms and tried to calm her down. The young woman kept saying that Jimmy was going to kill her and that he'd claimed she was having an affair. Catherine hadn't understood what Alice meant, but she instinctively recognized Alice's terror, and a second later Jimmy appeared in the doorway. Catherine couldn't remember what was said or from where the pistol had come that had appeared suddenly in Jimmy's hand, and the vision of her mother was always blurred whenever she tried to recall exactly what happened after that. The one distinct memory she had, however, was the sound of gunfire, a scream, and how her mother's body had fallen to the floor like a rag doll.

It had taken six months and a lot of love and coaxing

from her father before Catherine even spoke a word. She was thirteen before she was able to talk about that awful day. And now, once a year, around the anniversary of her mother's death, Catherine unwillingly relived the event all over again when a certain sound triggered the nightmare.

A loud boom of thunder rattled the house and jarred Catherine from her thoughts. Pulling the spectacles from her nose, she glanced up and saw the rain beating against the windowpanes. She loved storms with all their fury and noise, but tonight she hardly noticed how the trees rocked back and forth in the wind. She was still mulling over the same old idea that if that little girl hiding beside the credenza had only made her presence known that day, her mother would still be alive. Depressed, Catherine left her chair to find her piccolo, realizing there was nothing she could do to change the past. She could, however, soothe the ache in her heart by playing her mother's favorite song.

She had just finished executing the first movement and was about to begin the second, when she sensed someone was watching her. Turning, she saw Mr. Trumble, her father's butler, valet, and friend of thirty years, standing in the doorway with a silver tray holding a glass of milk balanced in one hand.

"Excuse me, Miss Catherine," he said in his usual straitlaced manner, "but I thought you might be wanting something warm to drink."

She hated warm milk, but for as long as she could remember, it was what Mr. Trumble had used as an excuse to check up on her whenever he worried she had been left alone too long. This time he was right, and she was grateful.

"Thank you, Mr. Trumble," she replied, laying aside her piccolo as she came to meet him and take the glass from the tray. "Sounds as though we're in for a noisy time of it, wouldn't you say?" She nodded toward the window and the storm outside when he seemed not to understand, took a sip of the milk, and returned to her desk, amazed at how much better she felt already.

"Yes, miss," he agreed, tucking the tray under his arm.

He watched her for a minute while she loosened the ribbon in her strawberry-blond hair, gathered up a stray curl, and retied the silky mane back from her face. Arriving at that precise moment hadn't been an accident on his part. He'd heard the high-pitched tone of the piccolo and he'd recognized the song. He also knew it meant Miss Catherine was caught in the memories of her mother's tragic death again, a ritual that always occurred this time of year, and although he doubted hot milk would chase away the bad images, he was sure his presence would distract her. Engaging her in conversation would do the rest.

"Will you be dining in this evening, Miss Catherine?" he asked, his soft green eyes raking in the sight of her as she readjusted the white cotton frock coat she always wore over her clothes. Her father had donned such garb whenever he was working on a project, and since father and daughter were so much alike, it seemed only natural that she would dress in the same manner. It didn't, however, add to her femininity, something about which Catherine Chase obviously didn't care. She hardly ever wore shoes in the house or fixed her hair in the latest Paris fashion, and bonnets were out of the question. Who had time for such nonsense? she would say, and Mr. Trumble always had to bite his tongue. How would she ever catch the eye of some young, available gentleman behaving the way she did? One look at her and she'd scare him off. A man didn't want a wife who was smarter than he was. Women were supposed to be soft and beautiful, and think only about pleasing their husbands and raising their children. Miss Catherine didn't fit into that category. Oh, she was beautiful, but all she cared about was solving a mystery or catching thieves, not a husband.

"It depends, Mr. Trumble," she answered, drawing him away from his thoughts.

"On what, miss?" he politely inquired.

She took another sip of milk, set down the glass, and reached for the book that had fallen to the floor. A moment or two passed as though she had drifted off into another world, and he had to clear his throat to bring her back again.

"On Preston," she advised, putting on her eyeglasses

again and thumbing through the pages in the book for the spot where she had been reading.

Phillip Preston was a thirteen-year-old street urchin, whom Mr. Trumble neither liked nor trusted. Miss Catherine was forever hiring the boy to ask questions she herself could not ask, and every time he sent word to the house that he'd stumbled across something, it meant Mr. Trumble would have to harness up the carriage and drive Miss Catherine to some unsavory part of town. He would never complain outright for the simple reason that she would go without him if he raised too big a fuss, but it didn't stop him from grumbling a little each time it happened.

"I take it to mean you're close to solving this one?" he commented, his nose held loftily in the air.

Catherine shrugged a shoulder and continued to browse through the pages of her book. Mr. Trumble always had an opinion, and even though she loved him dearly, his advice rarely helped solve anything, for the trick came in looking beyond the obvious, and Mr. Trumble never took the time to do that.

"If you were to ask me," he began, and Catherine hid her smile, "whoever stole the paintings would have left London by now. If he's smart enough to get into the British Museum after closing time, he's smart enough to know he'd have to take the artworks elsewhere to sell them."

Catherine pulled the glasses from her nose and set down the book. "That's exactly what Scotland Yard thinks, Mr. Trumble," she told him as she left her chair and crossed to one of the bookcases on the far wall. "I happen to disagree."

"May I ask why, miss?"

She rummaged through one of many boxes on the floor, found what she was looking for, and turned with it in her hand. "Take a look at this and tell me what you see," she instructed, handing him the article.

A puzzled frown drew his snow-white brows together. "It's a piece of cloth, Miss Catherine."

"What else?"

He failed to see the importance of her question, but since

she had been able to solve a lot of cases Scotland Yard could not, he would yield to her better judgment. "It's soiled and torn. There's a tiny hole in the middle of it. It's cotton . . . of a homespun variety." He turned it over in his hand and studied it a bit longer. Finally, he shook his head and gave the scrap of cloth back to her. "Is there more?"

Catherine smiled, pleased that he had noticed every detail. "Not on the surface, Mr. Trumble," she said. "That's all this is . . . a torn piece of soiled homespun cotton with a hole in it. However . . ." She returned the sample to the box and sat down in her chair again. "What would you say if I told you that I'd found the remnant on the ground beneath the window where the thieves had gained entrance into the museum?"

"*Thieves,* miss?" he interjected. "How do you know there was more than one?"

"By the size of the paintings they took. Several of them were too large for one man to carry all by himself," she informed him. "Now, what about the cloth?"

He thought about the information for a moment, then shook his head.

"Come on, Mr. Trumble, think harder," she encouraged, certain if he did, he'd discover her point.

He tried again. Several moments passed while he rubbed his chin and contemplated every angle. Then, almost as if someone had whispered the answer in his ear, he straightened his tall, thin frame and smiled, his green eyes glowing.

"By Jove, I think I've got it!" he proudly exclaimed. "The torn edges clearly mean the piece came from a larger section . . . a shirt, possibly. And a poor man's shirt by the quality, not to mention a dirty beggar by the stains on it. The hole is about the size of a nail head, which in all likelihood was the culprit in damaging the cloth, and since it was found at the scene of the crime, there's a good chance it belongs to the thief. Find the shirt and you'll find your man." Quite sure of himself, a broad smile lit up his lined face, until the vision of the stone building that housed the many works of art came to mind and spoiled his conclusion. "And then again, maybe I don't," he added, the frown returning and disappointment heavy in his tone. "The museum is made of stone, not boards and nails. Where would he have snagged the shirt?"

"On a crate," Catherine supplied.

"Of course!" he agreed. "On a crate." His enthusiasm was short-lived. "A crate?" he questioned.

"Well, you don't think the thieves would run down the alley with the paintings tucked under their arms, do you? Especially not something as valuable as what they took. They would have packed them in crates, not only to safeguard them, but to hide the merchandise before they loaded them into a wagon. And crates are made of boards and nails."

Mr. Trumble digested the theory, silently saw the logic in it, then raised his own supposition. "Which brings us back to the beginning. Why are you in discord with Scotland Yard?"

"It's quite simple, really. The thieves didn't take the first paintings they could lay their hands on. They took the most valuable. Meaning they knew what they were after."

"How could a couple of cadgers know that, Miss Catherine?" he mocked. "It had to have been a coincidence."

"Or someone told them what to take."

Forgetting his place, Mr. Trumble came all the way into the room and sat down in the chair beside her desk. "But that implies someone of means is behind the robbery."

Catherine bobbed her head and smiled impishly at him. "Precisely, Mr. Trumble. And that someone had to have visited the museum often enough to know where the paintings hung so that he could pass on the information to his cohorts."

"Good Lord, Miss Catherine," he murmured, stunned.

"It's also my theory that the gentleman intends to sell the paintings as soon as he possibly can." The serious look came over her face again as she settled the spectacles on her nose and picked up the book to reread a certain page. "If he hasn't already," she mumbled.

Overwhelmed by the workings of the young woman's

mind, Mr. Trumble failed to realize that she had dismissed their conversation for something more important as he ventured on to ask, "But what about the Preston boy? What have you hired him to do?"

When she didn't answer him, he suddenly noticed where he sat and that Miss Catherine's attention was off somewhere else. Jerking to his feet, he straightened his coat, then his shoulders, and raised his chin in the air. No one had to tell *him* when it was time to leave. After all, he'd only come here to get her mind off the past, and he'd obviously succeeded. He wasn't interested in helping her solve a case, and he certainly didn't care where that dirty ragamuffin spent his time.

At the doorway, he paused to glance back at the young woman bent over her work, and he sighed once he noticed the clutter surrounding her. Even though a housekeeper came in once a week to clean, Catherine would never allow Mrs. Tibbs to apply her talents to the study. What Mr. Trumble viewed as disorder, Catherine claimed was necessary. If Mrs. Tibbs put all the books back on their shelves, gathered the papers strewn about the desk and floor and on chair seats and end tables in one neat pile, and tossed out what the woman called junk, Catherine would be lost. She needed everything to stay right where it was if she was to do her job efficiently. Besides, Catherine didn't mind the dust. So why should it bother anyone else? she had often asked him. The parlor downstairs was for entertaining, not her study, and if he didn't like the mess, he shouldn't look.

How could I not? he thought, noticing that her breakfast tray was still sitting on the floor next to the settee where she had obviously put it. A blanket hung haphazardly draped over the back of the piece of furniture, and her shoes were shoved halfway underneath the tea table. Her behavior amazed him, for he had always assumed that once a little girl grew into a woman, her natural traits for neatness surfaced. They hadn't with Catherine Chase. She never saw the litter in which she lived and worked, and whenever he'd point it out to her, she'd argue that putting it all away would be a waste of time, since she'd only have to get it out again.

What a shame, he thought, his shoulders drooping. *Should a gentleman happen to show an interest in her, she'll be too busy analyzing a scrap of cloth to notice.* He sighed again, shook his head, and left the room.

Phillip Preston shivered in the darkness. He was soaked to the bone, and he could feel a sneeze coming on. Gritting his teeth, he pinched his nose and held his breath, waiting for it to pass as he huddled against the rain barrel in the alleyway. If he got caught, they'd club him over the head and toss him in the Thames, and no one would miss him. No one except Miss Chase, and he didn't want to disappoint her. She was counting on him.

As always, Miss Chase had elected not to give Preston all the details of the case she was working on, and he could only assume it was because she felt it was a way of protecting him from harm. The idea made him smile, since every aspect of his life put him at risk in some fashion or another, but Miss Chase didn't know that, and that was what he liked about her. She was smart and pretty, and very naïve in that respect, and even though she was quite a bit older than he, it was his dream that someday he'd court her in the manner she should be courted. In his opinion they'd make a perfect couple; he could do the investigating, and she'd do all the brain work.

A noise near the closed doors of the stable bristled the hairs on the back of Preston's neck. His assignment this time had been simple. All he'd had to do was find a wagon whose rear left wheel had a nick in it. Catherine had drawn him a sketch, scaled to size, for him to use once he'd found a possibility, and although it had taken him a couple of days to track down, the suggestion she had given him not to look for the wagon out in the open had cut the search by half the time. The danger came in not letting anyone know of his interest in their property, and so far he'd been successful. As a street urchin it wasn't uncommon for someone like him to seek shelter for the night inside, out of the cold and the rain, and a stable was one of the best choices. For Preston it had a double purpose, but before he'd been able to compare his drawing up close with the nick in the wagon wheel, the men who owned the wagon had returned and had thrown him outside in the alley. If they discovered that he was still hanging around, they'd get suspicious and probably kill him, rather than ask any questions. Men of their sort usually did. Therefore, if Preston was to finish his task, he had to get back inside the building.

"Excuse me, Miss Catherine," Mr. Trumble apologized, a displeased expression wrinkling up his face as he stood in the opened study doorway waiting for her to look up from her work.

Several moments passed before she obliged him. "What is it, Mr. Trumble?" she asked, taking the spectacles from her nose.

"Mr. Preston has arrived, miss. He's in the kitchen having a cup of hot tea and something to eat. He asked that I inform you of his presence."

Catherine could tell by the tone of Mr. Trumble's voice that the conversation between the boy and the older gentleman hadn't been as pleasant as Mr. Trumble made it sound. The two of them were forever at odds with each other, and Catherine could only blame it on the fact that they had never taken the time to get to know each other. Granted, Phillip Preston lacked manners, but she had always found his crudeness amusing. Mr. Trumble didn't, and once he'd seen the boy to the door, her father's companion and servant of more than three decades would return to the kitchen to count the silverware.

"Has he news for me?" she asked, slipping out of the white frock coat as she stood.

"He didn't say, miss," Mr. Trumble replied. "He seemed more interested in eating."

"That's probably because he hasn't had anything all day," she lightly rebuked.

Mr. Trumble's mouth twitched. "Well, at least he's had a bath," he mumbled, turning away.

Catherine took a breath to criticize the man's shortage of compassion and changed her mind. Nothing she could say would reverse Mr. Trumble's feelings for the boy. He'd have to do that on his own.

"Good evening, Phillip," she greeted a few minutes later as she entered the kitchen and found him hunched over the table and gobbling up every bite of food on his plate.

"Evenin'," Phillip answered with a wave of his fork as he reached for the cup of tea sitting in front of him. He took a swallow, set the cup back down, and helped himself to a second slice of bread to mop up the gravy on his plate. "I found it," he said between mouthfuls.

"You did? Where?" she asked excitedly as she pulled out a chair and sat down opposite him.

"In a stable, like ye said, just off Cleveland Street at Foley."

"That's close to the museum," she observed aloud.

"Aye, mum, it is," Preston agreed. "Does it make a difference?"

Catherine shook her head. Phillip didn't need to know. "Did anyone see you?"

He popped the last wad of bread in his mouth, chewed it a couple of times and swallowed. "Sort of."

Catherine frowned. "Sort of? What do you mean?"

"Well, there weren't nobody in the stable at first, so I went in. But before I could 'ave meself a look-see, two blokes came in and tossed me out on me ear." He wiped his mouth with the back of his hand, and added, "They thought I was just lookin' for some place ter sleep, so they paid me no never-mind after that. I 'id meself just outside the doors where I could listen, plannin' ter go back in once they'd left." He took another sip of his tea. "Ye got somethin' stronger ye can put in this?" he asked, holding out the cup.

"In another five or six years, I might. But not now," she firmly told him.

Preston didn't like her insinuation that he was too young for a touch of the spirits, and he opened his mouth to tell her that he'd been having his share of gin for a long time now, only to snap it shut again when she gave him a warning scowl. "Ye act like me mother," he grumbled, roughly setting the cup in its saucer. "Next ye'll be telling me it's time ter change me clothes."

Catherine looked him up and down. His red hair was matted to his head, and she could see where the rain had washed away some of the smudges from his freckled face. As for his clothes . . . "Well, they are a little dirty," she said with a smile.

"Not no more, they ain't," he jeered. "I got caught in the rain on account o' ye." He sniffed and rubbed a finger under his nose. "And I probably caught me death, too."

"I doubt it, Phillip," she argued, knowing that if he set his mind to it, *nothing* would catch him. "But if you're worried, I could have Mr. Trumble give you a teaspoon of his special elixir."

Phillip's eyes narrowed. He'd had a taste of someone's elixir before, and even though it had a touch of spirits in it, it still tasted horrible. "No thanks, mum," he declined. "If ye'll pay me what ye owe, I'll be on me way."

Slipping her hand into the pocket of her dress, she withdrew a gold coin and handed it to him. "Why not spend that on a nice, warm room for the night? You've already had something to eat."

"I'd like ter, mum," he said, rising, "but I 'ave ter eat again tomorrow, ye know." He started for the door and paused when an idea came to mind. "If ye're really concerned about me 'ealth, ye could give me another one o' these." He flipped the coin and caught it in midair.

"Oh?" she queried, smiling. "And are you planning to do something to earn it?"

Phillip shrugged. "I just figured ye'd be interested in learnin' what I 'eard while I was 'idin' in the alleyway."

Catherine's brow twitched. Of course she was interested in anything that had to do with the robbery. She just couldn't be sure Phillip had anything important to say. "It depends," she confessed.

Preston peered back at her through half-closed eyes. "On what?"

"On what you think you overheard."

If it had been anyone else making the comment, Phillip

would have been insulted. "Well, it made no sense ter me, since ye weren't of a mind ter tell me what those men 'ad done."

Catherine recognized his tone of injured pride. "It's for your own protection, Phillip, and nothing more. You know that. Now tell me what you heard, and I'll give you another coin whether it's useful information or not."

Money always meant more to Phillip Preston than his dignity, especially since he didn't have much of either one, and he smiled, very willing to recite every word of the strangers' conversation. "They're meeting someone . . . someone important by the sound o' it."

Catherine straightened in her chair. "When?"

"Tonight."

"Did they happen to say where?"

Preston raised his nose in the air, refusing to say more until he was paid.

"Phillip, this is no time for games," Catherine snapped as she bolted to her feet. "Where are they meeting?"

"Blimey, Miss Catherine. Ye don't 'ave ter—"

"*Where,* Phillip!"

"At the stable, mum," he quickly answered. " 'Round ten, it be. But ye're not thinkin' of goin' there yerself, are ye?" Miss Chase might never have confided in him, but it didn't take a genius to know that the men at the livery were dangerous, and Preston wished now that he'd kept his mouth shut. If he hadn't gotten greedy, she wouldn't be planning on going out this evening.

"Wait here," she instructed, brushing past him on her way out of the kitchen. A few minutes later she returned, handed him a another coin, thanked him for his help, and asked if he wouldn't mind seeing himself to the door. Before he could answer, she had left him again.

A light drizzle dampened the streets of London and anyone who ventured out in it. Inside her hansom cab, Catherine was quite warm and dry. Mr. Trumble, on the contrary, suffered the effects of the biting mist as he snapped the reins and guided the rig in the direction Miss

Catherine had instructed. He'd voiced his displeasure and his concern over his mistress's decision to leave the comfort of her home in his usual grumbling manner, but to no avail, and since he wouldn't trust Miss Catherine's safety to anyone else, he had harnessed the horse and had drawn the rig up to the sidewalk in front of the town house despite his own objections. She hadn't told him and he hadn't asked what awaited them at the end of their journey, but he suspected it had to do with Phillip Preston's visit, since it always seemed they took such a trip after the boy had spoken with her. However, this time Mr. Trumble had come prepared. He had loaded the carriage pistol and had it hidden under the seat where he rode, knowing that if the worst happened and Miss Catherine's life was put in danger, he wouldn't hesitate to use it.

Slight though it was, Mr. Trumble took comfort in the knowledge that this particular ride had a positive side to it. Instead of heading toward the river and the less respectable part of town, they were moving away from it. He had assumed the necessity of the trip—especially at this time of night—had been because of the case on which Miss Catherine was working. Now he wasn't so sure, though he couldn't imagine what other purpose was being served, and once they had neared the corner where Foley intersected with Cleveland Street, he pulled the hansom cab to a halt and opened the trapdoor on the roof in front of him.

"Do you wish for me to turn onto Foley Street, miss?" he asked, peering down at the top of her head.

"No, Mr. Trumble," she replied without looking at him. "Here will do just fine."

"Here, miss?" He glanced around, seeing only a row of houses on either side of the street and that very few had any light shining through their windows. He felt the rig bounce a little as its passenger descended to the sidewalk, and he hurriedly set the brake and tied off the reins, certain she would want him to escort her. "Miss?" he called, once he noticed that she was already several steps ahead of him. "Miss, shall I accompany you?"

The fullness of the dark, hooded cape she wore billowed

out around her when she stopped and turned back to look at him. "No, Mr. Trumble. I'd prefer you wait here for me. If I'm not back in . . ." She thought about it for a second, then advised, "One hour, drive into the alley behind Foley Street. I should be just around the corner."

"But, Miss Catherine," he objected, not at all pleased with the sound of it.

The wave of her hand as she turned her back on him ended any discussion they might have had, and Mr. Trumble begrudgingly pulled his watch from his pocket and checked the time. He'd give her only until ten-thirty, and then he'd come looking for her.

Catherine could hear a dog barking in the distance, but other than that, the streets were deathly quiet. Had she been a typical female, the eeriness that surrounded the night and the fact that she was alone and very possibly walking into danger would have frightened her. Such was not the case. She was simply too intent on catching the robbers *and* the man who hired them for any of it to scare her. At the corner, she stepped off the curb, crossed Foley Street, and continued down Cleveland, until she came to the alleyway where Phillip had said he had found the wagon. Pausing for only a moment to make certain she wouldn't be walking headlong into something, she felt a rush of excitement shoot through her when she realized how close she was to proving Scotland Yard wrong . . . again. Just as soon as she had all the facts and a list of names, she'd march into the commissioner's office and dump it all in his lap. The man would think twice next time before he laughed at the idea that one woman was smarter than his entire police force.

Midway down the narrow back street where only one rig could pass at a time, she noticed light coming from behind a partially closed stable door. Slowing her step, she moved cautiously, listening for voices or any other clue that would warn her in time of someone's approach. Drawing near the entrance, she stopped, wondering if the man the robbers were to meet was already inside and just how close she should risk it. From this distance she wouldn't hear a thing they said, and the light rain would mean the stranger would probably have his cape pulled up high around his neck and his hat down over his brow, preventing her from seeing his face. Yet, if she stood too near the door . . .

The right to make a sensible and logical decision was taken from her when the clip-clop of horse's hooves and the rattling of carriage wheels from in back of her disturbed the quiet, and a quick glance all around her revealed no recessed doorways or any other kind of alcove in which she could hide other than that of the half-open stable doors. The fleeting thought that she was making a dreadful mistake tickled the hairs on the back of her neck as she hurried forward, stole a peek inside to find the haven safe—at least temporarily—and dashed through the aperture just as the approaching rig rounded the corner and headed down the alleyway toward her.

The thump of a gold-handled cane against the roof of the hansom cab signaled the driver to stop. Shiny black shoes stepped to the cobblestone street, and the swish of the man's cape swirled the heavy mist out of his way as he moved to enter the stable. Once inside, he took the silk top hat from his head, the dark gray gloves from his hands, and laid them both beside his cane on the seat of the wagon as he walked by on his way to the rear of the rig and the crates he saw stored there. Finding them nailed shut, he looked around for something with which to pry them open, completely unaware of the wide blue eyes studying his every move.

The light from a single lantern hanging from the rafters cast long shadows about the stable. From her hiding place behind a stack of wooden boxes, Catherine watched the stranger and marveled at the odd sensation that warmed her insides. She had never seen a man as handsome as this one or as finely dressed, and she wondered if he had traveled a great distance to get here or if he lived in a mansion somewhere close by. His black hair shone in the pale light, and his jaw was rugged and lean. His eyes were such a dark brown that she was sure if he looked at her, she would see her reflection in them. There was an air of nobility about him, while at the same time a hint of recklessness, indicating that perhaps he wore the elegant clothes only to suit society. He was tall and muscular and seemed oddly out of place in this den of thieves. Yet, here he was, and that was all she really needed to know about him . . . except, perhaps, his name.

The door at the back of the stable creaked, then swung inward, and the man turned, his body rigid as if he were prepared to defend himself. A second later, two others joined him, and he relaxed his stance, obviously having recognized the pair.

"Had I been of a mind to," he growled at them, "I could have hitched up a horse and driven off with the wagon." He jerked his dark head toward the entrance he had used. "The least you could have done was bar the doors."

"Sorry, gov'na," the shortest of the two responded. "But we didn't want ye to think we changed our minds. We was only plannin' ter be gone a second or two." He nodded at his companion. "'Arry 'ad ter use the privy, and me, well—"

"Save your excuses," the tall one barked, motioning toward the crates. "Show me what you've got, and I'll decide if they're worth buying."

The two thieves hustled about and within minutes the first of the crates was opened and the painting held up for their customer to see.

I knew it, Catherine silently declared, once she recognized the work of art. *I knew the paintings were still in London. Now all I have to do—*

A rustling noise beside her in the straw absently pulled her attention to it. She saw the oversized rat, thought nothing of it, and glanced back at the men. A second later, a chill raised gooseflesh on the back of her arms, and she started, her body naturally recoiling at the delayed discovery of how close she was to the huge rodent. In turn, she bumped one of the boxes that shielded her presence from the gang of thieves, creating just enough noise to alert them.

"What's this?" the one named Harry said as he stepped around his companion and started toward the spot where Catherine hid.

Instantly recognizing the danger she was in, Catherine

bolted for the door. But long before she had reached it, her arm was seized and she was jerked back around. An ugly, pockmarked face loomed close, and just as she was about to tread heavily on the instep of the man's foot, a huge fist came up and struck her squarely in the jaw, snapping her head to one side and plummeting her into unconsciousness.

"The nosy wench," Harry growled, pulling the pistol from his waistband. "I'll teach 'er ter snoop where she ain't wanted."

"No, you fool!" the stranger shouted. "Fire that thing and we'll have all of Scotland Yard down our necks."

"But she saw us, gov'na. She knows who we are and that we stole the paintin's. We can't let 'er go."

"I have no intention of letting her go," the dark one admitted angrily as he scooped up his gloves and hat and put them on. "I'll take her to a secluded spot outside of town and then dispose of her. You two wait here." Bending, he easily swept the unconscious woman up in his arms. "And see that these doors are locked behind me. Your carelessness is what let her in." He glared at the pair one last time, before he turned and disappeared into the darkness.

CHAPTER 2

Dark brown eyes, their color intense with anger, stared across the room at the slight form lying on the bed. Soft curls of luscious strawberry-blond hair caught the red-gold light of the fire in the hearth and glowed with a brilliance of their own. Black lashes lay against alabaster skin, marred only by a slight pink flush in her cheeks and the ugly, dark bruise on her delicate jaw. The young woman's identity was unknown to him, though at the moment it really didn't matter. Her reason for being in the stable did. Had he not reacted quickly enough, she would have been dead now, and he'd have had that on his conscience.

Pushing away from the fireplace where he had stood with his arm laid along the mantel, T. J. Savage wandered aimlessly about the room, deep in thought, until he came full circle and decided to sit down in one of the wing chairs by the crackling blaze. Leaning back, he crossed an ankle over his knee, rested his elbows on the arms of the chair, and tapped his fingertips together in church-steeple fashion, while his gaze fell on the young woman again. It was quite possible that she had stepped inside the stable merely to get in out of the rain, but instinct warned otherwise. Although her clothes were not made of silk with a lot of satin ribbons and lace trim that spoke of wealth, their style indicated a more conservative kind of woman, rather than a harlot or someone down on her luck. Yet, none of that explained what she was doing in the stable or why she was out at night alone. The only hansom cab he could remember seeing had been stationed more than a block away, which either meant that it wasn't hers or that she had ordered the driver to wait a good distance away while she snooped. The muscle in his jaw flexed with the thought, and in a burst of renewed anger, he shoved himself out of the chair and went to the balcony doors, where he stood glaring out into the night with his arms crossed over his chest.

T. J. Savage had returned to London only a week earlier after a twenty-year absence and in a very different financial and emotional state from when he'd left as a boy of a half score and two. His mother, a laundry woman, had never married his father, and at one time she even admitted she wasn't sure which of the sailors from the American Navy ship had sired her son. T.J. never cared since they were perfectly happy without him . . . poor, but happy. He loved his mother very much, and he'd vowed one day when he was old enough, he'd earn the money it took to feed and clothe them so that she would never have to take in laundry ever again. Then she got sick and died two days before T.J.'s tenth birthday, and he was tossed out in the streets to fend for himself. Scared and alone, he had had to resort to stealing just to have something to eat. He was kicked and shoved, yelled at and slapped, and one time someone tried to shoot him. Within two short years, the hard life he was forced to live had turned him into a bitter and angry young boy. Then he met Christian Page.

A soft rap on the door broke into his thoughts. Turning, he glanced briefly at the beautiful young woman, who still hadn't regained consciousness, and crossed the room. Certain he knew who stood on the other side, he freed the latch and swung the door quietly inward as he swept out one hand and silently gave permission for Mrs. Witton to enter.

"Still 'asn't come around, 'as she?" the elderly woman inquired with a frown as she carried a bowl full of warm water and salts, and a cup of hot tea to the nightstand. "The poor thing. The scoundrel must 'ave 'it 'er awfully 'ard." She gave her companion a stern look. "Ye did call 'im out, didn't ye, sir?"

T.J. ignored the question as he gave the door a shove and went back to sit down in the chair again.

"Well, ye should 'ave, sir," Mrs. Witton continued with a short bob of her head as she dipped a cloth in the water and then wrung it out. "Imagine. 'Ittin' a woman." She clucked her tongue and shook her head disapprovingly as she tenderly dabbed the damp cloth against her patient's jaw, and asked, " 'Ave ye any idea 'oo she is, sir?"

"None," T.J. replied, resting his chin on one fist as he stared at the flames in the hearth. "I was hoping maybe you'd know her."

Hertha Witton straightened and cocked her head from one side to the other, closely studying the woman's face. "Sorry, sir. I've never seen 'er before. But I could ask around for ye, if ye want."

T.J. shook his head. "That won't be necessary, Hertha," he said, glancing over at the young lady who hadn't moved an inch or uttered a sound since he carried her into the house and laid her on the bed. "She'll come around before long, and then all I'll have to do is ask her myself."

Even as he spoke, his guest began to stir. Rising, T.J. told Hertha to leave the room and to close the door behind her on her way out. He needed the privacy to find out why the young woman had been in the stable and to point out how stupid she'd been, and he didn't intend to be polite when he asked. Whether she'd been there on purpose or by accident, he planned to scare her so badly that she'd never make that kind of mistake again. But with the housekeeper listening to every word, T.J. doubted Hertha would allow him the chance. He had only known the gray-haired lady for a week, but in that short span of time, T.J. had come to recognize the housekeeper's most apparent trait; she was sympathetic to just about everyone. If she were allowed to remain in the room, the instant T.J.'s manner grew harsh, Hertha would more than likely intervene and ruin everything. There was a time and place for kindness, and so far as T.J. was concerned, it wasn't now.

"But sir," Hertha objected when she refused to go of her

own free will, and he took her elbow and firmly guided her toward the exit. "It isn't proper—"

"It wouldn't be the first time I've been accused of being improper, Hertha. Just look at it this way; what this young lady did tonight wasn't very proper either, so I would imagine finding herself alone in a room with a man won't upset her all that much." He smiled lamely at her as he grabbed the edge of the door and slowly began to close it behind her, adding, "I'll ring if I need anything else. Good night, Hertha."

The latch clicking shut ended their discussion.

The dark shadows of a heavy sleep slowly lifted, and Catherine's world began to grow. It started with the taste of blood in her mouth where her teeth had dug into the flesh of her cheek. Close behind that came a dull ache that stretched from her chin to the joint beneath her ear. The smell of a warm fire filled her nostrils, and the sound of the crackling blaze made her think of home and of the black cat who always curled up at the bottom of her bed. Wiggling her toes in an effort to find his furry backside, she realized that she was lying on top of the covers instead of underneath them. The discovery didn't surprise her, since there had been plenty of times when she had gone to bed without changing into her nightclothes, but there was something startlingly different about it this time. Suddenly the sights and sounds, the unfamiliar voices of the men in the stable, penetrated her fog, and in a crashing brilliance, she remembered everything. With a gasp, she sat straight up in bed.

The room, its furnishings, and the tall, mysterious dark figure in the middle of it all whirled around her in that instant. Pressing cool fingertips to her temples, she waited until the sensation passed before carefully opening her eyes. At first, the sight of him sent a chilling alarm through every nerve ending in her body, until a wave of calm reasoning washed over her, and she was able to meet the piercing brown eyes staring back at her with a measure of quiet composure. He was angry, but not angry enough to kill her or he would have done so long before now. He stood at the foot of the bed with the fingers of one hand gripped tightly around one of its tall posts. The other hand was knotted in a fist and resting on his lean hip. His mouth was in a tight, straight line, and he'd lowered his chin enough that he had to peer out at her from under coal-black eyebrows. The width of his cheekbones gave him a sinister appearance that would have frightened just about anyone else had they been in her predicament. But it didn't frighten Catherine. The first lesson her father had taught her was that fear crippled a person's thought processes, and that if she allowed her emotions the upper hand, any deduction she might have made otherwise would never surface.

"You mustn't let anything distract you, Catherine," he had told her over and over again.

Although the advice had truly been in regard to laboratory experiments, she had applied the wisdom to her own work as she was doing right now with the stranger. The rage he displayed was real enough, but she doubted it went any deeper than a strong irritation over having been inconvenienced.

The aroma of tea sweetened with honey distracted her. Spying the cup on the nightstand next to her, she glanced back at the stranger for a brief second and then gingerly swung her legs off the bed as she picked up the teacup, certain the refreshment was meant for her. It it had been brought for her companion to drink, it would have been put on the table dividing the two wing chairs near the hearth, rather than placed so far out of reach.

The angry crimp to T.J.'s brow softened for an instant and surprise smoothed the hard lines in his face as he watched the young woman help herself to the tea. To all appearances she wasn't the least bit afraid . . . of him or of the situation in which she had gotten herself. Was there a chance she knew something about him? Something that assured her she was safe? Impossible! The only person who knew what he was up to was Lewis Rhomberg, and Lewis had given him strict orders not to interfere. He'd left London thinking that T.J. had listened to him. And even if Lewis hadn't been opposed to T.J.'s help, he certainly wouldn't have told anyone about it . . . and certainly not a woman!

"Who the hell are you?" he blurted out, when frustration became too much for him to handle. "And what the hell were you doing in that stable?"

Catherine made a mental note of the agitation she heard in his voice. It had the same undertones as her father's whenever she'd done something to upset him, and even though she didn't know this man or his moods, she sensed the only real danger she was in was the threat of a punctured eardrum if he continued to yell at her. She set down the teacup and looked around for her shoes.

"I was about to ask you the same thing," she calmly replied. Then, when she failed to locate the missing footgear that had always been a nuisance anyway, she glanced up and queried, "Do you know what happened to my shoes?"

T.J. started to raise a finger and point at the armoire where he'd put both her cape and shoes, when his temper exploded instead. "Sweet Mother of God, woman! Have you no idea how close you came to being murdered?"

Catherine considered the statement. "Since I was unconscious at the time, I'll have to assume by your question that I was very close to being murdered. I'll have to further assume you're the reason I wasn't."

T.J. could hardly believe what he was hearing. He dropped his arms to his sides, his shoulders drooped, and his mouth fell halfway open in astonishment. Wasn't she afraid of anything?

"I'll have to take that to mean my assumptions are correct," she added, rising off the bed and crossing to the armoire. His brief glance at the wardrobe earlier had indicated the location of her things even if he hadn't actually announced their whereabouts. Reaching for the ivory knob, she paused with her hand extended as she murmured, "I suppose I really should thank you."

T.J. snorted derisively. "Oh, think nothing of it. I do that sort of thing all the time." He watched her for a second longer, and when she bent to pick up her shoes from the floor of the cabinet, he shot across the room and slammed the door shut, nearly catching her hand inside. "Sit!" he raged, pointing a finger at one of the wing chairs.

Catherine wasn't quite sure what it was she had done to provoke him again, but rather than ask, she did as instructed. He seemed to have a mean streak in him and she had no way of knowing how far she could push him.

"I don't know what kind of game it is you think you're playing," he snarled through clenched teeth, his nose inches from hers as he leaned forward with his hands on the arms of her chair, "but I'm not in the mood. If I hadn't been in that stable tonight, your body would have been found floating in the Thames tomorrow morning. And if you don't start answering my questions, it still may turn up there!"

Catherine doubted he meant it, but just to humor him, she said, "All right. What is it you wish to know?"

"Let's start with your name."

Since there wasn't any harm in telling him and because she guessed he probably wouldn't know who she was anyway, she willingly answered, "Catherine Chase."

His tall, well-muscled, finely garbed body straightened instantly. "Chase?" he repeated. "As in Sterling Lloyd Chase, the professor of chemistry at Oxford University?"

Stunned by how wrong she'd been about him, she was unable to reply except for a nod of her head.

His dark brows gathered close over his eyes again. "Who was he to you?" he demanded.

Catherine gulped down the knot in her throat. "My father," she whispered.

His reaction was immediate as he slapped the heel of his hand against his forehead and spun away from her. "That's all I need," he howled, doubling up his fists as though he were about to hit something. "Catherine Chase, female sleuth, snoop, busybody, meddler—"

Something that rarely happened to Catherine, happened. She lost her temper. "I beg your pardon?" she hissed, bolting from her chair. "I am *not* a snoop or a busybody or a meddler as you claim. I may be a sleuth, but it's a title I've worked hard to achieve and one I well deserve." Without thinking, she grabbed a handful of his coat sleeve and jerked him back around. "Those paintings you were about to purchase were stolen from the British Museum. Scotland Yard had given up looking for them here in London because they assumed whoever had taken them had moved them out of the country by now. I took one look at the spot where the thieves had entered the museum and knew they hadn't." She raised her hand beneath his nose, the thumb and first finger held erect as she marked a small measure of space. "And I was this close to proving it."

"Oh, really?" he mocked, not at all impressed with her declaration. "And why is that?"

One of Catherine's shortcomings was hating to have to explain something complex to someone who didn't have the ability to figure it out for himself. Mr. Trumble was the exception. She liked him. Giving the stranger a cold look, she brushed past him on her way back to the armoire. "What difference does it make now?" she asked, pulling open the wardrobe door and reaching for her shoes.

"None, I guess," he jeered. "But I *am* interested in hearing how you arrived at such a conclusion."

"By looking for the obvious," she answered dryly, crossing to the bed and sitting down to put on her shoes. "All the clues were right there. Anyone with any common sense could have figured it out."

T.J. recognized the hint of aspersion aimed his way, and a vague smile sparkled in the dark depths of his eyes and disappeared as he turned and lowered himself down in one of the chairs. Lewis Rhomberg had told T.J. all about Catherine Chase the first time the two men had dinner together, and the subject of Lewis's work had come up. According to his friend, Miss Chase had an exceptional talent for uncovering evidence that eventually resulted in solving a crime. She had a brilliant mind in that respect, but when it came to everyday matters, Lewis doubted she could find her way home if someone pointed her in the right direction. Worse than that, he confessed, was her failure to realize how dangerous her kind of work really was. She seemed to think that her paper trail would never cross the real-life path of those who had committed a crime, or that if it did, she assumed those very same criminals would hold no grudge against her. That alone was the reason why Scotland Yard was reluctant to give her any information on an unsolved case. They simply didn't want it on their conscience if she got hurt or killed while helping them do their job.

T.J. remembered thinking at the time that Lewis was probably exaggerating, since most of the women *he'd* ever met were more interested in what they put *on* their heads instead of what went *in* them. Now that he'd met Catherine Chase personally, he knew Lewis had been telling the truth. That much was evident. All by herself she had not only concluded that the stolen paintings were still in London, but she'd tracked down their whereabouts. A sharp piece of work, he silently admitted. Yet, while he sat there observing how she was struggling to get her left foot in her right shoe, he also realized that she was her own worst enemy.

"Damn things," she muttered, throwing down the slipper once she'd recognized her mistake. "I don't understand why we have to wear them, anyway."

T.J. rubbed a finger along the upward curve of his mouth and fought with the laughter that tightened the muscles in his throat as he watched her collect the other shoe and proceed to make the same error as before. He liked Catherine Chase. She was different, and that was what made her interesting.

"Other foot," he instructed after a moment, and once he was sure she'd wear the shoe even if it didn't fit.

"What?" she snapped, peering up at him through the long strands of honey-colored hair falling in her face.

"It belongs on the other foot," he further explained as he left his chair and came to kneel before her. "Here, let me." He took the slipper from her hand, caught the back of her ankle and easily slid the footgear into place. "Do you always have this much trouble getting dressed?" he asked with a smile as he picked up the second shoe and helped her on with it.

Catherine could feel a flood of warmth spread upward

from where his hand touched her ankle all the way to the top of her head. She had never allowed a man to get this close to her before, and she found the experience both exciting and a little frightening, neither of which she could fully comprehend. Confused as well as feeling vulnerable and hating it, she jerked her foot away from the warm fingers encircling it, when it seemed he was quite content to hold it for as long as she would allow him the opportunity, and quickly left the bed to fetch her cape.

"I—I have to be going," she uttered nervously. "Mr. Trumble must be worried sick about me by now."

"Mr. Trumble?" T.J. repeated, not bothering to rise as he twisted around and balanced his weight with one knee touching the floor and his right arm draped over his other thigh. "Not your lover, I hope."

"Certainly not," she rebuked. "And you're rather brash in suggesting such a thing." She gave him a stern frown, pulled her cape from the armoire, and swung it over her shoulders. "He works for me. He's my guardian . . . so to speak."

The idea made him chuckle.

"You find that amusing?" she asked, watching him rise.

"Don't you?" he challenged.

"No. I don't. He's a very sweet man—"

"Who failed in his job."

His meaning was lost to her. "What job?"

"A guardian is someone who is legally responsible for the care of one who is considered by law to be incompetent to manage his own affairs. You've already proven you shouldn't be allowed out of the house, so where was he earlier, when you were trying your level best to get yourself killed?"

Catherine didn't like his attitude and his remarks were insulting, but he wasn't the first man to feel threatened by her intelligence. It had happened many times before, and she was sure it would happen again. Allowing it to annoy her was senseless. Smiling, she concentrated on tying the strings of her cape into a bow.

T.J. cocked a brow, surprised that she hadn't come at him with claws bared. "Well?" he baited.

"Well, what?" she asked, flipping up the hood of her cloak and wincing when she accidentally bumped the bruise on her jaw.

"Aren't you going to defend him?"

"Against what? The narrow-sighted ramblings of an arrogant fool? No, I'm not." She started past him. "Mr. Trumble is quite capable of defending himself. If you have an objection to the way he handles his *job,* as you call it, I suggest you speak to him. I'm sure he'll set you straight." She paused at the door and looked back. "Now, if you'll excuse me, I have to be going."

Realizing that she was about to make her exit, T.J. hurried over and slammed the door shut again before she could pull it all the way open. "And I'd be remiss if I allowed you to leave just now. I've heard a lot about you, Miss Chase, about how smart you are when it comes to dealing with material things. Beyond that, you haven't the wit to recognize how serious a problem you have."

"Really?" she mocked, leaning back and lifting an eyebrow at him.

"Yes, really. Until those paintings are back in the museum where they belong, you're not going to stop looking for them. You'll track them down again, hide yourself in a stable or barn or under someone's bed just to prove how smart you are. Well, you're not smart, Miss Chase. Otherwise you wouldn't be standing here with me right now."

The spark of anger she saw in his eyes seemed to enhance their rich color and add a certain kind of roguish quality to his good looks. He might live in a fine house and wear expensive clothes, but the rough edges around his manners belied his baronial appearance, and that bit of knowledge begged further probing.

"Are you listening to me, Miss Chase?"

The question brought her around. "Yes. I believe you said I'm stupid."

His shoulders slumped. "I did not say you were stupid."

"You said I'm not smart," she pointed out. "And if a person isn't smart, then they're stupid." She smiled softly at him. "You have a right to an opinion. Why are you so upset about about being called on it?"

He stared at her for a long minute, wondering just how much more of it he could take. Gritting his teeth, he seized her arm and marched her back to the fireplace where he shoved her down in the chair closest to him. "Why were you in that stable tonight?"

Catherine assumed the answer was obvious after everything they'd talked about in the last few minutes, and she said so.

"Then allow me to rephrase it. Tell me how—with all the stables in London from which to choose—you happened upon the right one."

"I didn't just 'happen' upon it. It took some investigative work."

"Go on," he urged.

"It had rained the night before the robbery. The runoff from the rooftops collected dirt and deposited it in a puddle in the alleyway behind the museum. By the next evening the mud had dried and when the wagon passed through it, it left a very clear imprint of a nick in one of the wheels. I drew a likeness of it, gave the sketch to a young boy who knows London better than I do, and had him search all the stables and liveries until he found the wagon."

"Very clever, Miss Chase, but how did you know that *that* particular wagon was the one involved in the robbery?"

"I didn't. But I couldn't just forget about it, either. I had a fifty-fifty chance of being right." She smiled lopsidedly at him. "And I was."

"Mmmm." He sneered. "So why didn't you send word to the commissioner at Scotland Yard instead of going to the stable by yourself?"

"I couldn't," she confessed. "Not until I was sure the wagon the boy had found contained the paintings. You see, all I asked of Phillip Preston was that he look for a wagon with a nick in the wheel. I wouldn't tell him why it was important to me because I didn't want to put him in any danger." When he opened his mouth to comment, Catherine interrupted, certain she knew what he wanted to say and that she didn't want to hear it. "Besides, there wasn't time to inform the commissioner. Phillip told me he'd overheard your partners say they would be meeting with you at ten o'clock. If I'd gone to Scotland Yard first, I'd have missed the meeting and the paintings would have been lost."

He gave her a long, hard look, then remarked, "You're too smart for your own good."

"Thank you," she said, knowing he'd meant it as an insult. "May I go now?"

T.J. threw his hands in the air and spun away. "Lewis was absolutely right about you. I truly believe you'd shoot yourself, if someone handed you a gun and told you to pull the trigger."

"I beg your pardon?" she asked, failing to understand his point. "Who's Lewis? And how does he know me?"

"It doesn't matter!" he exploded, turning back around. He glared at her for a second, then shook his head and sat down in the chair next to her. "Miss Chase," he began, fighting to control his simmering anger, "you're behaving as though I'm no threat to you, when by all rights you should be scared to death of me. I was there in that stable to buy stolen works of art. That makes me as guilty of the crime as the men who actually took them. Now, because of your interference, you know who we are. We could go to prison because of you. Do you honestly think I could just let you walk away?"

"Are you saying you won't?" she dared.

He started to reply, but she cut him off.

"If that were your intention, you wouldn't have bothered bringing me here. Nor would you have stopped your partner from killing me as you implied you did. And you wouldn't have served tea." She raised her brows at him and waited. When he chose not to answer, she continued. "I might have difficulty with putting on my shoes, sir, but I assure you it's only because I find such menial tasks a bother. The minute I woke up here, I knew finding those paintings again would be virtually impossible. And without them, what good would my testimony in court be to anyone? You're obviously wealthy enough to pay someone to lie for you, to swear you were fifty miles away at the time I claimed to have seen you in that stable. As for the other two you were with . . . Scotland Yard isn't interested in them. They're after the man who hired them. So, killing me would be a waste of a good bullet." She waited a moment, then asked, "Am I wrong?"

A smile challenged his stern expression, and rather than let her see that she had guessed correctly about him, he rose and moved away from her. Catherine Chase was an exceptional woman; so much so that her fact-finding talent would one day get her in a lot of trouble, if it hadn't already.

"This other man," he said, standing near the balcony doors looking out. "Have you given any thought to his reaction once he learns the sale of the paintings never took place?"

Catherine shrugged a shoulder. "He'll be angry, of course, but it doesn't mean he won't be able to set up another meeting with someone else."

His dark eyes captured hers. "You're taking a lot for granted, Miss Chase," he observed.

"Am I? How so?"

"You're assuming I'm no longer interested in owning them."

Catherine smiled. "You'd be a fool if you did."

"And why is that?"

She drew in a breath to tell him that even though he might be able to buy himself an alibi for tonight, he would never escape the constant scrutiny of Scotland Yard once they learned about his part in all of this. She started to tell him, and then she changed her mind. Especially once she saw the gleam in his eye and the crooked smile that lifted one corner of his mouth.

"Finally," he said. "You've actually realized your dilemma. Or perhaps I should say, it's my dilemma. What am I to do with you?"

A trickle of fear moved downward along her spine, but she quickly overcame it as her father had taught her to do. "Well, you have two choices as I see it," she calmly told him. "You can kill me as your friends wanted to do in the first place, dump my body in the Thames, and then sit back and wait for Scotland Yard to knock on your door." When he gave her a questioning look, she smiled. "I may have been the only person who actually saw your face, but I'm not the only one who knew about the meeting and where it took place. If Phillip could find you once, he'll find you again, and this time he'll have help. You'll be charged and hanged for murder.

"Your second choice is much simpler and less costly in the end. You can take me home. There's no guarantee I won't head right for the commissioner's office, but as I stated before, you can buy your way out of trouble. My word against the score of people you pay to lie . . ." She shrugged a delicate shoulder. "The worst that can happen is that you'll be hounded by Scotland Yard for a while. You might even be questioned every time there's a robbery. But in my opinion that's a lot easier to deal with than standing trial for murder."

While she talked, T.J. noticed how the firelight seemed to caress the soft curve of her cheek. The hood of her cape hid most of her hair, but for one defiant curl that lay against her smooth brow. He'd always been attracted to women whose hair was as dark as a midnight sky, and rarely gave any other a second look. Catherine Chase had managed to change his habits, and although he found that to be a bit of a surprise, he also realized that it was only one of several other stirring differences he was beginning to feel because of her. He admired her wit and her superior intellect, her courage in the face of danger, and how she remained calm despite everything. He liked the sound of her voice, her blue eyes, and the stubborn way she held her chin up high as if she might be daring him to prove her wrong.

Of a sudden, he realized he was staring at her and that a rush of color had darkened her cheeks. A hint of apprehension shadowed the look in her eyes, and the confident air with which she held her slender frame had faded. She appeared nervous, and although she had every reason to be, T.J. doubted it had anything to do with their discussion. Instead, he sensed it was his presence that unnerved her, and for that he felt a moment of fleeting regret. He wanted to frighten her, but only in the sense that she would recognize the foolishness of her pursuit. As a man, he truly wished her ho harm. A smile moved his lips ever so slightly as he thought how very much he would like to steal a kiss from her, and that perhaps *that* was what she feared.

The temptation grew stronger as he slowly closed the distance between them, his eyes never wavering from hers. Standing before her, he held out his hand.

"Come," he said softly. "I'll take you home."

The thumping of her heart drummed loudly in Catherine's ears, and a strange warmth spread through every limb. She felt faint and giddy, and she disliked the experience. Lowering her gaze from his handsome face to the lean brown fingers extended in a gentlemanly manner, she wondered if she dare touch him and what the result would be. Her father had never taken the time to teach her about personal things, womanly things, and she had never grown curious enough to ask simply because she had always assumed she would never need to know them. At a young age she had decided to devote her life to helping others, which meant she would have very little time for herself. Until this moment, the sacrifice hadn't been an issue.

"Miss Chase?"

The deep richness of his voice tickled her senses and startled her to awareness. Praying it wasn't a mistake, she took the proffered hand and stood, knowing in the same instant that she should have paid closer attention to her instincts. The warmth of his touch seared her with a branding heat that weakened her knees and nearly sent her tumbling back into the chair. Instead, a strong arm encircled her waist and held her steady, pulling her off balance and forcing her to look up into the handsome visage staring back at her. His nearness, the strength of his hardened frame pressed close against her, took her breath away. Then, before she could react or decide if it was what she wanted, he pushed the hood of her cape from her head, caught her face between his hands, and lowered his mouth to hers, tenderly kissing her parted lips.

A mad rush of dizzying pleasure attacked her from all sides. Not only hadn't she imagined such a sensation, she hadn't even *thought* about it. The scent of him, the feel of his body molded against her own, the moist fullness of his mouth claiming hers, and his warm breath caressing her cheek made her heart lurch in her chest and her blood pound through her veins. If this was heaven, she wanted to die right then.

T.J. meant for it to be nothing more than a tender kiss, a stolen moment of pleasure, before he took her home where she belonged. Yet, once she responded to his touch, he realized that this studious young woman *had* to be made aware of the risks she was taking each and every time she uncovered evidence that brought her closer to solving a crime. She had to be shown that clues weren't always material things, that sometimes it meant dealing with the criminal himself, and that by doing so, she would be putting her life in danger . . . just as she had done tonight. He had to be assured that once he set her free, she would heed his advice and forget about playing sleuthhound. He enjoyed the taste of her, the feel of her curves, and the sweet fragrance of her hair, but for her own good, he knew it mustn't end this way between them. He must give her something to think about. Drawing on every ounce of his reserve, he abruptly set her from him.

"You're a fool, Miss Chase," he harshly told her. "You play a man's game with a female's weaknesses. You carefully analyze everything you see and hear, and yet you allow your passion to influence you the second you're treated like a woman." He turned away from her and went to the dresser where he retrieved a silk cravat from the drawer. With it in hand, he came back to her. "Your only salvation *this* time is my lack of interest." He jerked his head in the direction of the bed. "Otherwise, you and I would be exploring the depths of your femininity." He seized her arm and cruelly spun her around in order to make it easier for him to cover her eyes with his makeshift blindfold. Once he'd tied the knot, he roughly caught her wrist and ushered her from the room.

CHAPTER 3

Lewis Rhomberg had been away from London for a little over a week, and yet so much had happened while he was gone that it seemed more like a month. There had been a rash of burglaries that had Scotland Yard running around in circles and the general public up in arms. The worst news he'd been given upon his return was that the break-in and subsequent theft of several valuable paintings from the British Museum had yet to be solved. The mastermind behind the robbery was still unknown, but several leads had the police certain that within a few days they would be closing in on the man. Yet none of that was what had Lewis Rhomberg in a sour mood so early in the day, and the closer his rig came to the mansion owned by the adopted son of a longtime friend of his, the shorter Lewis's foul temper grew.

When T. J. Savage suddenly appeared on Lewis's doorstep a few weeks earlier, it was the first time the two of them had seen each other in nearly eighteen years, and it wasn't until his visitor smiled a hauntingly familiar smile that Lewis was able to recognize the tall, good-looking man standing before him. A flood of memories had washed over him in that instant, the most vivid being the day he had said good-bye to the young boy at the dock in Sydney, Australia.

Lewis had left the untrusting and nasty-dispositioned youth in the care of Christian and Alexandra Page, and for several months afterward he wondered if his friend had done the right thing by taking T.J. in and raising him as his son. The young T.J. Savage had a grudge against the world, and Lewis doubted even the kindness and patience of two very understanding people like Christian and Alexandra could ever make a change in the hostile youngster. He'd been wrong . . . except for two minor character flaws. T.J. was still just as stubborn as ever and twice as independent.

Although Lewis had never sailed back to visit his friends in Sydney, they kept in touch through letters. Even T.J. wrote to him now and then, and Lewis had noticed that by the time T.J. was of marrying age, he'd grown restless with the uneventful life of raising sheep with his adopted parents. The last time he'd heard from T.J. was a little more than six months ago, when T.J. wrote to tell him what he'd been doing the past five years. He'd said he had left Australia in search of whatever it was that was missing from his life, that he'd lived in Capetown, South Africa, for a couple of years, then in Rio de Janeiro and other places in Brazil where he'd made his fortune in the diamond mines, but that for all his traveling and searching, he still hadn't found whatever it would take to fill the void in his life. He was restless, and he had thought coming home to London would be the answer. So far, it hadn't helped.

Turning off South Carriage Drive and onto Trevor Place, Lewis's rig passed several elegant mansions before the driver reined the horse up the lane that would take them to T.J.'s front door. Once the hansom cab had rolled to a stop, Lewis swung open the doors and stepped down, pausing a moment to stare at the magnificent, two-story brick house and to ponder, again, how the bastard son of a laundry woman had risen to such heights on his own. If only Christian and Alexandra could see what their boy had accomplished . . .

"I shouldn't be very long, Kenton," he advised the driver, before turning on the flagstone path and heading to the veranda.

"Very good, sir," Kenton replied as he tied off the reins and settled down in the seat for a short nap. Past experiences told him that even though Lewis Rhomberg meant what he said, it never seemed to work out that way.

The warm sunshine against his shoulders felt good as Lewis walked the short distance to the front door, and he paused before knocking to savor the sensation. In a few minutes he would no doubt be in a heated argument with T.J., and as a result the rest of his day would be ruined. Squaring his shoulders, he took a deep breath of fresh air and raised his knuckles to the oak panels in front of him.

"Good morning, Stewart," he greeted a moment later, once the butler had opened the door.

"Mr. Rhomberg." Stewart nodded.

"I'd like to speak to Mr. Savage, if he's in."

"He just sat down to breakfast, sir. He's in the dining room. Shall I announce you?"

Lewis shook his head and stepped across the threshold as he handed his top hat and gloves to the man and slipped out of his coat. "No, thank you, Stewart. I'll announce myself. Otherwise I'm sure Mr. Savage would cut short his meal and make a hasty exit out the back door." He laid his coat over the butler's arm, smiled at him, and then turned for the dining room.

Lewis had been working for Scotland Yard for most of his adult life. Although it was the kind of work he enjoyed and wanted to do, the pay was terrible and the hours sometimes stretched around the clock. Those two reasons alone were why he had never married, and why he always felt just a twinge of regret whenever he was in a house as fine as the one he was in right now. The marble floor in the foyer, the brass chandelier with its multitude of finely cut crystal teardrops suspended from the cathedral ceiling above him, and the black lacquered credenza and gold-framed mirror hanging over it were worth more than Lewis had earned in his thirty years on the force. The only comfort he took in that was knowing that it all belonged to T.J. Savage, a young man who, as a child, many times went without a meal simply because he had no money with which to buy a loaf of bread. T.J. deserved everything he had . . . and then some.

Bright sunshine filled the dining room through the open French doors on the opposite side of the room from where Lewis paused in the archway. Before him stood a forty-foot table lined with Duxbury chairs on either side. At the far end sat T.J., although Lewis was having a hard time seeing him through the score of silver candelabra and floral arrangements adorning the tabletop. Most men would envy one who had such wealth. Lewis experienced his usual moment of empathy for the man. T.J. might have all a man could possibly want, but he was still unfulfilled, and while T.J. had yet to figure out why that was, Lewis knew exactly what T.J. needed.

"Do you enjoy eating alone?" he challenged as he rounded the edge of the table and walked the distance to where his friend sat.

Having recognized Lewis's voice and because he'd been expecting him to pay a visit, T.J. didn't bother looking up. "I'd say yes, if I thought you would leave," he mumbled half to himself. He really wasn't in the mood for banter.

Lewis ignored the sarcasm and added a bit of his own. "I wouldn't be here if you behaved yourself." He smiled at the dark brown eyes that glanced up briefly at him, and then pulled out a chair beside his friend. Sitting down, he reached for a slice of apple from the bowl next to T.J.'s plate and popped it in his mouth. "They're out of season. Where'd you get them?"

T.J. wiped his mouth on the linen napkin and laid it aside to lean back in his chair. "Did you come here to discuss what I have for breakfast or just to annoy me?"

"I'm not the one who's annoying," Lewis rallied amiably.

T.J. cocked a brow. "That depends on one's point of view."

Lewis took a second piece of apple, chewed and swallowed it, then settled his attention on the man staring back at him. "The day I left you standing on the pier in Sydney I assumed that age would dull that sharp tongue of yours. I see that it hasn't. You're worse now than when you were a dirty little street urchin. Did Alexandra allow you to talk to her like that? I'm sure Christian didn't."

Whether Lewis knew it or not, he was one of only two men T.J. trusted and respected. His friendship meant a lot to him, but old habits were hard to break. His instinctive nature was to be defensive even when he knew he was wrong, and since he was sure Lewis wasn't there just to be sociable, he'd lashed out *before* Lewis had a chance to lecture him. It was a trait that still needed a lot of work, but at least he was trying. Lowering the protective shell that had always kept others at a distance, he smiled lopsidedly.

"No, she never did," he admitted, leaning to refill his teacup. "The day before I left, I said something that offended her. I don't even remember what it was now, but I do remember her slapping the back of my head." He laughed at the memory. "I was twenty-seven years old at the time."

Lewis could see the love shining in T.J.'s eyes. "If I thought it would work for me, *I'd* slap the back of your head," he remarked, grinning.

"I'm sure you would," T.J. said, lifting the cup to his mouth as he added, "but I wouldn't suggest it." He took a long drink, set the cup back down, and was quiet for a moment. "I'll never understand why God didn't allow them to have any children. They would have made the perfect parents."

"They had you," Lewis argued.

T.J. shook his head. "It isn't the same."

"Why isn't it?"

A feeling of guilt raced through him. "Flesh and blood don't desert their kin."

"Ha!" Lewis exclaimed. "Offspring are the first to leave. And besides, you didn't desert them. They weren't depending on you for their survival. You grew up, T.J. You wanted to be on your own. They understand that."

"I hope so. I just couldn't see spending the rest of my life raising sheep."

"How *do* you want to spend the rest of your life?" Lewis asked, certain he already knew the answer.

T.J. slipped back into his old self. "Outliving you so I'll know what real peace is," he jeered.

"Good idea," Lewis agreed. "And you can start by minding your own business." When T.J. started to reply, Lewis raised a hand to stop him. "Need I point out what happened to Christian when he pretended to be someone he wasn't? He wound up on a convict transport heading for Australia. Granted everything worked out for the best in his case, but you're not him!"

T.J. lowered his chin and glared back at his companion through dark eyebrows. "And need I point out that if he hadn't been put on that transport, I never would have met him. The result would have been the same—I'd have wound up in Australia, but as a convict working out the rest of my life for someone else rather than living with Christian and Alexandra."

Lewis could feel the same argument coming on. "Then talk to the commissioner. Let him hire you as one of his agents. But stop the charade before you get yourself killed!"

T.J. gave a short laugh and pushed himself away from the table. "What good would I be then?" he asked, turning to stand near the French doors where he absently studied the jagged flight of a pair of birds winging a path high above the treetops. "The only way you're going to catch an upper-class thief is to travel in the same circle. Now, correct me if I'm wrong, but not even the commissioner earns that kind of money. Even if he did, no one would talk to him. And I'm not interested in becoming an agent. I told you before, I'm only doing it because I lack something better to occupy my time."

Lewis gritted his teeth until his burst of temper passed. "Really? And here I thought you were just being noble."

T.J. smiled, but Lewis wasn't able to see it as T.J. continued to look outside.

"That's the difference between you and Christian," Lewis continued. "He risked his life by infiltrating the gang of cutthroats responsible for murdering his kin. And he did it to collect evidence. You're chasing criminals because you're bored!"

"And why are you doing it, Lewis?" T.J. asked, his back still turned to him.

"Because it's my job!"

T.J. gave his friend a dubious look. "Oh? Are you saying what you get paid is worth the risk? Are you saying it's *not* because of the danger and excitement that goes with it, the thrill you experience each time you catch a criminal?" He smiled knowingly, and when Lewis refused to offer a difference of opinion, he finished by saying, "Or perhaps you're just angry because you're afraid I'll show you up."

Lewis's lined face turned red almost instantly. "I most certainly am *not*! There's only one reason why I'm here wasting my breath on you, and that's . . ."

He couldn't quite get the words out and T.J. knew why. Lewis Rhomberg, after all these years, was still full of guilt and he didn't even know it. He was blaming himself because he hadn't foreseen the problems that would occur as a result of Lewis's agreeing not to tell anyone that Christian had infiltrated an outlaw gang. Then Christian got arrested for being in the wrong place with the wrong group of men while Lewis was in another part of England, and by the time Lewis had heard about it, Christian had been tried, found guilty, and shipped off to the penal colony in Australia with a hundred other prisoners. And he might *never* have known what happened to his friend, if Christian hadn't helped a young boy escape the convict transport, and in return for his freedom, T.J. had taken a message to Lewis. A year and a half had elapsed after that before Lewis was able to clear Christian's name, and even though Lewis honestly knew he couldn't have stopped Christian, even if he'd refused his help, Lewis had shouldered all the responsibility for what had transpired in his absence.

"Bad memories, Lewis?" T.J. baited. "Does this remind you of what happened with Christian? Is that what this is really all about?" He waited, but when Lewis wouldn't answer, he continued. "You're expecting me to make the same mistakes he made, and since you're still blaming yourself for what happened, you'll say or do just about anything to prevent it from happening again." He rushed on when Lewis drew in a breath to deny the accusation. "Christian's situation was totally different from mine. He joined that gang and pretended to be one of them to give himself the freedom to collect the information he needed to have them arrested. I'm not joining any gangs. And I'm not pretending to be someone I'm not. In all appearances, I'll be nothing more than a wealthy man interested in spending some of my money. I'm not going to be a part of the stealing or the conspiracy, nor will I give anyone cause to think otherwise. The deception comes from my willingness to talk to Scotland Yard and to name names. Any danger that might result will come from the Yard's failure to keep my identity a secret."

"No," Lewis contradicted. "The danger comes in making one mistake. And you, dear boy, have already made it."

T.J.'s brows came together in a puzzled frown.

"Allow me to correct that statement," Lewis added, once he'd seen T.J.'s reaction. "The danger comes in not knowing you made a mistake. Would you like to know what it was? I can sum it up to two words. Catherine Chase."

Caught off guard, T.J. failed to mask his surprise. Their chance encounter had happened more than a week ago, but T.J. hadn't stopped thinking about her. He'd been wondering if she had heeded his advice, and he'd been remembering their kiss, the color of her eyes, the delicate shape of her chin, and how she had stirred a deep desire in him, a feeling he'd never experienced with any other woman. The surprise came in hearing Lewis say her name. Leaving his place beside the French doors, he sat down in the chair next to his friend and added more tea to his cup.

"What about her?" he asked after a moment.

"She's been asking around about a man matching your description."

"So?" T.J. casually challenged as he lifted the cup to his mouth. "Describing me would be describing fifty other men living in London. Why should that concern you?"

"Because I happen to know what case she's working on. I also happen to remember the conversation we had before I left town last week. I told you to keep your nose out of the

British Museum theft. Maybe it's all just a coincidence, but from the look on your face a moment ago, I'm inclined to think otherwise." He leaned and braced his elbows on the table. "And I suggest you tell me everything you've learned and why Miss Chase is looking for you so I won't be surprised when they toss you in jail."

T.J. refused to give in. "What makes you think that could happen?"

Lewis laughed sarcastically. "Surely you don't think she's looking for you to invite you to dinner, do you? Catherine Chase doesn't socialize, and a romantic evening is the furthest thing from her mind. She finds men tedious. And *that,* my young friend, includes you."

T.J. would have liked setting Lewis straight on that issue. He'd kissed enough women in his time to know that Catherine Chase's response hadn't been even close to disapproval. Yet, explaining why he thought Lewis was wrong meant he'd have to tell the man everything that had gone on in his room that night, and T.J. wasn't the sort who talked about his personal affairs with anyone.

"T.J.," Lewis coaxed. "Where were you that Catherine Chase had the opportunity to see you?"

"And why do you feel you have to ask? If she went to Scotland Yard with her information—"

"I didn't say she talked to anyone at the Yard," Lewis cut in. "All I said was that she was making inquiries about a man who looks like you."

"Then—"

Lewis interrupted again. "Are we going to go on like this for the rest of the day? I have work to do. I'm not like you, you know. My landlady expects the rent at the end of the month, and the commissioner isn't going to pay me a shilling if he hears I spend most of my time talking to you. You're in this up to that stubborn chin of yours, T.J. Savage, whether I like it or not. So you might as well stop all this dancing around and tell me what you know."

T.J. noticed how tired Lewis's blue eyes looked and that the wrinkles at their outer edges were deeper. Knowing his friend as well as he did, T.J. surmised the man hadn't gotten much sleep the night before, and arguing with him was only wearing Lewis down. He wanted to keep his accidental meeting with Catherine a secret, since he was sure the telling of it would only upset Lewis. But since Lewis Rhomberg was the only man T.J. knew who worked for the CID and who was willing to let him in on their secrets, alienating himself from Lewis, because of a silly disagreement, would do more harm than good. If T.J. wanted to continue his efforts in helping to recover the stolen artworks without any interference by the Criminal Investigation Department, he knew he would have to confide in his friend. He took another sip of tea and set aside the cup.

"I went to the opera a couple of weeks ago, and while everyone was in the lobby during intermission, the subject of rare paintings came up. I let it slip that I was interested in buying a Rembrandt or something of equal value, and that I didn't care how much I had to pay for one. A day or two later a message arrived at the house, saying that if I was truly sincere, I would be able to make such a purchase, but that it had to be kept a secret. I was told to go to the southeast corner of Hyde Park and wait, that someone would meet me there with directions on where to go next. The man who approached my rig handed me another note, which said I was to go to a stable in the alley behind Foley off Cleveland Street."

"Did you get a good look at this man?" Lewis cut in.

T.J. shook his head. "He wore a hooded cape and kept his face turned away."

"Careful bunch, aren't they?" Lewis observed with a disgruntled twist of his mouth. "Go on."

"Inside the stable was a wagon loaded with crates, and before I had a chance to examine them, two men I'd never seen before entered through the back door. It's my opinion they were the ones who did the actual break-in. I ordered them to open one of the crates so that I could have a look at what they were offering to sell and to make certain they were the stolen paintings."

"Well?" Lewis urged when his companion took too long to finish.

"They were, but before I could make them a deal, a noise distracted us. It seems Miss Chase had gotten there ahead of me and was hiding behind some barrels in the corner."

"Good Lord," Lewis moaned. "Obviously no harm came to her, but how did she escape?"

T.J. had already decided to alter the end of the story. "Purely by luck. She was close enough to the door to get a good head start, but she might have wound up dead if I hadn't intervened."

"Why? What happened?"

"One of the two men pulled a pistol. He would have dropped her in her tracks if I hadn't warned him that the gunfire would attract too much attention. When he argued with me, saying that her testimony would put all of us in prison, I insisted he leave the matter of her disposal to me, and I left the stable appearing as though I were chasing after her."

"Smart thinking, T.J. You saved her life and she doesn't even know it," Lewis remarked. "But what happened to the paintings?"

"When I got back a short time later, the wagon, the paintings, and the thieves were gone. I've been waiting around here hoping someone would try to get in touch with me again. So far no one has. I guess that little episode has them nervous."

"And in the meantime, Miss Chase is looking for you because she's sure you're a thief. Or at least involved in some way."

T.J. nodded to the possibility, although he had another reason in mind, one he wasn't going to tell his friend. He conceded to the prospect that it might be a little presumptuous on his part, but he guessed she had enjoyed their kiss as much as he had. She was looking for him, all right, but if she had wanted to implicate him in the robbery of the British Museum, she would have told Scotland Yard everything she knew about him. She hadn't, and as far as T.J.

was concerned that meant her interest in him was strictly personal.

"You know it's only a matter of time before she finds you," he heard Lewis advise. "The woman's talent for finding things is uncanny."

"So what if she does? She can't prove anything."

"Not now, she can't, but just give her a while," Lewis agreed, a bit annoyed. "This is the very reason I told you I didn't want you sticking your nose into police business."

"So what do you suggest I do? Tell her the truth about me?" He gave his companion a challenging look, then added, "She wouldn't believe me. Why should she?"

"Of course she wouldn't believe you. That's why I'm here. I'm ordering you to back away."

T.J. laughed. "*Ordering* me? I'm not one of your agents." He abruptly left his chair and went to the buffet to retrieve a cheroot from the box sitting there. "You can order all you want, but it won't do any good. I'm hooked on this one. Besides, you need me. I can go anywhere I want to in London, and no one will think a thing of it. Name one other person you know who can dine with barons and twenty minutes later be talking to stablehands." He raised his brows and waited.

"Catherine Chase," Lewis answered without a moment's hesitation. "And she was as close to solving this case as you were, and *she* has Scotland Yard's protection."

"It didn't seem like it that night in the stable," T.J. scoffed, striking a match and lighting his cigar.

"Yes, well, she gets careless now and then. Besides, what I have in mind for you will serve two purposes."

T.J. squinted suspiciously back at his friend through the gray smoke he exhaled. For the past month Lewis had been rejecting T.J.'s help. Now all of a sudden it sounded as though he wanted it. "Tell me why I've got this feeling that I'm not going to like what you have to say."

Lewis shrugged and reached for another apple slice. "Just your nature, I guess." He grinned and popped the piece of fruit in his mouth.

"Mmmm," T.J. mocked, moving away from the buffet.

He returned to his chair and sat down again, waiting for Lewis to explain. But when it seemed his companion was more interested in the food than in easing T.J.'s curiosity, his patience grew thin. "Out with it, Lewis," he barked. "I haven't got all day."

If Lewis had learned one thing about T.J. Savage over the past month, it was that he didn't like being teased. Lewis, on the other hand, loved to torment, and rarely cared who his victim was. He enjoyed it more when he was able to rile the person, and he'd succeeded with T.J. "It concerns Miss Chase," he lazily replied while relaxing back in his chair. "As you've seen for yourself, she has a way of getting into trouble. Not unlike you, I might add." He smiled at his friend, but didn't wait for T.J. to comment. "Up until the night she met you, she had never come face-to-face with any of the criminals she was after, and I would imagine that from here on out, she'll be a little more careful." The spark of humor faded from his eyes. "But that's not what has her life in danger."

T.J. frowned. "What are you talking about?"

"A little over a month ago her father died in an explosion in his laboratory. Before the CID was brought in to investigate, the place had been relatively cleaned up. What was left showed no evidence that it was anything more than an accident. The university has accepted that, and so has Scotland Yard."

"But you don't," T.J. guessed.

Lewis shook his head.

"Why not?"

Drawing air into his lungs, Lewis exhaled a tired sigh and rose from his chair to pace the room. "It's all circumstantial, and there's a strong chance I'm wrong. But instinct is begging me not to ignore the feeling I have." He stopped his aimless trek and braced his hands on the back of one of the chairs. "The first time I had any contact with Catherine Chase was the morning she came to the Yard to speak with the commissioner . . . *two* days before the explosion. I was in his office when she knocked on the door, and once she asked to speak to him alone, I excused myself and waited outside. The commissioner told me later that she had come to report a break-in at her father's office at the university in Oxford, and that because no one there would do anything about it, she wanted Scotland Yard to look into it. The commissioner sent me. And you know what I found?"

T.J. shook his head.

"Nothing. Absolutely nothing."

"Did you talk to the professor?"

"Yes, but he claimed there hadn't been a break-in, and when I asked him why his daughter seemed to think so, he said I'd have to ask her."

"And did you?"

"The commissioner told me not to bother, that it wasn't the first time Catherine Chase had them running around in circles. In fact, he ordered me to drop it." Lewis gritted his teeth and returned to his chair and sat down. "I'm sorry to say I listened to him. Two days later Professor Chase was dead, and *I* learned what a narrow-minded bastard the commissioner is."

"Narrow-minded? About what?"

Lewis snorted. "About women who are smarter than he is. He feels threatened every time Catherine Chase solves a crime before he does."

T.J. couldn't say he'd felt any less a man because Catherine had gotten to the stable ahead of him, but he had to admit it had surprised him. He admired her knowledge even though he disagreed with how she applied it. The commissioner, it seemed, wouldn't and couldn't accept it under any terms.

"Some men are like that, Lewis," T.J. advised. "I just hope you're not blaming yourself for not having recognized it sooner."

Lewis shrugged. "Maybe. Maybe not. It's too late to change any of it now anyway. Time to worry about tomorrow." He crossed his arms and leaned in on the table, his gaze locked squarely on T.J. "That's where you come in. I had an idea on the way over here—"

"Wait a minute, Lewis—"

"Now, hear me out," he cut in. "If the break-in is in any way linked to the explosion, whoever's responsible isn't going to want to talk to me or any other member of the CID. He might be long gone for all I know. But I won't rest until I have some answers."

T.J. raised a brow. "Took you long enough to decide. The professor died some time ago."

Lewis straightened in his chair. "I decided the second I heard about the explosion, but no one else agrees with me that it's something to be checked out. I've been on my own, and since I didn't want Miss Chase to hear that I was looking into the matter, I've been a little restricted."

"What makes you think I won't run into the same problems?"

A broad, mischievous grin spread across Lewis's face. "Because you'll be working from the inside."

"I beg your pardon?" T.J. asked suspiciously. The silly smirk, along with the subtle implication in Lewis's statement, bode ill, and T.J. didn't like it.

"You're a handsome man, T.J. You're wealthy, and somewhere buried deep inside, I would imagine there's a charming side to you. If I'm right about this, that Professor Chase was actually murdered for something he had in his files, sooner or later his daughter is going to figure it out. And you know what that would lead to."

The muscle in T.J.'s cheek flexed. "You're asking me to be her nanny."

"No I'm not," Lewis objected. "I'm asking you to be her companion." He glanced away and added softly, "And her protector."

T.J. glared at his friend for several long minutes, silently daring Lewis to look at him. When he wouldn't, T.J. leaned and snuffed out his cheroot in the ashtray. Although Lewis hadn't voiced the consequence should T.J. decide against the proposal, T.J. was reasonably sure there was one. Finally, when it seemed Lewis would never speak again, T.J. asked, "And if I say no?"

Lewis reached for another piece of apple as he rose from his chair and turned to walk casually away. He was near the end of the table and only a few feet from the exit before he decided to answer. "I will personally put the word out that you're working for Scotland Yard."

By the time the full impact of Lewis's statement had registered in T.J.'s brain and he'd opened his mouth to retaliate, Lewis was gone.

CHAPTER 4

A warm blush pinkened Catherine's cheeks as the memory of her first sensuous kiss stirred again from deep in the recesses of her mind and caught her off guard. She blinked, straightened in her chair, and glanced up from the book she had been reading. Absently pulling the wire-rimmed spectacles from her nose, she looked guiltily around the study as if she half expected someone to notice, when in fact she was all alone. Seven days had passed since that wonderfully frightening moment, and she still couldn't get it out of her head. Nor could she excuse the bubbling excitement that poured over her every time the vision disrupted her thoughts. More disturbing than that was the realization that in all the while they had talked, she had never learned his name. To this day she still didn't know who he was. And not because she hadn't tried.

Leaving her desk, she went to the window to look out, the image of that night and how he'd blindfolded her before taking her home flooding her mind. She had tried to keep track of all the turns the hansom cab made and in which direction it went each time, but the nearness of the stranger sitting beside her had been too distracting. Although they barely touched, she could feel every detail of his masculine frame and to some degree the anger that hardened his muscles. Common sense told her he was upset because she had spoiled his meeting and because she was a witness he couldn't eliminate. She was thankful for that, but she also wondered if there might have been a more personal reason in letting her go. Perhaps that kiss had affected him the same way it had bothered her, and that had been her primary impetus in trying to find him these past few days and why she hadn't contacted Scotland Yard with the information she had on him and his partners.

Her gaze drifted away from the foggy, late afternoon scenery outside the window to the desk she had vacated only moments before. In a daze she returned to her chair and sat down to pull out a bottom drawer. It had been nearly impossible for her to locate the stranger on her own, and as a last resort she had hired Phillip Preston. She had instructed him to be very discreet when asking around about a tall, good-looking man in his early thirties with an expensive taste in clothes, the arts, and whatever else he owned or *wanted* to own. But like Catherine, Phillip had been unable to narrow down the list of names to a number less than twenty, and short of lurking in the shadows outside the home of each possibility until she caught a glimpse of him, Catherine knew she would have to come up with some other way of tracking him down. It was already too late for her to start over on the chance that finding the wagon again would give her the answer she wanted, since she was sure the paintings were already tucked safely away somewhere. It might produce the two thieves, and if they didn't kill her on sight, she might learn the man's identity, but she doubted it. They simply wouldn't risk turning him over for fear of retribution, even *if* she offered to pay for the information.

A vague, demure smile changed the thoughtful line of her mouth as she pulled the black cravat from the drawer and lifted it to her nose. The scent of his cologne still clung to it, and each time she smelled it, the vision of him filled her senses; his dark, angry eyes, the wide shoulders, the cut of his expensive clothes, his long, lean fingers and perfectly manicured nails, and even the tiny scar high over his left cheekbone. She could remember the firm hand that had helped her descend the rig, the deep voice that told her to stand perfectly still, a silence that had surrounded her for a moment while she felt him staring at her, and how a strange emptiness had overcome her once she knew that he had left her. Only then did she pull the cravat from her face. He had wisely chosen to drop her off a block from her house where he wouldn't run the risk of anyone inside happening to see him, and at the time Catherine had silently complimented his cunning. He had taken every precaution in keeping his identity a secret, and so far it had worked. His mistake had been in not realizing with whom he was dealing, for Catherine Chase made her living at solving the unsolvable.

Her smile widened into one of confidence as she studied the silk cravat she held. Perhaps it would take her a little longer than usual to figure it out, but this scrap of cloth was the key. Dreamily, she raised it to her nose again and took a deep breath, savoring the manly scent that filled her nostrils. Her father seldom used cologne, but on rare occasions and only after she argued long and hard with him, he would shed his white frock coat and don the formal garb of men in his position. The memory of how she had had to practically drag him to the tailor's made her chuckle. He hated dinner parties as much as she did, and if the university hadn't required he attend as a way of soliciting funds for his work, he would have refused to go. Not that she had ever blamed him. She didn't like stuffy politicians either, and they rarely understood what it was he was trying—

"Oh, Catherine!" she exclaimed when the answer to her dilemma suddenly exploded in her head. "How could you be so stupid?" She glared disgustedly at the cravat for a second, shook her head, and then laid the silk cloth aside as she rose and slipped out of her frock coat. If she hurried, she might make it to the shop before it closed, and from there . . . The confident smile returned.

A few minutes later found Catherine at the bottom of the stairs and reaching for her cape hanging on the hall tree. "Mr. Trumble," she called as she swirled the cloak over her shoulders and tied the strings at her throat. "Mr. Trumble, I'm going out for a while. I shouldn't be gone more than half an hour. Hold dinner for me, will you?" The sound of his footsteps in the hall behind her turned her around. "I have an errand to run."

"Very good, miss," he reluctantly replied, the frown on his brow deepening when his gaze drifted downward to her feet. "But don't you think it would be wise if you wore your shoes?"

A lock of strawberry-blond hair worked free of its ribbon when Catherine dropped her head forward to confirm Mr. Trumble's observation. "Mmmm," she murmured, wiggling her stockinged toes. "You know what I think, Mr. Trumble?" She glanced up questioningly at him. "I think you and I should take up residence in the West Indies."

"The West Indies, miss?"

"Yes. I read that the natives there don't even own a pair of shoes." She smiled impishly at him, then turned for the stairs, bounding up them at a surefooted pace to disappear back inside the study.

"Yes, miss," Mr. Trumble muttered with a sad shake of his head. What she really needed was a finishing school, a place where she could learn proper etiquette, and he remembered discussing that same suggestion with her father on the eve of her sixteenth birthday. But the professor hadn't agreed. He could see nothing wrong with Catherine's behavior, and Mr. Trumble concluded it was because Sterling Chase hadn't any idea how a young lady should act. They were two of a kind; the professor and his beautiful daughter. Neither one of them cared what others thought or perhaps they were simply too busy to notice. That was certainly the case with Catherine. Mr. Trumble doubted he could name another single woman in the whole of London who would put her life at risk every time she left the house on a case. A week ago was a prime example.

She had ordered him to wait for her while she went off snooping around where she didn't belong. Although she had never admitted to what had happened there in the alleyway behind Foley Street, Mr. Trumble was reasonably sure she had had to make a hasty exit; so hasty, in fact, that she'd forgotten all about him. Worried sick, after he'd gone looking for her and couldn't find her, he'd just about decided to inform Scotland Yard, when he remembered another incident similar to the one he was experiencing then. Catherine had been so caught up in her work that she'd walked back home before she had realized Mr. Trumble had accompanied her. Praying that that was all that had happened this time, he had returned to the town house to find her sitting in the kitchen having a cup of tea. From all appearances, she had seemed to be all right . . . except for the faraway look in her eye and the vague smile that wouldn't go away even while she apologized for scaring him.

A forlorn sigh passed between his lips as he watched the young woman skip back down the steps toward him. Her father had told him a long time ago that Trumble worried too much, that Catherine was an exceptional little lady who could take care of herself, and that trying to tie her down would only break her spirit. Mr. Trumble wanted to believe that. He also wanted to believe that Catherine had two guardian angels. With the chances she took, she needed all the protection she could get.

"Better?" he heard her ask, and he pushed aside his thoughts to concentrate on her question.

"Miss?"

Smiling playfully, Catherine lifted the hem of her skirts to show him the shoes she had donned.

"Yes, miss," he replied. He started to open his mouth and offer to walk with her, but Catherine had obviously second-guessed him. Before he could draw a breath, she waved a finger at him in a negative fashion, silently declining his offer before it was made.

"I won't be gone long," she promised, stretching up on tiptoes to place a light kiss on his cheek, something she had never done before.

Stunned, Mr. Trumble just stood there rather than open the door for her, and he remained unmoving for several moments afterward, until the sound of the latch clicking shut brought him around. He glanced at the closed door, realized she had left, and shook off the surprise that had numbed his entire body. Although he couldn't really put a finger on it, there was something different about Catherine Chase all of a sudden, and if he didn't know better, he'd swear she was acting like a woman suffering from her first bout with love.

"Impossible," he snorted as he turned back for the kitchen and the meal he'd been preparing when she'd called out to him.

It took Catherine nearly a quarter of an hour to reach the Baker Street Bazaar, and with only fifteen minutes to spare before it closed for the evening, she hurried inside. Glancing to her right, she saw tables lined with bolts of cloth, sewing needles, spools of thread, scissors, yarn, and other paraphernalia a seamstress might be interested in buying. Catherine looked past it. Suspended by hooks from the ceiling hung herbs and spices, copper pots and wicker baskets. She saw a bin of potatoes, and one filled with onions, and she moved farther on. Finally when it seemed she'd never find what she was looking for, she decided to ask someone for directions, and she crossed to where a man stood replenishing the empty candy jar on the counter.

"Excuse me," she said, touching his arm and drawing his attention to her. "But I was wondering if you could help me."

"I'll try, miss," he said, smiling as he dusted his hands together and turned to face her. "Are you looking for something in particular?"

"Yes," Catherine told him, digging into the pocket of her skirt and pulling out the silk cravat. "I'm interested in buying some of this cologne. Do you recognize its scent?" She held up the neck scarf for him to take.

"Oh, yes," he admitted. "But you won't find it here."

Catherine frowned, puzzled. "Why not?"

"It's a gentleman's cologne, miss. And a very expensive one. I'm afraid you'll have to try Sir Arthur's Shoppe or perhaps The Gentleman's Quarters over on Dorset Street."

Both haberdasheries were more than five blocks away, and Catherine knew she would never make it to either one in time . . . at least not on foot. Plucking the cravat from the man's fingers, she thanked him for his help and spun around, leaving the shop just as quickly as she had entered it. Outside, she flagged down the first hansom cab she saw and climbed in, issuing instructions on where she wanted to go and that she was in a hurry. A few minutes later she was paying the driver an extra coin for his trouble and his success in expediting her wishes, once they had rolled to a stop in front of The Gentleman's Quarters and she could see that there were customers inside.

The tiny bell over the door announced her entrance and brought an uneasy blush to Catherine's cheeks when everyone there turned to look at her. She smiled, bobbed her head, and moved to a far corner where she could wait with some degree of privacy. She knew it was uncustomary for a woman to visit a haberdashery, and ordinarily it wouldn't have bothered her. Following leads in any case almost always took her places where a lady shouldn't go, with or without an escort. But this was different. She wasn't on the trail of a murderer or a kidnapper. She was here because she wanted to know the name of a man who had kissed her, and that sudden realization had a startling effect on her. Up until a week ago, she hadn't given men a second thought . . . not in the romantic sense, anyway, and now, seven days later, she was acting like a love-struck fool. Whoever he was, whether she liked it or not, he was the only clue she had to finding the stolen artworks, and *that* was how she should think of him.

The tinkling of the bell interrupted her thoughts. Looking up, she discovered that the other customers had left the shop, and that the proprietor was on his way over to her. Silently restating her wont to consider the stranger as the opposition, she pulled the cravat from her pocket.

"My name is Catherine Chase, sir," she politely informed him, "and I'm working on a case in conjunction with Scotland Yard. A little over a week ago, there was a robbery at the British Museum and several valuable paintings were stolen. Perhaps you heard about it?" When he nodded his head, she handed him the cravat. "It's my belief that the man who owns this has some vital information that would help in recovering the artworks. Only he doesn't know it, and I'm at my wits' end trying to find him. I thought perhaps you could help me. Do you recognize the cologne?"

"Yes, miss, I do," he said, once he'd raised the cravat to his nose and breathed in its scent. "But I'm afraid it isn't going to be of much assistance. I know quite a few men who wear this particular fragrance."

Catherine's shoulders drooped.

"However," the man continued as he examined the silk cloth, "I can narrow it down a bit. I had a gentleman visit my shop two or three weeks ago who was interested in purchasing a black silk cravat with red stitching, just like this one. Of course, I didn't have such a thing ready-made, so I had to ask him to come back the next day. His name was T. J. Savage. *But,*" he hurried on when he saw the pleased smile cross Catherine's face, "he might not be the man you're after."

"Why not?"

He handed the necktie back to her. "Because the next week I was bombarded with at least a dozen orders requesting I duplicate Mr. Savage's design. Being the businessman that I am, I filled those requests and made a handsome profit in return. Now, if you'd like, I could check my records and give you a list of all the men who bought them, but other than that . . ." He shrugged his shoulders and waited for Catherine to accept his offer.

"Yes, please," she replied, "but perhaps I can save you a little time. The man I'm looking for is tall, lean, rather handsome, and in his early thirties with dark brown hair and brown eyes. Do any of your customers match that description?"

He thought about it for a moment. "I can't be sure. I mean, not all of them came in to the shop personally. Several sent their valets. I remember their names, but that's only because of the records I keep."

"I understand," Catherine assured him, hoping the disappointment wasn't too evident in her tone. "But do you recall any of those, whom you did see, fitting that description?"

He turned away from her as he headed toward the back of

his shop. "Well, Mr. Savage for one," he answered over his shoulder. "And Nigel Greenwood for another. Except I believe he's closer to forty. And then there's . . ."

It was nearly seven o'clock by the time Catherine's hired hansom cab pulled up in front of the town house, more than an hour later than she had told Mr. Trumble it would take for her to run her "errand." Her dinner, no doubt, would be cold or horribly overcooked, and even though neither possibility bothered her all that much, having to face Mr. Trumble's disapproving scowl was another matter entirely. She didn't like upsetting him, which of late it seemed she did with regularity, and each time it happened she always vowed to do better in the future . . . just as she would pledge to do in the next minute or two. Stepping to the sidewalk, she paid the driver and hurried up the flagstone path to the front door.

"Mr. Trumble, I'm home," she called as she pulled the cape from her slender body, haphazardly draped it on the hall tree, and kicked off her shoes. "I'm sorry I'm late, but it couldn't be helped. I was following up on a lead, and—" She cut short her explanation when she saw him step from the parlor, a somewhat anxious look on his thin face. "Is something wrong?"

"No, miss," he advised, moving closer to her and away from the open parlor door. "You have a guest."

Catherine leaned and looked past him as she asked, "I do?"

"Yes, miss. A Mr. Savage wishes to speak with you."

Catherine could feel the blood draining from her face. "T. J. Savage?" she inquired, noticing how the pitch of her voice sounded a bit higher than usual and that she had trouble saying the name.

"I believe so, yes." Mr. Trumble frowned. "Do you know him, Miss Catherine?"

"I'm not sure." She practically mouthed the words in the hope her visitor wouldn't hear. "Bring some tea, will you?"

She started for the parlor, remembered her shoes, and dashed back to slip them on again. Then, when she looked up and saw that Mr. Trumble hadn't moved, she scowled at him and waved her hand, silently ushering him to the kitchen, before she stepped in front of the mirror hanging over the cherrywood buffet to fix her hair. It needed to be brushed and have the ribbon retied, but there wasn't time for that. Her curiosity just wouldn't allow it. Taking a deep breath and squaring her shoulders, she braced herself to meet him, almost certain T. J. Savage was the man who had tormented her thoughts for the past seven days.

T.J. had come to his feet the instant he heard Catherine's voice in the hall, and he had remained standing after Mr. Trumble had excused himself to greet her. He'd had to do a lot of things in his life that he'd have preferred not doing, but of them all, this was the worst, and he honestly couldn't say why. Perhaps it was because he was being blackmailed into doing it, and he'd always rebelled whenever he was forced into acting out of character. A movement in the doorway caught his eye, and his irrational thoughts, along with the deep scowl, vanished the second he saw her. Catherine Chase was even more beautiful than he'd remembered. Her pale blond hair with its strands of red-gold highlights complemented the delicate shape of her face, her pink lips, and the azure color of her eyes, and the temptation to pull her into his arms and kiss her rose again as it had done that night.

Catherine wondered if he could see the effect he was having on her or at least hear how wildly her heart was pounding. The tingling that had started in her stomach had spread to every limb and she was sure the warmth that touched her face had turned her skin a bright red hue. She couldn't imagine why he had come, and even though it pleased her, she doubted it was for the same reason she had spent the better part of a week trying to track him down. She mentally shook off the notion that there might be even the remotest possibility that he had, while she sternly reminded herself that he was a criminal, one she had sworn to bring to justice. Gathering her wits about her, she pulled her gaze from his handsome face and stepped further into the room.

"I'm having trouble figuring out why you're here, Mr.

Savage," she announced, surprised by how calm and self-assured she sounded. "Would you care to share it with me?"

A fleeting smile crossed T.J.'s mouth and disappeared as he thought how he'd like to share something else with her. "I'm here to plead my case," he replied, waiting until she had taken a seat in the chair opposite his before he too sat down.

Catherine stared at him for a moment. She'd never met anyone with eyes as dark as his, and she wondered if he might have some French ancestry mixed in with his English blood. "You're here hoping to convince me that you had nothing to do with the museum robbery, but that you simply couldn't pass up the chance of owning a Rembrandt, even if it was stolen."

She raised one tawny brow, daring him to contradict her assumption, only to be interrupted by Mr. Trumble serving tea. She waved off the cup he offered her and waited until T.J. had been given his, before she thanked the older gentleman and asked if she and her guest might be left alone. His response was a disapproving frown, and as always she ignored it to settle her concentration on the man sipping his tea. Once she heard Mr. Trumble's footsteps fading down the hall toward the kitchen again, she restated her possibility.

"Am I right?" she asked.

He smiled and replied, "In part."

"Oh, let me guess," she challenged. "You're not a thief."

His smile changed to a soft chuckle. "That's right. I'm not a thief. I have no need to steal, Miss Chase. I'm wealthy enough to buy whatever I want."

"Except when it's not for sale," she corrected.

T.J.'s dark eyes glowed. "Everything has its price, Miss Chase."

His comment made her think of her father and how he had said practically the opposite. "Some things just can't be purchased," he had often told his daughter. "My work, for example. I would never dream of selling one of my formulas to someone for his private use. It's meant to be shared . . . with the world." Not everyone agreed with her father, and there were times when Catherine even doubted it. Yet, despite their differences of opinion, she had always admired his conviction.

"If my father were still alive, I'd introduce you to him. I'm sure he could show you the error in your thinking." She smiled at him, then urged, "So plead your case, Mr. Savage. I'm more than willing to listen. But allow me to warn you before you do that I'm a very difficult person to sway. Cold, hard evidence, in my opinion, speaks louder than words."

T.J. knew that up until this morning's confrontation with Lewis Rhomberg, all he would have had to do was tell her to pay his friend a visit and there'd be no more doubt. But things had changed since that discussion. Lewis wanted T.J. to get close to Catherine Chase, to protect her from whatever danger was out there waiting to grab her, and if he ruined it by telling her the truth, T.J. guessed Lewis would have him thrown in jail just for spite. No, he'd have to play along with this charade until he could prove to his friend that Catherine Chase was at no more risk than he was.

"What evidence, Miss Chase?" he asked instead. "About all you have on me is the fact that I was in that stable with two men who were willing to sell me something. You can't even prove I would have actually gone through with the deal or what I would have done with the merchandise if I had. You have nothing, Miss Chase, nothing that would hold up in a court of law."

"Then why are you here?" she asked. "Surely my good health isn't *that* important to you."

Quite the contrary, he thought, holding back a smile. *Or at least it's important to a friend of mine.* He took another sip of tea and set the cup down on the table beside him. "I'm here to offer my help."

Catherine wondered if the fragrance she could smell belonged to the cravat in her pocket or to the man watching her. It was such a pleasant scent that she guessed she would never tire of its odor. Or perhaps it had something to do with the man who wore it. Realizing her thoughts had strayed, she mentally reprimanded her carelessness and focused her attention on his statement. "Your help?" she repeated. "Doing what?"

"In recovering the stolen artworks."

Laughter pulled at the corners of her mouth and made her blue eyes sparkle.

"I'm serious," he vowed, his own features relaxed as he tried not to smile in response to her obvious skepticism.

Catherine nodded, pretending to believe him. "Of course you are. What better way to head me in the wrong direction?"

T.J. silently stared at her for a moment. She was quick; there was no denying it. But she was wrong, too. With a sigh he leaned back comfortably in the chair, one elbow braced on its arm and his chin cradled between his thumb and first finger, while his gaze slowly swept over her. She reminded him of the first diamond he had ever found, and how, after his initial examination, he was sure that once the rock was broken away, a gem of unequaled beauty would emerge. Catherine Chase was like that. He could see the subtle beauty she chose not to flaunt—if indeed she was even aware of it—and he was sure that with the right clothes and the perfect hairstyle, she would shine just like a diamond. He dismissed the idea once he realized she'd have to be willing for it to ever happen, and he wasn't really sure he wanted her to change. He already liked what he saw.

"How much do you really know about me, Miss Chase?" he asked, diverting his attention back to the matter at hand.

Catherine had been trying to read his thoughts. She wanted to know the real reason he was there and why, after a week had passed, he had decided he needed to see her. "You mean aside from the company you keep?"

He smiled and reached to pull a cheroot from his pocket, asking permission to light it before he struck a match. Exhaling a puff of white smoke, he murmured more to himself than to her, "I told Lewis you wouldn't believe me."

"Lewis," she echoed. "You mentioned him before. Who is he?"

"A friend," T.J. easily admitted, while in his thoughts he wondered how true that really was. A friend wouldn't blackmail a friend.

"Does Lewis know you're involved in the museum burglary?"

Her insistence made him chuckle. "I guess you could say he does. But not in the way you're implying. I was in that stable for much the same reason you were, Miss Chase. I was trying to find out who stole the paintings and to get them back."

"Oh." Her tone clearly marked her doubt.

He took a puff on the cheroot, exhaled, and watched her through the haze, while he tried not to grin. He'd known this wouldn't be easy. "Miss Chase," he began again, "I have no reason to lie to you, and if you'd like, you may accompany me home where you'll have the liberty to make a thorough search of the place. You won't find anything there that hasn't been paid for, I assure you."

"Of course not," she agreed.

"I meant you won't find the paintings," he amended.

"I'm sure I won't," she replied. "You wouldn't be offering, if you had them in your house."

"I'm offering because I don't have them . . . anywhere. And I'm here because I've been given a second chance to buy them."

Before she could twist his statement around to suit her own view, he dug into his vest pocket and pulled out a piece of paper. "This was delivered to my home about an hour ago. If you'd like, I could give you a sample of my handwriting so you'll know I didn't write it," he added, once he'd given her the note and she'd unfolded it to read.

"All right," she yielded, after she'd studied the poorly scripted message, "let's say I believe you and that this is authentic. Why show it to me?"

T.J. took another puff on his cheroot, knowing she was far from convinced, but that at least he had her listening.

"For two reasons," he began. "First, it's the only way I have of proving to you that I had nothing to do with the robbery. I spoke the truth when I said I was in that stable only to find out who had stolen the paintings and to get them back. We both know how that turned out."

Catherine could feel the blush rising in her cheeks, and rather than have him notice, she left her chair and went to the window to look out. The sun had slipped beyond the horizon, but its dying golden light still set the sky ablaze with an array of color. She had never noticed the beauty of a sunset before, having favored early morning to the ending of a day, and she couldn't understand what had happened to change her.

"Miss Chase?"

The purely masculine resonance of his voice tickled the flesh beneath her ear and down her neck, and she unwittingly touched her icy fingers there as she drew in a breath to speak. "This note," she managed to say, holding up the piece of paper and giving it a shake, while she deliberately kept her head turned away. "It says you're to meet these people in Hyde Park. They surely don't intend to conduct business in such an open arena."

T.J. could sense something bothered her, and while he wanted to believe it was as simple as his being in the same room with her, he couldn't be sure. Out of politeness he had risen with her when she left her place beside him, and since she chose to remain standing, he elected to do the same. Slipping his right hand into his coat pocket, he rolled the cheroot between the thumb and first two fingers of his other hand as he casually strolled to stand beside her at the window.

"I'm sure they don't," he supplied, tilting his head to one side while he boldly enjoyed the sensuous profile she had unknowingly offered him. "I would imagine I'll be met by someone with a second set of instructions telling me where to go from there. At least that's what happened the last time."

Catherine could feel her knees growing weak, and she

silently cursed her decision to send Mr. Trumble away. His presence would have helped her maintain an emotional distance from this man. Drawing on what strength she had left, she turned to him and held out the tattered paper for him to take.

"And your second reason?" she asked, wishing T.J. Savage had been a man of three score and ten with thinning gray hair, a bulging stomach, and a wart on the end of his nose. But he wasn't. He was the most incredibly handsome man she had seen in her young life.

Suddenly, warm fingers were wrapped around hers, and it took her a second to realize he was merely reclaiming the note she held out to him. Yet, when she tried to pull her hand away, it seemed as though she were paralyzed. And worse than that, she couldn't avert her eyes from his or stop the tingling that had her stomach twisted into a knot.

"You're a very beautiful woman, Catherine Chase," she heard him say. "One of the most beautiful women I've ever met. But you're also very foolish."

The spell that had weaved its magic around her desires vanished in that same instant. She blinked, then frowned and jerked her hand from his. "Am I?" she asked, crossing to the hearth where she took down a taper from the mantel and touched its wick to the crackling fire. Turning, she passed the flame onto the gas lamp sitting on the table, then to the sconces hanging on either side of the fireplace. Once the room was filled with light, she blew out the taper, returned it to its place, and faced her companion with her hands clasped in front of her.

"I'm not the one making up stories, Mr. Savage. *I* have nothing to hide."

"But I do," he finished, smiling crookedly.

"It certainly looks that way."

He watched her for a moment, before he crumpled up the paper and stuffed it in his coat pocket. He took one last puff on the cheroot, exhaled, and crossed to the chair he had abandoned earlier. Leaning, he snuffed out the cigar in the ashtray, then motioned for her to sit down again. Once she had, he took his seat opposite her and smoothed out a wrinkle in the knee of his trousers while he contemplated what he would say next.

"When I was only ten years old, my mother died, and since I had no idea where my father was or even *who* he was, I wound up having to take care of myself. I didn't do a very good job, I'm afraid, and as a result, I was arrested for stealing a pound of cheese. I would have been shipped off to the penal colony in Australia if a man hadn't helped me escape the convict transport just as it was about to weigh anchor. In return, I did him a favor, and that's when I met Lewis . . . the friend I mentioned earlier. I won't go into detail since it's really not important how it all came about, but the end of that chapter of my life found me living in Australia with two very special people who had taken me in and were raising me as their own."

He smiled at her, thinking he would see a flicker of compassion in the pale blue eyes, but when she neither said anything in return nor even blinked in recognition of the story, he cleared his throat and continued. "Five years ago, I got restless and I left Australia to find my fortune. I lived in South Africa for a while, then in Brazil, where I met up with a man mining for diamonds. I arrived with only the clothes I wore, and left with more money than I knew what to do with. Yet, I still wasn't satisfied. That's when I decided to come home . . . to London."

He paused again, waiting for her to comment. She didn't, and for a second he wondered if she had heard a word he'd said. "I've been here for a little over a month now. I haven't made very many friends, but I really don't care nor does it surprise me. Those born into wealth have a hard time accepting a man who had to work for his. Besides, I didn't come here to make friends." He thought he saw a glimmer of sarcasm in her eyes, and he quickly added, "The boy who left London over eighteen years ago might have been a thief, Miss Chase, but I assure you, the man you see before you now doesn't have to steal."

Catherine wanted to believe him, but she'd learned over the years that the ones who claimed their innocence the loudest were usually guilty. And they usually covered up their guilt by telling some outlandish tale. But the decree almost always came *after* they'd been arrested. There was no questioning his wealth—that was obvious—and there was even the possibility he'd earned it in the diamond fields as he'd said he had. Her doubt came from how he maintained it. She considered him a while longer, then replied, "Let's say I believe you. You still haven't explained why you were trying to recover the paintings. What business is it of yours?"

"None," he admitted.

Catherine frowned. "Then why—"

"Being wealthy has a lot of advantages, Miss Chase. You can sleep all day if you want. You never have to lift a finger to get something done. You can have breakfast served to you in bed, if you so desire. Why, you wouldn't even have to hold an umbrella over your head to keep the rain out of your face as long as there's a servant around." He sat up and leaned forward with his forearms braced against his knees. "The disadvantage is that all the free time you've acquired for yourself can drive you mad. I'm bored, Miss Chase. There's no excitement in my life anymore. I decided to catch the thieves just so I'd have something to do."

Catherine raised a dubious brow. "It's as simple as that."

"Yes," he answered without any hesitation. "Or it was until you stumbled into the middle of it."

Catherine sensed what he was about to admit and she didn't like it. "Wait a minute, Mr. Savage. Before you say something stupid and ruin my opinion of you, I'll let you in on a little secret. I never have been nor will I ever be a damsel in distress who's waiting for her knight in shining armor to come riding on his white charger. I've been taking care of myself for a long time now, and the fact that I'm a woman doesn't mean I need a man around to protect me. When I get myself in trouble, I can usually get myself out of it."

"Oh?" he challenged, a little miffed with her. "How would you have gotten yourself out of the trouble you were in the night we met? If I hadn't been there, I mean."

"That was different," she argued, leaving the chair.

"Different?" he barked, springing to his feet and grabbing her arm when she started to turn away. "The difference is that you'd be dead right now, and *that's* the reason I'm here, the reason I showed you the note. I want you to promise me you won't leave the house tonight, that you'll wait for me here where it's—"

"Safe," she cut in, wrenching her arm free of his grasp. "You really do think I'm addle-brained, don't you?"

"If you can't see the logic in my request, yes!"

"Oh, I see the logic, Mr. Savage. When all of Scotland Yard couldn't track down the paintings, I could. And if I could do it once, I could probably do it again. That makes me a threat, so you either have to get rid of me permanently—which you've already proven you're unwilling to do—or you've got to trick me into believing you're an honest man and win my oath that I won't interfere. With me conveniently out of the way, you're free to conduct your business and be on your way." She gave him an encouraging look to deny her assumption, and when he merely glowered back at her, she said mockingly, "Oh, I can just imagine the story you'd have to tell if I agreed and waited here for you. Well, it won't happen, Mr. Savage. The minute you walk out that door—"

The rest was never spoken, for at the very moment, T.J. turned away from her. Puzzled, she watched him scoop up his cape from the back of the settee where he'd laid it and march toward the exit. Once he'd stepped into the hallway, he called out Mr. Trumble's name, and Catherine all too quickly guessed his intent.

"No," she ordered, hurrying after him and catching his arm. "You can't involve Mr. Trumble."

"I can and I will," T.J. growled, bending slightly so that his face was only inches from hers. "If you won't listen to me, then maybe you'll listen to him."

He turned his attention to the butler, once Mr. Trumble had entered the hallway, wasting little time and even fewer words in suggesting that the man keep Miss Chase under lock and key, if necessary, that her life would be in danger if he allowed her to go out, and that he would return as soon as he could. The rest, he said, Miss Chase could explain to him, and once T.J. saw worry knit the man's brow, he felt confident enough to leave. Whirling the cape over his shoulders, he gave Catherine one last angry glare and stormed out of the house.

CHAPTER 5

"Mr. Trumble, please," Catherine softly begged. "I swear to you he was only trying to make you *think* my life would be in danger. I assure you it won't be . . . especially if you go with me."

The gray-haired servant frowned all the more as he considered her guarantee. He'd had only a few minutes to talk with Mr. Savage in private, before Catherine had returned home, and he had to admit that it wasn't long enough to learn much about him. But he had always prided himself on being able to judge a man's character within the first few minutes of a conversation, and he'd come to the conclusion that T.J. Savage was a good man. He couldn't say why he felt that way . . . maybe it was because the young man spoke without looking down his nose at him. Or perhaps it was how he laughed that made Mr. Trumble feel comfortable with him. And then there was the sparkle in Mr. Savage's eyes when he mentioned Miss Catherine. It might be a silly way for him to form an opinion of someone, but Mr. Trumble sensed the young man liked her. And if he liked her, why would he lie about something as important as her safety? Sighing heavily, he looked across the foyer at the closed front door.

"I realize, miss, that I am only your servant," he began, turning to face her, "and that I should keep my sentiments to myself. But with your father's passing, there is no one left to advise you. I have been with this household for more than thirty years. I was present the day you were born, and when your father laid his wife to rest—a sad time for all of us. I did my best to help him raise you, and when he too perished, I lost a very dear friend. Perhaps none of my blood runs in your veins, Miss Catherine, but that doesn't mean I can turn my back on you simply because you say I should."

In all the years she'd known him, Catherine had never heard him voice his emotions. She had sensed how much he cared, but until now, it had been nothing more than a feeling. She also realized, much to her shame, that she had never told him how much he meant to her.

"Nor would I wish it," she said, taking his arm and gently guiding him into the parlor. Crossing to the settee, she drew him down beside her despite the objection she saw in his green eyes. "And I apologize if I've ever given you the impression I think of you as merely a servant. I do not. You were my father's one and only true friend, and that isn't something I can ignore. He respected you, and so do I. I can only hope you feel the same about me."

"Of course, miss," he quickly promised. "I hold you in the highest esteem. Your talents, your intelligence, your concern for others, place you well above your peers. Forgive me if I made it sound otherwise."

"You didn't," she assured him. "And we've argued because I have failed to realize that by not confiding in you, my trips around town appear to be very perilous. I've been unfair to you, I know. But I hope you can understand my reason."

"I believe so, miss," Mr. Trumble replied. "To catch a thief, one must think like a thief. Then, if one has drawn the right conclusions, one must investigate the possibilities. It also means acting alone. A crowd only draws attention, and therein lies the danger."

"Precisely, Mr. Trumble," Catherine said with a smile.

"However," he continued, "there are certain situations in which a man is better equipped to handle himself than a woman."

"I don't disagree, Mr. Trumble. Yet, on the other hand,

a woman has an advantage a man can only wish to have."

Mr. Trumble frowned. "Miss?"

"Would a thief or a murderer ever assume he's being hunted by, shall we say, a less physically equal foe?" She smiled again once he saw the logic in her claim. "Of course not. And even if they suspected that might be true, they wouldn't see it as a threat, which in turn would make them careless. And *that,* Mr. Trumble, is what we have here with Mr. Savage."

His gray eyebrows came together in a perplexed frown. "I beg your pardon, Miss Catherine?"

"What reason did he give for coming to the house?"

He was quietly thoughtful for a moment. "I don't believe he actually said . . . other than that he wished to speak with you." Remembering his status compared to her late father's, he added stiffly, "But then, miss, it isn't my place to question."

"And he wouldn't have said if you had," she assured him, anxious to finish their debate and to convince him that T.J. had only used what he guessed was Mr. Trumble's guilt in helping him to keep her out of the way. "At least he wouldn't have been truthful with you. He's a thief, Mr. Trumble, and that also makes him a liar."

Her declaration not only conflicted with Mr. Trumble's first impression of the young man, it was a direct insult to his capabilities in judging people. Offended, he straightened in the settee and took a breath to complain, only to have Catherine cut him off.

"The night you drove me to Foley and Cleveland, and I had you wait while I walked down the alley?" she reminded him. "I was acting on the information Phillip had given me. I had hired him to track down the wagon used to haul the paintings stolen from the museum, and that's just what he did. There, in a stable behind Foley Street, I not only found the wagon and the paintings, but I found Mr. Savage and two men, obviously his partners."

"Good Lord, Miss Catherine," Mr. Trumble exclaimed. "Had I known—"

"Don't concern yourself," she urged, knowing he felt as

though he had failed her. "Everything worked out all right. I wasn't injured, was I?"

Mr. Trumble wondered about that. Although he hadn't noticed it when he arrived home to find her sitting at the kitchen table, the next morning there was no mistaking the dark bruise on her jaw. When he'd asked her about it, she had claimed a book, just beyond her reach in the tall bookcase, had fallen from a top shelf and struck her in the face before she could catch it. He'd dismissed the incident after that simply because Miss Catherine always seemed to be dropping one thing or another. But now . . .

"If he's a thief, as you say," he queried suspiciously, "why was he here? Why did he come to see *you*? How would he have known—unless he saw you—that you were there that night? And doesn't that mean—"

"I'm not frightened of him, if that's what you're getting at. Nor should you be frightened for me. He came for two reasons. First, he 'd obviously heard I was making inquiries about a man of his description, and secondly, he was hoping to convince me that he's innocent."

"Good God," Mr. Trumble blurted out. "You're not saying he actually admitted being there, are you?"

"Yes, Mr. Trumble, that's what I'm saying. He also pointed out that I have nothing legally sound on which to have him arrested, which is true, unfortunately. *But,*" she added as she reached over and laid one hand on his, "we can change that."

He looked askance at the young beauty sitting beside him, truly not liking the glint he saw in her pretty blue eyes. "How?"

"He claims to have a message that was sent to him by the men who stole the paintings. He showed it to me, but in my estimation, it doesn't prove a thing. He could have paid someone to write it. Anyway, it says he's to meet the two men in an hour at the southwest corner of Hyde Park, and from there he'll be given directions on where to go next."

"I don't understand, Miss Catherine," he confessed. "If Mr. Savage is a part of the group who—"

"He's claiming he was in the stable the first time only as a buyer."

"And you don't believe him."

"No," she easily replied. "It's too contrived. He was there to pay them off for doing a job, and nothing more." She saw a look of confusion wrinkle the man's lined face, and she urged him to voice whatever was bothering him. Without having him totally satisfied, she knew she would never get him talked into helping.

"Why would it be necessary to hold a second meeting? What happened that night that stopped him from concluding his business right then?"

Catherine wondered if the warmth she felt rushing to her face had actually turned her flesh a bright pink. She hadn't thought far enough ahead with her story to cover that particular angle, and she was about to get caught . . . unless she came up with something and fast. So why not the truth?

"I'm not sure, Mr. Trumble. Perhaps they did. Maybe there really isn't going to be a meeting, that Mr. Savage made the whole thing up hoping to throw suspicion away from him. And *that's* why you and I have to be at Hyde Park within the hour." She was quiet for a moment, then added dejectedly, "I really don't have enough proof to have him arrested, Mr. Trumble, but I'm certain he's guilty. Please. You've got to help me. I know this case doesn't seem as important as some of the others I've solved . . . there's no murderer running loose or a baby to be found. It's only stolen property, but think of the merchandise. Those paintings were meant to be shared with the world. Why should one man have them all to himself?"

Mr. Trumble considered the points she'd made, and he had to agree. He also knew that no matter what he said, she was going to the park. And if she believed that strongly in her intuition, then so should he.

"I'll have the rig pulled around out front in five minutes," he said, rising and walking toward the door. Once he'd reached it, he paused and turned back, the look on his face telling her he meant business. "This time, however, I will not stay with the hansom cab. Where you go, I'll be going with you. If you're right about this man, and I find that hard to accept, that makes him very dangerous, and I could never live with myself if I allowed something awful to happen to you just because of our differences in station."

Truthfully, Catherine was glad Mr. Trumble had taken a stand. Deep down inside she was scared. But not so much of the danger she would be in if she was right about T. J. Savage, more that she was about to prove her suspicions correct. He'd made a shocking difference in her life, and even though there was a very strong possibility he was evil, she couldn't stop the haunting desire he had awakened in her.

Lamplights cast a diffused amber glow as they struggled to shine through the dense fog swirling all around them. A chill embraced the air, and the streets glistened with moisture. Tucked warmly inside the hansom cab, Catherine hesitantly awaited their arrival at Hyde Park as she listened to the clip-clop of horses' hooves against the cobblestone avenues. London, it seemed, was always bustling with activity in some form or another, and although it made travel a little slower, it also promised to mask Catherine's presence as her cab moved within the mass of other rigs passing by the park. Then, once Mr. Savage had received his instructions and had pulled away for his next destination, the heavily traveled streets would allow her to follow unnoticed, since all the other hansom cabs were practically the same in appearance to hers. Yet, the closer Mr. Trumble drove them to the park, the more she found herself hoping it wouldn't be necessary to hide herself among the crowd.

The servant's comment earlier, that he was having difficulty believing Mr. Savage was a criminal, brought to mind several other instances when Mr. Trumble had voiced his opinion about someone he had just met. Catherine had always thought it took time to get to know a person, that speaking with a new acquaintance for only a minute or two wasn't enough to form an accurate evaluation of a man, and she had always stuck to that belief. Mr. Trumble never did, and what amazed her was that very often his first impression was right. She hoped he had guessed correctly about the man they were following, and that in the very near future she would have to apologize . . . both to Mr. Trumble for doubting him and to T.J. Savage for jumping to the wrong conclusion. It's what she hoped for, yet the memory of Mr. Trumble's firm rejection of Aaron Courtland kept coming to mind to ruin it.

Catherine had only just met Aaron and his mother, Edith, the summer past when she and her father decided he needed some time away from the university and from his work. They'd elected to stay in their town house in London, until the weather turned chilly and the professor's chemistry students took up residence on the campus again. Then they'd return to Oxford to live just as they had done every year. But that particular summer brought about some changes in Catherine's life, changes that saw Sterling return to Oxford alone, while she stayed on in London.

An associate of her father's, Harold Schumbacher, had come to the house early one June morning to tell Sterling the exasperating details of how he and his wife had returned home the night before to find that they had been robbed. Interested in hearing the story, Catherine had asked permission to sit with the men in the parlor while Schumbacher recited everything he'd told Scotland Yard that same night, and before the man had finished telling it, Catherine had a hundred questions, more, it seemed to Schumbacher, than the detective from Scotland Yard had asked. Amused, at first, by the young woman's fascination with the robbery, Schumbacher had easily supplied the answers, until a vague awareness of the direction in which she was leading him raised his own questions. Within minutes, they had come to the reasonable deduction that the houseboy Harold Schumbacher had fired the day before was the culprit in the case, and he'd raced off to tell someone at Scotland Yard. Later that afternoon, a package with Catherine's name on it was delivered to the town house, and inside she found a gold-handled magnifying glass, a gift from Harold Schumbacher for her help in seeing that his stolen property was returned.

Word of her talents soon spread, and before long, Catherine was having to turn people away simply because there weren't enough hours in the day for her to solve every crime given her. She became more selective in her choices, picking those that had to do with murder or kidnapping, arson, missing persons, or the kinds of theft that involved priceless articles. As her reputation grew, she acquired several enemies as well, the most ardent being the commissioner of Scotland Yard. But Catherine never seemed to mind. Commissioner Mays simply couldn't handle the damage to his ego, and the rest of those who complained about her usually spoke out because they were afraid of her . . . afraid she would prove them guilty of something.

By the middle of summer, Catherine and her father were the guests most often invited to any function put on by the wealthy, and it was at one of these parties that she met Aaron and Edith Courtland. She could remember thinking how extremely opposite in appearance mother and son were, but that their personalities were identical. Flashy, exuberant, and generous, the pair had won the friendship of practically everyone they met, despite their scandalous background. Edith, a short, plump redhead with wide blue eyes, had spent the youthful years of her life climbing in and out of bed with whichever man offered the most money. Aaron, tall, lean, and not unpleasing to look at, with dark hair and green eyes, was the product of one of those liaisons.

A vague smile lifted the corners of Catherine's mouth as she hugged her cloak around her and thought back to the first time she had been introduced to Aaron and his mother. Edith had taken an instant liking to her, and Catherine wondered if the woman had decided right then that Catherine would be the one Aaron married, for it seemed once a week from then on, Edith was inviting her over for tea or dinner or for whatever other excuse she could invent. Catherine, of course, had always declined, since her work would sometimes keep her busy until well past midnight, *and* for the simple reason that she wasn't interested in romance. It wasn't that she found Aaron unappealing—he was quite charming in fact and he'd become a good friend—but she had more important things to do with her time. And Mr. Trumble had agreed.

She chuckled to herself when she remembered the servant's comment in response to the statement. He had said that those who had too much money and nothing else to do but primp in front of a mirror were surely destined to do the devil's bidding. She was more than surprised to hear the words come out of Mr. Trumble's mouth, but at the same time his remark had made her laugh.

"How can you say something like that about a man you haven't even met?" she had challenged him.

"Perhaps I haven't," he had replied. "But I know something about him. He and his mother are trash, miss, and they're parading around like royalty. You'd be wise to stay clear of them, Miss Catherine."

She knew Mr. Trumble only meant to protect her reputation, since those born of noble rank seldom accepted those who were not, but in her opinion, Aaron shouldn't be held responsible for his mother's actions before he was conceived, and she had told Mr. Trumble that. "Aaron Courtland is a good man," she had argued. "He's provided for his mother and himself, learned to read and write, and to appreciate art, the opera, and fine wines. You must, at least, respect him for the initiative he took in bettering his life and that he did so without anyone's help."

Mr. Trumble hadn't replied, but the look Catherine could remember seeing on his face told her that respect was the last thing he had for Aaron Courtland, and she had never brought up the subject again. But now, as Hyde Park came into view, she was tempted to ask Mr. Trumble how he could find so much wrong with Aaron Courtland, and absolutely nothing about T.J. Savage to discredit. The idea, however, vanished when she felt the rig jerk to a halt.

"Do you see him, Miss Catherine?" Mr. Trumble's voice filtered down through the open trapdoor above her.

Turning her full concentration on her task, she scanned the crowded street for a sign of T.J.'s rig. Several minutes passed before she noticed that one had pulled to a stop at the curb and that a dark figure had stepped out from behind a tree.

"There!" she directed with a point of her finger. "Do you see them?"

"Yes, miss, I do," Mr. Trumble replied, just as the man handed something over and then turned on his heel and fled back into the darkness of the park. "But are you sure that's Mr. Savage?"

Before he had finished making the inquiry, the rig swung around to head down an adjacent street, placing the cab and its occupant in the dim light of a nearby street lamp. In that split second Catherine could see T.J.'s handsome face as he folded the piece of paper he'd been given and put it in his breast pocket, and a trickle of doubt seeped into her mind. Perhaps he'd been telling the truth after all. Maybe he truly wasn't a part of the trio who had broken into the museum . . . and maybe this was just part of a bigger plan to trick her into thinking so.

"Yes, Mr. Trumble, I'm sure," she answered, her words edged with anger and firm determination. "Don't lose him."

"I won't, Miss Catherine," Mr. Trumble promised as he snapped the reins and urged his horse to follow the rapidly departing cab.

When T.J.'s driver chose a less busy street to travel, the way opened up for Catherine and Mr. Trumble to keep a close eye on the rig while maintaining a safe distance behind them should either T.J. or the man who drove him happen to sense they were being trailed and look back. They made several turns and never slowed their pace, and before long Catherine realized they were heading toward the dock area and the River Thames.

Despite the late hour, the area around the wharf was still quite active. Scores of wagons, carts, and men carrying boxes and crates filled the street and impeded the pursuit, until an oncoming freight wagon, traveling at a dangerous speed, cleared a path of its own. Shouts of anger and colorful oaths followed the reckless driver as he plowed through the crowded street and forced Mr. Trumble to rein his cab out of the way simply to avoid a collision.

"Are you all right, Miss Catherine?" he asked worriedly, once the emergency had passed and he'd calmed his frightened horse.

"Yes, Mr. Trumble, I'm fine," Catherine called up to him. "Have you lost sight of Mr. Savage?"

"I'm afraid so, miss," he sadly reported, after a moment of scanning the busy, dimly lit avenue. "Shall we turn back?"

"Not yet, Mr. Trumble," she answered. "I don't give up that easily. We'll take our chances that he drove straight through. If we can't find him again in fifteen minutes . . ." She grimaced. "Then we'll head home."

"Very good, Miss Catherine," he agreed, snapping the reins and pulling the rig out into the street again.

They continued on for several more blocks, maneuvering their progress through the crush of wagons and dockhands busy at work and inadvertently blocking their path. Catherine had nearly lost hope, when for some reason she glanced off to her left at the alleyway they passed and spotted what she was sure was T.J.'s cab pulled to a stop at the far end.

"Mr. Trumble," she called excitedly. "I think I saw him."

"Where?"

"Down the alley we just passed." When she felt him stop the rig and sensed he was about to turn it around, she quickly instructed, "No, don't go in after him. He's sure to see us. Pull over there." She pointed to a spot at the side of the street. "We'll go the rest of the way on foot."

Although he wasn't about to say anything, Mr. Trumble highly disapproved of her decision, and with great reluctance he did as she ordered, positive his opinion wouldn't make a difference to her anyway.

"I hope the cab's still here when we return, miss," he grumbled, holding out a hand to assist her from the cab.

"If it isn't," she replied with a soft smile, "we'll have Mr. Savage buy us a new one."

He couldn't see the logic in her remark, but rather than

comment, he fell into step behind her as she fought her way along the crowded sidewalk.

Once they had neared the opening to the alleyway, they paused long enough for Catherine to sneak a look down the deserted avenue and assure their safety before continuing. With her back against the side of the building, she leaned slightly and glanced around the corner just in time to see a dark figure stepping out of a doorway. Thick fog swirled around the man's tall shape and, since he walked with his head down, the brim of the hat he wore hid his face. But even so, Catherine was almost sure she recognized T.J.'s muscular build and the somewhat cocky air with which he held himself. Then she faintly heard him order the driver not to waste a single second in leaving, and any doubt she had disappeared.

"Hurry, Mr. Trumble," she urged, turning to him and giving him a gentle shove. "He's leaving. Fetch the cab, while I watch to see which direction he goes. We mustn't lose him again."

More than willing to oblige, the gray-haired servant turned on his heel and quickly fled, failing to realize that he would be leaving his ward unprotected during his absence.

Most of Catherine's investigative success had to do with instinct. The other fraction came as a result of her curiosity, and the latter was what urged her to go to the building T.J. had exited before making a hasty departure. Perhaps Mr. Trumble hadn't noticed that T.J. had left the meeting place empty-handed, but Catherine had, and she wanted to know why.

Checking first to make certain Mr. Trumble was well on his way and that T.J.'s rig had rounded the corner out of sight, she grabbed her skirts in both hands and raced down the narrow back street to the half-closed door of the stable. A dim light seeped out through the cracks, and although she heard no sound coming from inside, experience had taught her not to take anything for granted, and she proceeded cautiously, despite the thunderous beating of her heart, the dryness in her mouth, and the fear that sent a shiver down her spine. Behind that door was the proof of T.J.'s guilt or innocence, and even if her discovery went against every conclusion she had drawn thus far, she simply had to know the answer.

Rusty hinges creaked when she pulled the wooden door handle toward her, and she froze the instant the sound seemed to ricochet off the walls behind her, certain those inside had heard and that before she could draw another breath, they would be on her. She'd placed herself in danger many times before, and she had always come out relatively unscathed. The risk was a part of her work. Yet, something about this particular case had her nerves on edge, and she couldn't quite figure out why. Several seconds passed, and once she was sure she hadn't warned the thieves of her presence, she pulled the door open far enough to stick her head in without actually having to go inside.

Since first becoming a detective, Catherine had seen her share of gruesome sights, but none of them had prepared her for what she saw just then. Caught as she was totally unaware, the vision of the two broken and bloodied bodies lying in the middle of the floor cut off her breath and turned her stomach. Certain she was about to retch, she jerked back, clamped her hand over her mouth and staggered away a step or two, while she sucked in a long breath of cool air through her nose and waited for the wave of nausea to pass.

No one deserves to die like that, she proclaimed in silent outrage. *No one!*

Weak and afraid her knees would give out from under her, she turned and leaned back heavily against the wall, a thousand questions whirling around inside her head. She wanted to believe otherwise, but one explanation above all the rest kept rising up to challenge her. Who, other than the man she had seen fleeing the scene, could have done this? And what she couldn't explain was why she had no intention of sharing her discovery with anyone.

"Nathan," Wallace Crandell called back as he and the rest of the men in his group headed for the door. "You coming with us?"

Looking up from his desk, Nathan Beecher waved his

fellow detectives on. "In a minute," he replied. "I've got a couple of things to do first. Where will you be?"

"At the White Horse Pub," Crandell advised as he shrugged into his coat and plopped his hat on his head. "You know, Nathan, working late won't get you anywhere, if you're thinking to impress the commissioner. He's more likely to notice you if you haul in some fiendish murderer." A playful smile followed the comment, then laughter, when Nathan curled his lip in response. "Just trying to make your life a little easier." Wallace grinned, turning and nearly colliding with the young boy coming in through the front door. "Hey, son, be careful."

"Sorry, sir," the youngster apologized. "I'm looking for Mr. Rhomberg. Do you know where he is?"

"I'll take you to him," Nathan offered, rising and motioning for the youth to follow him. "You in some kind of trouble?"

"No, sir," the boy replied. "I got a message for him."

The announcement didn't surprise Nathan. Lewis Rhomberg was always having messages delivered to him, and it always seemed that shortly thereafter Lewis would solve another case. Nathan had been with Scotland Yard for a little over a year now, and of all the men who worked there, the veteran detective was the one whose respect Nathan hoped to achieve. Crandell was wrong in thinking that Nathan wanted to win Commissioner Mays's attention, for in Nathan's opinion, Lewis Rhomberg was the one who really got things done. *He* deserved the title of commissioner of Scotland Yard, not Argus Mays.

"Excuse me, Mr. Rhomberg," Nathan interrupted, once he'd opened the door to Lewis's office and found him deeply engrossed in his work. "You have a visitor." He smiled, then corrected, "Or maybe I should say, you have a messenger."

Until Nathan's voice had disturbed his concentration, Lewis hadn't realized what time it was. Not that it mattered. He usually worked late, but he seldom skipped an evening meal, which was exactly what he'd done tonight. Falling back in his chair, he rubbed his eyes, stretched, then smiled at the young man who had disrupted his train of thought.

"Don't tell me you're learning bad habits too, Nathan," he teased. "One overdedicated fool is enough."

"I was just on my way out, sir," Nathan promised. "What about you?"

"I'll be right on your heels just as soon as I talk to this young man," Lewis vowed with a nod at the boy staring nervously back at him.

Nathan seized his chance. "A few of us are stopping for an ale at the White Horse, sir. We'd be honored if you'd join us."

Of all the young men working for the Yard, Lewis liked Nathan Beecher best. He could see in him the same kind of urgency and dedication to his work that had inspired Lewis in his early days, and there was a strong probability that in the future Nathan would aspire to the rank of commissioner, something Lewis realized was beyond his capabilities. His only hope was that he would still be around when Nathan took over. It would be much more enjoyable to work for someone who had the same temperament and ideas as Lewis had, rather than to have to tolerate the stupidity and bias of someone like Commissioner Mays.

"I appreciate the invitation, Nathan," he confessed, "and if time allows, I'll be there."

"Very good, sir," Nathan replied, smiling broadly. "I'll save you a chair." He motioned for his companion to step into Lewis's office, then closed the door behind him and hurried off to catch up with the others.

Noticing the folded piece of paper the boy held in one hand, Lewis nodded at it. "Is that for me?" he asked.

"Yes, sir," the boy answered, rushing to the desk. "I was told to wait until you'd read it just in case you had a message for him."

"Him?" Lewis asked, unfolding the parchment.

"The man who paid me to give it to you."

Even if Lewis hadn't recognized the handwriting, he would have known the message came from T.J. by the sarcastic way he'd signed the note. Chuckling, he reached into his pocket, withdrew a coin, and tossed it to the boy. "I'd say this calls for a face-to-face meeting, but thank you for your time."

"No trouble, sir," the youth admitted, grinning at the generous payment he'd received before he turned on his heel and made a hurried exit.

"Your dutiful slave," Lewis muttered as he stood and reached for his hat and coat from the peg on the wall behind him. "*That* will be the day."

As always, Lewis walked several blocks after leaving Scotland Yard, carefully noting who, if anyone, followed him, before he flagged down a cab and rode to within one block of the inn where T.J. had asked Lewis to meet him. He'd learned over the years to take extra precautions, no matter how innocent a rendezvous seemed to be. After paying the driver, he descended the rig, cut across the street and down an alley, before he paused outside the entrance to the inn to have one last look around. Positive no one was interested in where he was going, he opened the door and went inside.

Lewis had very little trouble picking out the location of the table where his friend sat away from everyone. None of the other patrons had the kind of presence that drew a man's attention the way T. J. Savage did, and although Lewis couldn't exactly explain just what that was, he was glad he'd talked T.J. out of pursuing a detective's line of work. Part of Lewis's success came from being able to blend in with his surroundings. T.J. could never do that. Hanging his coat and hat on the peg by the door, he closed the distance to his friend, silently stared at T.J. for a moment, and then pulled out a chair to sit down.

"Took you long enough," T.J. mocked, once the barmaid had left them alone again to fetch Lewis's meal. "Did you walk all the way here?"

"As a matter of fact, I walked a good portion of it, yes. A man can't be too careful, you know." He smiled at the young maid who momentarily interrupted them to place Lewis's mug of ale on the table in front of him. He took a long drink, ran his tongue over his lips to savor every drop, and then relaxed back in his chair, his fingers wrapped around the handle of the tankard. "And since when does a 'slave' criticize his master?"

T.J.'s brown eyes sparkled and a hint of a smile parted his lips as he reached into a pocket and pulled out a cheroot.

"So, why all the secrecy? Have you learned something about Professor Chase's death?"

Striking a match and lighting his cigar, T.J. took a long drag on it, exhaled, and watched the smoke rise toward the ceiling before answering. "That will take a little time," he announced. "I have to win Miss Chase's trust first, before I can get her to talk about anything so personal."

"And how is it you plan to go about doing that?" Lewis coaxed suspiciously.

T.J. studied the tip of his cheroot for a moment. "She believes I'm a thief, Lewis. Do you think I can get her to trust me when all she'd really like to do is have me jailed?"

Lewis narrowed his eyes. "I was afraid you'd say something like that." Disgusted, he took a second swallow of his ale and set the mug back down. "All right. So, tell me what you've learned about the robbery. That is why you sent for me, isn't it?"

T.J. forced back a smile. With the exception of the man who had raised him, he doubted any other had ever been able to get the better of Lewis Rhomberg. It wasn't necessarily something of which T.J. was proud, but he did find it amusing.

"I received a second message from the thieves this afternoon telling me where to meet with them. But when I got there, all that was waiting for me was two dead bodies."

Lewis frowned. "The thieves?"

T.J. nodded. "From the tracks I saw in the dirt floor, it's my guess they had the paintings with them and that whoever killed them drove off with the artworks."

"I don't understand," Lewis admitted. "What tracks?"

The vision of Catherine Chase flooded T.J.'s mind and he smiled. He had used the information she had given him and hadn't bothered telling Lewis about it. A minor detail, but one that had obviously confused his friend.

"Miss Chase told me that the wagon used to haul the paintings from the museum had a nick in one of the wheels. That's how she managed to be at the first meeting place. She'd hired a boy to find the wagon for her. Remembering that, I did a little investigating of my own after I'd found the murdered men, and the first thing I noticed was the marks in the dirt, fresh marks . . . of a wagon wheel with a nick in it."

Lewis's frown grew even deeper. "When did she tell you this?"

"About an hour ago," T.J. lied as he leaned and flicked an ash into the glass dish sitting on the table. "After our talk, I decided the only way I could prove to her that I wasn't the man she was after was to help her catch the real thief. Then the message came to the house, and I used it as an excuse to pay her a visit." He smiled, remembering Catherine's reaction to his claim and how he'd told Lewis in the beginning that she'd never believe him. Being honest had its drawbacks. If anything, he'd strengthened her conviction.

"Are you saying you *told* her about the second meeting?"

"I told her not to leave the house, that she'd nearly gotten herself killed the last time she went chasing after crooks."

Lewis snorted. "And you honestly think she listened to you?" He shook his head and added, "You certainly do underestimate the woman."

Feeling a bit insulted, T.J. offered a defense. "I made sure she wouldn't follow me."

"How?" Lewis quickly asked. "Did you tie her up and throw her in a closet? It's the only way you'd keep her home."

T.J. started to tell him about Mr. Trumble, when Lewis's suggestion evoked a humorous picture in his mind, and he laughed instead. "No, I didn't lock her in a closet. But that's not such a bad idea. I'll try and remember it, if I ever have trouble with her again."

Lewis gave his friend a sarcastic, one-sided smile. "Yes, well, to be honest, I doubt even that will work. But it's certainly a lot smarter than counting on Trumble's help."

T.J. could feel his stomach knot. "Trumble?" he repeated.

"Her servant . . . if that's what you want to call him. Don't get me wrong. I think Trumble's a very nice gentleman, but he doesn't know how to handle Catherine Chase." Lewis took another drink of his ale, then added, "No one does."

The barmaid arrived at that moment with Lewis's dinner. Distracted by the mouth-watering aroma of roasted lamb, baked new potatoes, gravy, and hot buttermilk biscuits, he failed to notice the odd look that had come over T.J.'s face or his meal might not have gained so much importance to him. Wondering how he could have been this hungry without even knowing it, he picked up his knife and fork, cut off a slice of meat, and popped it in his mouth, groaning with the sheer pleasure of its taste. He was nearly half finished with his meal when he remembered the real reason why he'd come to this particular inn and what the topic of conversation had been.

"So, what did you do with the dead bodies?" he asked, shoveling in another mouthful.

"Nothing. I left everything the way I found it," T.J. replied, once he'd shaken off the worry that he'd made a mistake in trusting Mr. Trumble. "Except for this." Digging deep into his pocket, he withdrew a tiny gold object and laid it on the table in front of his friend.

"It's a button," Lewis observed, failing to understand its relevance.

"And I believe it came off the killer's coat."

Suddenly very interested, Lewis put aside his fork and picked up the button to examine. "Why do you think so?" he asked after a moment.

"Because I had to pry it out of the hand of one of the dead men. From the look of things, I'd say both of them put up quite a struggle before their assailant got the better of them. I would suppose you'll be able to figure out exactly what the killer used to bash in their heads once you've had a chance to study the scene, but I can tell you this much, it wasn't the muzzle of his gun. This bastard had to have used a much heavier weapon than that. Why, their own mothers wouldn't recognize them after the beating they took." T.J. shook his head, remembering. "I've never seen so much blood."

Having lost his appetite, Lewis shoved his plate away with one hand, while he dropped the button in his vest pocket with the other. "You certainly know how to ruin a man's dinner."

"Sorry," T.J. apologized, once he'd realized how colorful his description had been.

"You're also not offering much hope of solving this case."

"Not unless you can find the wagon. Or the man who owns that button."

Reaching for the necessary coin to pay for his meal, Lewis admitted, "And I won't do either sitting here." He tossed the money on the table and stood, frowning when he noticed that his companion wasn't as eager to leave. "Aren't you coming?"

T.J. shook his head. "I have a problem of my own that needs my attention more, and it's something that can't wait until morning, unfortunately." He too threw a coin on the table and rose. "Besides, you and I really shouldn't be seen together, remember?"

He grinned and leaned to retrieve his cape and hat from the chair next to him, while he gave Lewis directions to the stable. When he straightened again, unbeknownst to him, the bottom button on his coat became wedged in the decorative groove on the table's edge, and before he realized it, he felt a tug, heard a slight rip and the dull clink of something hitting the floor at his feet. Stepping back, he looked down to find that he had torn a button loose, and the sight of it made him chuckle.

"It's a good thing you witnessed this," he joked, bending to scoop up the gold fastener and stuff it in his pocket. "Otherwise, you'd have just as many doubts about me as Catherine Chase."

"Don't get too cocky, T.J. Savage," Lewis warned, turning with him toward the door. "I have my doubts about you. They're just different from Miss Chase's. She doubts your innocence. I doubt your sanity."

"Really?" T.J. laughed. "And why is that?"

"Why?" Lewis echoed. "Setting aside the fact that you probably have enough money to buy half the European continent, your looks alone would win you the company of any beautiful woman you wanted. Yet you choose to chase around in the dark looking for crooks and having dinner with me. Wouldn't you say that's a little insane?"

T.J. playfully shrugged a shoulder. "Not really. Having money isn't everything, and as for beautiful women . . . I have yet to meet one who's interesting."

The declaration had barely passed his lips when the image of a blue-eyed, strawberry-blond-haired woman flashed before his eyes. Catherine Chase was interesting . . . and frustrating. And yes, she was beautiful . . . in an unpolished sort of way. Suddenly, the fragrance of her hair and skin filled his senses, and he sighed dreamily. He'd stolen a kiss or two in his time, and while they had always been exciting and had usually led to richer rewards, the passion had faded as quickly as he had disappeared into the night. Perhaps the memory of that kiss with Catherine lingered even now simply because he hadn't chosen to take advantage of the situation, and the result had left him feeling unfulfilled, like a morning without a sunrise; a rose without a thorn; or an artist's palette void of paint.

What more could it be than that? he asked himself as he settled his hat on his head and whirled the cape over his shoulders. Why, nothing more, he silently replied, following Lewis from the inn. Yet once he'd bade farewell to his friend and had climbed into the hansom cab with instructions for the driver to take him to Catherine's home, T.J.—like Lewis—was filled with doubt.

CHAPTER 6

A troubled, unhappy frown darkened Catherine's eyes as she stood looking out the window in the study. Fear, confusion, and worry darkened the sky-blue color of her eyes, and the soft curve of her mouth turned downward. For the past half hour she had been fighting off the image that would pop into her head every time she unwillingly allowed her mind to wander back to the scene in the stable. Her body would shake, and she would unknowingly clasp her arms around her until the trembling stopped, only to have it start again once she relaxed.

What truly bothered her more than the shock of seeing two brutalized bodies lying in a pool of blood was how deeply it had affected her. It hadn't been the first time she'd witnessed such a hideous sight. Some had even been more grisly. Yet this was the only time she'd been unable to distance herself from the victims, the crime, and the suspects.

"Suspects," she muttered disgustedly, folding her arms in front of her as she glared out the window. "Wrong word. There's no suspicion involved. I *know* he's guilty." The anger faded from her eyes, and a sadness replaced it. "And *that's* what has me fighting with my conscience."

The thump of a book hitting the floor turned Catherine around in time to see Satan leap from the edge of her desk to the floor, and she smiled. It seemed she was forever scolding the long-tailed cat and with no success, and she wondered why she even tried. The feline was as independent as she was, and *she'd* never accepted anyone's attempts to change her. Why should the cat?

Round gold eyes stared up at her once Satan had sauntered across the room and stood waiting at her feet to be picked up. When it seemed she hadn't responded quickly enough to suit him, he voiced his disapproval with a loud meow and the flick of his tail. The effort awarded him the prize he obviously wanted, and once Catherine held him snugly in her arms, he began to purr.

"I wish my life could be as simple as yours," she murmured, burying her face in the soft fur on the back of his neck. "Nothing bothers you. You don't even have to look for something to eat anymore. It's always waiting for you in the kitchen. You sleep on a nice, comfortable bed. You don't have to be out in the rain or the cold. What more could you want?"

She smiled at him, and as if he were trying to answer, he stretched and rubbed his nose under her chin, making her laugh.

"Oh, you're quite welcome, Satan. Is there anything else I can do for you?" she asked, scratching him behind the ears as she carried him to the settee and sat down with him cradled on her lap. "Maybe the next time Mr. Trumble brings me a glass of warm milk, I'll let you drink it for me. Would you like that?"

Satan squinted yellow eyes at her.

"No, really. I'd appreciate it if you would. I truly don't like warm milk." She stroked his head, his bony back, and the long length of his tail, wincing when her affection for him resulted in sharp claws curling through the fabric of her skirt and into her thigh. "Ouch," she half laughed, half scolded as she pinched his toes to make him stop.

Satan obviously didn't like the lesson she was trying to teach him, for he instantly bounded off her lap with a swish of his tail and swaggered from the room.

"I'm sorry, m'lord," she mockingly called after him. " 'Tis the price one must pay for love."

The smile faded from her lips once the temporary

distraction had pranced out of sight and her thoughts had returned to the dead men in the stable. All the diversions in the world weren't going to erase the fact that she had practically witnessed the murders or that she knew who had committed them. Rising, she left the settee to return to her desk and the notes she had been making to better clarify the clues she had found in the stable.

Once she had regained her composure and before Mr. Trumble had come with the cab, Catherine had steeled herself to go back inside the building. She had needed to examine the bodies and to look for any other telltale marks that might have been left behind in order to fully convince herself of Mr. Savage's guilt. Although in her heart she felt it wouldn't take a lot of doing, she had also taught herself that the obvious wasn't always the right answer. Just because she had seen him coming from the stable and had heard him instruct his driver not to waste any time in leaving, it didn't necessarily mean he was the killer. He could have found the men already dead . . . just as she had. Or perhaps the thieves had changed their minds about giving him the paintings and an argument had broken out, and in defense of his own life, T.J. had had to kill them. And then there was the possibility that he'd been telling her the truth all along. The thieves could have found out about his plan, lured him to the stable, and then jumped him once he'd stepped inside. There certainly was evidence of a struggle to back it up. Yet the flaw in that theory was the way one of the two men had died. He'd been struck over the head from behind, which meant he probably hadn't been aware of his killer's intentions. The second man's forehead had been caved in, and unless the murderer got some twisted satisfaction out of hitting a dead body, the cut lip, broken nose, and shattered left wrist, as well as the gash under the victim's left eye, indicated he had fought with his attacker before being killed.

Remembering those specific clues, Catherine leaned forward in her chair, picked up her spectacles and slipped them on, then reached for a pen and a blank piece of parchment on which to draw. Her stick figures hardly resembled real people, but once she had finished her sketch, she had discovered four very important facts. First of all, since all of the injuries to the second man had been on his left side, that implied the killer had held his weapon in his right hand. That alone wasn't enough to hang a man, but if T.J. was left-handed . . .

Secondly, because of the violence behind the attack, the murderer had to have been splattered with his victim's blood. It had been dark in that alleyway where she saw T.J. climb into his cab, making it impossible for her to see much of anything, but she could remember him never having fidgeted with his clothes the way someone would if they'd gotten soiled. She also recalled that he hadn't been carrying anything when he left the stable, and since she hadn't been able to find the murder weapon—a crowbar in her estimation by the width of the mark left in the damaged flesh and bone—she had to assume someone else had removed it. The real killer, perhaps?

Lastly and probably the most important of all the aspects involved was the location of evidence in comparison to the size of the room. The scuff marks in the dirt, the blood, the bodies, and every single footprint she could find were all concentrated to one side of the interior. The only logical deduction she could draw was that a wagon or coach or something of equal size had taken up the remaining space, and that it had been removed *after* the murders and *before* either T.J. or she had arrived. Common sense told her it had been the wagon used to carry the paintings, and if Mr. Trumble hadn't come with the cab when he had, she would have probably noticed the wagon tracks and more specifically the distinct mark one of its wheels made. Now all she could do was speculate, but in her opinion speculation was probably fact.

The clock on the fireplace mantel struck nine, drawing Catherine's attention to the time. She and Mr. Trumble had returned home more than half an hour ago, and T.J. had yet to pay them a second visit as he had said he would.

No doubt he's home changing out of his bloodstained clothes, she mused sarcastically as she pulled the eyeglasses from her nose and dropped them on the desk. The smug look on her face quickly disappeared. *And you're not listening to your own assessment of the facts, Catherine Chase*. Rising, she moved back to stand by the window. *You've found him guilty before he's even gone to trial. And if he did, there'd be too many contradictions to convince a jury. You know what your problem really is? You don't want to admit that your first instinct might be wrong.*

"And if it is," she murmured aloud, looking down at the dimly lit street and the sidewalk passing in front of her house, "why isn't he here? What's taking him so long?"

The question had barely crossed her lips before she noticed how the fog clinging to the street lamp at the corner began to swirl and lift upward. A second later a livery cab came into view, and as it pulled to a stop out front, Catherine could feel her heartbeat quicken. In order for T.J. to win her completely over to his side, Catherine knew that sooner or later he would have to talk with her again about tonight's meeting. What he had to say and how carefully he would word it would certainly give her a clear indication of his guilt or innocence, since he'd have no idea that she was already aware of the murders. What she probably wouldn't hear, however, was his explanation for the missing half hour.

A nervousness came over her as she watched T.J.'s tall shape unfold from within the cab and stretch to full height as he stepped to the sidewalk. Even in the darkness without a light touching his face, she knew how handsome he was, and for a second she wondered if there was another woman somewhere in London who thought the same thing every time she saw him, a woman who had a claim on him. Surprised by her thoughts, Catherine frowned and spun away from the window to look for her shoes. He'd be at the door in a matter of seconds, and she needed what little privacy offered her to gain control of her composure. If he suspected something was wrong, it would ruin everything.

"Miss Catherine?" Mr. Trumble's voice drifted up from the stairway outside the study. "I believe Mr. Savage is on his way to the door."

"Yes, Mr. Trumble, I saw him from the window," she called back as she stepped into her shoes and hurried out into the hallway. "Now, remember, we *never* left the house. He's not to know we followed him or that we observed him coming from that stable. It's the only way he'll feel safe in telling me whatever story he's decided to recite. If he's truthful with me . . . well, then . . ." She smiled lopsidedly at him and reached up to pull the ribbon from her hair, positive the truth was the furthest thing from T.J.'s mind.

She hadn't liked having to lie to Mr. Trumble by pretending she hadn't found anything significant inside the stable, but she had done so for various reasons, the most important being that she was sure the sight of those murdered men would have been too much for the man's gentle nature. She also knew that if Mr. Trumble was made aware of the kinds of things involved in her work, he'd become adamant about accompanying her from now on, and that would create a whole new set of problems for her. No, it was best he didn't know what was going on . . . for his sake and for hers. She'd rather he go on thinking he was right about T.J. Savage.

The knock on the door made them both jump, and while Mr. Trumble descended the trio of steps he'd climbed, Catherine brushed back her long hair with her fingers and held the heavy strands in place with the ribbon, her eyes riveted on the thick oak panels Mr. Trumble swung inward.

"Good evening, Mr. Savage," he greeted, moving to one side and holding out his hand. "Won't you come in?"

Catherine felt as if her heart had lurched to her throat the moment T.J. moved into the foyer where she could see him. His presence seemed to dwarf that of Mr. Trumble's, and the black cape, which fell in dark, rich folds from his wide shoulders, gave him a sinister appearance, almost as if the devil himself had come calling. Whether she actually gasped aloud or just imagined she had, somehow T.J. sensed she was there, and he turned to look at her while he doffed his top hat and cloak and handed them to Mr. Trumble. A warm smile parted his lips and made Catherine horribly uncomfortable. She'd read about the wild beasts in the African jungle, how they devoured human prey, and that folklore claimed the huge tigers smiled just before they attacked. Catherine had always known that wasn't true—a feline couldn't smile—but that fact did little to ease the sense that she herself was about to be gobbled up. Mentally shaking off the idea, she pulled her gaze from him and descended the stairs.

"We'll talk in the parlor," she instructed as she hurried past him in that direction. "Mr. Trumble, would you bring our guest a glass of wine or a snifter of brandy, perhaps?"

"Thank you, no," T.J. cut in. "Nothing for me. But if Miss Chase would like a glass—"

"I seldom drink," she crisply replied as she disappeared through the doorway and into the parlor.

"Why doesn't that surprise me?" he murmured, before glancing at the gray-haired servant who had silently listened to the cool exchange. "I suppose nothing about her surprises you, does it, Mr. Trumble?"

"No, sir," the man replied, turning to hang his visitor's garments on the hall tree. "I'll be in the kitchen, if you wish anything, sir."

T.J. didn't respond, nor did Mr. Trumble wait to hear his answer. He simply walked away, and T.J. watched the spry little man's departure until he too had vanished from sight. He'd never served in any man's army, but just then he certainly knew what it must have felt like to be in the enemy's camp. With a shake of his head and a crooked smile, he joined Catherine in the parlor.

The soft light of the lamp sitting on the end table warmed the room and drew T.J.'s immediate attention to the woman who stood with her back to him while she stared out the window. The drabness of the ivory-colored linen blouse and the dark brown skirt she wore failed to mask the beauty hidden beneath the attire, and T.J. openly stared, his gaze following the slender figure from the top of her head to the hem of her skirt while his imagination stripped her bare. Catherine Chase didn't have to clothe herself in lace and satin, low necklines and tight-fitting undergarments, to accentuate the fact that she was a woman or to stimulate T.J.'s male appreciation. The long, strawberry-blond hair, blue eyes, and her porcelain-smooth skin stirred all the desire he needed to be interested, and the knowledge that so little about her could arouse his want to explore the depth of her soul surprised him. Other women, some more than eager to fulfill his wishes, had never sparked the kind of fire in him that he experienced now with Catherine, and for a moment he both feared and questioned the cause. Perhaps it was her obvious dislike for him, her lack of interest in him as a man, that bruised his ego and challenged him to change her mind. Or maybe it had nothing at all to do with his pride. He'd never fallen in love before, which left him incapable of recognizing the feeling, and he honestly doubted that was the root of his strong attraction for her, but just the same he realized walking away from her wasn't going to be an easy feat.

While she stood absently scanning the dark street outside the town house, Catherine made a decision. She didn't like T. J. Savage because he was the first and only man capable of shattering the black-and-white way she looked at life. He'd added color and depth, feelings that were strange to her, and he'd made her acutely aware of her own vulnerabilities, and that not all men were put on this earth just to take up space. What irritated her was her failure to understand why he couldn't just blend in with everyone else. She'd been very happy and content until he came along. Now, he'd turned her world upside down and awakened emotions in her that made her distrust herself. Why, she couldn't even look at him without feeling warm all over and somewhat tongue-tied, and it frustrated her. How could she think sanely and logically if all she really wanted to do was stare at him like some enamored dolt?

"Have a seat, Mr. Savage," she ordered suddenly as she swung around, surprising herself as well as him with her sharp abruptness. Carefully avoiding the temptation to look at his handsome face, she crossed the room and sat down in one of the wing chairs before the hearth, watching from out of the corner of her eye as he took his place beside her.

"You've been gone quite a while," she stated. "Was there trouble?"

T.J. wondered if she was more angry with him for not allowing her to come along or with Mr. Trumble for enforcing T.J.'s wishes. In either case, he concluded, her temper would simmer even more once he told her what she'd missed. "I'm afraid there was," he announced, having decided on his way over not to hide a thing from her. "By the time I arrived at the location where the thieves were to have been waiting for me, someone else had obviously gotten there ahead of me."

Good heavens, Catherine thought, surprise pulling her tawny brows together as she lifted her eyes to meet his. *Is he going to tell me about the murders? I certainly wasn't expecting this. But wait, Catherine,* she silently warned. *He's bound to have an explanation to clear himself.*

"You mean the men and the paintings were gone?" she suggested, giving him the lie he needed to throw suspicion from himself.

"You're partly correct," he answered. "The paintings weren't there, but the thieves were. They'd been murdered."

Catherine's mind raced. What was he scheming? Why would he tell her the truth when there was no need? As far as he was concerned, she had no idea what he found. So what was to be gained by telling her?

"Murdered?" she baited. "By whom?"

T.J. shook his head and shifted in the chair to free one tail of the coat on which he sat. "I wish I knew. If I did, we'd have the man behind the burglary."

Catherine's brow wrinkled all the more. "Why do you say that?"

"Because I'm in agreement with you that those two dead men were working for someone else, someone who knows the value of art and who'd be willing to pay a steep price to own it." He sat back and placed an ankle across his knee. "I've done a lot of thinking about this affair, and I've come to the conclusion that I was part of a double-cross."

Interested in his theory, Catherine listened intently once she'd asked him to explain.

"Their job was finished the minute they drove the wagon away from the museum. Yet here they are several weeks later, still in possession of some very valuable merchandise. Why?" He could see by the expression on her face that she wasn't following his train of thought. "It's my guess," he continued, dropping his foot to the floor and leaning forward with his elbows braced on his knees, "that once all the excitement was over and they were safely away, they began to realize exactly what it was they had in their hands, and that by selling it themselves, they wouldn't have to be satisfied with the few pounds they would have been paid for breaking into the museum. All they had to do was find a buyer. I provided them that by spreading the word I was in the market for a Rembrandt at any price. And you know how servants love to gossip."

Catherine had to admit that she'd never given that angle a thought. But now that he'd brought it up, it made sense. If they *had* been hired by someone to do the job, then why would they still be in possession of the stolen property? And why would they be willing to sell the paintings to the first man who came along with the right amount of money? A seasoned art thief would sell them to the highest bidder. And he wouldn't leave them crated and bouncing around London for days, nor would he trust the likes of the two murdered men to make his transaction for him.

"So, what you're saying is that whoever hired the two men is the one who killed them?" she suggested.

"It's the only answer I can come up with," he confessed.

"But are you sure the men had brought the paintings with them this time? Just because they weren't there when you arrived—"

T.J. smiled. "You're not the only one who has an eye for detail, Miss Chase."

Catherine raised one brow at him.

"What do you think the odds are that there are two wagons in London or even in England with the identical nick in one of their wheels?"

Catherine had to bite the inside of her lip to keep from exclaiming out loud and giving herself away. She knew there had been a wagon in that stable, and she'd guessed it was the same one used in the robbery. T.J. just verified it for her. Rising, she motioned for him to stay seated while she appeared to be idly pacing the floor and giving his idea some consideration. She wanted to believe him, to believe everything he'd said, but her training and past experience told her never to fully trust anyone. The wiliest of crooks always seemed to have the right answers. And why shouldn't he? It was his neck at risk.

Turning to face her companion, Catherine stared for several seconds, while deciding how to test him. "Did you find any other clues? Some that are more tangible than speculation?"

T.J. instantly remembered the button he'd given to Lewis. It was probably the only piece of evidence worth considering, but by telling her about it, he would have to admit to his friendship with a detective for Scotland Yard. It would certainly clear any doubt she might have about him. Yet, at the same time, it would raise too many questions, ones he might not be able to answer. "Such as a murder weapon?" he asked, deliberately pointing her in a different direction.

Catherine nodded.

"No," he honestly replied. "But I can tell you one thing. It had to have been something heavier and bigger than the muzzle of someone's pistol."

"Why do you say that?" she asked, her eyes narrowed.

Unsure of how she could handle the gruesome details, he hesitated.

"Mr. Savage," she cut in, certain she knew what he was thinking, "my investigations haven't always been as mild as looking at tracks in the dirt. I've worked on a few murder cases already, so anything you say won't have me running to the washbasin."

A smile parted his lips with her response. "My apologies. I have a tendency to forget that you're an exceptional woman."

Catherine didn't like the subtle insult he'd voiced to include the whole of womankind. "You wouldn't have to apologize, Mr. Savage, if you took the time to compare the type of women who are usually in your company to the many who are not. If you did, you'd learn that the majority of us are smart, resourceful, strong-willed, and that other things are more important to us than what color ball gown we should wear. The sight of blood is not uncommon to us. It happens every time we give birth or nurse our soldiers' wounds. So spare me the condescending manner, and tell me why a pistol couldn't have been the murder weapon."

T.J.'s smile widened. With a shake of his head, he leaned back in his chair and eyed her for a moment. "You are a hard one, aren't you, Miss Chase? You take objection to my attempt at paying you a compliment and then turn it into a crusade against what you assume is bigotry. If I were anyone else, your remarks would anger me."

"It wasn't my intention to make you angry," she replied in self-defense. "I merely wanted you to realize that I'm capable of handling anything you might tell me."

T.J.'s gaze dropped from the stern expression on her face to the soft rise and fall of her bosom, to the pink fullness of her mouth, and back to the firm determination glowing in her pale blue eyes. "Anything?" he asked quietly.

A flicker of a frown shot across her brow and disappeared. "Yes. Anything." Her heart thumped and she unwittingly took a step backward when he lowered his gaze, placed his hands on the arms of his chair and pushed up.

"I wonder . . ." he said, slowly moving toward her, his dark eyes locked on her slightly parted lips. "If I told you that I found you to be the most beautiful woman I've ever seen, how would you handle that? If I told you that I've thought of no other woman since that night we met, how would you react? And if I told you . . ." He came to within a hand's breadth of her and reached up to entwine his finger within a stray tendril of pale blond hair lying against her brow. "If I told you how much I wanted to kiss you right now, would you let me?"

The bolt of red-hot, titillating fire that shot upward from

her loins to the pit of her belly took her breath away, and she was faced with the biggest challenge in her life. She knew he was only playing with her. She'd given him the opening, and he'd taken the advantage. She knew it, yet everything in her longed to give him the permission he sought, to feel his lips against hers, to experience again the ecstasy his kiss could bring.

The heady scent of his cologne, his presence, the anticipation of what was to come made her head spin, and as she watched his parted lips slowly descend toward hers, she unknowingly closed her eyes. In the darkness of her lowered lids the spell was broken and sanity returned. Straightening her spine and tightening every muscle in her body, she abruptly turned away, crossing to the buffet and the stack of unopened letters lying there.

"You certainly have a way of avoiding the subject, Mr. Savage," she charged, fidgeting with the pile of folded parchments and noticing that one appeared to be an invitation of some kind. "Are you trying to hide something?"

T.J.'s brown eyes sparkled. "As I've told you before, Miss Chase, I have nothing to hide." He smiled warmly at her when she cast him a brief glance. "In fact, if you'd think about it, you'd realize that I just made a confession of love."

"Love!" she exclaimed, laughing as she whirled to face him. "Oh, please."

"Is that so hard to believe?" he asked with a playful, boyish look of innocence. "Are you implying no one could fall in love with you?"

The humor disappeared. "I'm not implying anything, Mr. Savage," she said. "It's just my way of letting you know I won't be fooled by your charm and sweet words. As I see it, you're a thief and very possibly a murderer."

T.J. laid one hand over his heart. "You injure me, miss. I bare my soul to you, and in return you mock me."

Catherine started to reply when she realized the game he played would continue for hours if she let it. Instead, she gave him a disgruntled look as she absently picked up the letters from the buffet and returned with them in hand to sit down in her chair.

"Why, Mr. Savage?" she asked again, once he'd moved to stand near the fireplace. "Why wasn't the murder weapon a pistol?"

Not at all surprised by how easily she had regained her aplomb, T.J. studied the profile she presented him, before countering her question with one of his own. "And why do you accuse me of being a murderer?" He motioned at his attire. "Do you see any blood on my clothes?" He turned both palms upward. "Or on my hands?"

Catherine refused to admit aloud that she had already found flaws in her own earlier deductions about him, and instead looked him over from head to toe, noticing but not mentioning the button that was missing from his coat. "Blood?" she asked. "Why would there be any blood on you, if you took a length of cord and strangled the two men with it?"

T.J.'s brows dipped downward. "Strangled them? Who said anything about them being strangled? They were beaten to death, and it's my conclusion the killer used a metal pipe of some sort."

"Really?" she tested. "Why?"

For a second T.J. contemplated a more delicate way of putting it, then changed his mind. After all, she'd told him she was capable of hearing anything he had to say. "Because of the size of the wounds and the extent of damage to their skulls. A pistol might crack a bone but never shatter it that way. It also means that whoever swung the weapon had to have gotten blood on himself."

"What else did you notice about the bodies?"

"The man closest to the door was killed with one blow. The second man took more of a beating."

"What makes you think so?"

"Aside from the cracked skull, his left wrist was broken, his lip was split, and he had a gash under his eye."

"What about his nose?"

"What about it?" T.J. asked suspiciously.

Catherine shrugged as if it weren't important once she'd

realized how close she was to admitting she'd already inspected the bodies. "Nothing, really. It's just that many times a man's nose is broken during a fight. I thought perhaps his might have been." She picked up one of the letters in her lap and tore it open, hoping her answer was enough to satisfy him.

"I suppose it could have been," he guessed. "I didn't really pay that much attention."

"You should," she lectured, "if you ever intend to find the man who did this. Every detail has to be taken into account when you're investigating a crime. Otherwise you might miss the one clue that can solve it." While she spoke, she absently perused the gold-embossed invitation she held.

T.J. thought of the button he'd given Lewis, and he silently decided that knowing if the dead man had a broken nose or not was of little importance. Who owned the button was the key to this mystery . . . that and who had the paintings. He watched her for a moment as she studied the note in her hand, before he elected to sit in the chair next to hers. He couldn't deny the enjoyment he experienced bantering with her and testing her mettle, but the time for games was over. He wanted to find the man responsible for all of this just as badly as he was sure Catherine did, and the only way either of them would achieve that was if they were to join forces. She might not agree, since it was obvious she still had her doubts about him. But if he worded it right, he might get her to at least agree to a truce.

"Miss Chase," he said softly, breaking into her thoughts, then frowning when he saw her crumple up her letter, rise, and toss it in the cold fireplace. "Bad news?" he questioned, politely leaving his chair again.

"Hardly," she responded with a shrug of one shoulder. "It's an invitation to dinner."

T.J. smiled crookedly. "From an overzealous suitor?"

The question made her laugh. "An overzealous matchmaker, perhaps."

"Mmmm," T.J. murmured with a grin. "I know what you mean. I have a friend who's constantly hinting that I need a woman in my life."

The comment surprised her. "You mean there isn't one?" she asked before she realized how it might sound.

T.J. shook his head. "I'm sure you'll find this hard to believe, but until I met you, there was never a woman who caught my interest for longer than a day or two."

Catherine could feel the blush rising in her cheeks. Turning her face away from him, she returned to her chair to sit down. "You're right. I don't."

"Well, it's true," he guaranteed her, noticing the heightened color along the crest of her cheekbones. "And I apologize if it sounded as though I might be patronizing you. I'm not. You're a very intelligent woman, so intelligent that I'd be a fool for not openly admitting it."

Her embarrassment passed. "You want something," she stated, one tawny brow arched higher than the other. "What is it?"

"A truce," he confessed without hesitation as he came to sit down on the edge of his chair seat, his knees apart, and his elbows resting on them. "I won't deny how guilty I must look to you." He paused, grinned, and added, "If I were in your place, I'd probably think the same way. But even you must see the flaws in the evidence you've gathered so far. Otherwise, we wouldn't be here talking. You'd have had me arrested by now."

Catherine slowly bobbed her head, silently yielding to his observation, but only in the part that indicated his conviction was inevitable.

"Then allow me to prove my innocence," he invited. "Let's work together on this . . . as a team. Let's combine our resources, find the stolen artworks and the man who murdered those two men."

"How?" she asked. "If you're right about the double-cross, then whoever has the paintings has probably shipped them out of London by now . . . along with himself. Robbery is one thing. Murder is a death sentence."

"I agree. But we're not dealing with an ordinary thief. This man is well educated, probably wealthy, and very self-confident. I doubt he even blinked while he beat those men to death, and that's why I'd stake everything I own on the probability that he *and* the paintings are still in London. He's arrogant, Miss Chase. He's positive he'll never get caught."

Catherine shook her head. "The second he sells one of the paintings, Scotland Yard will hear about it."

"Who said he intends to sell any of them?"

That was a point Catherine hadn't considered.

"I doubt that's why he stole them," T.J. quickly added, once he saw the worry cross her lovely face. "But just in case it is, and he's planning to hang them in one of the rooms in his house under lock and key, our only way of finding them would be to play against his smugness."

"I don't understand," Catherine willingly admitted.

T.J. smiled encouragingly. "Why does any thief get caught?"

"Because he makes a mistake."

T.J. nodded. "Rich or poor, smart or stupid, no one's immune. And this man's already made one mistake. He failed to realize that the men he'd hired to do the job might become greedy. He corrected the error by killing them. His second mistake. Now he's feeling cocky . . . and very safe. There's no one alive who can link him to the crime."

Catherine was still having trouble figuring out his idea. "You're not very optimistic, Mr. Savage."

T.J. grinned. "Oh, but I am. You see, as far as our thief is concerned, he's committed the perfect crime. Or should I say, *two* crimes? And *that* is his third mistake."

Catherine frowned. "How so?"

"Let's go on the assumption that he stole the paintings purely for his personal pleasure, that he never planned to sell any of them. His life continues as before with one exception. The topic of conversation, no matter where he goes, will invariably turn to the robbery. He'll listen quietly, maybe even offer a word or two, then return home to privately applaud his cleverness. But before long his ego will cause him trouble. The mysterious thief—even though they're talking about him—will start to upstage him, and when that happens, he'll break. He'll be forced to share his secret just to get the credit for a crime that has all of

Scotland Yard baffled. Now, either he'll confide in someone and prove it by having a private showing or he'll make an even bigger mistake by deciding to sell a couple of the paintings. It'll be a lot easier for us if he does the latter, but in either case, we'll be there when he trips up."

"It all sounds very logical, Mr. Savage," she said after a moment's thought. "But I have one problem with it."

"What's that?"

"How will we manage to 'be there when he trips up'?" she asked. "You make it sound as though we'd be the ones in whom he'd confide."

T.J. grinned. "I'll admit it's a poor bet, but I had just as much of a chance in making a connection the first time as we do now." He chuckled and reached up to pull on his left earlobe. "The results weren't what I wanted, but if the method paid off once, it might work again."

Catherine suddenly realized it was a topic they'd never discussed, and that perhaps it was the reason she couldn't accept his story. If he truly hadn't been involved with the robbery from the start, then how did the two thieves know to get in contact with him? "What method?" she asked, anxious to hear his explanation.

T.J. leaned back in his chair. "It's quite simple, really. Whenever the topic of the missing paintings came up, I'd hint at how much I would like owning a Rembrandt . . . and that cost was of no significance."

Catherine had trouble believing that was all there was to it. "You mean all you did was spread a few rumors around, and a day or two later you were setting up a meeting place? Whom did you tell?"

"The right people," T.J. replied.

"Obviously," Catherine said. "But could you be a little more specific?"

"There wasn't anyone in particular," he explained. "I just made sure whoever I told was wealthy." He could see by the way she squinted at him that she still thought he was being too vague. "Every dinner party I attended, each time I went to the opera, or whenever I was visiting the tailor's I made sure to mention it to anyone who was listening. I'm sorry, but I can't be any more specific than that. Look," he said, leaning forward again, "this man isn't stupid. If I'd have shown any interest other than wanting to make a purchase, I wouldn't have gotten as far as I did. Now all I can hope for is that he'll remember who it was who made the offer and try to deal with me directly."

"So you're saying we just have to sit back and wait?"

"Not at all," T.J. said, shaking his head. "If this is to work, I have to behave as though nothing is wrong."

"By doing what?"

"By continuing to go to the opera, the tailor's, and anyplace else where I might meet up with him."

A sarcastic half-smile lifted the corner of her mouth. "I keep saying 'we,' and you keep saying 'I.' Why is that?"

T.J. hadn't realized he'd been omitting her presence in his plans, but apparently that was exactly what he'd been doing. Smiling, he rested comfortably in his chair as he looked her up and down. "Do you own something a little more fancy than that?" he asked, waving a finger at her attire.

Catherine glanced down at her clothes, frowned, and looked back up at him. "What has a fancy gown to do with any of this?"

"Well, if you intend to go to the opera with me, you'll have to dress up a little."

"Opera?" she echoed. "I don't like the opera."

"I didn't say you had to like it. You just have to attend." His dark eyes sparkled as he held back a smile and waited for her to respond.

Catherine's mouth twitched. "I suppose you'll want me to go to the tailor's with you, too."

Somehow T.J. managed not to laugh. "If you'd like," he calmly replied, for which he received a scalding look.

"And what would you say if I told you that you'd have to go places I wanted to go?" she challenged, suddenly remembering the invitation she'd thrown in the dark fireplace. "I might not look it, but I have rich friends too, Mr. Savage." Rising, she retrieved the parchment and handed it to him before sitting down again. She gave him a moment to examine the crumpled piece of paper, then added, "Since I'm not fully convinced you're as innocent as you'd like me to believe, I think *I* should be the one to choose which party we attend and whether or not being seen at the opera is all that important. In fact," she added, pointing at the invitation he held in his hand, "we'll start by accepting Edith Courtland's generous offer to dine at her home next week."

It wasn't until he agreed without any hesitation that Catherine realized what she had done. Edith hadn't invited her just to be social. She wanted Catherine and Aaron to have the chance to get to know one another better. T.J.'s presence would certainly put a strain on that possibility, but if Catherine had had the choice, she wouldn't have gone at all. Now she'd have to come up with a sensible explanation for the uninvited guest she'd bring with her as well as try to soothe Edith's hurt feelings.

Is all of this really worth it? she mused dejectedly, her gaze settling on the man sitting next to her. *Of course, it is. T. J. Savage knows where the paintings are and you have to get them back.*

Warm brown eyes lifted to look at her, and Catherine's pulse quickened.

CHAPTER 7

Catherine had spent a restless night thinking of T. J. Savage, the two murdered men, and the changes that had evolved in her thinking over the past few days. Ever since that tall, good-looking antagonist had walked into her life, she'd been questioning what she normally took for granted. She'd found flaws in her deductions, and she'd been fighting strange new emotions that startled and confused her. Day-to-day events had been routine until she'd met him. Now, the first thing that popped into her head the moment she opened her eyes in the morning was the vision of T.J. with his dark features, that warm, seductive smile, his rich baritone voice, and how much pleasure she'd gotten from her first kiss. She was thinking of him now as she flipped off the covers and touched her feet to the floor. Had she slept at all?

"I don't feel like it," she muttered to herself, wincing at the stiffness in her back as she rose and crossed to the wash-basin.

The mirror above the small table reflected an image that caused Catherine's upper lip to curl once she noticed how red her eyes were and that there were tired circles under them. Her long, strawberry-blond hair fell in a wild, tangled mess about her face and shoulders, and her skin seemed exceptionally pale. There were faint hollows beneath her cheekbones, and as she leaned closer to the silvered glass, she wondered why she had never noticed how thin her nose was and that her lips were a soft pink even though she wore no rouge. It wasn't an unpleasant-looking face, she conceded, but it was by no means beautiful as T.J. had claimed.

Suddenly realizing how she was wasting valuable time on something as unimportant as appraising her looks, she bent and irritably splashed cool water on her face. How silly! What did it matter whether or not her nose was too thin, her eyes too blue, or her lips too pink? What had that to do with the case she wanted to solve? Nothing! It had nothing to do with it. Yet, once she'd toweled the moisture from her skin and she was brushing the snarls from her hair, she absently wondered what it would be like to be a brunette.

She was shaken from her musings when something touched her leg. Glancing down, she smiled guiltily at Satan as if she thought the sleek black cat had read her mind and he was asking for an explanation.

"Good morning, Satan. Has Mr. Trumble given you something to eat yet?"

The cat meowed as if to complain that he was tired of waiting for his breakfast, and she laughed.

"He hasn't? Well, shame on him."

The feline meowed again.

"Of course I'll feed you, if you can wait a minute longer while I dress."

Round gold eyes blinked up at her as Satan sat down on his haunches, obviously deciding that whatever his mistress had said suited him just fine. Yet within only a moment or two, while Catherine pulled fresh undergarments from the dresser drawer and shed her cotton nightgown behind the trifold screen, the cat bounced up again and padded noiselessly from the room. He seemed uninterested in a human's needs, and Catherine, lost in thought again, failed to see his departure.

The details of the conversation she'd had last night with Mr. Savage had surprised her, but now that she'd had the time to think about it, his dominating manner and the way he'd rushed right in and dissected the crime and put each fact and element in proper order irked her. What made him think he had the talent for solving such an intricate puzzle?

And what right had he to choose how they would go about investigating the clues left them? He was just like all the rest. She was a woman, so that made her incompetent. Her upper lip curled unflatteringly as she wriggled into her petticoats, pulled on a starched white blouse and buttoned it up the front, then slipped an olive-green skirt down over her head and shoulders and secured the fastening at her waist. Let him think what he wanted. Once this crime was solved and the culprit was in jail, everyone in London, including T.J. Savage, would know her worth, and she wouldn't have to say a word!

The tiny lines between her eyebrows faded once she realized how distraught she was becoming. She never had before, and *that* was what had made her job so simple. She'd always been able to examine all the clues with an impartial eye, and now all of a sudden she was behaving like a six-year-old child arguing over whose idea it was to play with dolls. Arguing never solved anything. It merely drained a person's energy and clouded one's mind, obscuring what was really important. Closing her eyes, she took a deep breath and exhaled very slowly, while she allowed all the tension to leave her body. The Courtlands' dinner party wasn't for a week yet, which meant she wouldn't have to see T.J. Savage for seven whole days. She could get a lot done by then, and she'd start by paying Nathan Beecher a visit.

Twenty minutes later Catherine's hired cab pulled up in front of the three-story brick building that housed Scotland Yard's offices, the coroner's examination room, and a dozen jail cells on the lower floor. Stepping down from the rig, she paid the driver and told him not to wait, that once she'd finished her business inside, she planned to walk home. It seemed like the first sunny day in a long while, and although the air was crisp and stung her cheeks, she needed its fresh scent to help clear her mind.

As usual a bustle of activity greeted her once she'd opened the front door and stepped inside. Straight ahead was the sergeant's desk, although she had always wondered why it wasn't called a counter, since the man had to sit on a tall stool just to see over the top of it. His job was checking in prisoners, keeping the files up-to-date, and answering questions whenever the Yard was bombarded by reporters or a string of victims there to report a crime. It was customary for all visitors to register with the sergeant rather than roam the halls on their own, but it was a ritual Catherine seldom acknowledged. She already knew where to find Nathan Beecher, and she was well aware of Commissioner Mays's orders not to allow her to talk to anyone. Stealing a look at the man busy with half a score of people crowding around him, Catherine pulled the hood of her cape further down over her brow and hurried off to her left where she knew she would find Nathan at the end of the corridor.

"Miss Chase!" The young man beamed once he'd looked up from his paperwork and saw her smiling back at him.

"Good morning, Nathan," she greeted. "Busy as always, I see."

"Yes'm," he replied, rising and holding out his hand to the empty chair beside his desk. "Have a seat and tell me what I can do for you."

Long, pale red-gold hair shimmered in the morning light shining through the windows, once Catherine pushed back the hood of her cape and shook her head to free the thick locks of their restraints. "I was just wondering if there's been any progress on the museum robbery," she said, sitting down.

Just the mention of the top-priority case brought the young man back to earth. He knew the only reason Catherine Chase ever came to see him was because of her work and that of all the detectives at the Yard, he was the only one who ignored the commissioner's direct orders to keep closemouthed with her. He knew it, but every time he saw her, he hoped that *this* time she had come for personal reasons. Of course it never really bothered him once he'd been reminded that she saw him only as a man who shared a common interest with her. After all, he was asking too much, since Miss Chase had no idea how he felt about her.

Someday he'd work up the courage to change that. Someday . . . but not today.

"It seems just when we take a step forward, something happens, and we're knocked off our feet again," he admitted, once he'd glanced across the large room he shared with six other detectives and saw that the door to the commissioner's office was closed.

"Oh?" she asked, feigning ignorance. She'd come to see Nathan in the hope of finding out whether the murders had been reported and if the Yard had been smart enough to conclude from the clues that the deaths were related to the robbery. If neither had happened, she intended to pay Phillip to "accidentally" discover the crime and turn it in. From there she would drop subtle hints to Nathan until he drew his own conclusions and she wouldn't have to admit to a thing. If she was really lucky, all she'd have to do right now was pretend to be surprised.

Nathan had never known Miss Chase to react to the news of a violent crime with any other emotion besides interest. He'd even been with her on a few occasions when the body of a murder victim had been found, and she'd hardly blinked at the sight. She had nerves of forged steel in comparison to some of his fellow detectives and even the commissioner at times. But for some reason he was hesitant to tell her the details.

"Nathan?" she said, breaking into his thoughts. "What's wrong?"

The young man sighed resignedly. He knew Miss Chase wouldn't leave until he confessed, so there was no point in trying to protect her. "Last night one of our detectives received an anonymous tip about a meeting that was to take place near the wharf, and that if he was interested in recovering the stolen artworks, he should check into it."

Catherine's brows dipped downward. "A tip?"

Nathan nodded. "A young boy came in just as I was ready to leave for the night. He asked to see Mr. Rhomberg, and since that's not an uncommon occurrence with him, I thought nothing of it. I wish now that I'd stuck around. I could have gone with him. Not that it would have made much of a difference."

Catherine knew the answer, but she asked anyway. "Why?"

"He got there too late. All he found was two murdered men and an empty stable."

Catherine tried to concentrate on what Nathan was saying, but she couldn't. She'd already done her own investigation, and she doubted Mr. Rhomberg had uncovered any more clues than what either she or T.J. had found. What she *hadn't* known about was the message someone sent to the inspector and the boy who delivered it.

"Nathan," she said, once he'd finished reciting the story. "Has Mr. Rhomberg questioned the boy?"

"What boy?" he asked.

"The one who gave him the message."

Nathan shook his head. "I don't think so. Why do you ask?"

She was quiet for a moment. "You said the message wasn't signed, which tells us that whoever wrote it doesn't want to get involved. But he, or she, already is. If this person knew where to find the paintings and about the meeting, then he might know who the murderer is." A faraway look came over her as she mumbled, "The boy's our only lead."

"No he isn't, Miss Chase," Nathan happily supplied. "Weren't you listening? I said Mr. Rhomberg found a button clenched in the hand of one of the dead men. It's his guess it was torn off the killer's coat during the struggle."

The vision of T.J. exploded before her eyes. She heard the conversation they'd had. She remembered the way he'd stood before her and asked if she saw any blood on his hands . . . or on his clothes, and she remembered how her gaze had swept over him. More than any of it, she remembered the row of buttons on his coat . . . gold buttons . . . and that one of them was missing. She wanted to tell herself that it was only a coincidence, that the button had been off his coat *before* he'd gone into the stable. She wanted to believe he'd been telling her the truth.

Feeling weak of a sudden, Catherine raised a trembling hand to her brow. She couldn't recall thinking how stuffy the building had been when she first came inside, but the air seemed *very* tight right then. She closed her eyes.

"Miss Chase?" Nathan called to her, his voice full of alarm. "Miss Chase, are you all right?"

Nodding her head, she asked weakly, "The button . . . may I see it?"

"Mr. Rhomberg has it and he's not here."

"Can you describe it?"

Nathan frowned and scratched his temple. "It's gold with two thread holes, and it has a tiny design—like leaves or ivy—around the edge. Why? Do you know something about it?"

She wanted to answer him, but for some odd reason no words would come out when she opened her mouth to speak.

"You look faint," he observed, rising hurriedly from his chair. "Sit still. I'll get you a glass of water."

He was gone before Catherine could stop him.

In the silence that surrounded her, T.J.'s dark eyes and handsome smile came to mind, followed by a clearing of her thoughts. Her heart ceased its rapid pace, her head stopped spinning, and her stomach unknotted itself. Firm determination and a touch of anger replaced them. She'd been right about him all along. Now all she had to do was show her evidence to Nathan.

No, she thought, pushing herself up from the chair with the aid of one hand against the desktop. *I'll personally give it to the commissioner. I'd like nothing better than to show him* and *Mr. Savage that I'm not as inept as the two of them seem to think I am.*

Flipping the hood of her cape up over her head, she turned around, ready to depart without waiting for Nathan to return, when the door to the commissioner's office opened and two men stepped out. She instantly recognized the taller of the pair and how angry he would be if he saw her, and since she wasn't in the mood to exchange heated words with him—at least not just now—she lowered her head and started to walk away. Before she had taken three steps, however, his voice boomed out to stop her, drawing her attention as well as everyone else's in the room.

"Miss Chase," Commissioner Mays loudly rebuked. "I thought I made myself clear the last time I found you snooping around this building. Amateurs are not welcome here."

His insult failed to irritate her as she was sure he meant it to do. Holding back a smile, she glanced over at him, amazed to discover that she had never really noticed the details of his appearance before today. And now that she had, she wondered why, all at once, it made a difference. He was as tall and thin as always. He still sported a thick mustache and long sideburns. And his narrow-set brown eyes continued to mirror his contempt for her. So what was it about him that caught her eye this time? Might it be that this was the first time she could actually see his arrogance distorting his face, or was it simply because that up until now she'd never bothered to give him two seconds of consideration? She should continue the practice. She should nod politely at him the way her father had taught her to behave and leave without comment. Stating her qualities as an investigator wouldn't impress him, so why waste the effort? He was an ignorant man and any attempt to educate him would be fruitless. Maybe she just felt like handing back the sarcasm he always seemed so eager to give her.

"And why is that, Commissioner? Are you afraid an 'amateur' will show you up?" she asked, quoting the term he'd used.

Mays's mouth twitched as he suppressed his heightening rage. "Amateurs get in the way, Miss Chase," he snarled. "They destroy evidence with their clumsiness and then claim it's the Yard's fault. They're the first to criticize when it takes too long to solve a crime, and they take all the credit once it is. I don't like amateurs, Miss Chase. I don't like you."

"I'll try not to lose any sleep over it, Commissioner," she remarked with a faint smile. "And I'll try to pretend *you* were the one who knew all along that the stolen paintings hadn't left London the way everyone else at Scotland Yard thought they had. I'll remind myself that it was *your* idea to track down the wagon with a nick in one of its wheels, that you knew from the start that the prints in the dirt near the broken window at the museum had something to do with the robbery. And when an arrest is made for the murder of those two men last night, I'll assume it was *your* brilliant detective work that uncovered the killer's identity." She raised both eyebrows at him. "You are about to make an arrest, aren't you?"

A bright scarlet hue began to creep up Mays's neck from just above his shirt collar all the way to his receding hairline. He stammered and fumed, ground his teeth and clenched his fists, obviously enraged over how everything she'd said had been just the opposite of the truth. He'd laughed at her idea about the wagon-wheel imprints, and he'd all but given up looking for the paintings in London. Now she was suggesting *she* knew who was behind it all.

"A-arrest?" he finally managed to grate out. "We don't even know the names of the dead men. How can we arrest anyone?"

Catherine glanced from Mays's angry face to the embarrassed expression on the man standing beside him. Ferris Hargrove, the commissioner's assistant, seldom disagreed with Mays, but from the look in his eyes, Catherine could see this discussion made him uncomfortable.

"Are their names of any real importance?" she asked, looking back at Mays. "They may have been the ones to actually break into the museum, but it wasn't their idea. An amateur could have figured that out. And they died because they were no longer of any use. Spending one second trying to learn their names and who their next of kin is would be a total waste of time. But go right ahead and follow up on it, Commissioner. Waste your time. It's what you do best."

"Get out!" he exploded, one arm raised, the hand extended and a finger pointing toward the exit at the end of the corridor. "Now!" He turned to his companion. "Mr. Hargrove, show our unauthorized visitor to the door and make sure she uses it!" He glared at Catherine a moment longer, then turned on his heel and retreated back into his office, slamming the door behind him with a deafening crack.

Nathan had returned with the glass of water just in time to witness the commissioner's last burst of temper. He knew Mays resented Miss Chase's interference—or more precisely, her ability to solve crimes faster than anyone else on the force—but he'd never seen the man publicly berate her. He'd been rude, and Nathan wanted Miss Chase to know that the rest of the men didn't feel the same way about her. He set the glass on his desk and started after her.

"Miss Chase," he called, stopping her midway down the hall, Hargrove at her side.

"It's all right, Nathan," she promised with a smile. "I don't blame you. I shouldn't have come. Go back to work. I don't want you paying for my mistake." She smiled again, then turned away.

"I think what he wanted to say, Miss Chase," Hargrove speculated as they headed for the door, "is that the commissioner had no business talking to you like that. We appreciate your help. And he should, too. The objective of Scotland Yard is to solve cases and bring the guilty to justice. It shouldn't matter how it's done, just that it is." When they reached the door, Hargrove paused and touched his hand on her elbow, delaying her departure. "If it's any comfort, Miss Chase, I think I should tell you that your being a woman isn't really what upsets him."

The remark surprised her. "Oh?"

Hargrove glanced toward the sergeant to make sure the man was too busy to hear what he had to say. "I've heard rumors," he admitted, then added quickly, "Now mind you, that's probably all they really are—someone's gossip—but the story going around is that Mays despised your father."

Catherine knew Argus Mays thought the world would be better off if she weren't in it, but she never suspected his opinion might have stemmed from something her father had said or done to him. "Are the rumors any more detailed than that?"

Hargrove shrugged a shoulder, obviously hesitant to repeat it.

"Please?" she asked. "If I can understand him, I might be able to deal with him."

Ferris Hargrove, a man in his early fifties, looked much younger than his years. Yet, today, Catherine noted, he appeared tired and drawn.

"It makes sense, I suppose," he said with a half-smile. "I mean, it would explain his attitude toward you . . . to some degree."

"What, Mr. Hargrove? What happened between my father and the commissioner?" she urged when it seemed he would never tell her.

Hargrove took a deep breath and exhaled in a rush. "It's rumored that years ago the commissioner was seeing your mother—romantically speaking—until she met your father. He blamed the professor for stealing his lady love and for her unnecessary death."

Catherine laughed in spite of the seriousness of the charge. "That's absurd, Mr. Hargrove. My father never mentioned it to me. And he certainly couldn't have prevented Mother's death."

Hargrove bobbed his head. "I said it was only a rumor. But you must agree it explains why seeing you upsets him so."

Mr. Trumble had oftentimes told her how much she resembled her late mother, and if what Hargrove proposed was valid, then it stood to reason Argus Mays hated the memories the very sight of her stirred up. Yet, she still couldn't understand why her father or Mr. Trumble had never told her about Commissioner Mays's past connection to the family . . . especially with all the trouble she had because of him.

No, she mused. *That's all it is—a rumor—and it's not worth my time even thinking about it.*

Right now it was more important for her to pay T. J. Savage a visit without his knowledge. She had to get her hands on the jacket he had worn last night . . . the one that would not only prove where he had gone after leaving her town house, but that he had committed a horrendous crime.

Thanking Ferris Hargrove for his kindness, Catherine hurriedly left the building in search of Phillip Preston.

"Ye wanna do what?" the young boy exclaimed sometime later as he and Catherine sat having lunch at the Triple Street Inn.

"Shhh!" Catherine warned, glancing around to see if anyone close by had heard his outburst. "I can't explain any more than I already have, Phillip. You've got to take my word for it."

"But Miss Chase," he argued, dropping his half-eaten biscuit back on his plate, "ye ain't no thief. 'Ow do ye plan ter get yerself in the man's 'ouse without someone seein' ye?"

She chewed and swallowed her last bite of apple pie, dabbed her mouth with a napkin, then reached for her cup of tea. "Simple. I'll do it tonight . . . when it's dark."

Phillip squinted one eye at her. "All right. Nobody *outside* will see ye. What about Mr. Savage or 'is servants?"

"Mr. Savage won't be home," she answered confidently, after taking a sip of her tea and returning the cup to its saucer. "You'll see to that. As for his servants . . . well . . . I'll have to figure something out."

Phillip collapsed back in his chair with a shake of his head. "And what if ye get caught? Ye willin' ter go ter the jail, mum?" When she started to open her mouth and claim it wouldn't happen, Phillip quickly interrupted. "I've been in the jail before. Don't bother me none. So tell me what ye're goin' after, and I'll do it for ye."

"No," she firmly objected. "I won't risk it, so don't ask." She frowned, withdrew a coin from her skirt pocket, and slapped it on the table in front of him. "All I want from you is for you to come up with a way of getting Mr. Savage out of his house for half an hour or so. Can you do that for me?"

The offer of money never failed to alter Phillip's loyalty. The gold coin and the knowledge that Miss Chase would simply find someone else to help her if he refused prompted him to forget his warning. "Yes'm," he replied disgustedly as he reached to scoop up the payment. "What time?"

She thought about Mr. Trumble and how she'd have to explain to him why she was going out after dark, and the answer to her first problem came to mind. If Mr. Trumble went to bed *before* she left the house, he wouldn't know about her late-night escapade, and if she waited until after *he'd* retired, then there would be a strong chance Mr. Savage's servants would be sound asleep at that time, too.

"Eleven o'clock," she announced, certain her idea would work. Now all that was left for her to figure out was how she'd get into the house and which bedroom was T.J.'s. She couldn't afford wasting precious time looking through every room in the mansion.

"A little late, ain't it?" Phillip challenged. "One little sound, and—"

"Let me worry about that," she instructed as she grabbed her cape off the chair next to her and stood, slipping the cloak over her shoulders. "And make it eleven-thirty," she corrected after a moment's thought.

Phillip drew a breath to question what difference a half hour would make, only to have Catherine cut him off when she turned her back on him and headed toward the door.

A frown creased T.J.'s brow as he waited for the livery cab to roll to a stop outside his friend's flat. The late hour worried him. Lewis Rhomberg seldom stayed up past ten unless he was working on something important, and even then it rarely had anything to do with T.J. But the message that had been delivered to the house a short while earlier told T.J. that Lewis needed to see him right away, and T.J. could only assume it had something to do with Catherine Chase.

Alighting from the cab, he told the driver to wait and headed for the rear of the building where his friend rented rooms on the lower level. At the door, he knocked, waited, and rapped again before he heard the key turn in the lock and the hinges squeak as Lewis responded to the summons.

"I'm sorry if I got you out of bed," Lewis apologized as he closed the door behind T.J. and took his cape and hat. "Would you like a glass of brandy?"

"No, thank you," T.J. replied as he sat down in one of the chairs before the fire. "I'd rather just hear what it is that couldn't wait until morning."

Lewis glanced at the clock on the mantel. In his younger days, half-past ten wasn't late, especially if he had been in the company of a young and willing woman. He'd only apologized to T.J. because he assumed he had probably interrupted a romantic moment. Grinning, he sat down beside his friend.

"*Did* I get you out of bed?" he asked devilishly.

T.J. instantly caught his meaning. "I don't think that's any of your business, and I certainly hope you didn't drag me all the way here just to find out."

Lewis shrugged it off, knowing that if T.J. wanted to settle down, he'd do it without Lewis's help and most definitely without his approval. "We've got a problem," he announced, dismissing T.J.'s harsh reply to mean he'd been alone when the message came, and that he hadn't liked being reminded of it.

"What kind of a problem?"

Leaning back in his chair, Lewis stretched out his legs and watched the flames dancing in the hearth. "I had a lot of work to do at my desk tonight and didn't leave the office until an hour ago. Since I hadn't had anything to eat all evening, I stopped off at the White Horse Pub on my way home and I ran into Nathan Beecher there. I've talked about him before, haven't I?" he asked, looking at his companion.

Remembering the detective's name, T.J. nodded.

"He told me Catherine Chase had paid him a visit this morning. She was asking about the museum robbery, and according to Beecher, when he mentioned the button we had in evidence, she became quite pale . . . something she's never been known to do."

"Wait a moment," T.J. said. "Are you saying Beecher openly discussed the case with her? She's not a member of the force. I thought it was the Yard's practice not to talk to outsiders."

"It is. And Beecher's been warned several times, but he . . . well, he's smitten with her."

T.J. cocked a brow. "So she bats an eye at him and he tells her everything she wants to know."

Grinning, Lewis scratched his nose. "She's the exception, T.J. Telling Miss Chase can only help, not hinder our investigation. She's very smart. And she's always willing to share *her* information with us."

T.J.'s dark brows came together. "Then she's told Beecher about me."

Lewis shook his head. "Not yet. At least he never mentioned your name to me. If she ever does tell him, then we'll have a problem."

T.J. sensed that wasn't all that concerned his friend. "There's something else, isn't there?"

Pulling his legs in, Lewis sat up in the chair and nodded. "Her reaction to the news about the button you gave me. I could be completely wrong about this, but I've been thinking of nothing else since talking to Beecher."

"Wrong about what?"

"She asked to examine the button, and when Beecher told her I had it and that I wasn't in the office, she asked him to describe it. She didn't say so, but Beecher got the impression she might have seen it before and she merely wanted to make sure it was the same one."

T.J. frowned. "I'm not following you."

"Last night when we talked about the murders, you said you'd told her about the second meeting and that you'd warned her not to investigate, that you'd take care of it yourself. Are you absolutely sure she didn't get there ahead of you?"

"Positive. She didn't know where it was to take place. Neither did I until I was met by the man in the park. She could have followed me, I suppose, but even so, she wouldn't have known about the button."

Images of all the events of the past night whirled before T.J.'s eyes: talking to Catherine, then Mr. Trumble; the man at the park; the bodies; how he'd found the button and given it to Lewis; returning to Catherine's and the discussion they'd had. Suddenly, it hit him.

"Oh, dear," he half moaned, half laughed.

"What?" Lewis demanded. "You've thought of something. What is it?"

"After meeting with you, I went back to see Miss Chase."

"I guessed that much. Otherwise, she wouldn't have known about the murders. Beecher said it didn't seem to surprise her. Didn't you tell her about the button you'd found?"

"How could I? I'd given it to you."

Lewis shrugged. "So?"

"I haven't been totally honest with her, Lewis, ol' boy. You made it very clear how quick-witted she is, and I thought if she knew you and I were friends, she'd wonder why I continued to stick so close to her if I'd proven my innocence. That's what you wanted, wasn't it? For me to come up with a reason to stay close to her, to protect her, to learn what I could about her father's accident? I used the museum robbery for that purpose." He smiled and flicked a piece of lint off the knee of his trousers. "It's had its repercussions, I'm afraid."

"In what way?" Lewis asked, hesitant of the answer.

"I haven't been able, yet, to convince her that I was only a buyer in this case and not the mastermind. She finds fault with everything I say, and hearing about the button that was taken from the dead man's hand, she's positive now that I'm not only a thief, but a murderer."

When Lewis frowned at him, obviously confused, T.J. reached for the bottom button on his coat and pretended to pluck it free. The gesture immediately reminded Lewis of the incident at the inn and the comment T.J. had made about how guilty he would look if Lewis hadn't witnessed the damage done to his jacket. Apparently Miss Chase had noticed the missing button that night, but hadn't made the connection until Beecher revealed the damning piece of evidence they had.

"Well, I know you're innocent, T.J.," Lewis teased. "And I promise I won't let you sit in jail too long before I come to your rescue."

"Very funny, Lewis," T.J. jeered. "But I'm not really worried about it. I've got my housekeeper to verify that she saw me take the button from the pocket of my coat, when I told her about the mishap and asked her to have it repaired as soon as possible. In fact, it's at the tailor's right now."

"Mmmm," Lewis murmured with a twinkle in his eye. "Miss Chase would think that's awfully suspicious."

"What is?" T.J. shot back, his temper short. He was getting very tired of defending himself.

"That the man who admits to having been at the scene of a crime suddenly sends the coat he was wearing at the time to the tailor's for repairs. And not just to mend a tear, but for the replacement of a button. Or did you have them all replaced so they'd match?" He rubbed the side of his mouth and added, "It's just too much of a coincidence, don't you agree?"

T.J. gave his friend a tired look. "I'd love to stick around and let you have your fun, Lewis, but I've got better things to do. Are we finished?" He stood, not bothering to wait for an answer.

"Yes, we're through. All I really wanted was to warn you," he said, rising and following T.J. to the door. "I don't think you totally appreciate Miss Chase's talents. If she's convinced you're guilty, she'll find a way of proving it even if she's wrong. There are a lot of men in prison, I'm sure, who were victims of circumstantial evidence. I don't want your name to be added to the list."

T.J. grinned. "As long as I have you . . ."

Lewis's upper lip curled. "An awfully thin piece of ice, T.J. I could drop dead the instant you walk out that door, and then where would you be?"

T.J. thought about mentioning Newgate Prison and changed his mind. Lewis wasn't teasing anymore. He was genuinely concerned, and T.J. knew he shouldn't make light of it. "Don't worry about it," he suggested, opening the door and stepping outside. "I can take care of myself."

"It's not you I'm worried about," Lewis murmured as he watched his friend's tall frame disappear into the darkness. "I'm wondering who'll take care of Miss Chase?"

Hidden within the shadows of the tall hedges surrounding T.J.'s property, Catherine waited and watched. The entire second story of the house was dark, which she hoped meant T.J. had retired. She needed to know which room was his, and the only way she would find that out was to be there when T.J.'s servant knocked on his door with Phillip's bogus message and T.J. lit a lamp in response. Then, once he had left the house, her next feat would be for her to get inside.

A movement on the sidewalk out front drew Catherine's attention. Silhouetted in the light of one of the street lamps, she easily recognized Phillip's slender form, and her heart started thumping. It was a simple enough plan—lure Savage out of the house for a half hour or so, let herself in, find the jacket with the missing button, and then flee before anyone was the wiser—but the closer the time came to executing her scheme, the more nervous she became. She'd done this kind of thing over and over again with only one mistake; the time T.J. and his partners had caught her. Perhaps that was why she sensed her mission wouldn't go as smoothly as she hoped it would. T.J. Savage had broken her string of good luck, and it was very possible he might do it again. Shaking off the worry, she concentrated on the young man approaching the front door of the mansion.

Since Catherine was too far away to hear what was said between Phillip and whoever greeted him, she had to assume by his hesitant manner as he turned, started back down the walk, then paused and looked all around that something was wrong. Not willing to hear that there was already a kink in her plan, she stood there a moment wishing it would simply disappear before she surrenderingly moved along the hedgerow toward her associate.

"Phillip!" she called to him in a harsh whisper. "Phillip, over here!"

Ducking into the bushes beside her, Phillip crouched

down and gave the dark house a quick look as though he feared someone might see them. “I think ye better forget sneakin’ into ’is ’ouse, Miss Chase,” he advised.

“Why? What happened?”

“Nothin’ ’appened. ’E just ain’t there, that’s all.”

“Not there?” she repeated. “Is that what you were told?”

Phillip nodded. “ ’Is maid said Mr. Savage left about an ’our ago and that she isn’t sure when ’e’d be back.”

“Did she say where he went?”

“No, mum, and I didn’t ask.”

“Damn,” Catherine fumed, glancing up at the house.

Every ounce of common sense told her to wait, to do it another time when she was sure he wouldn’t walk in on her. Yet she also knew that once he heard about the incriminating evidence Scotland Yard had against him, he’d more than likely have the coat destroyed. Commissioner Mays wouldn’t arrest him on her word alone. She needed that coat as proof, and tonight might be her only chance to have it.

“Thank you, Phillip,” she said with a dismissing pat on his arm. “You may go now. If I need anything else from you, I’ll send word. All right?”

“Miss Chase,” he replied skeptically, “ye’re not thinkin’ ter—”

“Go, Phillip,” she ordered a bit more strongly. “I haven’t got the time to discuss this with you, and I can’t have you standing around. You understand me?”

The boy frowned, debating whether he should listen to her or not. If she got herself in trouble and he’d abandoned her . . .

“No,” he announced, drawing a startled look from his companion. “I won’t try and stop ye from goin’ in,” he said, “but I ain’t leavin’, neither. I can keep a lookout for ye and ’oller up if I see somethin’.”

Catherine didn’t want him anywhere around, but she could see by the determined look in his eyes that he meant what he said. “All right,” she said, yielding, “but stay in the shadows. Once I’ve found his room, I’ll signal you. Then if someone comes, you can toss a pebble at the window. But don't call out to me. They'll hear you. Understand?"

Phillip nodded.

"Then you're to run like the dickens, Phillip Preston," she ordered, her nose close to his and a finger thrust in his face. "You're not to wait for me. Is that clear?"

"Yes'm," he answered, a little shaken. Catherine Chase had never talked to him like that before, and it not only surprised him, but frightened him.

Pointing at a spot in the bushes where she was sure he wouldn't be seen, Catherine waited until the boy had hidden himself there before she concentrated on the task at hand. Certain all the doors and windows on the ground floor were locked, she was left with no other choice but to enter through one of two balcony doors above her. Thick ivy clung to the side of the house, but she doubted it would hold her weight. The widespread limbs of a huge oak tree growing close to the two-story mansion offered a simple solution as they arched over the wrought-iron railing of the small porch and promised a safe descent. And climbing trees had been one of her childhood pleasures. Of course, that had been a few years ago, but how much more difficult could it be for her now? While she eyed which route to take through the maze of branches, she kicked off her shoes and shed her stockings. Her skirts would be enough of a problem without having to deal with the slippery-soled footgear as well. Giving Phillip one last look to make certain he had stayed put, she started up the tree.

T.J. considered stopping off at the Hound's Tooth Pub for a mug of ale and decided against it. He wasn't in the mood to be sociable, and at this time of night everyone in the place was sure to be in a jovial frame of mind, which meant he wouldn't escape being drawn into a friendly conversation. What he needed was some peace and quiet, a couple of hours alone to sort out his thoughts. He really wasn't worried about Miss Chase ever being able to collect even a shred of evidence to have him arrested, but he certainly wasn't winning her favor, either. Last night while they talked over the clues he'd found in the stable, she seemed to have believed he hadn't had any part in the killings. But that had been before she had spoken with Nathan Beecher.

"Driver," he called, rapping on the roof of the livery cab, "pull over here. I'd like to walk the rest of the way."

"Very good, sir," the man replied, reining the horse in alongside the curb.

Stepping down, T.J. withdrew two coins from his pocket and handed them to the driver. Even though he could afford to pay for any service he required, T.J. had never been able to forget his humble beginnings, and paying for a ride when he was quite capable of walking always seemed to be a waste of money. More than that, however, he thought the stroll would do him good. Since acquiring his wealth a few years back, he'd hardly done anything more strenuous than issuing instructions to his staff.

At the corner, he turned and headed down the sparsely lit avenue toward his home at the end of the block. What he specifically liked about the property he'd recently purchased was that although he had neighbors on both sides and across the street from him, the boundary was sealed off by tall hedges and the house sat toward the back of the spacious lawn, offering some degree of privacy. He wasn't necessarily a recluse, but at times like tonight, he enjoyed his solitude, and the huge house and half acre of land provided just that.

Turning up the long drive that circled around to the front door, T.J. noticed that Mrs. Witton had left a lamp lit in the parlor for him, and he smiled. He liked the gray-haired lady and the motherly way she treated him, even though at times he felt she lectured him a little too often. She complained most whenever he stayed out late since she thought he needed his rest more than socializing with the kinds of women usually found at such an hour. She'd complain tonight if she was still up. If she wasn't, then he'd have no trouble getting into the house without disturbing her. Mrs. Witton's hearing wasn't what it used to be. Chuckling to himself, he started up the cobblestone walkway to the front door.

When he was to think about it later, T.J. would wonder what it was that made him look off to his right at that moment. Perhaps it was the movement in the shadows that caught his eye or the sense that something wasn't right. Whatever it was, he came to an abrupt halt once he spotted a young boy's shape step out from within the hedges and move toward the house, totally unaware of T.J.'s presence. Frowning, T.J. started toward him, guessing yet fairly certain the boy was there to rob him, and before the child broke a windowpane to gain entry, T.J. planned to stop him. His mission changed, however, when he noticed how the youngster continually stared up at the second story rather than at a more accessible form of entrance at ground level, and he paused to contemplate the reason. Drawn to look for himself, he glanced up in time to see the doors to the balcony of his bedchambers being shut, and he was instantly filled with rage.

If you're supposed to be the lookout, he silently fumed, his gaze shifting back to the boy, *you're doing a very poor job of it, and I'm about to show you just how poor that is.* With fists clenched, he started off again.

The hair on the back of Phillip's neck suddenly stood out. It wasn't that he'd heard a sound or saw someone coming toward him. It was the sense that he wasn't alone and how the cool night air had thickened with an omen of danger that made it nearly impossible for him to breathe. Miss Chase had succeeded in scaling the huge oak tree and in finding which room was Mr. Savage's bedchambers, and since he'd been paid only to deliver a message and not to stand guard, he quickly decided it was time for him to leave. With a short, fearful glance toward the front of the house just to make sure his instincts were right, he spotted the tall, dark figure of a man rapidly closing in on him, and he bolted, spinning around and racing off into the darkness before his attacker could grab him.

T.J. broke into a run, sprinted halfway across the side yard, then came to an equally abrupt halt. It didn't matter where the boy went or that T.J. didn't know who he was, and catching him didn't mean he had to be out of breath.

There was a much simpler way of getting his hands on the boy. Turning back, he glanced up at the balcony doors to his bedchambers. A *much* simpler way. Smiling, he started for the front of the house again, glad he hadn't shouted at the youngster running away from him and that the boy hadn't thought to call out a warning to his cohort. Catching *this* one wouldn't take any effort at all.

He had just passed the base of the oak tree with his eyes trained on the direction he was going when his toe connected with something lying on the ground and kicked it away. Reluctant to stop yet curious, he paused, glanced down, and saw what he thought was a shoe. Bending, he picked it up to examine.

"I don't believe it," he murmured, surprised and amused, once he'd realized it was a woman's slipper he held and he had guessed who owned it and what it was doing under a tree on *his* property. "She's got spunk. I'll have to give her that," he added, grinning. A quick look around produced the mate and a pair of white stockings, and with them held tightly in his grip, he hurried off again as he promised devilishly, "And that's not all I'll give her."

Catherine's luck had been both bad and good. She'd had no trouble climbing the tree and reaching the railing, and the second room she'd tried had all the earmarks of belonging to T.J. The faint scent of cheroots and especially his cologne lingered hauntingly in the air, and the wardrobe full of men's clothes rather confirmed whose room it was. Her problem came in not being able to see all that well. There was a full moon and only an occasional cloud now and then to block its light, but it still wasn't enough. She'd found a tin of matches on the mantel, but she'd decided lighting a candle would be too risky. If, for some reason, one of the servants came down the hall, he or she would see the yellow flooding out from under the door, which left her with no other alternative but to use the muted light from a single match. The process was slow and awkward, since it seemed T. J. Savage owned more clothes than the King of England.

"This will take forever," she muttered, shaking out the hot flame an instant before it reached her fingers. "I've never seen so many clothes in one person's wardrobe in my life." Adding the match's charred remains to the others she stored in the lid of the tin box, she stood back, looked the armoire up and down, and added with a playful smile, "Of course, I've never snooped through very many closets, either."

Realizing the extent of the man's wealth, she took a moment to glance around the room. Many considered her father to have been rich, but his holdings paled in comparison to this. The room was large enough to hold *two* full-sized feather beds, twelve chairs, six wardrobes, three or four trifold screens, a half-dozen dressers, and anything else one might decide to store in it. Mr. Savage chose to have only one of each with the exception of the two wing chairs by the hearth. But even so, she felt the settee sitting opposite them was a bit too much and totally unnecessary. Did he really entertain guests in his bedroom?

The disparaging question made her blush once she envisioned the kind of guests he might have, and she turned back around with such a flourish the tin of matches slipped from her fingers and clinked on the floor. Muttering an unkind word, she stooped to retrieve them, placing herself in direct line with the bedroom door. At that moment she heard the sound of someone's footsteps on the staircase and how they seemed to be growing louder as the person headed her way. Scrambling to collect the rest of the wooden sticks, she stuffed them in the tin box, hurriedly set it on the mantel, and closed the wardrobe doors before turning to the balcony. She couldn't be sure if T.J. had managed to slip past Phillip and was preparing to retire or if a maid was on her way to turn down the bedcovers, but in either case, Catherine decided it would be better if she waited outside.

Her direction made a sudden detour, however, when she heard the doorknob rattle, and she was forced to take refuge behind the trifold screen in the corner. At the same moment she crouched down and gathered her long skirts in around her feet, the door to the room opened and a stream of light from the hall sconces flooded in across the floor. A second later and before she could peek through a slit in the screen to see who it was, the portal swung shut and plummeted everything into darkness again.

Catherine gritted her teeth, certain that if she didn't, they would chatter and give her away as she listened to the sounds of the intruder moving about the room. She started at the noise of the draperies being pulled shut over the alcove to the balcony doors, and she silently cursed her lack of time to make a safe departure. It didn't take an educated person to know who was in the room with her. T.J. had come home, and Phillip had failed to warn her.

The smell of sulfur reached her almost as quickly as the light from the candle he lit, and she squinted her eyes until they had adjusted to the change. She stayed perfectly still, fearing any movement would apprise him of the company he had. It was quiet for a moment before she heard the bed squeak as he sat upon it and what she thought were his shoes thudding on the floor, and she cringed. Dear God, he wasn't going to bed now, was he? He couldn't! She'd be trapped if he did . . . at least until he fell asleep, and then she'd have the challenging task of sneaking from his room without awakening him.

The creak of hinges told her he was at the armoire, which meant he had his back to her since the wardrobe stood on the other side of the room. Drawing on her reluctant courage, she shifted slightly and stole a peek between the panels of the screen, and her heart thumped with the sight of him removing his coat. Soft candlelight bathed his tall form in a warm, alluring glow and shimmered in his raven-black hair, and for a moment she forgot her reason for being there. The excitement faded, and she closed her eyes and leaned her head back against the wall behind her. T. J. Savage was a murderer. Two men had died because of him, and she had no right seeing him in any other aspect than that.

The sound of water filling the washbasin jerked her upright again, and every nerve ending in her body came alive with all sorts of images racing through her mind. Without realizing she had, Catherine stretched as far to her left as she could possibly get until she could see him again through the narrow slit in the screen's framework. From all appearances, he planned to wash before retiring and Catherine's untapped curiosity about a man's toiletry refused to allow her to look away. She had never so much as seen a man's bare arms, let alone his shoulders, chest, or back, and her imagination had always left her feeling cheated. Of course there had been the corpses at the morgue, but a dead body hardly paralleled warm, healthy flesh and flexing muscles. Now was her chance to observe without anyone knowing it.

Her heart seemed ready to burst from her chest when he tugged his shirttail free, and she unknowingly pressed a hand to her bosom. With his back to her, she could only assume he was unbuttoning the front as he tipped his head forward and watched his fingers work down the row of fastenings. A second later he stretched and slipped the garment off one shoulder, then the other, as he dropped the silky white fabric down his back and flung it to a nearby chair seat. Catherine's breath caught in her throat. Wide, bronzed, well-rounded shoulders subtly emphasized the narrowness of his waist, but it was the rippling muscles across his back that held her gaze and made her tingle all over. She'd never seen anything so exquisite in all her life. Were all men built the same? she wondered.

He bent forward then and she noticed how the muscles moved in the back of his arms as he scooped up two handfuls of water and splashed his face with it. Droplets clung to his hair and glistened in the candlelight as he rubbed more water across the back of his neck. When he stood erect again, Catherine's eyes followed the crystal drops that trailed a moist path over the well-defined crests and sharp valleys in his back before they gathered along the smooth curve of his spine and disappeared at the waistband of his trousers, leaving only her imagination to guess what was hidden beneath. He turned slightly and reached for a towel, presenting her with his profile. Dark, wet curls fell against his brow, and the fact that he needed a shave only added to his rakish good looks.

The beat of her pulse seemed to keep time with each brisk movement of his hands as he roughly dried his hair, and when he haphazardly hung the towel back on the rack and turned her way, her hand flew to her mouth to squelch the gasp that nearly escaped her lips. A thick mass of tiny black curls covered the magnificent expanse of his chest and trickled down to a fine line across his flat, hard belly. Shadows played beneath the taut sinews that flexed with each move he made, and Catherine suddenly doubted there was another man anywhere in the world who looked this good.

The subtle torture she endured changed to sheer panic in the next instant when his hands caught the fastening on his trousers and popped it free. Good God, he wasn't— He didn't intend to— Oh, he mustn't! Not now! Not while she was— She clamped her eyes shut and dropped her head forward against her knees. What had she gotten herself into?

A moment passed before she heard what she thought was the rustle of a garment being laid aside and a whimper tightened the muscles in her throat. *If only he'd extinguish the light* . . . she silently moaned.

Several more seconds ticked away, and before she realized it, she opened her eyes, lifted her head, and looked again. Her face flamed the instant she saw his naked profile, but she was too numb to do anything more than stare. The long, lean silhouette of his *very* masculine body against the amber glow of the candle behind him stirred a warmth deep in the pit of her stomach and spread to her loins and every nerve fiber in her. She couldn't breathe. Her flesh tingled. And strangely enough she felt an ache to have him hold her in his arms.

Suddenly the light went out, robbing her of the pleasure that had turned her practical thinking into irrational desires. She heard the crinkle of sheets as he slipped into bed, heard him sigh, and imagined the sight of him lying back against stark white pillowcases, his eyes staring up at the ceiling and perhaps his fingers interlaced behind his head. Was he thinking of her? Or someone else? How would he react if he knew she was there? Would he be angry? Or would he fulfill her fantasy? Ashamed of her wantonness, she frowned and settled herself in to wait. As soon as she was positive he had fallen asleep, she would make a quiet and hasty exit.

A smile teased T.J.'s mouth as he lay in bed staring up at the ceiling, his head cradled in the palms of his hands. He could only imagine the torment he'd caused the little snoop hiding behind the screen, and although he ordinarily wouldn't strip out of his clothes when he knew someone might be watching him, he'd felt it was what Catherine Chase deserved.

Instinct had told him the instant he'd entered his room that she was still there. One of the doors on the armoire would always drift open again if it wasn't solidly closed, and it was still in motion as he stepped across the threshold. The fresh scent of burned matches had been his second clue, and the empty moonlit balcony across from him plainly revealed her lack of time to descend the tree. That left only the trifold screen in the corner, and he'd confirmed her hiding place once he'd stepped up to the alcove to pull the draperies shut. A stream of diffused ashen light fell across the floor and touched the hem of her green satin skirt, and he pretended not to notice by not turning his head that direction. Instead, he'd lit a candle and proceeded to disrobe, thinking that she'd be the one to stop him. When she didn't, he'd wondered how much of it was pure terror or bold curiosity that kept her silent. And now, as he lay in bed, he could only assume that she planned to make her escape the instant he was asleep.

Should I take pity on her and not drag it out? he mused wickedly, his dark eyes glowing. A moment passed while he considered his choice. *Absolutely not,* he concluded, as devilish laughter threatened to spoil his game.

CHAPTER 8

Faint sounds, the warmth of sunshine falling into the room, and stiff and aching muscles worked against the peaceful serenity of Catherine's sleep-benumbed mind. She stirred, lazily moved her head in an effort to ease the kink in her neck, then came fully awake when the thud of a door being closed echoed off the walls and ceiling, and instantly triggered all the memories of the night past. Afraid to move or even draw a breath, she sat still and listened to the deafening silence closing in around her until she was sure the sealed door signaled T.J.'s departure from the room. Yet, before she dared to leave her hiding place, she leaned and made a quick examination of the chamber just to be sure. Satisfied she was alone, she slumped back against the wall and glared at the sunlight streaming in through the opened draperies of the alcove. How could she have fallen asleep? Had she been that tired, that relaxed that she hadn't even felt threatened? Good Lord, what would have happened if she had stretched in her sleep and knocked the screen over?

Realizing it was foolish to waste time thinking about what *might* have been, she absently reached for her shoes and stockings sitting next to her on the floor and started to put them on. Climbing a tree in the dark had been hard enough. Now she'd have to work her way down in the full light of day while running the risk of being seen by one of the servants or a neighbor out for his morning walk. Next time she came up with a harebrained idea and her instincts warned her not to follow through on it, she'd—

A chill suddenly shot up both arms, crossed her shoulders to her neck, and buried itself in her scalp the instant she realized what she held in her hands. As if the stockings were diseased or covered in blood, she flung them away, her pale blue eyes wide and full of terror. She had left them on the ground outside at the base of the oak! How could they have gotten— Her eyes narrowed as the only explanation came to mind. Their presence—here in his room on the second story—could only mean one thing. T.J. knew she had been hiding behind the screen! But when? When had he discovered his unannounced and uninvited guest? This morning? Sometime during the night? Or—

A slow, boiling rage began to bubble up inside her, and with a deep-throated growl, she snatched up the white mesh stockings and put them on. The bastard! she silently seethed, jamming her feet into the slippers. He'd stripped out of his clothes knowing full well he was being watched and by whom! He'd done it to deliberately provoke her, and he probably had to fight with himself to keep from laughing out loud. The detestable reprobate! Had he no morals at all?

Furious, she started for the balcony and changed her mind. Since she doubted he would keep their secret anyway, there was no sense in her trying to save what was left of her reputation by sneaking out of his house. No, she'd do exactly the opposite of what he expected her to do. She'd show him that she was just as brazen as he was. Executing a crisp about-face, she marched to the door with her chin held high, not missing a beat as she seized its brass knob, flung the portal wide, and stepped out into the hallway. She would have liked it better if there had been someone there to see her, but since there wasn't, she squared her shoulders anyway and headed for the stairs.

At the bottom she paused. She could hear voices coming from an open doorway a short distance away, and that they were discussing the weather. Her nostrils flared, her chin came down and her eyes narrowed once she recognized T.J.'s deep voice and she realized how at ease he sounded . . . as if nothing out of the ordinary had happened to him in a month or more. She hated his cockiness. In fact, she loathed everything about him. Suddenly wanting nothing more to do with him—or his house—she turned abruptly for the front door and nearly collided with a gray-haired woman coming from the parlor.

For a second Catherine was embarrassed by the surprised and stunned look she received until she heard T.J.'s rich, warm laughter spilling out into the foyer behind her. Reminded that all of this was *his* fault, she nodded politely at the still silent woman and brushed past her for the door. Not bothering to close it behind her, Catherine marched down the cobblestone path with her eyes trained straight ahead, unaware that Mrs. Witton had followed her to the threshold and stood watching her departure, her arms filled with clean towels, her mouth hanging open, and a perplexed expression deepening the lines in her face.

By the time Catherine neared the front walk of her town house, the end of her nose and her fingertips were numb. She'd been so angry with T.J. and his fiendish prank that she hadn't realized she had walked all the way home until the iron fence surrounding her property had come into view. With it flickered the knowledge that Mr. Trumble would be waiting for her, and unless she planned to tell him everything, she knew she'd have to come up with a lie that was totally believable. She wasn't sure, yet, how she would deal with T. J. Savage, let alone Mr. Trumble, if she failed to convince him that she'd only just left the house this morning rather than last night. If she had to, she could avoid ever seeing Mr. Savage again, but her lifelong companion was another matter entirely.

Glancing up at the front entrance just to make sure Mr. Trumble hadn't already spotted her, Catherine roughly gathered her long, silky mane back into its ribbon, dusted off her skirts, and threw back her shoulders, ready to face whatever was in store for her. She might have felt better if her mission had been a success, but since it hadn't been, she could only hope her failure didn't somehow manage to reflect itself in her eyes. Mr. Trumble was always able to see that something was bothering her just by the expression on her face, and this was one time she hoped she could mask it.

She had hardly closed the door behind her when a nervous Mr. Trumble appeared in the hallway before her, his gray brows pulled down in an anxious frown.

"Miss Chase," he whispered with a short glance over his shoulder at the parlor door, "are you all right? You left before I had a chance to serve your breakfast."

"Yes, Mr. Trumble, I'm fine," she answered, forcing a smile as she removed her cape and allowed him to hang it up for her. "I didn't sleep well last night—too much on my mind, I guess—so I decided to go for a walk. I apologize if I frightened you."

Although this had actually been the first time she'd left the house so early in the morning without telling him, Mr. Trumble had come to expect such behavior from the young woman. He would have preferred she announce her intentions beforehand, but that was not what had him so uneasy. It was the guest who waited for her in the parlor.

"Yes, miss," he said, glancing over his shoulder again, a gesture that did not go unnoticed by his companion.

"Mr. Trumble," Catherine accused, "you're acting like an unfaithful spouse who's afraid he's about to get caught. What's wrong?"

The bold suggestion made him straighten sharply. "You have a visitor, miss," he whispered, taking two steps past her and farther away from the parlor door in the hope she would understand how important it was that they not be overheard.

Catherine's first thought was that Mr. Trumble meant T. J. Savage was there, but once she'd managed to still the rising panic, she realized he couldn't have gotten there ahead of her without her having seen him. "Who is it?" she asked, hoping he was too busy with his own nervousness to notice hers.

"A Miss Cherry Hammerand, miss," he replied, his composure restored. "If I may be so bold to assume, I believe she's a . . . a harlot by her manner of dress and speech."

"Did she say what she wanted?"

"Yes, miss. She wishes to hire your services." His tone implied his disapproval.

"Thank you, Mr. Trumble," Catherine replied as she headed away from him, totally unaffected by his subtle reproof of the woman. "And would you be so kind as to bring us some tea?" She wasn't sure about Miss Hammerand, but Catherine knew *she* could use a hot drink to rid her bones of their chill.

The instant she saw Cherry Hammerand rise from her chair, Catherine understood how Mr. Trumble had arrived at his conclusion that the young girl spent her nights working at a pub. Although she was quite pretty under all her makeup, she wore too much rouge on her lips and cheeks to suit Catherine, and her eyebrows were charcoaled almost black. And the ebony patch she had glued on the outside of her left cheekbone near the corner of her eye was the same, in Catherine's mind, as hanging a sign around her neck stating her profession. Her clothes were frayed and wrinkled, which told Catherine that Cherry didn't cater to rich clientele, and Catherine thought how easily that could change if the young girl would only wash her face and purchase a fancy but modest dress to wear.

"Miss Hammerand," she politely greeted, her hand extended, as she crossed the distance to where Cherry stood. "I'm Catherine Chase. What may I do for you?"

Cherry timidly shook the proffered hand and sat back down as Catherine motioned for her to do. "Call me Cherry, Miss Chase," she corrected. "Everybody does."

Catherine smiled and nodded her acceptance as she took a seat beside the girl.

"I probably shouldn't 'ave come," she began, dropping her gaze to her hands folded neatly in her lap. "Scotland Yard said I shouldn't worry, but I do."

"About what?" Catherine coaxed, sensing as well as seeing the dismay in the girl's dark eyes.

"It's me friends, Miss Chase, Molly and Laura. They're

missin', and I'm afraid somethin' awful 'as 'appened to 'em."

"Missing?" Catherine repeated.

"Aye, miss. The last time I saw Molly was two days ago. She left the pub early that night 'cause she wasn't feelin' well, and I 'aven't seen 'er since. She never made it to the flat she, Laura, and me share. Then last night—" She stopped suddenly to swallow the tears that had tightened her throat. "Last night Laura said to me that she 'ad an idea where Molly might be and she left to go look for 'er. That was shortly after ten, it was, and now she's gone, too." She clutched her hands and raised them against her bosom, her eyes on Catherine, and her lower lip trembling. "I'm afraid, Miss Catherine. It ain't like 'em ter go off without tellin' me where they'll be."

Mr. Trumble appeared at that moment with the tea, and Catherine hurriedly fixed the girl a cup, placed it in her hands, and insisted she drink some of it.

"What did Scotland Yard tell you, Cherry?" she quietly asked once Mr. Trumble had left them again.

"That they'd turn up sooner or later. They said me friends were probably off visitin' relatives." Her tears spilled over the rim of her lashes and fell down her cheeks. "But I don't think so, miss. They never took their clothes or nothin', and I'm not sure either of 'em 'ave any relatives . . . at least not 'ere in London. Oh, please, Miss Chase, you've got to 'elp me find 'em."

Catherine was well aware of the attitude of the men at the Yard and that they wouldn't waste their time looking for two prostitutes even if foul play was suspected. What really irked her was knowing that many of those very same men used the services of women like Cherry and her friends whenever the mood struck them, but that if the girls were in trouble, they'd look the other way. After all, those sorts of women asked for what they got.

That alone was enough reason for Catherine to take the case, but something else prompted her to accept. She needed the distraction. She needed to get away from everything and anything that would remind her of T. J.

Savage. Until now she hadn't been able to bring herself to admit that the museum paintings were lost, but in good conscience, she was sure the death of those two men had subsequently brought a momentary end to her investigation. And since Scotland Yard had the only tangible piece of evidence to connect T.J. to the murders, she knew she might as well let them handle it. They couldn't mess it up any worse than she already had.

"Yes, Cherry," she announced, "I'll help you find your friends."

Catherine decided that perhaps it would be wise of her not to stay at home for any length of time that day just in case T.J. felt inclined to pay her a visit. She started out by making an appointment to meet Cherry at her flat a little later, after Catherine had bathed, changed her clothes, and had eaten breakfast, and within an hour of agreeing to find Cherry's friends, Catherine was on her way to the dock area where Miss Hammerand lived.

For the next two hours they talked and Catherine jotted down notes. She learned that both Molly and Laura were blond, tall, thin, and two years apart in age, a disappointing discovery for Catherine, since their descriptions weren't much different from each other except that Molly had brown eyes, and Laura's were green. Both girls had been born and raised in the same neighborhood where they lived now, and they both worked at the same pub with Cherry.

Once Catherine had written down all the pertinent information she needed, she asked permission to examine the girls' personal belongings, telling Cherry that getting to know a person's habits and their individual likes and dislikes many times helped Catherine with her investigation. When she'd finished, she asked Cherry if either Molly or Laura had a special male friend or anyone else aside from Cherry whom Catherine might question. From there they visited the tavern owner and they talked with two other girls who knew Molly and Laura, none of whom offered much direction.

Catherine and Cherry had lunch together, then parted

company. Cherry needed to sleep for a few hours since her job required she stay up most of the night, and Catherine wanted to speak with Nathan Beecher at Scotland Yard. From the information she'd collected thus far, she feared the girls' disappearance could mean only one thing.

The ride across town took longer than Catherine liked. It gave her too much time to think with very few diversions. Memories of the night past kept coming to mind, her embarrassment at having been caught, and more so the image of T.J.'s long, lean body bathed in candlelight. Even now a hot flush rose in her cheeks as she fought to dissolve the vision that continued to stir a titillating warmth along her spine. She couldn't comprehend the pleasure it gave her when the sight of a naked man should—by all rights—scare her to death.

She sighed a quiet breath of relief when the three-story brick building belonging to Scotland Yard came into view, and she very nearly didn't wait for the cab to come to a complete halt before getting out. She paid the driver, told him not to wait, and hurried inside to find Nathan.

As always, the young man was pleased to see her. Once she had sat down in the chair next to his desk, he voluntarily reported that no further developments had occurred in the museum robbery, and a frown appeared on his face after she admitted that that wasn't the reason she had come. Instead she told him about the missing girls and that she was hoping their bodies hadn't turned up in the morgue.

His hesitancy in replying gave her a queasy feeling. It turned to pessimism once he revealed that three new murders had been reported overnight and that each victim had been a woman. Even though their bodies had been identified, the additional information he gave her indicated that in his opinion it was only a matter of time before Molly's and Laura's names were added to the undertaker's list.

"Why do you think that?" she challenged.

"The dead women were all prostitutes, Miss Chase," he advised, "working the dock area, and the similarities among the women are a little unnerving."

"What kind of similarities?" she asked.

"All three were blond, pretty, in their early twenties, and they all lived within five blocks of each other. From our investigation so far, we've learned they weren't acquaintances, but we've also noted that their bodies were found in separate abandoned buildings near the waterfront. And before you ask," he hurriedly added, one hand raised to stop her before she could, "yes, we went door to door but there really wasn't much need." Once he saw the curious look on her face, he finished, "They weren't murdered where their bodies were found."

"How can you be so sure?"

"Each one had put up quite a struggle before she died. They were bruised and cut, yet we didn't find any blood anywhere except on their clothes, no scuff marks or pieces of their torn clothing."

"So you're saying they were dumped in these buildings *after* they were killed?" she concluded.

"Yes. And all three were killed by the same man," Nathan continued, his voice lowered as he leaned closer to her with his arms folded and lying against the desktop. "Or at least the same weapon was used."

"Weapon?"

Nathan frowned and looked quickly around the large room to see who might be listening. "I shouldn't be telling you this, Miss Chase. You know how the commissioner can get."

"Yes, I know," Catherine agreed. "But I'm not trying to solve these murders. I'm looking for two missing friends. And *you* know that anything you tell me never goes any further than this room."

He smiled at her, and Catherine thought how—for just an instant—his smile seemed to hint at a warmer feeling than simple friendship.

"Each of them was strangled. From the bruises on their necks, we've determined the killer didn't use his hands."

"You mean he used a rope or cord of some kind?"

Nathan shook his head. "We're not sure what he used," he confessed, reaching for a pen and piece of paper. After sketching out an odd design, he pushed the paper across the desk at her.

"Were any of the victims wearing a necklace?" she queried, frowning at what she saw on the parchment.

"No. Why do you ask?"

She laid the paper down and twisted it around for Nathan to study. "See how you've drawn tiny half-circles? I'd say your weapon was some sort of chain, the kind women wear as necklaces. Perhaps the killer strangled them with their own jewelry and then stole it from them after they were dead."

"Good heavens, Miss Chase," he exclaimed after a moment, "I think you've hit on something." He smiled crookedly, almost as if he'd thought of something wicked. "Wait till the commissioner hears who figured it out. He'll have to change his mind about you then."

Catherine quickly shook her head and stood. "It was your discovery, Nathan, not mine. I don't want my name mentioned. Promise?"

"But Miss—"

"Promise?" she asked more sternly than before.

Reluctant, Nathan was quiet for a moment. "I promise," he finally pledged as he sprang to his feet. "But I'll be indebted to you just the same."

Catherine smiled warmly at the pleasant-looking face staring back at her. "All right," she said, turning to leave.

Every muscle in Catherine's body ached. Her eyes were itchy and she couldn't seem to stop yawning during the entire trip home. As the town house came into view, she considered eating supper and then taking a nap before she went back to Cherry's again. Otherwise, she might fall asleep in the middle of a question, and she certainly didn't want Miss Hammerand to think that whatever happened to her friends was so unimportant that she couldn't even stay awake. She changed her mind about all of it once she entered the house and Mr. Trumble met her in the foyer.

"Mr. Savage was here to see you, Miss Chase," he casually announced as he took her cloak and hung it on the hall tree. "He asked when I expected you home, and since I wasn't sure, I suggested he come back around seven."

Catherine's gaze shot to the tall grandfather clock standing at the base of the staircase. It was nearly six already, which meant she wouldn't have time for a nap.

"Is dinner ready?" she asked, heading for the stairs.

"Yes, miss," Mr. Trumble replied.

"Good. Then I'll eat in the kitchen," she told him as she hurriedly mounted the steps on her way to her room. "I promised Miss Hammerand that I'd speak with her again this evening."

"But what about Mr. Savage? He seemed very anxious to—"

"You'll have to extend my apologies, Mr. Trumble," she called back over her shoulder. "Tell him I already had a previous engagement and that I'll get in touch with him when it's convenient we meet."

At the top of the staircase she paused and grabbed the newel post to steady her balance. She seemed light-headed of a sudden, and her knees wouldn't stop trembling. She took a deep breath, straightened her back, and started off again. She couldn't imagine his reason for wanting to talk with her, but she was sure the subject of last night would be at the top of his agenda, and she just wasn't ready to deal with it, yet.

Closing the door behind her, Catherine crossed to her dressing table and sat down. Late afternoon sunshine spilled in through the window, and while she looked at her reflection in the mirror, she wondered if her complexion was really that pale or if the golden rays of light only made it seem that way. She also noticed how tired and drawn she appeared, but she accredited that to her lack of sleep and where she'd spent last night.

Sighing, she braced her elbows on the table and propped her chin in her hands as she stared into the silvered glass. Her life had been so simple until *he* came along. She'd been content with spending her time helping others, arguing with Commissioner Mays, and irritating Mr. Trumble. She'd wanted nothing more beyond the satisfaction of knowing she'd done the best job she could. Now, all of a sudden, she was paying attention to trivial things . . . like how pale she looked or whether or not she wore shoes. And worse than that, *he* had made her aware of the fact that she was a woman with feelings, deep-rooted feelings that played games with her mind.

Her gaze drifted away from the mirror and spotted Satan lying on the windowsill, his head down, his long tail curled around him, and his gold eyes staring at her as if he'd heard every thought in her head.

"Oh, what do you know?" she snapped, jerking up from the stool. "You're just a cat."

Crossing to the washbasin, she poured water into the bowl, and splashed cool droplets over her face. Her problem with T. J. Savage wasn't going to go away no matter how much she wanted it to evaporate. He was responsible for the change in her, and even if he disappeared tomorrow, she'd never be the same again. There was a restlessness stirring inside her, a reserve of totally feminine emotions begging to be explored, and the idea that she might even be considering it provoked her beyond belief. And what really made her angry with herself was her cowardice. Rather than face him, she was plotting ways to avoid seeing him. For the first time in her life, she was afraid of someone.

"No I'm not!" she stubbornly denied as she reached for a towel. "I just have more important things to do right now."

She caught sight of the black cat again, and her temper flared even higher when she noticed how he had lifted his head and was staring at her as if to challenge her declaration. Snarling back at him, she wadded up the towel and tossed it on the floor, silently daring him to prove his allegation before she turned on her heel and stalked from the room.

"Oh, Miss Chase, I can't let ye do it!" Cherry objected, her brown eyes wide and full of fear as she stared disbelievingly at her guest.

"But I see no other way, Cherry," Catherine explained.

"I've questioned the few people who might be willing to help me with my investigation, and I've gotten nowhere. I really have no other choice." The clock on the mantel struck seven, drawing Catherine's nervous gaze, and she blinked away the image of T.J. knocking on the front door of the town house. She crossed to the settee and sat down beside the young girl. "Even though I'm not working for the Yard, people seem to think I am whenever I ask too many questions. If they're at ease with me, they might open up and allow me to learn something about Molly and Laura that we don't already know. Don't you agree?"

Cherry's frown deepened.

"I'll be all right," Catherine promised. "I know how to handle myself."

"I don't mean no disrespect, Miss Chase," the girl dared to say, "but does that include 'andlin' drunks? And what if one o' 'em wants more than 'is mug of ale? I'm sure ye've seen a lot o' gory things, miss, but 'ave ye ever dealt with a man 'oo wants ter toss ye on yer back and won't take no for an answer? Pretendin' ter be one of us is one thing, Miss Chase, but bein' convincin' is quite another."

Catherine clearly understood what Cherry was politely trying to point out to her, and although she had to admit she had never been in that kind of situation, she was still very sure her dexterity and quick wit would shield her from any major problems. The memory of the first time she'd seen T.J. came to mind and she flinched. *That* was different, she silently claimed, and nothing Cherry could tell her would make her think otherwise.

"I appreciate your concern, Cherry," she said, smiling softly, "but I'm at risk everytime I take a case. They're never the same, and this one will be a new one, but I can't let it stop me. If I allowed the dangers of my job to make up my mind for me, I'd never leave the house." She reached over and squeezed the girl's hand. "You want to find your friends, don't you?" When Cherry nodded, Catherine finished, "Then lend me something to wear and show me how to fix my hair. All right?"

Cherry still didn't approve, but she saw no way out of it.

If Miss Chase was willing to put herself in that kind of a predicament, who was she to stop her? With a surrendering sigh, she stood and crossed to the wardrobe.

"We'll start with your clothes," she instructed, pulling out a low-cut dress and holding it up for Catherine to see.

A smile parted Catherine's lips when Cherry looked at her, but once she'd glanced away again, a twinge of apprehension turned the gesture into an unflattering grimace.

I hope you know what you're doing, Catherine Chase, she silently scolded. *God, I hope you do.*

CHAPTER 9

Catherine wasn't sure if it was the cool night air that made her tremble or the expectation of what she was about to face once she followed Cherry inside the pub. She hadn't quite realized just how big an undertaking to which she had agreed until *after* Cherry had helped her dress, style her hair, and apply the right amount of rouge, and Catherine had looked at the finished product in a mirror. About the only thing that slightly resembled the old Catherine Chase was the color of her eyes, but even they seemed different with all the black liner darkening her lashes and brows. The black patch Cherry had decided would look best at the corner of Catherine's mouth and the purple plume jutting out from the mass of curls piled high on top of her head added the finishing touch to her disguise and drew her attention away from the rather revealing neckline of the dress she wore. If all Catherine wanted was to be accepted as one of the "girls," Cherry had seen to it in grand fashion. Her only concern now—as Cherry opened the front door to the pub—was that perhaps the young woman had gone to the extreme. Catherine wanted to blend in, not stand out as she was sure she would.

"Mr. Bassett," Cherry said, pulling the tavern owner and barkeep away from eavesdroppers, "ye remember Miss Chase, don't ye?" She watched the rotund, balding little man glance at the woman standing beside her and how his eyes widened as they swept Catherine from head to toe. "She's 'ere ter 'elp out."

A frown crowded his dark brows together. "'Elp out?"

"Aye," Cherry replied, grabbing his arm and pulling him in close. "She wants ter serve drinks, but no one is ter know 'oo she is."

"Why?" Bassett asked, his eyes glued on the lovely face marred by too much black pencil.

"She doesn't want anyone to know 'oo she really is so's she can ask questions without them gettin' suspicious," Cherry whispered.

"What the bloody 'ell for?" he echoed.

"Shhh! It's what she does when she's workin' on a case," she quickly explained. "If the customers think she's nothin' more than a barmaid, they'll talk to 'er, and she can find out where Molly and Laura are. Ye'll let 'er, won't ye, Mr. Bassett? Ye want ter 'elp find me friends, don't ye?"

His frown deepened as he gave Catherine a second once-over. "Is that all she'll be doin'? Servin' drinks?"

Catherine blushed instantly, certain she understood what he implied.

"Aye," Cherry snapped, irritated that her employer even had to ask. "She ain't no 'arlot, Mr. Bassett. She's only pretendin' so she can ask questions."

"And scare off me customers?" he objected, not at all sure he liked the idea. "I lost two o' me best girls and now ye're askin' me ter offend me customers?"

"I swear that won't happen, Mr. Bassett," Catherine quickly promised. "And I'll work for nothing."

His eyes lit up. "Nothing? Ye'll work all night and not ask for a shilling?"

"Not even a farthing," she pledged with a smile. "And if I offend even *one* customer, you may tell me to leave." She could see by his expression that he was weakening. "All I want is the freedom and opportunity to uncover clues that might help us find Molly and Laura. You've got nothing to lose, Mr. Bassett, and everything to gain."

He thought about it for a moment longer, then agreed. "Ye got a deal, Miss Chase."

"Faith," Cherry cut in, and at his questioning look, she explained. "We're ter call 'er Faith." She smiled and glanced at Catherine. " 'Twas me idea—the name, I mean, 'cause I 'ave faith she'll find me friends."

"All right." Bassett yielded. "Faith it is. Now get ter work, both o' ye."

Getting the men to talk about the missing girls proved easier than Catherine had anticipated. Apparently Molly and Laura were well liked—both for their personalities and the favors they willingly offered anyone with the right amount of coin. The instant the men realized there was a new face among them, they asked—with obvious disappointment—if one or both of the girls had quit their job and moved on. Catherine would explain that her employment was only temporary and that she would tell Molly and Laura how much they were missed. But other than that, no one ventured a guess or even hinted at where they thought the girls might be, and after an hour of being on her feet and enduring pinches, pats, and bold caresses to her rump, Catherine's disappointment showed in the slump of her shoulders.

"Anything?" Cherry hopefully asked when business slowed and they had the chance to sit down.

Catherine sighed and shook her head. "But it's still early. And there's always tomorrow night."

"Tomorrow night?" Cherry repeated, surprised. "Ye mean ye'll do this again?"

Stretching the tired muscles in her back, she winced at the sudden sharp pain near her spine and laughed. "If I live through tonight, I will. I don't know how you do it, Cherry."

"Ah, ye get used to it," the girl guaranteed.

A commotion at the door drew their attention, and Catherine frowned as she watched a group of sailors stumble in. "Is it always this busy?"

Cherry laughed as she picked up her tray and stood. "No. It's usually busier."

"What?" Catherine called after her.

The pub's limited space grew even more crowded as the night progressed, and it was close to midnight before either girl had the chance to sit down again. Catherine continued to subtly ask her questions with no helpful results, and the men's affection toward her became even bolder. Her bottom had been pinched so many times she was sure her entire backside would be black and blue by morning. One drunken sailor even had the audacity to lay his hand over one of her breasts and squeeze when she protested. Cherry came to her rescue, for which Catherine swore she would be eternally grateful, and all the while neither her new friend nor Catherine were aware of the dark figure sitting in a far corner watching every move the blond-haired waitress made.

"How long does this keep up?" an exhausted Catherine asked of Mr. Bassett as she plopped her tray of empty mugs on the bar.

"Sometimes until the sun comes up." He chuckled, knowing how hard the work was on a newcomer. "It depends."

"On what?" she questioned, watching him refill each tankard with ale.

"On whether or not a ship just anchored."

Catherine briefly scanned the crowd, noting that the majority of patrons weren't dressed in cropped pants, striped shirts, and caps. "Thank God," she mumbled, noticing for the first time how one customer preferred sitting alone in the darkest corner of the tavern and that he hadn't removed either his cape or his hat. With his head down and turned slightly away, she couldn't see his face, but from the quality of his garments, he seemed horribly out of place. Deciding to get a better look at him, she started toward him when Mr. Bassett called out and halted her in her tracks.

"These are ready," he said, tapping a fingertip on the tray. "Ye better serve 'em before we 'ave a riot on our 'ands."

"Yes, sir," Catherine agreed, thinking that once she'd delivered the ale, she would wander over to the well-dressed man in the corner and ask if he'd like his glass refilled.

She executed her task with a minimum of trouble, but when she turned to approach the customer who had piqued her curiosity, her blackened brows dropped downward once she discovered he had already left the pub. Perhaps she was making more of it than was really there, but that was what made her good at her job. She never let a possibility slip by without exploring every angle, and since Cherry had obviously been the one to serve the man his drink, Catherine would ask her about him.

"Over there," she said, pointing. "I never saw his face, but from the way he was dressed, I would say he isn't your usual kind of customer."

Cherry shook her head, frowning. "I don't know," she reluctantly admitted. "I've waited on so many. . . . Ter tell ye the truth, I seldom look at their faces unless—" She stopped abruptly and a slight blush rose in her cheeks.

"Unless what, Cherry?" Catherine pressed, failing to notice the girl's embarrassment.

Cherry cleared her throat, glanced up briefly at her companion, then back at the tray she held. "Unless 'e wants more than a drink."

The intensity of the moment vanished, leaving Catherine terribly uncomfortable. "Oh," she murmured.

"I'm sorry, Miss Chase. I 'ope I didn't ruin somethin'."

"Oh, no," Catherine quickly assured her. "Not at all." She forced a smile as she tried to dismiss the image she had of Cherry and a total stranger leaving the pub together and why. "Well," she said, deliberately changing the subject, "I guess we better get back to work."

Cherry nodded weakly and walked away, but it wasn't enough to stop the train of thought racing through Catherine's head. Only recently had she given any thought to men in the romantic sense, and while it was difficult enough for her to imagine what it was like for two people in love, it was impossible for her to understand how a woman could give herself to someone she didn't even know. Of course, Cherry did it for money, but not every woman did. They were the ones she questioned. Was the reward that wonderful? She shuddered, doubting *anything* could be that sensational that she'd want to crawl into bed with the first man who asked. Suddenly, the picture of a tall, dark-haired, extremely handsome man with a bronzed, perfectly sculptured, very masculine body flashed before her eyes, and she could feel the heat flaring up her neck to her face. Foolishly thinking that everyone in the room knew what had crossed her mind, she glanced guiltily around and saw that no one was paying any particular attention to her. Thankful, yet certain they were only being kind, she turned her concentration on clearing off the table of empty glasses the last patrons left behind.

"Faith," Mr. Bassett summoned some time later, "I think ye could go 'ome now. Cherry can 'andle the rest of the customers. Ye look tired."

"I am," Catherine admitted with a long sigh as she leaned heavily against the bar. "I never would have guessed serving drinks could be so much hard work."

Bassett laughed. "And I never would 'ave guessed ye'd keep up. But ye did." Grabbing the dirty glasses from her tray, he dunked them in the pan of hot, sudsy water as he asked, "Did ye learn anythin'?"

"No, I'm afraid I didn't," she replied with a disappointed glance toward the young girl flirting with a group of sailors. "And if it's all right with you, I'd like to come back tomorrow night and try again."

Bassett raised one brow. "Are ye sure?"

Catherine nodded. "It's the only way I know of to find out what happened to Cherry's friends."

"Then I'd be honored ter 'ave ye, Faith," Bassett teased. "If ye'll wait a minute, I'll rouse me son out of bed and 'ave 'im walk ye 'ome."

"I wouldn't think of it," Catherine objected as she untied the apron she'd been given to wear and laid it on the bar. "Cherry's flat is only a couple of blocks from here, and after I change into my own clothes, I'll hire a cab."

"I doubt ye'll find one this time o' night," he advised.

"They ain't too fond o' workin' this part o' town even in the daylight."

Catherine frowned. Walking two or three blocks to Cherry's flat was one thing, but walking all the way to the town house would take her a good hour or more. Perhaps she should stay with Cherry for the night or at least until the sun came up. Wondering if the young girl would mind the company, Catherine glanced across the room at her and realized the answer to that one without having to ask. A gray-haired man twice Cherry's age had dragged the girl onto his lap and was smothering her with kisses, an obvious declaration of his intentions once Cherry was allowed to leave the pub. Catherine would much prefer walking home even if it took her the rest of the night rather than witness Cherry's after-hour work habits.

"Tell Cherry I'll talk to her tomorrow afternoon," she instructed the man behind the bar as she headed toward the door and her cape hanging on a peg beside it, her eyes affixed to the amorous couple in the far corner.

Catherine hadn't realized the stench of the place until after she'd stepped outside and the cool night air filled her lungs. A heavy mist clinging to every lamppost promised to wash the offensive scent of ale from her hair, face, and clothes, and although it meant she would be damp by the time she reached the flat, Catherine honestly didn't mind. Cherry and Mr. Bassett might be nice people, but Catherine didn't like anything else about the pub, its patrons, and what went on inside, and if she hadn't given her word to investigate the disappearance of Cherry's friends, Catherine would have nothing more to do with the place.

A dog barking in the distance turned her head that way. Although she wasn't very fond of dogs, she wished she had one with her right then. She'd been relatively safe from groping hands the entire time she'd been in the pub with Cherry and Mr. Bassett around to step in, but out here . . . alone . . . on a dark, deserted street . . . in an unfavorable part of town . . . The dog might not be able to fully protect her, but he certainly could offer a distraction should someone misjudge her for a . . . She cringed at the thought. Plucking the amethyst feather from her hair, she grabbed the edges of her cape, pulled it tightly around her, and started off toward Cherry's flat.

She had traveled nearly a block before she realized her mistake. Cherry had said the last time she'd seen Molly was at work, that the girl had left the pub early because she had been ill, and that she had never arrived home. Catherine wasn't sure, but she guessed it must be close to two o'clock in the morning, later than when Molly had taken this route, yet the circumstances were the same. Molly had been alone. And so was Catherine.

A mixture of uneasiness and irritation poured over her. How could she have been so caught up in other things that she hadn't seen this coming? What set her apart from everyone else was her ability to avoid a situation before it happened, and here she was trapped in the middle of one!

You're getting careless, Catherine Chase, she silently scolded herself as the image of T. J. Savage came to mind. *And he's the reason why!* Muttering a few censorious remarks about the man, she lowered her gaze and concentrated on the sidewalk ahead of her.

The thick fog and biting mist did little to ease Catherine's sour mood as she hurried along. In the past the excitement of working on a case had always sharpened her skills and focused her full attention on the details of an investigation. Nothing else had ever managed to wedge its way into her thoughts. Lately, since meeting T. J. Savage, she'd been distracted, and she didn't have to be told how dangerous that could be.

At the corner she crossed the street. She remembered Cherry's insistence earlier that they not cut down the alley even in the bright sunlight since the worst of degenerates always seemed to hide there, but Catherine was in a hurry. The sooner she got to the flat, the sooner she could change her clothes and be on her way. Nearing the avenue, she paused with a last-minute doubt, and in that instant she heard the echoing footsteps of someone behind her. She jerked around, her heart thundering in her throat, but the heavy fog prevented her from seeing much of anything. Was it merely by accident that someone had chosen to walk the same street as she had taken? Or was she being followed? She clumsily backed away, fear trembling the muscles in her legs.

"Don't let him scare you," she whispered to herself. "If you can't see him, he can't see you. You've got the advantage. Use it!" Spinning on her heel, she dashed off down the street.

Her steps quickened, but it wasn't the click of *her* shoes against the cobblestones that caught her ear. Whoever was behind her had hurried his pace as well! She raced past a lamppost and its muted yellow light, silently calculating how long it would take for the man to approach it and place himself in the dull glow. There really was no need for her to see him to know he was there, but the panic that was rapidly engulfing her crowded her common sense, and once she'd traveled the estimated distance, she glanced back over her shoulder. A second later the tall, dark figure of a man in cape and top hat moved into the pale, befogged light, and a tiny whimper escaped her lips. She'd seen him before . . . at the pub, not more than an hour ago! Could he possibly be the man responsible for the deaths of the three murdered prostitutes? Did he intend to make her his next victim? Was she about to share the same fate as Molly and Laura?

"Absolutely not!" she bravely stated, turning her back on him and racing off again.

The coupling of fear and the urgency to succeed muddied Catherine's sense of direction. All that crossed her mind was using the dense fog as cover so that she could get away. Thinking to fool her pursuer, she dashed back across the street and headed down an alley, planning at the other end to turn left and wind up back at the pub. If the man was intent on catching her, she might trick him into coming inside, and once he did, she, Mr. Bassett, and Cherry would jump him. Surely the three of them would be able to hold him until the police came.

When the echoing of footsteps behind her seemed to be getting louder, panic threatened to overcome her. Careless, she glanced back over her shoulder, and in the process she stubbed her toe on something. Unable to keep her balance, she fell and landed hard on one hip. Pain shot through her body, and she would have liked sitting still a moment until it went away, but she knew that every second was precious to her. Calling on every ounce of strength she had, she pushed herself up to her feet and limped off. At the end of the narrow alleyway, she staggered to a halt, breathless and confused. Must she turn right or left?

"Damn," she fumed, angry with herself for not having paid closer attention, while her mind raced to retrace her steps and give her the answer she needed.

She had just about decided to turn left when off in the opposite direction she heard the faint voice of a preacher man heralding the word of God. Even though she thought it was strange for him to be out at this time of night, she also concluded that she couldn't be much safer than in the presence of someone like him. After a quick glance back down the alley, she hurriedly headed his way. Perhaps he could help her find the pub where Cherry worked.

She had traveled only half a block before she could see him standing under the street lamp on the corner, a book in one hand, the other held out as if he spoke to a crowd of people hanging on his every word. A chill embraced her, for there was something terribly odd about the man, but her steps never slowed as she moved closer to him. After all, what choice did she have? At least with him, her life wasn't in danger.

"Good evening, Reverend," she called out to him, and that same chill slithered down her back when he turned cold, dark eyes on her. "I was wondering if you could help me." She jutted a thumb over her shoulder. "I'm being followed, and I fear the man means to harm me. Would you be so kind as to walk me to Mr. Bassett's establishment?"

The preacher's brows came tightly together. "Mr. Basset harbors sinners, child," he accused, his gaze sweeping the length of her. "If it is a refuge you seek, ask God's forgiveness and He shall take you into His fold."

At first Catherine couldn't comprehend what he meant until she remembered how she was dressed and that her appearance could only make him think the worst of her.

"You misunderstand," she said, smiling. "I'm not a . . . a . . . sinner."

"Only God is without sin!" he exploded.

Startled, Catherine took a step backward. "Well, yes, of course. That wasn't what I meant . . . exactly. We're all sinners. Some of us more than others. But—"

"When was the last time you attended services?" his deep, blaring voice demanded.

Catherine blinked, trying to remember. "I—I'm not sure."

"Think, girl! Was it last week? Last month? When?"

She knew it was only her imagination, but Catherine could have sworn the preacher's tall, thin frame grew even taller as he towered over her. "Last week," she replied, thinking it was best she lie to him. How would he know differently anyway?

"You lie!" he shouted. "I can see it in your eyes . . . in the way you wear your hair . . . in your clothes!" A hand shot out and seized her chin as he roughly wiped the rouge from her lips. "You work for the devil. You're a child of Satan. See this?" He held up his thumb. "Red. Lucifer's color. He has cast his spell on you, child, but I am here to save you. Come!"

He turned his back on her and started to walk away, and for an instant Catherine hesitated. The preacher was crazy; she was sure of it.

"Where?" she asked.

"To wipe away your sin," he called back. "To purify your soul. To chase away the demons living inside you. Only then can you meet your Maker on bended knee."

As far as Catherine was concerned, he was talking gibberish, but if he wanted to cleanse her soul, it was all right with her, since the only place she could think of that would be appropriate would be a church. And being in a church with a crazy man was a lot more appealing than taking her chances with the stranger in the dark cape and hat. Thinking of the one who had been following her, she shot a glance back over her shoulder and saw nothing but the swirling fog. She wanted to believe he had given up trying to catch her now that she was in the preacher's company, but she doubted it. A man who hated prostitutes—for whatever reason—wouldn't back down so easily. He'd find some other way of catching her alone.

"Well, good luck," she murmured, turning back. She wasn't leaving the preacher's side until the sun came up.

Catherine had to practically run to keep up with the parson's long strides, and even though he was heading in the opposite direction from the pub, she didn't mind . . . more so once she heard the third set of footsteps behind them beating a rhythm in time to their own hurried pace. They walked several blocks, turned a corner, then walked several more, and by then Catherine was totally lost. The only time she'd ever been in this part of town was when Mr. Trumble drove her, and he always seemed to know exactly where they were. From now on, she vowed, she'd pay strict attention to her surroundings. That way if she ever found herself in a similar predicament again, she'd be able to get herself out without having to rely on anyone's help.

"Is it much farther, Reverend?" she asked, when it seemed they'd traveled for hours. She'd been on her feet all evening, and the spill she'd taken a short while earlier had given her a new ache with which to contend. She longed to sit down and rest, but she also preferred doing it inside the church.

The preacher came to an abrupt halt, so sudden in fact that Catherine stumbled into him. She drew a breath to apologize and gasped instead when he cruelly grabbed her arm and yanked her sideways into an alleyway. Had he just now heard the presence of the man behind them? Was he frightened, too? She opened her mouth to voice the questions, when all of a sudden the parson spun her around, doubled up his fist, and hit her across the jaw with the back of his knuckles.

"Harlot!" he screamed at her as Catherine tumbled to the cobblestones. "Scarlet woman! Whore! Prostitute! Satan's mistress! My work is never done. I rid the earth of one, and two more come to take her place. But I shall not be defeated. I shall continue to send them back from whence they came until they are no more."

Dazed, Catherine listened to his ranting, trying desperately to understand him while she shook off the numbing pain he'd caused her. What did he mean he'd rid the earth of one? Was he fantasizing or did he speak the truth? And what method did he use to change a sinner into a saint? Fear? Or did he beat them? The last thought helped her lift her head. Through a haze she saw him toss down his book, then reach inside his coat with both hands. A second later he was pulling something up over his head, and once the dull light from a second-story window above her fell upon the object he held, everything became chillingly clear.

"You will join the others," he declared, twisting the gold chain and cross around his hands. "By your death your soul will be cleansed and only then will God forgive you."

The pain that had clouded her thoughts only seconds before cleared the instant Catherine recognized that her survival depended solely on her ability to outsmart the man planning to kill her. Fear tightened every muscle in her body and panic made them tremble, and she very nearly caved in to the paralyzing emotions. Then her father's voice rang loud and clear inside her head.

"Get up, Catherine. Don't let anything beat you. Use your wit and cunning! Prove to the world that you're an exceptional woman. Make me proud."

She knew it was only her subconscious making the demands, but it was enough to spur her into action. Rolling onto her backside with her arms braced behind her for support, she waited until the parson moved closer, the necklace pulled taut between his fists and his eyes blazing with madness. In one quick movement she drew up her legs and kicked out with her feet, ramming them in her assailant's knees. The blow threw him off balance and knocked him backward long enough for Catherine to twist around, clear her skirts from under her and come up on her feet. She bolted off, planning to run as hard and as long as she could and in any direction her legs would carry her. But she had traveled only a few steps when she felt the unyielding entrapment of her cape in the parson's hand and the pull of its strings around her throat. Frantic, she tugged at the cords and freed the knot the instant the reverend's other hand caught her shoulder. His fingers dug deep in her flesh and brought tears to her eyes, but she refused to let it defeat her. Striking out, she knocked his hand away as she wriggled from her cape and charged off again.

She could hear his thunderous footsteps racing behind her and how her heart seemed to beat in the same rhythm. Up ahead she could see the muted light of a lamppost and the end of the alleyway. With any luck at all she'd happen upon a pub or some other business still open at this hour that would offer sanctuary. If only her legs would hold out! But long before she had reached the intersection, she was struck painfully from behind when the parson hurled himself through the air, caught her around the waist, and tumbled them both to the hard surface of the street.

Catherine felt as if every bone in her body had broken and for a second she couldn't breathe. Then he rolled her onto her back, his legs straddling her hips, and the flicker of light against a gold cross brought her back to life. She grabbed his wrists and pushed with all her might when he started to lower the chain toward her throat. Her strength was no match for his, and she knew that within seconds *her* name would be added to the growing list of murdered women.

"No!" she howled, tears blurring her vision. "Damn you, no!"

An evil laughter filled the air and hammered against her eardrums, a sound that gripped her heart and marked her imminent demise. In that moment she remembered her mother and the shot that had ended her life. She envisioned the explosion in the laboratory that killed her father. She thought of Mr. Trumble, her black cat, the silver piccolo, and the rope swing her father had hung from a tree in their backyard.

"No," she cried again, closing her eyes and blocking out the sight of the menacing dark form hovering so very close.

Her arms ached, but she continued to struggle, gasping when she felt the cold metal press against her neck. Within seconds, her head began to spin as she fought to pry her fingers under the chain that bit into her flesh. She was close to passing out and regretting ever having assumed she could handle any adversity given her, when all of a sudden the weight of the man was jerked from her by some unexpected force. The rush of air that filled her lungs burned all the way down, and she coughed as she clutched her throat and awkwardly sat up. Several moments passed before her vision cleared and she was able to breathe comfortably again, and in that second she heard the sounds of a violent struggle only a few feet away. Straining to see in the darkened fog, she could barely make out the image of two figures battling each other, and once she realized how close she had come to dying, she began to cry, her body shook, and she lost all self-control as she watched the taller of the two shapes swing a fist and send his opponent crashing to the ground, unconscious.

Fear suddenly emerged within her again when the victor turned her way and stepped closer. Certain the crazed preacher man was about to finish what he started, Catherine kicked out her feet at the one who approached and struck him in the shin, forcing him to retreat a step or two, lest he receive more of the same. Darkness and the heavy fog swirled about his head and shoulders, but Catherine was sure she could see the fire burning in his eyes and the evil twist to his mouth when he called out her name. Then he leaned and reached out for her, and she screamed.

"Catherine!" he sharply called again, the deep resonance of his voice penetrating her hysteria. "Catherine, you're safe now. I'm not going to hurt you."

The dark figure slowly materialized into a shape she recognized. First it was the man from the pub with the black cape and hat, the one who had been following her, and she cowered away from him, certain he had lied just now and that he truly *did* want to hurt her. Then his form changed again and in the muted light of the street lamp behind her, she could see his dark eyes, his handsome face, and the grim set to his mouth.

"T.J.?" she whimpered, still unsure. "T.J.?"

"Yes, Catherine, it's T.J.," he softly said as he leaned again and held out his hand.

Hesitant, she glanced at the dark shape lying deathly still on the ground behind him.

"He won't hurt you, either," T.J. swore. "If he isn't dead, he won't have the strength to get up." He leaned closer. "Please, Catherine, take my hand."

The instant her fingers touched his, she sprang to her feet and threw herself into his arms. "Oh, T.J.! He . . . he was going to kill me!"

A torrent of emotions raged through T.J. in that moment while he held her trembling body close in his arms and stroked her hair. He was angry with her—for several reasons—but more than that he was relieved that he had arrived in time to save her. Common sense told him that none of this was truly his fault, but he couldn't help feeling he was partly to blame. That little trick he'd played on her last night in his room had been cruel, although at the time he'd felt she deserved it, and as a result she'd been too embarrassed to face him. He had deliberately waited until afternoon before paying her a visit just to prolong her agony, and by then she'd found a way to remedy her problem without his help. He hadn't thought much of it when Mr. Trumble told him about the young woman who had hired Catherine's services until later that night when he'd come to the house a second time and was told Catherine had gone to Miss Hammerand's flat near the waterfront *and* that she'd gone there alone. His disapproval must have shown on his face, for Mr. Trumble was quick to voice his opinion and his worry when T.J. simply stood there without comment. His temper flared once the servant admitted that by eavesdropping he'd learned Miss Chase had agreed to look for two missing prostitutes, and it had raged even higher after talking with Lewis Rhomberg.

"From everything I've heard about Catherine Chase," Lewis had admitted with a worried frown, "she's smart enough to know when to back away. But she's also a very determined young lady. If she thinks she's close to solving something, she won't let up. Now, I'm not saying that it's a matter of time before these two girls she's looking for turn up in our morgue, but there certainly isn't much hope they won't, either. As of an hour ago, five prostitutes had been murdered and, until the killer is caught, no woman is safe on the streets."

Once Lewis had given him all the facts, T.J. had drawn his own conclusions, and he hadn't liked the frightening coincidences. Each girl had been young, blond, and pretty, and their bodies had been found in the same general area of the waterfront . . . a place close to where Mr. Trumble had said Catherine was going. It hadn't taken him an hour to learn from old friends where Cherry Hammerand worked, and he'd gone there to talk with her. But the second he'd stepped through the door and spotted the new barmaid, it had taken every ounce of self-control he had not to march right up to Catherine, grab her by the scruff of the neck, and drag her pretty little derrière out the door. Instead he'd decided to sit back and watch, to protect her from a distance without her knowing it. Seeing him right then was probably the last thing she wanted, and when he had realized how close that was to happening, he'd secretly left the pub to wait outside. If she had known he was there, she would have done one of two things; she'd have found some excuse to have him arrested or she'd have sneaked off when he wasn't looking, and in either case she'd have put herself at the mercy of not only a drunk who would mistake her for a prostitute, but the man bent on ridding London of its scarlet women. The latter had very nearly come about even with his attempt at preventing it, and while he held her sobbing form in his arms and softly swore everything would be all right, that she was safe now, his anger continued to wedge its way in between his compassion for her state of mind and his natural instincts to comfort her. What he truly felt like doing was giving her a rough shake.

Any decision he was about to make was delayed in that moment when he heard the racing footsteps of someone on the street coming toward them, and he turned slightly to place himself in front of Catherine and to shield her from whoever was coming just as a figure stepped into the yellow glow of the street lamp. It took him a second to distinguish the uniform of the police constable, but once he had, he relaxed. The bobby would see to it that the preacher was escorted to jail while T.J. took Catherine home.

His temper wasn't any less assuaged by the time the livery cab rolled to a stop at the front walk of his house than when he'd first flagged it down. Nor was his companion any calmer. Catherine was still sobbing, and when she stumbled getting out of the rig, he swept her up in his arms and carried her inside. Hoping none of the staff and especially Mrs. Witton hadn't heard his return, he gently nudged the door shut behind him with the heel of his shoe and quietly mounted the circular staircase two steps at a time, spontaneously turning into the first room at the top once he'd reached it. His chambers, unlike the others, had a settee where he planned to sit with Catherine and discuss the error in her judgment once she had regained her composure enough to talk rationally about it.

Hurrying into the darkened room, he instinctively carried her to the bed and laid her down before he turned to light a lamp. A second later a warm glow chased away the shadows, and while he shed his top hat and cape and tossed them on a nearby chair, he glanced briefly at the huddled form on the huge feather mattress. She looked so pathetic that for a moment he forgot why he was angry with her until he saw the bruises on her neck. His irritation flared anew and, with a low growl, he headed back out the door.

Moments later he returned with a wine decanter and glass that he took with him to the bed. He'd give her a drink and, once its warming effects had done its job, he'd suggest they sit by the fire. They needed to talk . . . about tonight and last night and how—if she weren't careful—she'd wind up as dead as Miss Hammerand's friends probably were. He stared at her for another moment or two before he lifted the decanter and poured a good measure of wine into the glass.

"Here," he said, once he'd set the crystal bottle on the nightstand and had gingerly eased himself down on the edge of the mattress, "drink this. It will help."

Round blue eyes looked up at him, and he felt the

muscles in his heart tighten. This was the second time he'd rescued her from the clutches of a catastrophe, and although both instances weren't really all that different from one another, his feelings for her right then weren't the same. Oh, he was angry—just as he'd been that night he'd stopped the men in the stable from shooting her—but there was something else, an ache deep inside him, one he couldn't quite pinpoint.

He helped her sit up when it seemed she was too weak to do it on her own, and once he saw how her hand trembled, he insisted on holding the glass to her lips, those bright red, overrouged lips that distracted from her natural beauty. He frowned while he waited for her to finish the wine, and when she had and he could see that she had relaxed a little, he stood, slapped the glass on the night table next to the decanter, and crossed to the washbasin where he poured water into the bowl. Wringing out a white piece of cloth, he came back across the room with it gripped in his fist and handed it to her.

"Wash your face," he tersely ordered.

Not since before her father died had Catherine felt so safe. She'd been enjoying the sensation that someone was willing to care for her and that he'd shown no tolerance for the one who'd tried to hurt her. It didn't matter just then that her savior was the very man she'd tried with all her heart and soul to prove was a criminal. At that moment she didn't see him as a thief and murderer. He'd risked his life to save her, and she was grateful. But the sharp disapproval in his tone and the furious look on his handsome face ruined the illusion and brought her back to reality. Glaring at him for a second, she scooted off the bed and went to stand before the washbowl.

T.J. watched her while she scrubbed the paint from her mouth, cheeks, and forehead, recognizing by the short, jerky moves she made that Catherine Chase had returned to her old self again. If he were to ask right now, she'd claim she saw nothing wrong with what she'd done, and they'd wind up arguing until daybreak.

"All right," he announced, leaning a shoulder against the

tall bedpost, his arms crossed over his chest, "I'm listening."

Catherine shot him a cold look, tossed down the washcloth, and moved to the dresser where she could see her hair in the reflection of the mirror. "I don't owe you an explanation, Mr. Savage. In fact, I think it's the other way around." She glared at the image of him she could see over her shoulder in the mirror, then concentrated on removing the pins from her tangled curls. "You can start with last night."

The muscle in his cheek flexed. He'd known this wasn't going to be easy. "You mean after I came home to find your shoes and stockings on the ground below the balcony of my bedchamber?"

A shiver worked its way up the backs of her arms and she gritted her teeth, hoping he wouldn't notice how his question disarmed her. She had guessed he'd known all along that she was hiding behind the screen. Now, he'd confirmed it, and her embarrassment began all over again. "I've heard of people like you," she bravely charged. "I just never thought I'd meet one."

"People like me?" he queried.

She shook out her long hair and ran her fingers through the gnarled mess. "Yes. Someone who enjoys undressing in front of someone."

"And what does that make you?" he countered.

Catherine's face flamed, and she spun around to stare openmouthed at him.

"Don't try denying you weren't watching," he dared to say. "How else would you have drawn such a conclusion? Did you get a good look? Was your virginal curiosity appeased?"

"You're disgusting," she seethed.

"And you're probably one of the most foolish women I've ever met," he returned, pushing away from the bed. "Or just plain stupid. Don't you ever learn?"

Catherine drew in a breath to defend herself, but he cut her off.

"You damn near got yourself killed that night in the

stable, and you turn right around and try some other way of achieving it. What were you thinking, Catherine?" He waved his hand at her. "Look at you, for God's sake. You paint yourself up, don a dress that invites a man to see what's underneath and leaves very little to the imagination, and then you go for a stroll as if you're immune to the dangers in the street. And if that isn't bad enough, you ignore the fact that all the murdered prostitutes were young, pretty, and *blond*!"

Without realizing it, Catherine touched a silky curl falling over her shoulder, her face pale, and a shocked look darkened her eyes.

"I don't believe it!" T.J. exclaimed. "You've got the talent to unravel the most embroiled clues, and yet you never once saw what was right under your own nose!" He clamped his teeth together and inhaled a long, deep, agitated breath. "Is that it, Catherine? Were you so intent on finding Miss Hammerand's friends that you didn't realize you were a prime candidate for the madman running loose around the docks? Or did you deliberately set yourself up?"

"Of course not!" she retorted, angered he would even think it. "I wasn't out to trap a murderer. I was simply investigating the disappearance of two women. All I wanted was to look like one of the girls so I could ask questions without anyone thinking a thing of it. I might not have learned anything, but it worked."

T.J. nodded in sarcastic agreement. "You can say that again. It worked so well you almost got yourself killed."

Her temper exploded. "That was your doing!"

"*My* doing?" he echoed, taking a few steps closer to her, his body rigid with fury.

"Yes! If you hadn't been following me, I wouldn't have gotten scared and run. I would have walked the two blocks to Cherry's flat, changed my clothes, and gone home. It's *your* fault I got myself into that mess."

T.J.'s eyes narrowed and he practically spit out his reply. "If I hadn't been following you, you'd be dead now. But go ahead and blame me, if it'll make you feel better. You've been blaming me for everything all along, so why change now?"

"*Blaming* you?" she parroted. "You make it sound as though you're completely innocent."

T.J. started to reply and decided against it. What good would it do to argue? She'd made up her mind about him and nothing he could say would change it. Glowering at her for a second, he turned to the nightstand and refilled the glass with wine. With it dangling from his left hand, he crossed to the fireplace and plopped down on the settee.

A frown gathered Catherine's brows together as she watched him raise the goblet to his mouth and take a long drink. Why hadn't he answered her? An innocent man would have been outraged over the implication. He would have shouted his denial long and loud. But T.J. hadn't. He'd simply clammed up and poured himself a drink. What really confused her was his anger. He was behaving as if he really cared what happened to her. And why should he? She was the only one who thought him guilty of the museum robbery and the subsequent deaths of his partners, so why hadn't he just let the preacher finish her off? It would have ended all his problems. Or wasn't he aware of her success in bringing criminals to justice? Curious, she studied his profile for a moment, then moved to sit down in one of the chairs near him.

T.J. could feel her penetrating stare and, rather than look at her, he leaned and retrieved a cheroot from the box on the table. Striking a match, he inhaled a long puff of smoke, then blew out the flame and tossed the charred stick in the ashtray. Several moments passed and when she continued to stare, he glanced at her from out of the corner of his eye. It was late, he was tired, and he really didn't feel like arguing with her.

"If you're feeling better," he announced, "I'll take you home."

Catherine shook her head. "I'm fine. But I'm not ready to go home just yet. We have some things to discuss."

T.J. gritted his teeth, sighed, and looked away. "I think we've said about all there is to say. I've got a lot of work to do tomorrow and I need my rest. We can talk some other time." He started to rise.

"Now," she replied, stopping him midway out of his seat. She waved a finger at him, motioning him back down, and he was slow to comply.

"You mean you're not tired?" he mocked. "I would think you would be after being on your feet all night." He raised the cheroot to his mouth, paused, and corrected, "Or part of it anyway. When I found you, you were flat on your back." He sneered at her. "Oh, I forgot—that's what prostitutes are supposed to do—lie on their backs." He cocked a brow. "How much money did the new girl make tonight before I got there, hm?"

Catherine had grown used to being insulted whenever she confronted someone she suspected was guilty of something, but T.J.'s attitude puzzled her. "You sound jealous."

"Jealous?" he exploded in a harsh laugh.

"Yes, jealous," she returned quite calmly. "Your whole disposition tonight has been one of resentment. What I can't figure out is why."

T.J. stared, openmouthed and speechless. She *had* to be joking! Jealousy had nothing to do with his rage, and she was crazy to think so. "I take it back," he grumbled as he reached for the wineglass. "You're not stupid. You're conceited."

"Oh?" she asked, unaffected by his barb. "Why do you say that?"

He finished off his drink and set the glass down. Twisting on the settee, he faced her. "Because, Miss Chase, had I been of a notion to bed you, I would have done so long before now. I certainly wouldn't have waited my turn or asked permission."

"Really?" she replied with a vague smile. "Now who's conceited?"

His dark brows dipped downward. "Not conceit, Miss Chase. Fact."

Perhaps he thought so, but Catherine wasn't as convinced as he was that getting her into bed would be no contest, and if the stakes weren't so high, she'd call him on it. Yet even if they weren't, she wasn't really interested in finding out. However, one thing bothered her. "Are you saying you find me unappealing?" she inquired, instantly surprised that she even cared to know if he did or not.

The conversation was becoming awkward. If he didn't point it in a different direction fairly soon, he'd be telling her things she didn't need to know. "What is it you really want from me?"

"Proof," she answered right away, glad he'd changed the subject.

He stared at her, took a puff on the cheroot, and glanced away. "About what?"

"That you're really innocent of killing those two men in the stable." When he looked at her again, she rushed on. "Let me see the jacket you were wearing that night."

"Why?" he asked, even though he already knew the reason.

"I need to examine the buttons."

The discussion he'd had with Lewis Rhomberg came to mind. His friend had kidded him about having the repairs done on the coat so soon after he'd accidentally torn off a button, that if Catherine ever found out, she'd never believe that he'd only had the original sewn back on rather than a whole new set. He knew the button he'd given to Lewis wasn't even close to matching the ones on his coat, but just as Lewis had pointed out, he'd never be able to convince Catherine of it if he showed her the garment with a full set.

"I don't see the purpose," he lied as he came to his feet, snuffed out the cigar, and headed for the armoire, "but if that's all it will take for you to stop accusing me of things I haven't done, then I'll gladly show it to you." Deliberately blocking her view, he opened the doors and searched inside for the coat Mrs. Witton had hung there just that morning after returning from the tailor's with it. "Ah! Here it is," he declared, one hand grabbing the hanger, the other reaching for the newly sewn-on button. With a quick twist, he popped it off and slipped it in the pocket without her seeing him do it. Feigning ignorance as he turned back around, he asked, "What's so special about the buttons?"

Catherine quickly stood up and met him halfway across the room. "This is what's special," she said drearily, holding up the right side of the coat to show him the mending that needed to be done. She'd been right about the missing button. Now all she could hope for was that the design work differed from Nathan Beecher's description.

"Damn," he remarked, pretending to be irritated with himself while he watched her examine the remaining gold fasteners. "I meant to tell Mrs. Witton about that. I caught the silly thing on something and tore it off." He reached inside the pocket. "I put it in here so I wouldn't lose—yes! Here it is." He withdrew his hand, held it out to her, and slowly uncurled his fingers.

Oddly enough, disappointment was the first emotion Catherine felt. She hated being wrong. It never failed to fill her with self-doubt. Frowning, she dismissed the egotistic thought when a new thought crowded its way into her head. This had been the proof she needed to assure herself that T.J. wasn't a murderer and she knew she should be pleased, but she wasn't. She was suspicious. He always seemed to have an answer for everything, and people like that demanded close scrutiny.

T.J. had seen the various expressions cross her face, and he knew he hadn't totally won her over to his side. The question still remained as to whether or not he'd been a part of the gang who broke into the museum. He could understand that. He hadn't exactly given her a lot of reason to think otherwise, and until the paintings were recovered, she'd more than likely go on suspecting him. And that was all right with him . . . for now anyway. It gave him an excuse to hang around. She wouldn't much like it if she knew, and she'd probably bring up that old argument that she was able to take care of herself, but after tonight, T.J. was positive she needed supervision whether she thought so or not.

"Just a moment," he proclaimed as if just discovering her reason for breaking into his house. "Is this why you were in my room last night? To look at the buttons on my coat?"

Embarrassed, she turned away.

"You could have just asked, you know," he scolded, smiling openly and enjoying the torment he caused her. "I would have shown it to you."

"You wouldn't have if the button hadn't been in the pocket."

He rubbed the tip of his nose with a knuckle, his grin widening as he fought not to laugh out loud. "Oh? And why not?" he asked, anxious to hear her explanation. Should he be outraged once she told him? Or should he just pretend to be injured? The smile vanished instantly when she turned back around.

"I went to the yard the morning after you told me about the two murdered men," she began, suddenly finding it hard to look at him. Averting her eyes, she went back to sit down in the chair. "I wanted to know if they could tell me any more than you'd already told me, if they had a clue to what happened to the paintings." She paused while she listened to him return the coat to the armoire, cross back to the settee, and sit down, but she still couldn't bring herself to look at him. She studied the fire in the hearth instead. "A friend there told me that it looked as if one of the two dead men had tried to fight off his attacker and that in the process he had—"

"Wait," T.J. cut in, acting as though he'd been smart enough to figure it out before she told him. "He tore a button off the killer's coat."

Catherine glanced sheepishly at him and nodded.

"And because you had obviously seen that there was a button off *my* coat, you assumed—" He threw his hands in the air and stood to pace the floor, feigning anger and frustration. "So you hired some ragtag boy to help you get into my house to steal the coat. You were so positive I killed those two men that you thought nothing of your own safety just to have the proof."

Catherine frowned. "My safety?" she repeated.

"Yes, Miss Super Detective Chase," he barked, truly annoyed with her now. He stopped his pacing and faced her. "What if you'd been right about me? Don't you suppose I would have guessed what it was you were after? And if I had, do you honestly believe I would have let you walk away? Just because you're a woman doesn't mean you're exempt from the brutalities of life. Innocence never wins compassion . . . not from an individual who doesn't even know what it is. And a man who would deliberately take a human life is incapable of feeling much of anything at all. I would think, Miss Chase, that that alone would have told you more about me than all the material evidence in the world."

She didn't like hearing the truth about her shortcomings. It made her feel like a failure. Still, she wasn't quite sure that that was what was at the root of her unrest. Yes, she had blindly rushed in with all the conviction of someone possessed. She just *had* to prove he was a murderer, and she simply couldn't wait until all the pieces fell into place on their own. She *had* to make it happen. The question was why. Why was it so important? She'd never let her emotions run away with her before. What was different about this particular case?

"I apologize," she murmured when the answers to her questions wouldn't surface. "And yes, I realize now that I took too many chances. I don't know why. I just did."

A weak smile parted her lips and she glanced up at him. In that instant—with the firelight sparkling in his deep brown eyes and bathing his coppery complexion in a healthy glow—that same strange, perplexing sensation warmed her insides. He was so handsome, so masculine, so . . . tempting. She blinked and turned her head away, when she realized how her thoughts had strayed. Dear Lord, *that* wasn't the reason why she was so intent on putting him in jail, was it? Because he had awakened feelings in her that frightened her and threatened to shatter her perfect, safe, content little world? Was that it? Was his very existence challenging her unspoken declaration that she could do without men and everything that went with them?

Hot all of a sudden, she wiped the back of her hand across her brow. "I—I had better go home now," she said, her voice almost too low for him to hear as she rose from her chair and looked about the room for her cape.

"In a minute, Catherine," he promised, coming to his feet. "But first I'd like us to agree on something."

The scorching heat rose further up her neck. What did he mean? Agree on what?

"I want us to stop fighting each other about this," he explained, frowning and wondering what was going through Catherine's head when she turned startled eyes on him. "What did you think?"

Defensive and not wanting him to draw the right conclusion, she fired back with a touch of sarcasm, "With you it's hard to tell."

T.J. exhaled disgustedly. "I might say the same about you. Trying to outguess you is harder than—" Distracted, he frowned when he noticed how she seemed to be looking for something. "What are you doing?"

"My cape . . . where is it?"

T.J. thought about it for a moment. "I don't remember seeing you wear it . . . at least not when I put you in the cab." His frown returned. "It's not important anyway. Forget about it and sit back down so we can talk."

"Forget about it?" she repeated. "I can't just forget about it. Not everyone has your kind of wealth, Mr. Savage. Besides, it was one of my favor—"

"I'll buy you a new one," he snarled. "Now sit down."

Catherine faced him. "Is everything that simple to you? If it causes you a problem, you just pay to have it fixed?"

His shoulders drooped. "All right, I won't buy you a new one. I'll go back to the alley and look for your old one. But not until *after* we talk."

"It isn't *old*, Mr. Savage. I just had it made last week. I'd only worn it a couple of times, and I'd like to wear it again. But—"

"Catherine, sit down!"

The rage in his tone nearly shook the windowpanes, and had she not been through so much already, Catherine might have challenged him. Instead, she sank into the chair, her eyes round and her heartbeat a little noisier than usual.

Her compliance surprised T.J. He stared at her for several

seconds, blinked, then took his own seat. Had he found the trick to controlling her? He mentally shook off that wonderful idea. He'd merely caught her off guard, that's all.

"I realize you have every reason to doubt me, Catherine," he began, absently noticing the pale red strands of hair sprinkled through a lush, thick mane of platinum and how the firelight sparkled in them, "and I can't do anything to change that until we find the paintings and the man who had them stolen." She looked so much better without all the paint. She was a natural beauty, and by darkening her eyebrows and rouging her cheeks and lips, she had turned herself into something unpleasing to the eye. He forced his thoughts back to what he'd said. "In order to do that—to catch the real mastermind, I mean, you and I have to stop pointing fingers at each other." He'd never seen eyes the color of hers before, and the image of a three-year-old Catherine materialized in his head. She had probably been the kind of little girl everyone wanted to steal. "I know we agreed on this before, but so far it hasn't worked." He wondered if her skin was as soft and silky as it looked. And those lips! God, how he wanted to kiss them.

Warm of a sudden, he rose and quickly shed his coat, tossing it haphazardly over the back of the settee on his way by. Crossing to stand at the balcony doors looking out, he forced himself to concentrate on what needed to be said, but only a second passed before he was imagining her perilous hike up the oak tree of the night past. A smile worked on his mouth and, unable to hold back, he chuckled out loud.

"Tell me, Catherine," he beckoned without turning around. "Do you always attack something with as much zeal as you did trying to break into my house? You could have fallen, you know."

Catherine's pale brows came together. "I thought we were discussing an agreement."

"We are. I just happened to think of your little adventure last night and how utterly senseless it was."

"Senseless?" she threw back at him. "It might have turned out that way in the end, but if I hadn't tried, I would still be thinking—" She fell quiet, too ashamed to admit she was wrong.

T.J. smiled secretively. "You'd still be thinking what?" he asked, glancing over his shoulder at her. "That I was a murderer?"

She nodded.

"You still do," he dared her.

She glanced at the fire. "I'd like to, but I can't."

"But you suspect me."

She remained quiet for several seconds. "Perhaps not of murder, but certainly of stealing the artworks."

"Why?"

She bobbed a shoulder, knowing her reasons were groundless. She had absolutely no proof of guilt except her instincts, and she was even beginning to doubt them. "May I go home now?" she asked tiredly as she came to her feet.

"As soon as you tell me why you still think I'm the one you're after."

"Let's just say I don't have anyone else to accuse right now. If I ever do, I'll make it a point to apologize to you."

"In front of witnesses?" he teased.

Catherine's eyes narrowed. "Be careful, Mr. Savage." She glared a moment longer, then moved for the door.

"You really don't like me very much, do you?" he ventured as he followed her to the door.

"No, I don't."

"Why?"

"Because you're arrogant."

He laughed. "Arrogant? What makes you think I'm arrogant?"

She paused with a hand on the brass doorknob and looked up at him. "I don't *think* it. I *know* it. You've decided that just because I'm a woman, I'll believe everything you tell me. Well, I'm not *just* a woman, Mr. Savage. I have a brain and I know how to use it."

"I never said or assumed you didn't," he willingly admitted.

"I can reason. I'm intelligent, well educated, and aware of men like you." Her eyes flashed with an indignant fire.

"I don't swoon or giggle when a man flirts with me. And I'm not the type to be frightened off by threats."

"And you're beautiful," he added, studying the stray tendril of yellow hair falling against her brow. "Don't forget that."

Catherine's upper lip started to curl. "You're doing it again, Mr. Savage."

He straightened. "Doing what?" he asked, wide-eyed and innocent.

"You're treating me as you would one of your lethargic female companions."

T.J.'s dark eyes sparkled with humor. "And how would you know what kind of female companions I have? Have you ever met one?"

"I don't have to meet them. Your attitude plainly speaks of your preference."

A smile dimpled his cheeks. "But I prefer someone like you."

"Ha!" she exploded. "Do you really expect me to believe that?"

"You don't have to believe it."

"That's good . . . because I don't."

He shrugged a shoulder. "I could prove it to you, though . . . if you'd like."

"I don't like," she countered, twisting the knob. She jumped when his hand caught the door and firmly pushed it shut again. "What are you doing?"

It was a question he couldn't answer . . . not specifically anyway. All he knew was that he didn't want her to go . . . at least not just then. He'd been hoping for some time alone with her, although he wasn't sure just what he intended to do except perhaps to explain his side in all of this, and that if he were to play the part of a gentleman right now, she'd leave and he'd never have his chance again. But was that really all there was to it? he wondered. Unaware of what he was doing, he raised his left hand and brushed the backs of his knuckles along her jawline, marveling at the velvety softness of her skin.

His nearness, the scent of his cologne, the subtle power

behind his insistence dulled her reactions. With her gaze locked on his full, sensuous mouth and only slightly aware that he had slipped his hand behind her head at the nape, she numbly watched his parted lips descend, and her pulse began to pound. A warmth spread from a spot close to her heart and fanned outward, tingling the muscles across her chest, her abdomen, and thighs. Her head began to spin. Her flesh seemed on fire, and before she realized it, she had closed her eyes and had tilted her head back, expectant of his kiss.

Surprised by her surrender, he hesitated. His conscience told him to stop before it went too far, while everything else inside him urged him onward, to welcome the chance, and to enjoy every second of it. It wasn't that he'd regret it later or feel ashamed. Hardly that! He wanted her. He had since the first moment he saw her. It was the teachings of his adopted father that haunted him. Christian had said that T.J. should treat the woman of his dreams with respect, that he should place her on a pedestal where he could protect her from harm. Hadn't he done that much already? Then what was holding him back? Was he afraid *she* would regret it later? Would she feel ashamed?

Of course, she would, he silently conceded with a disgruntled frown as he closed his eyes, lowered his head, and gently touched his lips to hers. *That's why it must end with a kiss. One kiss, that's all.*

The scent of her freshly washed skin, the warmth of her curvaceous body, and the feel of her slightly parted lips attacked his senses and flooded his mind with contradictory thoughts. His heart began to race, and a liquid fire coursed through his veins almost instantly. He'd kissed many young women and had bedded a few, but *none* of them had ever excited him this way, and he wondered if Catherine was feeling it, too.

It was a sweet kind of suffocation that stole her breath away. It made her dizzy and soft and giggly. She could feel her knees trembling and a chill shooting through her body despite the heat that scorched her flesh. Although it was nothing more than a kiss, she felt as if she were doing something wicked, and she loved the sensation. What she couldn't understand was the desire for more, as if the feel of his lips against hers weren't enough, that the gentle touch of his hand cradling her head wasn't fulfilling, and that if she let it end too soon she would never be allowed the experience again.

Suddenly and without warning, he slanted his mouth across hers and pushed his tongue inside as he pulled her close with both arms wrapped around her. At first, the thrill frightened her and she brought up her hands to shove him away. But only a second passed before the bliss of it challenged her will and she melted in his embrace. She could taste the faint essence of wine on his lips and she wondered if its intoxicating effects were what made her feel weak or if the mystery behind their intimacy was playing havoc with her senses. It scared her, yet that ever-present curiosity about the unknown refused to let her spoil the chance to find out what it was that tempted her. The vision of Cherry Hammerand and the man Catherine had seen kissing the girl came to mind for a brief second, and she wondered if a kiss was the same no matter who one shared it with, a question that needed answering. And who better to ask than the man holding her in his arms?

"T.J.?" she asked breathlessly once she'd pulled her lips from his. "T.J., is it always like this?"

A smile curved his mouth as he stared down into her darkened eyes. How could she do the kind of work she does and yet be so innocent at the same time? "Is what always like this?"

"A kiss," she explained, leaning heavily in his arms.

A puzzled frown marred his brow. "You've never kissed anyone before?" he asked.

"Only you," she admitted, remembering the first time he'd held her in his arms in much the same way and that he'd left her feeling faint from the pleasure of it. "If I kissed someone else, would it affect me so?"

He smiled again. "I don't know. How does it affect you?"

She closed her eyes and sighed. "Wonderfully."

A warning went off in his head. She was vulnerable. All

he'd have to do was take advantage of it, and they'd spend the rest of the night in bed. Disturbed by the conflicting thoughts racing through his head, he gently let go of her. "I think it's time I took you home," he said, frowning, "before—" He gritted his teeth, silently cursing himself for the near slip of the tongue.

His sudden change surprised her. Had she said something wrong? Had she angered him for some reason? She had to know. "Before what?" she pressed.

Uncomfortable standing so close to her, he turned for his coat as he replied, "Before Mr. Trumble sends an army of men looking for you."

"That's not it," she challenged, catching the crook of his arm and firmly pulling him around. "You forget, T.J. I'm very good at reading the expressions on a person's face. You're not worried about Mr. Trumble. What is it?"

He stared at her for a long while, wondering if he should be honest with her and if she'd laugh at him, if he told her the truth. Or worse . . . scare her off.

"Before what?" she asked again, her pale blue eyes full of determination.

He sighed resignedly. "Before I do more than just kiss you," he confessed in a rush of words. "Before I forget you're a lady and that I was raised to always act the gentleman. Before I ignore what Christian tried to teach me. Before I give in to these strong feelings I have." He raised dubious brows at her. "Satisfied?"

Catherine couldn't explain the warmth she felt just then. Smiling, she dropped her gaze. She'd never had a man talk to her like that before, and although she should be shocked by his bold declaration, she found herself enjoying it instead. For the first time in her life she felt the power a woman had over a man, and she rather liked it. She had been seen through the eyes of a lover rather than a foe, and the thought of it was exciting. In fact, it was so exciting she didn't want it to stop.

"No," she murmured, peering up at him through lowered lashes. "No, I'm not satisfied."

T.J.'s frown deepened. What did she mean?

Reading his thoughts, Catherine raised her chin. "I want more," she whispered, reaching up to drape her arms around his neck and pull his mouth to hers.

The instant their lips met T.J. forgot all the things he'd been raised to believe. He forgot about his earlier acknowledgment that Catherine would later regret having overstepped the boundaries of what was right and proper. He forgot his pledge that it would end with one kiss. He forgot that he was a gentleman and that Catherine Chase—though womanly and innocent—was still a lady.

Catherine realized the vagueness of her decree the moment she felt his arms come around her. He'd obviously mistook her confession to mean she wanted more than just a kiss, when in fact all she wanted was to enjoy again the bliss it had aroused. A tremor of fear shot through her with the thought that she might not be able to stop him if she let it go too far, yet at the same time she wondered if she'd actually refuse him should he try. There had been a few secret occasions when she'd allowed her mind to wander over romantic images of a man and a woman and how it felt to be in love, to *make* love, to be held in the arms of someone strong and masculine and demanding, to know *she* had the power to make him crumble. She sensed that control right now. She also felt herself weakening when his kisses moved from her lips to her throat, along the delicate line of her jaw, and upwards to tickle the soft flesh beneath her ear. She sucked in a quick, silent breath and her head began to spin when his hand cupped her breast, and for only a second she thought about pushing him away. She knew it wasn't right or decent, yet the warmth of his touch was pleasurable and she didn't want it to end.

His mouth captured hers again and took away any chance she had to protest while his fingers quickly unfastened the buttons up the back of her dress. The searing heat of the kiss spread all the way to her toes, and while she reveled in the ecstasy of it, she wasn't aware that he had freed the top of the garment from her shoulders or that she hadn't resisted until his moist, hot kisses fell across bare flesh. The shock of it made her gasp, but rather than show her outrage as she was supposed to do, she closed her eyes and tilted her head back, willingly allowing him to continue.

His lips found hers again, and while they moved hungrily, demandingly over hers, his fingers caught the ribbons on her camisole and plucked them loose. Cool air brushed her naked breasts while he hurriedly removed his shirt then pulled her close, one arm encircling her waist, his other hand trapping the back of her head as he kissed her with a passion that bespoke of urgency. The feel of rock-hard muscles against her bosom sent a white-hot charge of electricity through every inch of her body and she fleetingly wondered if she had reached the height of rapture in that moment or if there was more to come. Enthralled and eager to learn—forgetting all modesty and abandoning her moral upbringing—she kissed him back with all the wantonness of a vamp.

"Teach me," she whispered breathlessly against his mouth. "Show me how to be a woman fulfilled, T.J. Take me now."

The flame of desire darkened her pale blue eyes when he bent and caught her up in his arms. He carried her to the bed where he tenderly set her down and stripped away the rest of her clothes, then his own. Bathed in the amber glow of the fire in the hearth, he studied her oval face, the long, silky strands of strawberry-blond hair, the curve of her cheek and neck, the full, perfect swell of her breasts, the tiny waist and slender hips, before he encircled her delicate frame with one arm and slowly lowered them both to the bed.

Giddy with delight, Catherine smiled back at the handsome face pressing close. She had never imagined the kinds of sensations coursing through her mind and spirit just then, for if she had, she might have decided much sooner than now to explore them. But would they have been the same with just anyone? Or were they special because it was T.J. who made her feel this way? Was *he* special? And when it was over, would he forget all about her? Would he think of her merely as one of many before her? She tried not to frown, but the perplexing thought curled her brows with little effort, and she quickly closed her eyes that he might not see the doubt she was sure was reflected in them.

It's too late to worry about that now, Catherine Chase, she told herself. *You've made your choice. You'll have to live with it.*

The sadness that had begun to creep into her emotions vanished the second his warm, sinewy body touched hers full length and his open mouth claimed hers again. Without any hesitation she wrapped her arms around him and returned his kiss with unequaled yearning and fire, marveling at the overpowering want to draw him into her, to be as one with one thought, one desire, one purpose. Be it only for this night, she vowed, she would willingly give herself to him and mask the awful fear that in the morning they would part, never to share this wonderful torture again. She would live with the memory of it and be content with that.

A sigh escaped her lips when he trailed hot kisses down her chin and throat. But when they moved even lower, her eyes came open and she fought just to breathe, paralyzed by the hot sensation of his mouth covering one taut peak and how his tongue played lightly there. A rush of embarrassment mixed with pleasure burned her cheeks, and she started to cross her arms, when she felt his hand move along the crest of her hip and thigh, and a new trepidation beset her and changed the course of her thoughts. Panic started to build and nearly burst upon her when his caress grew bolder and slipped to the inside of her knee and started upward. She'd excused herself thus far, but this . . . ! *This* was too much.

"T.J.," she whispered huskily. "I don't . . . think . . . You shouldn't . . . *Ohhh!*"

The last came as a weak protest, a shriek of surprise, and a startled exclamation of both enjoyment and subtle bliss when the warmth of his fingers touched her in the most private of places. Had she been of a mind to demand that he stop, she wasn't allowed the chance to voice it, for in that moment he straightened and pressed his lips to hers again. The sultry kiss was almost more than she could bear, but it became of little consequence once his caress ignited a fire deep inside her that shot with wild abandonment through every nerve fiber in her body. She groaned deliriously in spite of herself, and when he nudged her thighs apart with his knee, she fervently obeyed, unsure yet positive that to do so would bring her the ultimate ecstasy.

The first wave hit her like the forging of steel; hot and hard. Her eyes flew open and a small cry of pain caught in her throat. But only seconds passed before a new and glorious feeling erupted and her womanly instincts guided her response. Arching her hips, she moved beneath him with the practiced grace of an experienced demimondaine, giving as much pleasure as she received. Her breathing quickened. Her pulse raced, and her heart thumped loudly as her imaginary world began to spin out of control. Whirling faster and faster, it carried her beyond the limit of her dreams. Then suddenly the fire that had consumed her exploded in a spectrum of color, and for a long moment she drifted through space, suspended in time, breathless and at peace.

The sensation of a gentle kiss beneath her chin brought Catherine back to earth. Giggling contentedly, she rolled onto her hip when she felt T.J. lift from her and fall on his back beside her. He lay staring up at the ceiling, his eyes dark with the memory of their passion and a pleased smile on his lips. He looked more handsome than ever in the flickering light of the fire, and Catherine wondered why it had taken them this long to admit to their feelings for each other. So much time had been wasted.

Shocked by her errant thoughts, she blushed and snuggled close when he shifted and cradled her in the crook of his arm. This wasn't something they could share whenever the moment was right and they were both willing. It really shouldn't have happened now, even though she was glad it had. If a woman wasn't married to the man with whom she made love, then she was a whore, and although Catherine truly didn't think of herself as one, it was a title she couldn't easily dismiss. What bothered her even more was her worry that T.J. might draw the same conclusion. It would kill her to see the accusing look in his brown eyes if he did. Frowning, she traced a fingertip along his thickly muscled ribs and fought the urge to ask him. He'd lie, of course. He was a gentleman, and a gentleman wouldn't deliberately shame a woman. He'd be polite and probably ask to see her again, but in time—and not very much time—he'd come around less often, until one day she'd suddenly realize that a month had passed since he'd last paid her a visit.

Tears emerged and Catherine quickly shut her eyes to trap them against her lashes. She mustn't cry. If he saw her sadness, he'd question it, and then she'd have to lie. Oh, he'd pretend compassion for her state of mind if she told him, she was sure, but the coldness behind the look he'd give her would betray his honest feelings, and that was something she couldn't bear. She mustn't allow him the advantage. He must be made to think it was *her* decision they never see each other again. It was the only way she would be able to hold her head up high; it was the only way to ease the pain, to help her forget.

Filled with a loneliness she hadn't experienced since her father's death, she willed herself the strength not to give in to the turbulent emotions roiling inside her. They would have to wait . . . until later . . . when T.J. was fast asleep . . . and she had stolen away into the darkness. . . .

CHAPTER 10

"Sometimes you have to sleep on it," Catherine could remember her father advising whenever she'd come to him with a decision that had to be made. "What seems to be the simple answer isn't always that simple. Give yourself the time to think it over first. That way you won't be disappointed and you'll run less of a risk of making a mistake."

How many times had she heard that particular recommendation? And how many times had his counsel proven accurate? More often than not. But Catherine's problem *this* time couldn't be so easily solved as some of her earlier dilemmas. T. J. Savage wasn't just a problem waiting for an answer. He wouldn't go away merely because she'd made up her mind never to have anything more to do with him. The only way she would ever be able to get rid of him was to have him thrown in jail until he was too old to remember who put him there or to even care!

"Damn!" she exploded, bounding off the bed and returning to her dressing table. "Everything used to be so uncomplicated."

Plopping down on the bench, she stared dejectedly at her reflection in the mirror. She'd hardly slept at all, and if Mr. Trumble had left her alone, she would have spent the whole day in bed. But he hadn't and it really hadn't been his fault he'd had to disturb her. Nathan Beecher had arrived at the house shortly after daybreak full of apologies, yet insisting he speak with her. Catherine hadn't honestly minded the invasion since she hadn't expected to get much sleep anyway. But once he'd told her his reason for coming, she would have liked nothing better than to crawl under the covers and pretend that the past two days had never happened.

The Reverend Matthew Johnson, it seemed, wasn't really a minister after all. He was a potter by trade and a very strict disciplinarian to his only child, a daughter of sixteen. His wife had left him shortly after the birth of their child, and although he'd never seen her again, he'd heard rumors that she earned her living as a prostitute. Certain his daughter would follow in her mother's footsteps if he didn't keep a tight rein on her, his fears soon overshadowed his common sense. Then one day he snapped. He decided that the only way to protect his daughter from such an immoral influence was to eliminate the source. With a Bible in one hand and his fingers clutching the gold cross hanging from a chain around his neck, he stalked his victims; young girls whose descriptions matched that of his wife's.

"He confessed to everything, Miss Chase," Nathan had sadly informed her. "He even told us where he'd dumped the bodies. In all he murdered eight prostitutes; two just last night. You were lucky. If Mr. Savage hadn't come along when he had . . ." He let the rest go unsaid. "Anyway, I need you to bring Miss Hammerand to the morgue. Two of the victims haven't been identified, and since you said her friends were missing . . . well . . ."

Catherine hadn't liked the assignment she'd been given. She'd grown fond of Cherry in the short time she'd known her, and delivering such news was something she'd have rather not done.

She had skipped breakfast, since she'd lost her appetite for it anyway, and had hired a cab to take her to Cherry's flat. The moment the young girl saw her Cherry started to cry. She wept all the way to Scotland Yard, while she viewed the remains of her friends, and all the way home again. Catherine had offered to stay with her a while, but Cherry had politely refused the kindness, saying that she'd rather be alone. She had cried even harder when Catherine turned down the girl's attempt to pay her for her time and trouble, and on the return trip to her town house, Catherine had cried.

Mr. Trumble had been as sympathetic as was possible for him once she'd explained the reasons for her tears. He'd suggested that a glass of warm milk might soothe her dismay, and Catherine had quickly declined. She had another matter on her mind besides the deaths of Molly and Laura, and trying to ignore it wouldn't make it go away. She had thanked him for his concern, excused herself with the idea of lying down for a while, and had gone back to her bedroom. But hardly a minute had passed before the vision of T.J. had filled her head, and she'd reluctantly resigned herself to the fact that sleep was out of the question.

Maybe I should just shoot him, she mused drearily, her elbow braced on the edge of the dressing table and her chin propped on the fist she'd made with her right hand. *And isn't that a smart solution? You'd be rid of him, but if they didn't hang you for it, you'd spend the rest of your life in prison.* Sighing dolefully, she pushed up from the bench and crossed to the window to look out. *You could always sell the house and live somewhere else,* she considered in a more hopeful vein. The south of France? Scotland? North America? She mentally shook her head. She didn't want to leave England. This was her home. If anyone should leave, it was T.J. He had no real ties to London. In fact his family lived in . . . . where did he say? Australia? Yes, that was it. Australia. He should go back to Australia and leave her in peace. She was here first. Her brow wrinkled. Well, she'd lived here longer, anyway.

Her thoughts were disrupted when she noticed a very expensively built brougham turn the corner and head down her street. It rolled to a stop at the end of the sidewalk, and Catherine's stomach churned, positive she knew who was inside. A second later, its door was opened and she straightened nervously as she watched the tall, lean frame, draped in a black cloak, unfold and step to the ground. He had his back to her and the top hat obscured his profile, but she was sure T.J. had come to torment her.

"He can't if he thinks I'm not home," she declared,

jerking away from the window. All she had to do was tell Mr. Trumble not to answer the door. And to achieve that she had to reach the servant before T.J. knocked.

She had dashed out into the hall and was starting for the stairs when she suddenly realized how she was dressed, and she spun back around. It really wouldn't bother her all that much if Mr. Trumble saw her in her undergarments, but since she was relatively certain the sight of her would strike him mute, she elected to don a robe, then seek him out. The task proved more time-consuming than she thought it would when she had difficulty finding it. And once she'd stepped back into the hall, it was too late. The sound of the brass clapper hitting its plate was already fading in the foyer, and Mr. Trumble's footsteps put him near the entrance. To call out to him now meant T.J. might hear the man's response, and she certainly didn't want that! Mumbling under her breath, she turned back to her room.

"Excuse me, miss," Mr. Trumble's voice beckoned through the closed door a few minutes later. "But you have a visitor."

"Who is it?" she mocked, hooking the last button on her dress.

"Mr. Savage, miss. He says it's important."

"I'm sure *he* thinks so," she muttered to herself as she grabbed for her hairbrush and added loud enough for Mr. Trumble to hear, "Tell him I'll be down shortly."

"Yes, miss," the servant replied. "Shall I serve tea in the sunroom?"

Catherine started to say no but realized they would probably have more privacy where Mr. Trumble wouldn't hear them if she closed the doors to the porch behind him. "Yes, Mr. Trumble, that would be fine." She frowned and added, "And cinnamon rolls if you have some." She was hungry of a sudden, and even though T.J. had probably ruined her life, she wasn't going to starve to death because of him.

She took an extra minute to brush her hair until it shone, but rather than tie it back as she usually did, she let it fall loose over her shoulders. Turning left, then right, she checked her appearance in the mirror from several different angles, nodded her approval, and headed out the door, her slippers still sitting on the floor next to the dressing table where she'd put them.

The closer she came to where T.J. waited for her, the more nervous she became, a new kind of emotion that had her totally unprepared and a little irritable. Until this happened, she had never been one to let anything upset her. She couldn't. To look at things objectively she always had to have a clear mind. So how was she going to deal with this situation when all she really wanted to do was hide?

One step at a time, I guess, she silently told herself as she passed through the dining room and approached the small enclosed porch jutting off the back. *Let him do all the talking—just as you would someone you were investigating. Listen to what he has to say, how he says it, and then judge how you should respond. Perhaps you won't even have to answer him.*

The doors to the sunroom stood open, and because she was barefoot, T.J. hadn't heard her coming. The sight of him as he leaned a shoulder against the window frame and stared out across the lawn took her breath away, and she paused to study him from a safe distance rather than make her presence known. The gray pin-striped trousers hugged his lower body just enough to define well-proportioned legs and narrow hips. His coat, unbuttoned, fell away from the white ruffled shirt he wore, and the black cravat around his neck lay in silky folds, shimmering each time he took a breath or moved just the slightest. The sunlight caressed his dark hair and bronzed complexion, and the troubled frown that drew his brows together gave him a rugged, intense appearance. Yet underneath the handsomely disarming façade Catherine had seen a quiet strength and subtle tenderness anyone else wouldn't have guessed was there. Perhaps that was the way he wanted it—to make people leery of him—but she knew differently. What she questioned was his opinion of her now that they'd shared his bed.

The stubborn thought that refused to die brought a hot

flush to her face. If her sentiments about herself were unflattering, then his must be, too. So why had he come to see her? Knowing there was only one way to find out, she drew in a deep breath and moved to the open doorway, the swish of her skirts catching his attention.

From the moment his valet had awakened him from a sound sleep by knocking on the bedroom door and he had first discovered Catherine's absence, T.J. had been rehearsing what he would say to her. He wanted her to know that last night had been very special to him, that *she* was special to him, and that if she thought otherwise, she was wrong. He'd debated telling her the truth about himself, about everything concerning him, his friendship with Lewis Rhomberg, the reason he was involved in the museum robbery, and why he hadn't told her before now. He'd almost made up his mind to bare his soul to her when the butler announced he had a visitor, and T.J. had dashed to the parlor expecting to find Catherine. Instead he found Lewis, and from the look on T.J.'s face, Lewis had surmised his friend wasn't all that happy to see him. His mood darkened all the more after Lewis had told him about Matthew Johnson, that the deranged man had murdered eight women, two of them being Cherry Hammerand's friends, and that Catherine would have been number nine if T.J. hadn't intervened. Lewis had gone on to draw a parallel between what Catherine had done for a virtual stranger and the kind of danger in which she would voluntarily place herself if she ever suspected her father's death had been something other than an accident. He also stressed the importance of T.J. staying close to her and that under no circumstances should he ever let on why. T.J. had wanted to argue the point, and he'd gone so far as to disagree with his friend, and it was at that moment that Lewis had suddenly realized T.J. was more than just infatuated with Catherine Chase.

"T.J.," he'd warned, "if you tell her the truth right now, she'd hear it as nothing more than a desperate attempt to save your own hide. It would give her all the more reason to go after you. The only way you'll get her to believe you is to tell her the *whole* truth . . . about our being friends and why I asked you to look after her. And if you do that . . ."

He hadn't bothered to finish explaining it, assuming T.J. could do that much for himself. And T.J. had. Catherine would surmise, as any woman would, that bedding her had been a part of his job, that he would have done anything to keep her from stumbling onto the truth about her father's death. That wasn't how it had happened. He knew it, but getting her to believe it would be next to impossible. Catherine dealt with facts, not people's emotions. And until this whole mess—the robbery, the murders, and the mystery around the explosion in Professor Chase's laboratory—was solved and the criminals behind it all were named and imprisoned, T.J. would have to let Catherine go on thinking the worst of him. But would it be that simple?

I don't think so, he mused, pushing from the window to face her as she stepped out into the sunroom. He knew Lewis was right, that there were a lot of problems to be solved before he could even consider courting Catherine, and that even then she might not accept him. After all, he'd done nothing but lie to her.

"Good morning, Catherine," he said softly.

"Mr. Savage." She nodded with a quick glance his way before she crossed to the white wrought-iron table and sat down in one of the chairs.

T.J. cringed at the formal use of his name and chose to remain standing where he was. She was obviously upset with him, and he didn't want to aggravate the situation. He studied her profile for a moment—the color of her hair and how it flowed like liquid gold over her shoulders and down her back, the delicate line of her jaw, and the soft arch of her brows—and was just about to ask her why she had left without waking him, when Mr. Trumble appeared and distracted him.

"May I get you anything else?" the man offered once he'd set down his tray.

"No, Mr. Trumble, that will be all," Catherine assured him as she reached for the teapot.

Following the servant, T.J. waited until Mr. Trumble had gone back inside and then closed the doors behind him. He wanted to talk privately with Catherine and without any further interruptions.

"What happened last night?" he asked, returning to his place by the row of windows. "Why didn't you wake me? Or do you take pleasure in walking the streets unescorted?" The instant the question passed his lips, he regretted it. "I'm sorry," he quickly apologized. "That wasn't fair and I know it. I'm just . . . just . . ."

"You're what, Mr. Savage? Unaccustomed to waking up alone?" came the sharp accusation.

T.J. frowned, stunned by the response and the cold way she had answered him.

"I thought you knew by now that I'm not like the kind of women you're used to . . . seducing." She glanced up at him and smiled dispassionately. "I forgot myself for a moment last night—due to your charm, I'm sure—but it won't happen again." She took a sip of her tea and added, "At least not with you."

He continued to frown while he watched her select one of the sweet rolls on the plate and take a bite of it. "What is that supposed to mean? 'At least not with you'?"

"Just that. What happened between us last night will never happen again." She took a second bite of the roll and gazed out across the lawn.

"Sweet Mother of—" he raged, storming the table and grabbing the chair next to her to sit down. "You make it sound as if it's something you do every night—with a different man each time—that *I* was a mistake."

Her blue eyes narrowed as she glared back at him. "You were."

T.J. drew in a quick breath to reply, exhaled instead, and fell back in his chair, his shoulders sagging. "Maybe I was . . . for you. But it wasn't a mistake on my part. I don't regret making love to you, Catherine, and I never will. What I regret is that it wasn't right for you. I suspected you'd feel this way . . . afterward, and I should have paid attention to my instincts. I apologize for that. But I won't apologize for the feelings I had . . . for the feelings I still have."

A tingle shot across the back of her shoulders. If she didn't know better, she'd swear he meant he'd fallen in love with her. Steeling her will not to show any reaction, she took the last bite of the cinnamon roll and washed it down with a sip of tea before she looked at him again. "And what feelings are those, Mr. Savage? That you very nearly had me convinced of what a nice fellow you are?"

"I'll never convince you of that, will I?" he shot back. "I could be lying on my deathbed with a Bible in each hand, swearing to God that I had nothing to do with the museum robbery, and you still wouldn't believe me. What would it take, Catherine? My blood?"

The idea made her flinch, but she managed to hide it with a soft smile. "Nothing so drastic, Mr. Savage. All you'd have to do is find the paintings and the man who stole them." She leaned to pick up the teapot and refill her cup. "Would you care for some?" she casually asked.

Her indifference and lack of emotion grated on his nerves. Either she was an incredible actress or last night honestly meant nothing to her. He stared at her for a second, then shook his head, declining the offer of tea. He had more important things to do than to exchange caustic remarks and stinging innuendos as to whether or not she cared about what happened between them.

"All right," he finally replied, rising from his chair, "I'll find the paintings and personally deliver them *and* the man who stole them to you. I'll pretend— as you're doing—that last night never happened. I'll go about my life as though you and I have never shared more than a few hostile words, since that's obviously what you prefer. What I *don't* intend to do, however, is stand back and watch you try to get yourself killed." His nostrils flared while he straightened his coat and hooked the buttons up the front. "I believe Mrs. Courtland's dinner invitation was for Saturday evening, was it not?" He didn't wait for her to answer. "I'll call around seven, since arriving separately would raise suspicion otherwise." He nodded politely at her, turned on his heel, and exited the sunroom.

Until he mentioned it, Catherine had forgotten all about the dinner party they had agreed upon attending. Yet even so, his announcement that they'd be going as a couple wasn't what made her heart race. It was the finality with which he had left her.

And isn't that what you wanted? she silently asked herself, awkwardly setting down her teacup with a trembling hand. *Isn't that what you were trying to tell him all along . . . that you didn't want to see him anymore? That last night had been a mistake? That once this case is solved—whether he's innocent or not—the two of you will go your separate ways?* Tears choked her, and she swallowed hard. *No. That wasn't what you wanted. You wanted him to take you in his arms and kiss you, to swear his undying love for you, to tell you that no other woman in the world or in his past had ever or could ever mean as much to him as you do. That's what you wanted, Catherine Chase. You fool.*

A thick fog and heavy mist blanketed London for three long days. Each night the temperature dropped and snowflakes swirled around the lampposts in an attempt to cloud their light. Warm fires burned brightly in every hearth and chased away the cold emptiness hovering just outside the door.

The only time Catherine left the town house was the day of Molly and Laura's funeral. Mr. Trumble had accompanied her, and she'd left right after the service despite Cherry's invitation to have supper with her. Burying two murdered girls wasn't exactly the kind of excuse Catherine had been looking for to distract her thoughts, but even then it was better than staying cooped up in her room with nothing else on her mind except T.J.

At first she had thought that being away from him was all it would take to have her thinking straight again, that she'd be able to sit down at her desk, read her notes on the museum robbery, and pick up on something she'd missed the first time around. For a while it had worked, and even her black cat hadn't been able to draw her attention away from the papers on her desk, not even by standing in the middle of them. As always, she had simply read around him while she pushed the eyeglasses back up to the bridge of her nose with one hand and gently shoved Satan to the floor with the other. But when she got to the end of her notes and had to rely on her memory for the rest, the image of T.J. erupted in her thoughts and shattered her hope that he was someone in her past.

Trying to sleep at night was close to impossible. Each time she shut her eyes she saw him, his dark hair, his smile, the rakish sway of his hips when he walked. Then she'd remember what it had been like to kiss him, the warmth of his lips against hers, the manly scent of him, the feel of his muscular arms enveloping her, and she'd moan in frustration and throw off the covers. She would try pacing the floor until she was so tired she could hardly stand up. All that got her was tired limbs, for the instant she lay down again, being alone in her bed reminded her of the pleasure she had found wrapped in his embrace.

Her relief came on the morning of the fourth day. She had eaten breakfast in the dining room and had just returned to the study when she heard someone knock on the front door. Knowing Mr. Trumble would greet the visitor, she sat down at her desk and laid out her papers in front of her again, thinking that perhaps today would be the day she'd be able to concentrate completely on her work. But within a few minutes a frown wrinkled her brow as she slumped back in her chair and questioned again her ability to continue solving difficult problems, and why facts, clues, and shreds of evidence were no longer easy for her to find and piece together. Why was this particular case causing her so much trouble? Why couldn't she look objectively at the material, weigh the differences, and then draw the proper conclusion? Was it possible that T.J. was truly innocent and she simply refused to accept it?

"But all the evidence points right at him," she said aloud, not realizing that Mr. Trumble was standing in the doorway.

"Excuse me, Miss Chase," he apologized, waiting for her to look up. "I don't mean to intrude, but I thought perhaps you'd like to see this."

"What is it?" she asked, rising and meeting him halfway across the room.

Shifting his grip on the huge box he carried, he set it down on the floor near the settee. "The university sent it."

"The university? Father's university?" she questioned, tucking her skirts against the backs of her knees as she squatted down to examine the contents.

"Yes, miss," Mr. Trumble replied. "And this was delivered along with it." He pulled a letter from his inside pocket and handed it to her.

Rising, Catherine tore the seal and unfolded the paper to read. "It's from Chancellor Wycliff," she advised as she scanned the rest of the note. "He expresses his apologies for not having had this sent to me sooner, but that he was only just recently made aware some of my father's things were still at the university." She glanced up at Mr. Trumble, started to say something, and changed her mind. "What do you suppose is here?" she asked, laying the parchment on the end table as she crouched down again and began to sort through the articles.

The first item she recognized was the miniature of her mother, and Catherine smiled when she remembered how her father had carried it with him whenever he had to travel to another town on business. At night he'd put it on the table next to his bed, and when he went to work each day, he'd place it on the desk in his office.

"He loved her very much, didn't he, Mr. Trumble?" She sighed, tears blurring her vision as she stared at the likeness of the woman who had given her life and who had had her own cut short.

"Yes, miss," Mr. Trumble answered quietly. "Almost as much as he loved you."

"I don't believe that, Mr. Trumble," she denied with a smile, "but thank you for saying it."

He nodded, his own eyes glistening as thoughts of his

friend and employer flooded through him. Realizing how close he was to allowing his emotions to show, he straightened sharply, tugged on the hem of his coat, and cleared his throat. "If that will be all, miss," he said in his usually stiff manner, "I must speak with the cook about this evening's meal."

Too caught up in her own memories to notice the servant's discomfort, Catherine merely waved a hand, silently dismissing him as she set aside the gold-framed miniature and began to sort through the rest of the contents of the box. She hadn't realized until now that after her father's death, she had failed to contact the university about his personal belongings, and she assumed her inner self had decided it would have been too much for her just then. She wasn't sure she could handle it now either as a terrible loneliness began to engulf her. Tears would threaten each time she retrieved something from the box and recognized it as being a trinket of her father's. She found scribbled notes in his handwriting, a stickpin, one glove, a lace handkerchief, a snuffbox and pipe, a book of poetry she recalled was his favorite. She recovered a dried flower pressed between its pages and could only assume it had come from the funeral spray on her mother's casket. And at the bottom, buried under a score of papers, diagrams, and chemistry books, she found something that made her cry unashamedly. Clutching the tiny baby shoe in both hands, she sank to the floor and held it pressed against her cheek; *her* baby shoe. It had always embarrassed her to see how her father treasured it. Like the miniature, he carried it with him wherever he went, and Catherine had asked him several times to at least not put it on display for his friends and colleagues to see and question its owner. For as long as she could remember she had always wanted to be grown-up, even at the young age of twelve, and in her opinion exhibiting the baby shoe would prejudice everyone's view of her. It had taken her until her seventeenth birthday to realize that that wasn't true, and that none of those who saw the shoe ever thought that way. Now it symbolized her father's love for her and his absence was even more difficult for her to accept.

"Oh, Papa," she wept. "Why did you have to die?"

A black furry tail brushed her face and she opened her eyes to find Satan rubbing his long, lanky body against her. She seldom cried, but whenever she did, the cat always seemed to sense her sorrow, and he wouldn't stop pestering her until he'd made her smile.

"Yes, Satan," she laughed through her tears as she grabbed his sinewy torso and hugged him close. "I know tears never solve anything, but sometimes I can't help it. And it makes me feel better."

As though he understood and even agreed with her, Satan began to purr, his long, sharp claws curling around to lightly pierce her arm.

"How about some milk?" she announced suddenly as she dropped the baby shoe back in the box and stood with the cat still held in her arms. "Would you like that?" She laughed when he meowed right away. "I'll bet you would," she remarked, rubbing her cheek along the back of his neck as she carried him to the door. "Well, we'll just have to see if we can't find you some."

Catherine spent the rest of the morning and part of that afternoon working in the study once the chalkboard she'd ordered from the Baker Street Bazaar had been delivered. She made notes on it, drew a diagram of the area around and including the British Museum, the livery where the murdered men had been found, and a list of every clue she had so far. When she'd finished, she stood back, pulled her eyeglasses from her nose, and studied everything she'd written down, hoping that something before her would spark an idea. It didn't, and out of frustration she yanked the white frock coat from her shoulders and tossed it down, and headed for the kitchen to eat her supper. A half hour later she was staring at the board again with the same result.

"I think you're losing your edge, Catherine," she said with a sigh as she plopped down on the settee, her legs stretched out in front of her, her feet resting on their heels, and her hands, palms down, lying on the seat on either side of her. "I know the answer's there. I just can't see it." She glared at the chalkboard a moment longer, then looked disgustedly away. "Damn," she muttered. "Maybe I should just go to bed and try again in the morning." Sitting up, she glanced one last time at the board and just when she was about to rise, a particular group of words caught her eye. "Of course!" she exclaimed, jumping to her feet. "The wagon! Phillip found it once; he can find it again."

Excited now that she might be on to something, she turned abruptly for the door, missed seeing the box of her father's trinkets on the floor in front of her, and tripped over it. Unable to catch herself, she fell, tipping the box over in the process. Certain she'd broken her toe, she rolled onto a hip and hiked up her skirts to examine the injured appendage, and at that same moment her attention was drawn to the red leather-bound book that had slid across the floor and lay open only a couple of feet away. The first time she'd gone through the items in the box, she hadn't bothered reading any of the books since chemistry had never been one of her strong points, and she probably would have ignored this one if it hadn't been for the folded piece of paper she saw sticking out from between the pages. Forgetting about her sore toe, she twisted and stretched to retrieve the volume.

The color drained from her face once she'd recognized that the tome wasn't a textbook on science, but a diary written by her father's own hand. She'd been aware that he always kept notes on whatever project he was working on, but she never would have guessed he kept a journal detailing his personal feelings. Clutching the book and the folded paper against her midriff, she came to her feet, circled back to the settee, and sat down.

The first few pages, dated at the beginning of the autumn semester at the university, told about his excitement with some of the new students in his chemistry class, the weather, and how he still missed his wife, more at this time of the year than any other. He wrote about Reginald Hastings, his laboratory assistant, and how the two of them were close to making a breakthrough in one of their experiments. He also expressed his concern about the aftermath of success, that in the wrong hands, it could have devastating effects. A twinge of suspicion hit Catherine as she recalled the explosion that had killed her father. It was possible his death might have been the result of misjudgment on his part and that he'd been testing this particular experiment. Yet if that were true, why hadn't Mr. Hastings been in the laboratory with him? And why so late at night? She knew her father didn't always share every aspect of his work with his assistant, and that he'd done that as a safety precaution, but he had never worked alone in the laboratory . . . and never after dark. Although he refused to wear spectacles, he had admitted to her that his eyes weren't what they used to be, and that he hated working in artificial light.

Frowning, Catherine glanced up and looked absently across the room. It had to have been her grief over losing her father that had made her miss such important and obvious questions. Otherwise, she would have asked Mr. Hastings to explain. Perhaps she should still ask him to explain. Snapping the diary shut, she laid it on the table along with the folded piece of paper she had yet to read and started to rise. But the realization that whatever was written on the parchment must have been of some significance or her father wouldn't have tucked it in the pages of his journal made her hesitate. Settling herself back down, she reclaimed the paper, smoothed out the folds, and began to read.

It was a letter to her father from a Swedish chemist named Gustaf Valdemar, and he was asking the professor to reconsider teaming up with Valdemar in his research on the stabilization of nitroglycerin, that selling the patent on it would make them both rich and very famous. She could remember her father mentioning the project he'd started and his explaining that it was dangerous work because he was experimenting with explosives, but he'd never told her there was an outside interest pressuring him to share his ideas.

"You wasted your time, Herr Valdemar," Catherine murmured with a shake of her head. "Money and fame were never in my father's vocabulary. And selling a discovery was the last thing he'd ever do."

Wondering why her father had even kept the letter, she began to read again, taking note with little interest that the chemist had advised her father about his plans to relocate his laboratory to Paris, and that the professor could contact him there. The rest of the letter said little else of importance, and Catherine was about to refold it and put it away, when she noticed the postscript at the bottom. The tone of Valdemar's message had, until the end, been light and friendly. His last notation, however, made Catherine frown, when the mood of the correspondence made a sudden change.

I urge you not to ignore this second request, Professor Chase, as the consequences of your refusal could have serious repercussions, it read, sending a chill through her.

Yet that wasn't what bothered her the most once she saw the date posted at the top of the page and she realized her father would have received the letter shortly before his death.

"It's probably just a coincidence," she muttered angrily as she haphazardly refolded the letter and jammed it back in the diary. "It has nothing to do with my father's accident. You're letting your suspicious mind get carried away again."

Unshed tears burned her eyes, and she gritted her teeth and swallowed hard. There was no sense in crying. It wouldn't bring her father back. She pushed herself up from the settee and bent to collect the things that had fallen out of the box. Her father's death had been the result of carelessness. No one would have wanted him dead! No one!

Then why was he working alone that night . . . after sundown? that tiny voice inside her head challenged. *Why wasn't Hastings with him? And what project was he working on when the explosion occurred? Had he been testing nitroglycerin?*

"I don't know," she hissed, tossing the scattered items

back into their container. "But I'm going to find out. I'm going to pay Chancellor Wycliff a visit first thing in the morning. I'm going to ask him all the questions that should have been asked the day my father died!" A defiant tear rolled down her cheek. "And I won't stop asking until I have all the answers."

CHAPTER 11

As the brougham rolled to a stop outside the Chases' town house, T.J. wondered if the excuse he'd give Catherine for paying her a visit would be believable. He knew it wasn't his real reason for wanting to see her, and he feared she might guess it too, and ask him to leave. It had been four days since he'd seen her, and the time had passed so slowly, he'd felt as if he'd lived each minute of it a hundred times over.

The day he'd left her he'd been angry . . . with her and with himself. He'd decided that since she'd made it quite clear the intimacy they'd shared meant nothing to her that he'd stay away, that he'd try and forget it happened. He would concentrate on finding the stolen paintings and the man who had schemed its theft, and then plan a trip to Australia to see Christian and Alexandra. If his adopted father couldn't explain the feelings T.J. was having, then maybe Alexandra could give him a woman's point of view and help him to understand Catherine.

For the next couple of days, he had busied himself with the arrangements for his six-month voyage, and just yesterday he had gone to see Lewis Rhomberg. Unaware that his temper had been short and his conversation crisp and stinging, he'd been surprised when Lewis asked what had him in such a foul mood.

"Who said I am?" he had snapped, his dark brows pulling together in a fierce scowl.

"Oh, no one in particular, I guess," Lewis had replied, his eyes twinkling. "I was just assuming by that frown on your face and how you haven't said a pleasant word to me that something was bothering you. It wouldn't be female by any chance, would it?"

"No!" T.J. had shot back.

Lewis shook his head. "I didn't think so. Women have never been a problem with you. Love them one minute; walk away from them the next. That's T.J. Savage."

"Yes, it is. And if she thinks I'll treat her any differently, then she's mistaken."

"Who?" Lewis baited.

"Catherine. Who else?"

Lewis fought back his smile. "Catherine. Catherine Chase?"

"Yes, Catherine Chase. Do you know any other Catherines?" he growled, leaving his chair to walk the floor of the parlor in Lewis's small flat. "Twice, now, I've stepped in before she got herself killed, and was she grateful?" He shook his head and kept pacing. "Of course not. She still thinks I'm the one who robbed the museum, and she's not all that sure I'm not the one who murdered those two men. Can you imagine? Why, the little twit even broke into my house the other night."

That was the first Lewis had heard of it. He couldn't even begin to guess why, and he opened his mouth to question her purpose, only to have T.J. cut him off.

"That's right," he offered. "She broke into my house with the help of a street urchin. And you know why?" he asked, but not because he expected his friend to answer. "I'll tell you why. She was after the coat I had on the night of the murders. She had seen that it was missing a button, and she was so sure I was the killer that she climbed up one of the trees in my yard, hopped onto the balcony, and then let herself into my room." He gritted his teeth and inhaled a long, deep breath. "The little fool! She could have fallen and killed herself."

When T.J. seemed to lose himself in thought rather than

finish the story, Lewis grew impatient. "How, T.J.? How do you know she did all that?"

The dark-haired young man spun around to face his companion. "How do I know?" he echoed. "Because I caught her; that's how I know. I came home earlier than she expected and walked right in on her." The muscle in his cheek flexed as he ground his teeth again and took up pacing the floor once more. "My mistake was in not jerking her out from behind the screen and scaring the very life from her. If I had, she might not have dressed up like a whore and gone looking for trouble. No, I had to pretend I didn't know she was there."

Lewis, more confused than ever, frowned, drew a breath, and started to ask T.J. if he'd go into a little more detail, when the young man whirled on him.

"And then the other night! I can't believe I let it go that far. And you think women have never been a problem for me. Well, you're wrong, old friend. I've never been able to understand a one of them." He threw his hands in the air and plopped back down in the chair next to Lewis. "How can they go from warm and responsive one minute to cool and nonchalant the next?"

Uneasy, Lewis hoped he'd misinterpreted his friend's meaning of letting "it" go too far. If T.J. and Catherine had become romantically involved, there'd be nothing ahead for them but problems. He thought the world of T.J. Savage, but at the same time he doubted the young man would ever devote himself to one woman. And especially not to Catherine Chase. She wasn't the type to let him . . . simply because she was too independent. So was T.J., and the combination would never strike a happy medium. And then, of course, there was the fact that T.J. had been lying to her all this time. Once she found that out, it would ruin any chance they might have had to work out their differences.

Frowning, Lewis had struggled for the gentlest way of wording his concern. "T.J.," he had said, "you're not trying to tell me that you and Catherine . . . that the two of you . . ." He had paused, scratched his forehead, and had begun again. "Letting it go too far doesn't mean you did more than just kiss her, does it?"

Until that moment, T.J. hadn't realized how much he had actually told his friend. The intimacy he and Catherine had shared was meant to be private, and he had regretted even the implication that something so personal between the two of them had occurred . . . despite the fact that he knew Lewis would never repeat a word of it to anyone. Angry with himself, he had glowered at the man rather than answer him, had turned on his heel and had stalked out of the flat without so much as a simple farewell.

T.J. had returned home then and had gone into the study to write a letter to Christian and Alexandra. He guessed they'd be happy to see him under any circumstances, but that they'd appreciate a warning of his arrival, especially since he hadn't been home in over two years and the last letter he'd written had been shortly before his departure for London some six months ago. Yet it wasn't long before his mind had wandered and he couldn't concentrate on his task. The vision of Catherine kept interrupting him. His good intentions were shattered when Stewart appeared in the doorway to tell him that someone was there to see him, and for a second he hoped the butler meant Catherine. Then he realized that if he had, Stewart would have announced her. His spirits low, T.J. had gone to the parlor to greet his guest, and a few minutes later he had the excuse he needed to see Catherine.

As he stepped to the sidewalk and asked the driver to wait, he paused a moment to straighten his attire before walking to the front door, and it was then that he realized the news he brought Catherine wouldn't do him any favors. He'd hired a man to hunt down the wagon used to transport the artworks, and even though his agent had been successful to some degree—he'd found the wagon at the bottom of a ravine at the edge of town, but not the paintings—Catherine would assume it was merely another ploy on his part to cover up evidence that would incriminate him. He also knew he wouldn't argue with her simply because it wouldn't do him any good. But then, that wasn't the reason he'd come to see her, anyway. He was hoping for another chance to explain that he cared about her . . . that he hadn't just made love to her because he'd been in the mood . . . and so had she. With a firm set to his jaw, he squared his shoulders and started up the walkway.

"Mr. Savage," Trumble greeted in surprise once he'd opened the door to find him standing there. "We weren't expecting you."

"Mr. Trumble." T.J. nodded. He hadn't really expected to find himself standing on Catherine's doorstep either, but here he was, and he didn't intend to leave until he'd had the chance to talk to her. "I'd like to speak with Miss Chase. It's important. I have some information about the museum robbery."

The butler shifted uneasily. "I'm afraid she's not at home, sir," he regrettably informed his visitor, "but if you'd like to wait, I'm sure it won't be long before she returns."

T.J. wasn't known for backing away from a situation, but Mr. Trumble had given him the opening, and since T.J. was already having second thoughts, he drew a breath to decline the invitation. "Thank you, but—"

"I insist," Mr. Trumble cut in, moving aside and swinging the door all the way open. "It will give us time to talk before she arrives."

T.J. had been so caught up in his own emotions that he'd failed to notice anything else going on around him. Now that Mr. Trumble had gone from displaying the traditionally stiff manner of a butler to that of someone unwilling to comply with a guest's wishes, T.J. sensed something was wrong. Without answering, he took the top hat from his head and stepped into the foyer while he pulled the strings of his cape free. Once he'd given the garment to Mr. Trumble and had removed his gloves as well, he motioned for the man to lead the way.

"You seem upset, Mr. Trumble," T.J. observed, once they'd both taken a seat near the hearth. "I assume it has to do with Miss Chase."

"Yes, sir, I am," the butler replied. "And yes, it has to do with Miss Chase. Ordinarily I would mind my own business, but since you seem to have taken an interest in her well-being and because I don't know what else to do, I've decided I will have to go with my instincts."

"On what, Mr. Trumble?"

"On you," he easily replied. "Miss Chase and I have different opinions of you, Mr. Savage. That's why she won't confide in you and I will. Yesterday morning a box was delivered to the house from the university where Professor Chase was employed. In it were personal things belonging to the professor. I didn't help Miss Chase sort through them, but this morning she came to me with a letter she had found in her father's diary. Although she didn't let me read it, she told me some of what was in it and how it raised some serious questions about her father's death . . . unanswered questions that everyone, including her, had overlooked. I have to agree, Mr. Savage, that once she pointed them out to me, I too began to suspect there was more to the accident that took her father's life than what appeared on the surface. What worries me the most, however, is that she's gone to the university in Oxford to investigate . . . and she's gone there alone."

Sometimes finding nothing at all could be a bigger clue than finding the murder weapon or a ransom note, and even though Chancellor Wycliff had suggested that her father's research notes could have been destroyed in the blast, Catherine wasn't so sure. That alone hastened her need to return to London after talking with the chancellor and anyone else who had helped clean up the laboratory after the explosion. She wanted to talk with Nathan Beecher at Scotland Yard to find out what the CID had found during their investigation and if they had, perhaps, come across her father's notes. What really bothered her even more, however, was the startling discovery of why Reginald Hastings, her father's assistant, no longer worked at the university. All the chancellor could tell her was that Professor Chase had fired the man only a few days before the accident and that no one there had seen Hastings since the funeral.

"A coincidence," Chancellor Wycliff had guessed, once she'd pointed it out to him.

"One too many," she had politely replied, deciding then not to mention Gustaf Valdemar's letter. There was no sense in upsetting the man with the possibility that something dreadful had happened right under his nose. She'd wait until later to do that.

Determined to find the missing pieces of the puzzle, Catherine had set out for London. What she didn't like thinking was that Reginald Hastings might be at the bottom of it. He and the professor had worked side by side for nearly two decades. Every Christmas he spent the holidays with the Chases since he had no family of his own. And she couldn't even begin to count how many times the man and her father had closeted themselves off in the study to map out some project or another. Whatever reason had caused her father to dismiss his associate after so many years must had been very serious, but not serious enough to keep Hastings away from the funeral, and she could remember how hard the man had cried over the loss of his friend and mentor that day. Yet the more she thought about him, the more he became an important clue to solving the mystery leading up to her father's accident. The trick, however, would be in finding him.

"Driver," she called, once the rig approached the outskirts of town, "take me to Scotland Yard, please."

"Yes, ma'am," he replied, snapping the whip to hurry the mare along.

Catherine doubted Nathan Beecher would have any information on the man, but it would be worth asking. She would also like to discuss her theory with him. He might not agree that any of it had anything to do with the explosion, but an unbiased mind certainly might help her to see things from a different angle. And then, of course, there was always Phillip Preston. The street urchin could most assuredly assist her in areas her friend at the Yard could not, and once she'd visited Nathan Beecher, Catherine planned to locate Phillip and ask him to find her father's missing assistant.

"Shall I wait here for you, Miss Chase?" the driver asked, once he'd pulled the rig to a halt outside the Yard's headquarters.

"Yes," she replied, stepping down. "I shouldn't be too long, I think."

The day had turned sunny after a dark, cloudy morning, but there was still a chill in the air. Wrapping her cloak tightly around her slim frame, Catherine elbowed her way across the crowded sidewalk to the main entrance of the huge brick building and went inside. As always a throng of people was gathered around the sergeant's desk, enabling Catherine to sneak by unnoticed. But once she'd traveled the narrow corridor to the large room Nathan Beecher shared with several other detectives, her luck ran out. The young man wasn't seated at his desk nor was he anywhere to be seen. Instead, she spotted Commissioner Mays standing amid a group of his agents in the center of the room, and Catherine quickly turned back around to make a hasty exit. What she didn't want right then was a confrontation with the man. She wasn't in the mood and she was sure that if he said anything at all to her, she'd lose her temper and tell him what she really thought of him.

She had just stepped back into the hallway that would take her past the sergeant's desk and out the front door, when she heard someone call out her name in a harsh whisper. Certain the commissioner wouldn't be so polite or secretive, she paused and glanced over her shoulder to find Ferris Hargrove hurrying toward her.

"Nathan isn't here," he said, "if that's who you're looking for."

"I am," she replied. "And I guessed as much. Will he be gone long? I'd really like to talk to him."

Hargrove shrugged his shoulders. "Hard to say. He's out on a case . . . could take a couple of hours. Perhaps I could help you."

Catherine didn't know Ferris Hargrove all that well to judge him, but since he was the commissioner's assistant, she feared anything she might tell him would go directly back to Mays.

"Or I can give him a message," Hargrove offered instead, once he'd sensed the reason for her hesitation.

Catherine smiled, embarrassed that he'd deduced why she hadn't accepted his offer to help her out. "It concerns the accident at the university that took my father's life."

Hargrove's face paled considerably. "What about it?"

Catherine glanced past him to make sure the commissioner was still occupied with his other men. "I need to know who was in charge of investigating the explosion and what the CID found in the laboratory."

Hargrove shifted uneasily from one foot to the other, his gaze dropping away from her. "That could take some doing, Miss Chase. The file's in the commissioner's office. But I'll tell Beecher you asked. It'll be up to him to get it." He nervously ran a hand over his forehead, glanced back at Mays, then took her elbow and guided her toward the front exit. "It's not that I don't want to help, you understand, but—"

"But it could mean your job if the commissioner ever caught you," Catherine finished, smiling softly. "I know that. Nathan knows it, too. His career would be over if Commissioner Mays ever learned he was helping me. It's bad enough that I impose on Nathan. I wouldn't ask it of you." When they reached the door, Catherine faced him. "If you'll just give him the message, that's all I'd ask of you. And tell him to be careful. If it's too risky, I'll find some other way of obtaining the information I need. All right?"

Hargrove consented, but his curiosity wouldn't allow him to let her walk out the door. "Miss Chase, there's no reason for you to investigate the explosion, you know. It was an accident. The reports say so, and the chancellor at the university was satisfied with the Yard's findings. That is what you're doing, isn't it?"

Every once in a while Catherine's reputation got in her way. Whenever she asked a question about something, people assumed she was working on a case. Ferris Hargrove was right in guessing that she had suddenly decided to look into the facts concerning her father's death, but she didn't want him to be absolutely positive. The fewer people who knew what she was up to, the better off she'd be.

"I know how it looks, Mr. Hargrove," she replied, "and I assure you that I have no reason to doubt the CID." *Not yet, anyway,* she added in her thoughts as she smiled at him, thanked him for his help, and headed out the door.

Irritated and busy mulling over her next course of action, Catherine neither saw the man pushing his way toward her through the crowd on the sidewalk nor heard him call out her name. If she had, she might have walked a little faster. To her misfortune, however, Aaron Courtland caught her arm just as she was about to ascend her rig.

"Good morning, Catherine," he chaffed with a broad grin, his green eyes sparkling. "If I didn't know better, I'd swear you were deliberately trying to get away without having to say hello to me."

It wasn't that she didn't like Aaron Courtland. In fact she had always enjoyed what little time they spent together. Who wouldn't? He was charming, handsome, witty, and full of the devil; the kind of man who could make a woman like Catherine forget about her troubles. What bothered her about being with him was what other people would think, especially Edith, Aaron's mother.

"I'm sorry, Aaron, I didn't see you," she apologized, moving with him to the edge of the sidewalk where they could avoid the crush of bodies around them. "I was concentrating on something."

"Another case?" His handsome face warmed with his smile. "You know, a beautiful woman like you shouldn't hide herself away the way you do. You need to get out, to enjoy yourself once in a while. Say tomorrow night, for instance?"

With the thought that the Courtlands' dinner party was so close at hand came another thought that tingled her insides. Short of death there was no getting out of having to see T.J. again.

"You *are* coming to dinner, aren't you?" he teased.

"Mother will be very disappointed if you don't. You know how hard she works at getting the two of us together." He frowned, rested a fist on one hip, and tapped his chin with a fingertip as if he were trying to recall something. "Let's see . . . it's been how long? A month? Two?" His lean face wrinkled when he chuckled. "Don't get me wrong, Catherine," he continued in a more sympathetic vein. "I'm not complaining about Mother's matchmaking. Quite the contrary. If I were the type to settle down, I'd want someone like you to share my life. But I'm not, and Mother has yet to figure that out. So humor the ol' girl, will you?"

His nonchalant manner never failed to ease the tension she always felt whenever she was with him. Smiling, she said, "I'll try."

"Good." He beamed. "Then I take that to mean you'll be coming for dinner tomorrow night." When she nodded and started to tell him something else, he decided to change the subject, since he knew how uncomfortable she was about the whole situation. "You know, Catherine," he began, cocking his head to one side as he closely studied her face, "you seem different to me. Maybe it's because I haven't seen you for a while, but you look radiant . . . despite the sadness I see in your eyes. Has something special happened in your life I don't know about?"

Catherine could feel a blush rising in her cheeks, and before she could tell him otherwise, Aaron laughed.

"Good heavens, you haven't fallen in love, have you?"

"No!" she exclaimed, highly irritated that he could even think such a thing. "I'm like you, Aaron. I'm not the type to settle down. It's obvious your mother doesn't agree, but I would have thought you of all people would understand."

He shrugged a shoulder. "Falling in love and settling down are two different things, Catherine. I've been in love many times, but that doesn't mean I ever want to get married. I'm sorry I offended you."

He raised his dark brows at her, his eyes twinkling, and a smirk crimping one side of his mouth. He waited for her to say something, and when it appeared he'd have a long wait, he decided it was best to change the subject . . . again.

"Have you eaten?" he asked.

"No, but—"

"Good, then give me a few minutes to talk to the sergeant, and we'll go somewhere for lunch."

"I can't—"

"Of course you can," he argued, turning to her rig with the intention of dismissing the driver.

"Aaron, no!" she firmly objected. "I have things to do and no time to eat just now. Please, don't make a scene."

His shoulders slumped as though he were truly injured by her rejection, and the sight of him made her chuckle.

"Then let's compromise," he suggested. "I'll fill out my report with the desk sergeant; you take care of your business, and then meet me somewhere later."

"What kind of report?" she asked, forever curious.

He exhaled wearily. "One of the vacant houses I own was broken into last night. There wasn't anything in it for them to take, but they did cause some damage . . . broken windows and the like."

"What do you suppose they were after?"

"A warm night's sleep," he replied. "It's happened before."

"Must be frustrating."

He nodded. "I doubt the police will do much good after the fact, but I really wish they could catch the little beggars."

Catherine immediately thought of Phillip Preston and how many times she wondered where he slept at night. "Are you sure it's children?"

"From the size of the footprints below the window . . . yes." He bobbed his head at someone he recognized walking past them on the sidewalk, then turned his attention back to his companion. "Will an hour give you enough time to finish up your business?"

Finding her ill-tempered cohort could take all day, and now that Aaron had mentioned food, she realized how hungry she was. Besides, with any kind of luck at all, maybe T.J. would see her with Aaron. "I'm sure an hour will be plenty of time," she replied. "Where shall we meet?"

"How about the tearoom at Montagu's?"

"Perfect. I'll see you there in one hour." She smiled warmly at him, allowed him to help her into the rig, and then waved at him while her cab pulled away from the curb.

"Until then, my sweet," Aaron murmured, the smile fading from his lips.

He remained there on the sidewalk for several moments watching her rig disappear within the crowded thoroughfare, until another cab pulled up where hers had been and blocked his view. The distraction brought him around, and while a boy descended from the rig, Aaron turned and went inside police headquarters, unaware that the youth was following close behind him.

"Excuse me, sir," the young boy said to him, once they'd joined the others waiting to speak with the sergeant, "but do you know where Mr. Rhomberg's office is?"

Before Aaron had a chance to answer one way or the other, a man standing nearby looked up from the paper he'd been reading.

"You looking for me, son?" he asked, his gaze taking in the ragged appearance of the boy.

"Only if you're Lewis Rhomberg."

Guessing that perhaps the child had a message for him that wasn't meant to be overheard by anyone, Lewis jerked his head toward the hallway where it wasn't as crowded, and once they were relatively safe from eavesdroppers, he asked who had sent him.

"He didn't tell me his name," the boy admitted. "He just said I was to come in here and ask you to meet him outside."

"Outside? Where?"

"He's waiting for you in his cab . . . out front."

Assuming T.J. had sent the youngster, Lewis reached in his pocket and handed the boy a coin with instructions to tell the gentleman he'd be right there just as soon as he got his coat.

"It must be rather important for you to run the risk of coming to headquarters yourself," Lewis commented a few minutes later as T.J.'s cab rolled down the street away from Scotland Yard.

"It is," T.J. admitted. "So important, in fact, I decided we should keep moving while I told you about it."

"Does it concern Catherine?"

T.J.'s frown deepened. "Yes," he said, glancing up at the trapdoor above them to make sure it was securely closed. "I went to see her this morning, but she wasn't home. Mr. Trumble asked me in to wait, and when I started to decline, he insisted."

"Oh? I'd say that's a bit unusual. Wouldn't you?"

"Yes, it is. And that's precisely why I accepted. I don't know the man very well, but I could see he was worried about something, and since the only thing we have in common is Catherine, I guessed his need to talk had to do with her."

"So what did he say?"

"He told me a box of Professor Chase's personal belongings had been delivered to the house yesterday, items he'd kept at the university."

"What kind of things?"

"A miniature of his wife; Catherine's baby shoe; things like that." Inhaling a deep breath, T.J. silently studied the scenery they passed by while he figured out the best way to explain. "According to Mr. Trumble, there had been a diary too, the professor's diary. In it Catherine found a letter written to her father from a Swedish chemist named Valdemar, Gustaf Valdemar, and it was dated a short time before Chase's accident. He had asked the professor to reconsider his decision not to work with the chemist on his latest project . . . nitroglycerin."

"Whew!" Lewis exclaimed. "Dangerous work."

"In more ways than one, possibly," T.J. interjected.

"What do you mean?"

"Mr. Trumble told me that Herr Valdemar had made a veiled threat in his letter, that if the professor refused to help, he'd regret it."

"Dear God." Lewis moaned. "Are you thinking what I'm thinking?"

"Yes," T.J. answered glumly. "And so is Catherine."

"Damn it!" Lewis growled. "This is exactly what I was afraid would happen. Where is she now?"

"She left this morning for the university. She told Mr. Trumble that some questions needed to be answered; such as why her father had been working alone at the time of the explosion and why he'd been doing his research at night."

"Meaning?"

"Meaning he always worked with an assistant and *never* after dark."

Lewis sighed heavily. "Oh, this isn't good."

"I doubt she'll find anything at the university," T.J. went on. "Your agents from the CID didn't, but that doesn't mean she'll stop there. She'll try to contact Herr Valdemar."

"Does she know where he is?"

T.J. nodded. "His letter said that he'd taken up residence in Paris."

"Paris?"

"Yes, and that's why I've booked passage in three days."

"Why not go right away?"

T.J. chuckled sarcastically. "You know Catherine," he said. "She's suspicious of everything and everybody. If I told her I couldn't keep our dinner engagement for tomorrow night—especially after I'd been so emphatic about going—she'd demand to know why."

"What dinner engagement?"

Visibly drained, T.J. reached up to remove his top hap and run his fingers through his dark hair. "The Courtlands'. Edith Courtland. Do you know her?"

"I know *of* her. She and her son are quite wealthy." Both men were quiet for a moment before Lewis asked, "Why would you insist on going?"

"For several reasons. The most important was simply because I wanted to stay close to Catherine . . . as you suggested I do," he reminded his friend. "I was also hoping the party would include the kind of guests wealthy enough to be interested in buying a stolen Rembrandt. I was planning to guide the conversation that way and then hint that I'd been looking for just such a piece of art for my own collection. That's how I joined up with the thieves in the first place . . . by spreading hints."

A tired smile worked its way across Lewis's mouth. "That's the way you met Catherine, too."

T.J. snorted. "Yes, it was. Funny how trouble has a way of following her around, isn't it?"

Lewis shrugged. "I suppose you could call it that."

"What else would you call it?"

Sighing, Lewis replied, "Fate, my friend. Fate."

CHAPTER 12

"Fate," T.J. grumbled as he stood before the mirror tying a knot in his cravat. "You think fate is what brought Catherine and me together? Well, if it is, Lewis, old friend, it's a twisted kind of fate." His dark brows dropped in a disgusted frown when it seemed the neckgear had a mind of its own and refused to hang properly. With an irritable jerk, he pulled the lopsided knot free and started again. "Or maybe I'm being punished," he concluded, staring at his reflection while his fingers agilely worked the satiny fabric one more time. "Maybe it's God's way of telling me that no matter how much money a man has, his past will always haunt him. After all, that's how Catherine sees me . . . once a thief, always a thief. Damn!" The last exploded from his lips when his second attempt at fixing the cravat failed. "Denton!" he shouted at the valet. "Would you come in here, please?"

Hurrying from the adjoining room where he had been disposing of T.J.'s bath, the gray-haired servant rushed to T.J.'s side. "What is it, sir?"

"I can't seem to get this blasted thing tied," T.J. barked, flicking the shiny black cloth with his fingertips. "Would you do it for me?"

"Certainly, sir," Denton agreed as he quickly set aside the wet towels and reached for the cravat. "I have to say, sir, this dinner party must be very important. I'm never seen you this nervous."

"It's not the party." T.J. sighed. "It's the company I'll be keeping."

A smile crossed the servant's mouth. "Ah, yes, Miss Chase."

T.J. had been watching Denton's progress in securing a knot in the reflection of the mirror until the last comment was made. Leaning back, he looked the man in the face. "What's that supposed to mean? 'Ah, yes, Miss Chase.'"

Denton had been one of the first servants T.J. had hired after moving into the house, and although they didn't talk about very many personal things, Denton had come to know his employer rather well by observing his many moods. Catherine Chase affected Mr. Savage differently from everything else in the man's life, and Denton—as well as everyone else on the staff—had drawn the same conclusion. T. J. Savage was in love.

"Nothing, sir," he replied, wisely deciding not to voice his opinion.

"Denton," T.J. warned. "I asked you a question. What did you mean?"

Uncomfortable and wishing he'd kept his mouth shut, the valet straightened the perfectly tied cravat and stepped back. "I simply meant, sir, that a woman as lovely as Miss Chase would have any man's nerves on edge. There's no shame in that."

T.J.'s dark brown eyes narrowed as he watched the man retrieve the coat from the armoire and hold it out for him. "Oh really? And is that the common opinion of the entire staff? Or just yours?"

Without thinking, Denton replied, "The entire— I mean, just mine, sir."

T.J.'s shoulders sagged. "That's what I thought. I've become the topic of gossip in my own home."

"Gossip, sir?" Denton echoed as he helped T.J. on with the coat. "Oh, no, sir. We don't gossip about you."

"No? Then what do you do? Talk about me?"

"Yes, sir." Denton's face whitened. "I—I mean, we—ah—we—"

T.J. shook his head. "Don't bother trying to explain. I understand."

"No you don't sir," the valet quickly suggested. "We talk about you, yes. But not in the sense you mean. Everyone here thinks a lot of you, sir, and all of us agree that you shouldn't be living alone in this big house."

T.J. raised his brow at him while he tugged on the cuff of his shirtsleeve. "Oh? Are you saying I should get married?"

"Yes, sir."

T.J. found the idea amusing. "And who do you think I should marry?"

"Why, Miss Chase, of course."

T.J. couldn't have been more shocked if someone had come right up to him and had thrown a bucket of cold water in his face. Numb, he just stood there staring at the servant. He was just now coming around to accepting the possibility that he might be falling in love with Catherine, but the notion of marrying her had never crossed his mind. He didn't know why. Love and marriage went together . . . or at least he had always assumed they did. But he had never imagined himself as the sort to take a wife.

Blinking, once he realized several moments had passed and that Denton was still waiting for him to reply, T.J. glanced down to watch his fingers hook the buttons on his coat. "Miss Chase, hmm?" he asked. "And why Miss Chase? Why not one of the other women I've been seeing?"

"Why, it's very simple, sir," Denton admitted, pulling the clothes brush from his pocket and whisking it across T.J.'s shoulders. "You're in love with Miss Chase."

T.J. burst into laughter. "I'm what?" he challenged, turning around to stare at the man.

"I said you're in—"

"I heard you," T.J. interrupted. "I'm just confused as to why you think that."

"We all do, sir."

"The entire staff," T.J. supplied.

"Yes, sir. We came to that conclusion some time ago."

T.J. laughed again. "Oh, you did? Well, that's very

astute of you . . . considering that I'm not really sure myself." Interested in knowing how Denton, Stewart, Mrs. Witton, and everyone else in the household had decided something he was having trouble recognizing, he asked, "Would you mind telling me how the lot of you arrived at such a verdict?"

"Well, it was a little difficult at first, sir," Denton began as he reached for the gray gloves and scarf lying on the dresser. "We all noticed a change in you." Turning back, he handed the items over and watched while T.J. draped the scarf around his neck. "You seemed more at ease . . . content, if you will. None of us could understand why, until Miss Witton saw the young lady in the foyer that morning."

T.J. paused with one hand shoved halfway into a glove. "What lady? What morning?" he asked, puzzled.

"Miss Chase, sir. Mrs. Witton was on her way upstairs with fresh linens when she met Miss Chase near the front door . . . about a week ago, sir."

T.J. could feel a stinging in his cheeks, and he cursed under his breath. The last thing he wanted was for Catherine's name to be tossed around among the servants.

"Don't worry, sir," Denton quickly assured him as though he'd read his mind. "None of us think ill of her . . . or of you. I would suggest, however," he continued as he returned to the armoire and selected a black silk top hat from the shelf, "that you not waste any time in making your feelings known to her." He glanced up at his employer and added, "It would be the proper thing to do, if you get my meaning."

Oh, I get your meaning, Denton, T.J. thought, sighing wearily. *The problem is Catherine. With the way she feels about me right now, she'd laugh in my face if I offered to marry her.*

"You did *what*?" Catherine exploded, jumping up from the chair behind her desk, blue eyes blazing and her chest heaving.

"I'm sorry, miss, if you object," Mr. Trumble replied,

firmly standing his ground, "but I did it for your own good."

"How can telling a thief that I'm investigating my father's death be for my own good?" she demanded, slamming a book shut and scooping up the papers from on top of the desk and shoving them in a drawer.

"Because unlike you, *I* don't believe Mr. Savage is a thief. There's genuine concern in his voice whenever he talks of you."

Catherine's upper lip curled. "I guess that's why you're the butler and I'm the investigator."

Mr. Trumble's spine stiffened and his chin came up a few degrees. "And perhaps that's why I'm able to see things you can't. I don't have to have everything explained to me. I trust my instincts."

"And so do I," she countered. "And my instincts tell me he's a thief."

"Your instincts are wrong, miss."

Shocked by his straightforwardness, Catherine stared, openmouthed.

Knowing he had already overstepped the boundaries of decorum, Mr. Trumble rushed on. "I've managed thus far to keep my thoughts to myself, Miss Chase. I've tried never to interfere with your work, since it seemed you knew what you were doing. I can no longer do that, I'm afraid. The museum robbery has become dangerous work whether you'll admit it or not, and I fear looking into your father's accident will prove to be just as perilous. You need a man to help you, and since—"

"I do not!" she raged.

"And since I'm not as young as I used to be," he continued without missing a beat, "I took it upon myself to ask Mr. Savage for his assistance. *If*—and I strongly emphasize the word—if I believed he was involved in the robbery or any other unlawful act, I never would have put my faith in him . . . or risked your safety. *That,* Catherine Chase, is how strongly I feel about him. Now," he added, turning for the door, "I suggest you finish with your preparation for this evening's dinner party. Mr. Savage should be here shortly."

Catherine couldn't remember a single time her *father* had talked so sternly with her. To hear Mr. Trumble use such an authoritative tone left her speechless. Mouth agape, she just stood there watching him exit the room, and several minutes passed before she was able to gather her composure and get her feet to move. She had already been dreading this evening's activities, and with the news Mr. Trumble had just given her, she dreaded spending the time with T.J. even more. Having an amateur stumbling along behind her when she was investigating a case was bad enough. But when that person was someone she'd rather not be with, it made her job that much more difficult. If she didn't have to waste time explaining everything to him, she'd surely have to listen to his sermons!

The clock on the mantel struck seven and brought Catherine's attention to the fact that she wasn't ready to leave for the party as yet. She'd gotten dressed, all except for her shoes, but she hadn't fixed her hair, and the chiming of the clock warned her T.J. would be there any moment. Exhaling an irritable groan, she headed out the door of the study and down the hall to her room, wishing some perfectly timed emergency would present itself and give her the excuse she needed not to have to spend the evening in T.J.'s company. The thought had barely crossed her mind when the sound of the brass knocker tapping against its plate filled the foyer and brought her to a halt as she listened to Mr. Trumble cross the tiled floor and open the door.

"Good evening, Mr. Savage," she heard him say, and she grimaced despite the quickening of her pulse.

"Mr. Trumble," T.J. responded, and Catherine's heart thumped as she fought the temptation to go the top of the stairs and steal a look at him. "I pray I'm not too early."

"No, sir. You're right on time. Come in and warm yourself by the fire while I tell Miss Chase you're here."

The announcement sent her racing off, and by the time Mr. Trumble appeared in the open doorway of her room, Catherine had already pulled the long strands of strawberry-blond hair high upon her head and had secured them there with pearl-tipped pins.

"Excuse me, miss," he politely said, "but Mr. Savage is waiting in the parlor for you."

"Tell him I'll be down shortly," she instructed, hoping to sound totally at ease, when in truth she was as nervous as the first time she'd been told he was waiting in the parlor for her.

"Very good, miss," Mr. Trumble replied with a curt bow, his gaze dropping to the stockinged toes he saw sticking out from under the hem of her satin skirt. Straightening up again, he cleared his throat and waited for her to look at him. Once she had, he nodded at her feet.

Following his direction, Catherine instantly realized what he meant. "Don't worry," she promised, turning back to finish up with her hair. "I won't forget."

"Yes, miss," he skeptically agreed as he turned and disappeared from sight.

Rising, Catherine stepped back to better appraise the overall result of her work in the mirror. Of the few fancy gowns she owned, she liked the green satin the best simply because of its modest neckline and absence of furbelows. The tight-fitting bodice showed off her slender waist, but the crinoline petticoats masked her long, slim legs and narrow hips, something of which she approved. It wasn't that she hoped to disguise her curves from her escort for the evening—she couldn't hide something he'd already seen—but the less she showed him, the more comfortable she'd feel.

Picking up the silk rose from the dressing table, she secured the hair ornament in place with a pin, lifted her mother's strand of pearls from the jewelry box and fastened them around her neck, and reached for her fan. Unfolding it, she fluttered it beneath her chin as she gave herself one more look in the mirror.

A shy smile moved the corners of her mouth while she stared, recalling T.J.'s claim that she was beautiful. She didn't agree, but it was nice to know someone thought so . . . even if it was a man she was trying very hard to hate. Taking a deep breath, she squared her shoulders, fluffed up her curls, and started for the door, coming to an abrupt halt once she remembered her shoes. She was in for a long night.

The sound of T.J.'s warm laughter floated up to greet her, and she paused at the bottom of the stairs to collect her wits. It reminded her of another time not so long ago when she had chosen to show him the strong side of her character by marching out the front door of his home as though being there made no difference to her. And it would have worked if she hadn't run into his housekeeper there in the foyer. The sight of the woman, staring openmouthed and confused, had clearly shown Catherine the error in her thinking, and she had barely left the house before she regretted being so bold.

"Too late to worry about that," she mumbled as she descended the stairs and braced herself for the evening ahead.

At the doorway of the parlor, Catherine halted. Her hands were shaking and if she didn't sit down once she entered the room, she was sure T.J. would hear her knees knocking. In all her young life she had never had anyone affect her this way, and dealing with it promised to present her the greatest feat so far. One smirk, one taunting word from him, and she'd crumble. God! How could she have been so foolish?

The rustle of satin skirts and the flash of green in the doorway stole the attention of both T.J. and Mr. Trumble as they stood near the fireplace having a private discussion. A long silence followed while the men each silently studied the beauty who had graced them with her presence. Gone was the studious, book-smart Catherine Chase, who, no matter what she said or did, expressed by the mere look in her eyes that she was no simple woman to be taken for granted when it came to the matter of intellect. In her place was a beautiful, soft, alluring creature who, without a word or blink of the eye, took their breath away. T.J., however, knew that underneath the layers of satin and lace was the soul of a woman waiting to be explored. His only hope was that she would allow him to be the one to set it free.

As hard as she tried, Catherine couldn't pull her gaze away from the handsome man staring back at her. She wanted to believe the separation she had imposed upon them was the reason why he appeared even more attractive than ever . . . in an untamed way. The cut of his black coat hugged his wide shoulders and trim waist. The gray pin-striped trousers accentuated his narrow hips and long legs. Suntanned hands contrasted with the whiteness of the cuffs on his shirtsleeves, and his raven-black hair, full and rakishly combed, fell softly against his brow, while dark eyes looked deeply into hers. No smile curved his lips, yet even so, Catherine felt as if he mocked her with his intense stare, and only then could she turn away from him.

"I don't imagine we'll be very late, Mr. Trumble," she told the man standing closest to her. "You know how tedious I find these sort of affairs."

"Yes, miss," he replied, waiting until she glanced away to grin at T.J. "Perhaps tonight will be different."

She sighed. "I doubt it," she said, missing the suggestive tone in his words or the way T.J. fought the smile tugging at his mouth. If she hadn't, she would have questioned the topic of their conversation before she interrupted them. "Shall we go?" she asked, glancing briefly at her escort for the evening.

T.J. nodded, leaned to set aside the goblet of wine he'd been drinking, and followed Catherine from the room. Once the three of them were in the foyer, he thanked Mr. Trumble for his hospitality, donned his top hat, cape, and gloves, and picked up the cane he'd laid on the credenza, while the servant helped Catherine on with her cloak and handed her a white fur muff.

"You look exceptionally beautiful tonight, Miss Chase," the old man murmured as he watched her shove her hands deep into the fluffy rabbit-fur cylinder.

"Thank you, Mr. Trumble," she politely replied, then added for T.J.'s benefit, "I hope Aaron will think so."

The remark did not go unheard by the one for whom it was intended, but rather than give the obvious reaction she had wanted to evoke from him, T.J. smiled as he reached around her for the doorknob and whispered close to her ear, "If he doesn't, he's either blind or a fool."

The warmth of his breath falling against her cheek made Catherine shiver. Hit with the chilly night air once they'd stepped outside, she continued to tremble even after they had climbed into the brougham and had traveled down the avenue for several blocks. Praying her salvation would come once they arrived at the Courtland manor and she could lose herself among the many other guests, Catherine readjusted the cape around her shoulders, buried her hands in the fur muff on her lap, and turned her concentration on the scenery in the hope her companion wouldn't notice her discomfort.

"Are you cold?" he asked only a second or two later, and Catherine cringed inside.

"No," she answered brusquely.

T.J. raised a brow. "Then why are you shaking?"

"I'm excited about the dinner party," she lied, refusing to look at him.

T.J. grinned. "Oh?" he challenged. "When did you change your mind?"

Confused, she frowned and looked askance at him. "About what?"

"About the dinner party. I was there when you read the invitation. Remember? You told me you didn't like going to Mrs. Courtland's because she's always trying to match you up with her son. Have you decided differently?" A devilish smile curled his mouth. "Or is it because I'm going with you this time?"

Catherine took a quick breath to respond, realized he was toying with her, and snapped her mouth shut instead as she turned her head away and stared out at the lights of London's streets. Several minutes passed during which time she debated being honest with him or saying nothing at all for the duration of the evening. The latter, she concluded, would be impossible simply because he wouldn't allow it, and she decided that perhaps she should get in the first word before he had the chance to say something that would have her all jittery again. It was what she wanted to do—to tell him that after tonight, they should part company for good—but once she opened her mouth, she couldn't bring herself to say the words.

T.J. had sat by quietly watching her and wondering what was going through her head. He could only guess what her real feelings were about him, since Mr. Trumble hadn't been of much help when he'd asked, and instinct told him that she was full of doubt . . . about him and about herself. He wanted to believe she cared, that because she was a lady, she regretted having given herself to him in a moment of heated passion, and that her doubt came from the possibility that lust had ruled her head instead of her heart. What he refused to accept the last time they spoke was her attitude and how she'd made it sound as if their affair had been an accident. Catherine Chase never did anything by accident, and that included allowing him to make love to her. Yet, aside from all of that, he was torn between offering his solution now or after the party. If her answer wasn't what he hoped for, he'd need the time and the privacy to convince her otherwise. With an inward sigh, he decided to wait. Perhaps later she'd be more at ease with him *and* willing to listen.

Other than the short conversation he'd had with Lewis about the Courtlands, T.J. hadn't had the presence of mind to do some investigative work on the family before tonight, something he usually did to prepare himself for any problems that might arise during the course of an evening. He supposed he'd let it slip because of Catherine and her personal knowledge of mother and son, but now—as their cab turned down the lane leading to an elegant two-story brick mansion—he was regretting his oversight. Instinct could sometimes make a fool of a person, but his was telling him that he was in for a surprise before the night came to an end, and it made him a little uncomfortable.

"Have you decided how to explain my presence?" he asked Catherine as their rig rolled to stop at the end of the long walkway.

"I won't have to," she replied, wishing she didn't have to

touch his hand as he helped her from the cab. "Aaron said he'd take care of it."

"Oh?" T.J. questioned, frowning. "When did you speak with him about me?"

"Yesterday," she answered, glancing around and wondering why there were no other guests arriving with them. "We had lunch together."

Struck with a twinge of jealousy, T.J. fidgeted with the edge of his cape, hoping Catherine wouldn't notice how her announcement had bothered him. "I thought you didn't like Mr. Courtland."

"I never said that," she replied, starting for the front steps. "Aaron is a very nice, very handsome man. Any woman would be honored if he showed an interest in her. What I don't like is how his mother is always trying to push us together."

"And why is that?" he asked, feeling a little better with the idea that perhaps *her* interests were centered around someone else . . . and more specifically, him.

Pausing just outside the front door, Catherine turned to look at him. "Can't you guess? I'm not the type to get married. I thought you'd figured that out by now. What man could tolerate me? Or better said, what man could possibly change my mind about settling down and acting like a wife?" She sighed, shook her head, and glanced away. "I'm only here tonight because you insisted we come. I've never been one to socialize, and I could never organize and execute a dinner party merely for the sake of being cordial. That sort of thing doesn't interest me. I'd rather spend my time catching criminals." She cast him a look that so much as told him he was included in the group before the sound of the door opening pulled her attention away.

"Good evening, Harold," she greeted sweetly as she stepped past the butler and into the foyer.

"Good evening, Miss Chase," the man returned. "It's been a while."

"Yes, it has. I hope you've been well," she commented while allowing the servant to take her wrap and muff.

A brief frown flitted across his brow. "Yes, miss, I

have," he said, puzzled by the inquiry. Miss Chase hardly ever spoke more than two words to him and she'd never been concerned about his health. "Mrs. Courtland and Mr. Aaron are in the parlor," he said once he'd taken T.J.'s things as well and stood with them draped over his arm. "Shall I announce you?"

"No need, Harold," came the cheerful command from a short ways away. "I can do that myself. Hello, Catherine." Smiling, Aaron reached for her hand and placed a light kiss on the back of it. "You look lovely."

"Thank you, Aaron," Catherine returned, pleased—for T.J.'s sake—that Aaron showed the formal affection.

T.J. hardly noticed the gesture made by his host. He was more caught up in the odd feeling he had about the man. There was something vaguely familiar about him, and T.J. was having a difficult time trying to figure out what it was. The sensation grew stronger once Aaron looked at him, his green eyes sparkling as if they held a secret, and his mouth curled in a mocking smile.

"Hello, T. J. Savage," he said, draping Catherine's hand over his left arm while he held out his other hand toward his guest in anticipation of a warm response. "It's been a long time. Or are you having trouble remembering who I am?"

"You *know* each other?" Catherine gasped, certain she had just lost her only ally.

"Yes." Aaron grinned, his gaze locked on T.J. "But he, obviously, hasn't quite placed me."

Hesitant, yet sensing no threat from the other, T.J. reached out and shook Aaron's hand. "Perhaps you'll enlighten me," he encouraged.

Aaron laughed good-naturedly, and the sound of his voice sparked a memory for T.J. Frowning, he squinted his eyes and leaned closer as he studied the man's face for a clue. Then it hit him. Standing before him was a childhood friend he hadn't seen in years.

"I'll be damned. Arnie?"

"The very same," Aaron admitted with a devilish smirk as he let go of Catherine and grabbed T.J. in a rough but meaningful hug.

Laughing once they broke the embrace, T.J. stepped back and gave Aaron a quick once-over. "Not quite," he disagreed, grinning. "The last time I saw you, you were a dirty little street urchin with big ideas." He shook his head. "I'd say from the looks of things, they weren't just ideas. What happened? Did a rich uncle die and leave you all his money?"

"I was about to ask you the same thing, friend," Aaron chaffed. "You've obviously come a long way from the back streets of London."

"In more ways than one," T.J. chuckled.

Turning, Aaron gently placed his hand to the back of Catherine's elbow and nodded toward the parlor. "We've got a lot to talk about, and I want her to hear every detail. But it would be rude of me to make Catherine stand the entire time. Come. I'll reintroduce you to my mother."

The mention of Mrs. Courtland brought a vivid picture to T.J.'s mind, and for a second he wondered how much Catherine knew about the pair's earlier days. Deciding to let Arnie tell her as much as he wanted her to know, T.J. fell into step behind them and followed the couple into the parlor. The instant his gaze fell upon the woman who waited for them there, he was reminded of the good times and the bad that growing up near the wharf had brought him. Arnie's mother still wore too much makeup, still had flaming red hair, and she was just as plump as he remembered her. She looked older, but the warmth he saw shining in her blue eyes when she glanced up and smiled at him told him that the goodness in her soul hadn't changed, either.

T.J. had probably been only ten or so the last time he'd seen her, and his friendship with Arnie had only lasted a couple of years, but he still remembered how kind-hearted and friendly Mrs. Courtland had been to him . . . especially after T.J.'s mother had died. But times had been tough back then, and rather than burden the woman with an extra mouth to feed, T.J. had set off on his own. Things might have turned out a little differently if he'd stayed, but he honestly had no regrets.

"Thomas," Edith Courtland cooed as she came to her feet and held out her arms. "Let me give you a hug."

"Thomas?" Catherine echoed with a frown as she watched T.J. and the woman embrace. "His name is Thomas?"

"Thomas Jefferson Savage to be exact," Aaron enthusiastically supplied, his eyes gleaming with mischief as he escorted Catherine to one of the wing chairs and waited for her to sit down before offering her a glass of port. "He always hated the name. That's why he chose to use his initials. You mean he never told you?" he mocked, glancing at his friend with an impish wrinkle in his brow.

"I never asked," Catherine murmured, then, "Why did you hate it, T.J.? Mr. Jefferson was a United States President."

"It's Arnie's story. Let him tell it." T.J. grinned with a shake of his head as he took a seat next to Edith on the settee.

Pouring another glass of port, Aaron crossed the room and handed it to his friend. "He hated it because it was always getting him into fights as a boy," Aaron began, picking up his own glass and walking back to sit down near Catherine. "The English are very unforgiving sorts, especially after having lost two wars to the Americans, and being reminded of it in any way always provoked a strong reaction . . . and most didn't care who did the reminding. It never bothered me, however," he declared, raising the glass to his lips and taking a sip.

"Of course not," T.J. interjected. "You weren't the one getting his head bashed in."

"If his mother had known what trouble it would cause," Edith assured, "she wouldn't have given it to him. Allison loved her son, and she dreamed of great things for him . . . she dreamed of taking him to America where she'd heard people weren't poor. Of course, that's all it ever was . . . a dream. So when Thomas was born, she did what she thought was the next best thing. She named her son after Mr. Jefferson."

"But why did she pick him? Why not George Washington

or Patrick Henry or someone like that?" Catherine asked, truly interested.

"Because she saw a painting of him one time, and she thought he was the handsomest man she'd ever seen. And, of course, she knew her son would be just as handsome."

Aaron raised one hand and made a circling motion with his finger. "Give us your profile, Thomas, old friend. Let Catherine and I decide if there's any resemblance."

"Aaron!" his mother snapped. "Stop teasing or I'll tell him whom you're named after."

"Why everyone knows that, Mother," Aaron claimed. "I'm named for the brother of Moses, first high priest of the Hebrews."

"Piffle!" Edith exclaimed, her blue eyes gleaming. "I named you after Aaron Burr."

T.J. had just taken a sip of his port and nearly choked on it. "Aaron Burr?" he questioned, a smile quivering his mouth. "Well, we all know what happened to him." He took another drink, while he stared over the rim of the glass at his friend, and then added, "You always did enjoy goading someone into an argument. Must be something in the name."

"Perhaps," Aaron agreed, truly not bothered by the drollery. "But at least I never got myself killed because of it."

"You came close a couple of times," T.J. reminded him. "Are you telling me you've changed since then?"

A slow smile worked the edges of Aaron's mouth. "No," he finally admitted. "I'm just more discreet about it."

The conversation turned to a string of detailed adventures the pair had had as youths, and Catherine listened intently. Aaron had never taken the time to tell her anything about his past, and she had always assumed it was because he wasn't proud of it. But the more the two men talked and laughed, the more Catherine realized that wasn't true at all. Apparently he'd guessed she wouldn't be interested in hearing how the bastard child of a prostitute fared during those times, and he couldn't have been more wrong. There was a wild kind of freedom and love for life hidden under the surface of what T.J. and Aaron said they had shared, and Catherine found herself a little envious of them. And she came to have a new respect for both men. Neither one of them had allowed their poor beginnings to stand in their way. They had risen up, grabbed what they wanted, and had never looked back. Perhaps their manners weren't as polished as those of men born to wealth, but they were gentlemen just the same.

That thought made her smile suddenly. There were probably a few aristocratic friends of hers who felt her manners lacked a little something, too. After all, wasn't she always forgetting her shoes? And didn't she choose to track down murderers rather than take a husband and raise a brood of children? She hated the opera and attending fancy social functions, and if it hadn't been for T. J. Savage, she still wouldn't know what romance was all about.

A hot blush rose in her cheeks, and even though the two men continued to watch each other as they spoke, and therefore missed the pinkening of her face, Catherine unfolded her fan and fluttered it beneath her chin, hoping her flesh would cool before either of them noticed. She doubted Aaron would understand the reason she suddenly found herself uncomfortable in T.J.'s presence, but T.J. would know the second he looked at her.

She was saved from having to explain to anyone in that moment when the butler appeared in the doorway and announced that some of the other guests had arrived. Instructing Harold to show them into the parlor, Aaron set aside his glass and stood, ready to greet the newcomers. A second or two later, four couples joined the group and introductions were made. Within the next half hour, a party of six made an appearance, and while Catherine knew everyone, T.J. was meeting them for the first time. What surprised her was that even though the other guests hadn't personally met him, everyone had heard of T.J., of his wealth, and that next to Aaron, he was probably the most eligible bachelor in London. A strange feeling had shot through her when the comment was made, and while Aaron joked that with the succession of beautiful women certain to be following T.J. around, there was no need for T.J. to ever settle down, Catherine wondered if it were true. She also wondered why it mattered to her one way or the other.

"They haven't seen each other since they were little boys," Edith remarked as she walked alongside Catherine and led the way into the dining room, "and it's as if it were only yesterday. I must say, however, that Thomas doesn't appear to be as bitter as he was the last time we saw him."

"Bitter?" Catherine repeated. "About what?"

"His mother's death. He was only nine or ten when she died, and it was hard for him to accept the fact. He blamed her for leaving him alone, and to be truthful, my dear," she added in a whisper as she glanced over her shoulder to make sure T.J. wasn't close enough to hear, "it wouldn't surprise me to learn that he still doesn't trust women."

"Because his mother died and left him alone?" Catherine couldn't believe a grown man would feel that way.

"She was all he had, and after she died, he was left to fend for himself. I wanted him to stay with us, but he wouldn't. He was bound and determined to prove he could take care of himself."

"Well, he's certainly done that," Catherine replied.

"Yes, he has," Edith agreed, chuckling. "You're a very lucky woman."

The statement was slow to sink in, but once it had, Catherine turned a frown on the woman at her side. "Lucky?" she echoed. "What do you mean?"

"Oh, you don't have to pretend with me, my dear," Edith claimed as she reached for Catherine's hand and patted the back of it. "I was wishing you'd fall in love with my Aaron, but Thomas has always been like a son to me. So I can't really complain."

Catherine started to ask her to explain, but wasn't allowed the chance when those behind them caught up and crowded into the dining room. Catherine was escorted to the right end of the long table where Aaron helped her with her chair, while T.J. followed Edith to the opposite end and took his place next to the hostess. The others filled up the rest of the vacant chairs, and once everyone was seated,

Catherine realized the only way she'd be able to see T.J.—providing she wanted to, of course—was to lean forward and look past the guests who separated her from him. An hour ago she would have considered herself fortunate not to have to meet his eyes, but now . . .

A lavish dinner was served, and everyone enjoyed the meal, the company, and the conversation as it seemed T.J. and Aaron dominated the latter of the three. They freely discussed their humble beginnings and how they lost track of each other after T.J.'s mother succumbed to a fever and he set out to conquer the world. He told of living in Australia, South Africa, and Brazil before he made his fortune and decided to return home to England. The women around the table saw him as a charming and handsome adventurer, while their husbands saw him as an astute businessman, someone they wanted to get to know a little better. Only Catherine noticed how cunningly he turned the discussion to the recent museum robbery by stating how very much he'd love to own a Rembrandt at any price.

"Well, maybe Catherine can help you out," Aaron said, a wide grin making his green eyes sparkle.

"Me?" she returned as she set down her fork and pushed away the last few bites of dessert on her plate. "How can I help?"

"Aren't you working on the British Museum case?" He watched her nod her head, then daintily blot the corner of her mouth with her napkin before he explained. "I would imagine that whoever has them would be very eager to sell them if he thought you were getting too close. You do have a reputation for solving difficult crimes, Catherine. The man would be a fool to hang on to them for too long."

"But surely you're not suggesting that Mr. Savage would buy stolen property?" Arnold Greenwood proposed, his lined face wrinkling into an unflattering frown. He simply couldn't believe Aaron would assume such a thing about his childhood friend and a man Arnold had just now come to respect for his hard work and honesty.

"I don't know," Aaron replied, casting T.J. a questioning look. "Would you?"

In the short while the two of them had gotten reacquainted, T.J. had realized Arnie Courtland hadn't changed a bit since the last time they were together. He was still mischievous and he always loved a good prank at someone else's expense. With that in mind and not caring if anyone else at the table would misinterpret his reply should he play along, T.J. decided to throw it back Arnie's way.

"Are you asking because you know someone who's anxious to sell? You, perhaps?"

Several of the women gasped. Nearly all of the men stared in wide-eyed nervousness, certain Mr. Savage had just insulted their host. Catherine, however, had heard the underlying mirth twisting the seriousness of T.J.'s questions, and she wondered which of the two friends would win this match of wits.

"Really, T.J.," Aaron playfully scolded. "If I had a Rembrandt or a da Vinci, do you honestly think I'd be willing to sell them?"

T.J. shrugged a shoulder and lifted his wineglass. But before he took a drink, he parried, "If you were low on funds . . . yes."

Aaron waved a hand to indicate their surroundings. "Come now, T.J.," he challenged. "Does it look that way to you?"

Never one to let his friend have the last word, T.J. studied the room for a moment, analyzed its worth, then countered, "I'd be foolish to say no, Arnie. You always were good at putting up a front. Appearances can oftentimes be misleading."

For some inexplicable reason Arnold Greenwood felt the need to switch sides and defend the man he'd known for close to ten years. "Mr. Savage, I assure you that Aaron Courtland has never done a dishonest deed in his life." The man's pale brown eyes grew darker with the frown that dipped his brows downward, unable to fathom the reason why the man he addressed and the one he had exonerated suddenly burst into laughter.

"My apologies, Arnold," Aaron quickly atoned, once he'd gained control of his manners and had realized that no one at the table other than his mother knew the reason why the man's remark had struck a humorous chord. "T.J. and I were childhood friends. He knew me when I had a penchant for testing authority, if you will. Not unlike most boys my age, I'm sure. We didn't mean to laugh, but saying that I've never done a dishonest thing in my life is stretching the truth a bit." He glanced at T.J. and winked. "And I apologize to everyone for leading you on. We were only playing. Weren't we, T.J.?"

"For the most part," T.J. agreed, waiting for Aaron to look questioningly at him. "I truly would like to own a Rembrandt."

This time the entire group of guests joined together in a hearty round of laughter, easing the tension that had grown very thick in the course of a few minutes. Catherine too found the humor in their playful bantering, but despite the smile curling her lips, she also knew T.J.'s clandestine reason for restating an earlier desire. He was hoping that someone within the group would pass the word along, and that it would reach the right ears. Catherine hoped so, too. Deep in her heart she wanted the matter put behind them. She wanted to clear T.J.'s name. She wanted all doubt she had about him to vanish so that she might look differently at him, so that she might listen to her heart instead of her head.

CHAPTER 13

"She's a very beautiful woman," Aaron declared as he and T.J. stood off to one side of the library observing Catherine with his mother. The other guests had bid their farewells and had gone, and Catherine and T.J. would have left too, if Aaron hadn't insisted they stay a while longer. He always enjoyed Catherine's company, but having found his best friend again after such a long absence prompted Aaron to offer the couple one more drink before the evening came to a close. Catherine had no objection, but T.J. seemed reluctant . . . as if he had other plans and wanted to execute them as soon as possible. Aaron didn't ask, but he assumed by the look on T.J.'s face every time the man's eyes found Catherine that his plans concerned her.

"Beautiful and stubborn," T.J. finally replied as he watched her pick a book from the shelf and leaf through it.

"Most women are," Aaron comforted. "What makes Catherine different is her intelligence. She's too smart for her own good."

"I'll have to agree with that," T.J. added before taking a sip of his wine.

Aaron cocked a brow. "Do I hear a twinge of sarcasm in your voice, old friend?"

T.J. hadn't meant to let his feelings be known and if it had been anyone else, he would have made light of the comment. But this wasn't just anyone else. This was Arnie, the best friend T.J. had ever had as a boy. "Not sarcasm, really," he admitted, keeping his voice low. "'Concern' would be a better word."

"Oh? Concern for what?"

The only person in whom T.J. could confide was Lewis Rhomberg, and even though they had gone over the topic of Catherine Chase time and time again, T.J. had never come away from their discussions feeling good about the decisions they'd made. Lewis thought as a detective would think—about angles, clues, and possibilities—not as a man with feelings for the foolhardy little risk-taker. "What she doesn't know won't hurt her," was how he viewed Catherine Chase. T.J. didn't, and he doubted Aaron would agree with Lewis's deduction, either. What Catherine didn't know, she dug after until she found it. And that included the truth behind how her father had died.

"T.J.?"

Arnie's voice broke into T.J.'s thoughts, and he smiled halfheartedly. They had been close friends at one time, sharing their deepest, darkest secrets with one another. But that had been a long time ago and a lot had happened since then. Arnie seemed not to have changed all that much and T.J. really needed that trust and friendship at the moment, but . . .

Recognizing T.J.'s reluctance to answer and concluding it had to do with Catherine being so close by, Aaron nudged his friend with an elbow, waited for T.J. to look up, then nodded toward the door. If T.J. wanted privacy, he'd give it to him. Leading the way, he guided his companion out into the hallway, past the dining room, then into the study, closing the door behind them once they were inside.

"If you're worried, I guarantee you nothing you tell me will leave this room," Aaron promised, doubling up a fist and laying it against the left side of his chest the way two young boys always did whenever they made a pledge.

T.J. chuckled and mimicked the gesture before sitting down in the chair next to Aaron's desk. Even now his friend had a way of making the worst of problems look minor, and T.J. was glad they had found each other again.

"She told me the two of you had lunch together," T.J.

began, relaxing back and crossing one ankle to his knee, "and that she told you I'd be accompanying her tonight. Did she tell you anything else about me?"

"Such as?" Aaron asked, choosing to stand by the hearth, one shoulder leaning against its stone face.

"How we met, for instance."

Aaron thought for a moment. "I honestly don't remember if she did. The second she said your name . . ." He smiled fondly. "Well, I was swept away in memories and didn't really listen to her, I'm afraid." He sensed the seriousness of their discussion and frowned. "Why? How did you meet?"

T.J. brushed a piece of lint off the sleeve of his jacket after setting his wine goblet on the desk. "I was trying to make a purchase of some stolen artwork. The details are a little involved, but the gist of it is that she got it into her head that I wasn't there as a buyer but as one of the thieves."

Aaron chuckled. "If you were still ten years old, I'd have to say Catherine had good reason to think so."

"Hmmm," T.J. murmured. "And if I had known then that a person's past has a way of following him around, I might not have been so quick to steal."

"T.J., you and I both know why you stole. If you hadn't, you would have starved to death. No one, including Catherine, could blame you for that."

"Oh, I don't think she blames the boy . . . just the man." Weary of a sudden, he rose and went to the window to look out as he explained in detail the events that had brought them to this moment, carefully omitting the intimacy they had shared and his connection with Lewis Rhomberg. Arnie didn't need to know everything.

"There's something else," Aaron suggested, once T.J. had paused in his story-telling and appeared unwilling to continue. "I see no reason for concern in what you've said so far. It won't take her long to prove you're not one of the thieves. So what has you frowning like a condemned man?"

T.J. remained silent for a moment longer. Then, with a tired sigh, he faced his companion. "She has reason to believe her father's death wasn't an accident, and she plans to investigate."

Aaron's complexion paled a bit. "What?"

"She just recently found a letter from a chemist threatening her father if he continued to refuse his help. That, along with a few oddities on how he died, has her looking into it."

"And you're afraid that if it's true, she could get herself into a lot of trouble," Aaron finished.

"Trouble?" T.J. said. "I'm afraid she'll get herself killed. You know Catherine. She never thinks about herself when she's working on a case. She just dives blindly into it and won't stop until it's solved." His scowl deepened. "And if this chemist murdered her father, he wouldn't think twice about killing her."

"So what are you planning to do?"

"I'm planning to stay one step ahead of her."

Aaron shook his head. "I'm not following."

"I'm going to do a little investigating of my own . . . without her knowing it. In fact, I'm leaving tomorrow for Paris."

"Paris? What's in Paris?"

"The chemist, I hope."

Reaching for his glass of wine, T.J.'s expression turned thoughtful and several moments passed before either of them said anything. T.J. was the first to speak.

"Swear to me you won't breathe a word of this to Catherine or your mother."

"Of course not," Aaron assured him. "But T.J. . . . "

Sensing what his friend had difficulty saying, T.J. smiled. "Don't worry. I'll be careful. I've been in situations much rougher than this."

"I know that. And I'm not really worried. I suppose I'd just like it better if you weren't going there alone. Safety in numbers, and all that." He sighed and raised his brows. "You are going alone, aren't you?"

T.J. grinned. "Yes. Unless you'd like to go with me."

Aaron snorted. "Twenty years ago you couldn't have stopped me. But I'm a respectable businessman now with investments to take care of. I'm still struggling for my wealth, T.J., my boy. If I had money stashed away as you do, I'd say to hell with business and pack a few clothes. Ah, I wouldn't even pack some clothes. I'd buy new ones in Paris." He laughed, then grew serious again. "Just don't get yourself killed. Catherine would never forgive you for it."

Finishing off his wine, T.J. set the empty glass down. "I really would like to believe that, but I can't. If anything, she'd be glad to be rid of me."

A lopsided grin parted Aaron's lips. "Are you trying to get some sympathy? Because if you are, you won't get it from me."

Realizing how it sounded and that there was a strong chance Arnie cared more for Catherine than she assumed he did, T.J. glanced briefly at his friend, smiled sheepishly, and looked away. "She means a lot to you, doesn't she?"

"As a friend, yes," Aaron replied, drinking the last of his wine and setting the glass on the mantel. "Mother would like it to be more, but it isn't. And it probably never will be. Besides, Catherine's interested in someone else now." He laughed at the startled look T.J. gave him. "I'm talking about you, Thomas Jefferson Savage. Are you so blind you haven't realized it yet that that woman is in love with you?"

T.J. might have believed it if he'd heard the confession coming from Catherine's lips. As it was, he could only smile in return and wish it were true.

Aaron recognized the doubt in his friend's dark eyes. "I've known her longer than you have, T.J. If what I see in her face whenever she talks of you or watches you when you're not looking . . . well, if it isn't love, I don't know what it is." He chuckled and shook his head. "The idea doesn't scare you, does it?"

Feeling a warmth rise in his cheeks, T.J. grinned. "I'm sure it scares her," he predicted. "She thinks I'm a thief. I'm the sort of person she puts in jail. To fall in love with someone like that would go against everything she believes in."

"Well, you're not a thief, old friend," Aaron replied, pushing away from the stone mantel and crossing to where

T.J. stood. "And as soon as she proves that to herself . . . well . . ." He raised a hand and cupped it behind his ear as if he were listening to something in the distance. "Are those wedding bells I hear?" he mocked, draping an arm across his companion's shoulders.

Giving in to the gaiety of the moment, T.J. laughed as he allowed his friend to pull him toward the door. But the laughter was quick to die when Aaron posed the next question.

"So, are you going to ask her tonight?"

"Ask her what?" T.J. queried, jerking away from him.

"To marry you, of course. *You* might have trouble seeing, but I don't. You're as mad about her as she is about you, so why wait?"

T.J. was about to respond when a soft rap on the door interrupted, followed by Edith's tiny voice asking if there was trouble.

"Now why do you suppose my mother thinks of trouble and instinctively connects it to us?" Aaron joked as he opened the door and grinned back at the two women on the other side.

"Because they go hand in hand, Aaron," his mother scoffed. "Just because you're grown men doesn't mean the two of you still can't be up to no good."

"Don't listen to her, Catherine," Aaron begged. "She never has understood that a man sometimes has to tell a white lie to succeed in business. That's not true at all in T.J.'s case, however. You can't lie about a fistful of diamonds." He grabbed T.J. around the neck again. "And speaking of diamonds—"

Knowing exactly what Aaron was about to say, T.J. cut in before he had the chance to finish. "Edith, I want to thank you for a lovely evening, but it's getting late, and Catherine and I really should be going."

"Why, thank you, Thomas," she politely replied as she gave her son a disapproving scowl that prompted him to release his hold and to keep any further comments to himself. "Perhaps we can do this again soon."

"You have my word." T.J. smiled back at her.

They said their good-byes at the front door, and while Aaron and his mother stood at the threshold watching, T.J. helped Catherine into the livery cab, climbed in beside her, and waved one last time to the couple silhouetted by the light in the foyer. They rode several blocks before T.J. drew up the courage to speak.

"Catherine," he began, "I know it's late and you're probably tired, but I was wondering if we could go somewhere private to talk."

The evening hadn't gone at all the way Catherine had expected it to go. She'd actually enjoyed herself, and while listening to T.J. and Aaron reminisce about their childhood days, she had softened her opinion of T.J. That, along with the extra glass of wine she'd had, made her wish the night wouldn't end just yet. Now T.J. was giving her the excuse not to let it.

"We can go to the town house if you'd like," she offered. "I'm sure Mr. Trumble has gone to bed by now. But even so, if I tell him, he'll leave us alone."

"That would be fine," he answered, a soft smile parting his lips as he studied the delicate profile she unknowingly gave him. He couldn't be sure if it was the wine she'd had that made her relax or if something about the evening had caused her to change her mind about him, but whatever the reason, the angry little lines at the corners of her eyes were gone and her mouth was tilted in a vague smile. Perhaps he was reading too much into it, but if Aaron was right, Catherine just might be receptive to his proposal, and if she was, his life was about to make a change for the better.

They rode the rest of the distance to the town house in silence. Catherine, feeling the effects of the wine, was simply enjoying the fresh night air and the company she kept. T.J. was lost in thought as he vigorously debated just how he should go about wording his offer. He had very nearly made up his mind when the rig rolled to a stop, but the moment he stepped down and turned back to assist Catherine, each and every idea he'd had disappeared. The mere presence of her, the touch of her gloved hand in his, and the scent of her perfume undermined his confidence and left him feeling doubtful. Even a twinge of fear was beginning to wedge its way into his thoughts. What if she refused? Would he be able to walk away with dignity? Could he accept her decision and be content with it? A sadness came over him as he opened the front door and waited for her to step inside. He could accept it. But he would never be content.

Shedding her cloak and muff, Catherine kicked off her shoes while she waited for T.J. to hang his cape on the hall tree. With a smile, she nodded toward the parlor and led the way. Once they were inside, she motioned for him to take a seat near the hearth and the warm blaze burning in it while she closed the door behind them.

"Would you care for a glass of sherry?" she asked, crossing to the decanter.

The only response T.J. could manage, while he stood beside his chair, was a slight nod of his head.

With two glasses in hand, she joined him by the fire, held out one for him to take, and then settled herself down, quite satisfied to spend the next few minutes watching the dancing flames. The last time she could remember feeling so comfortable in a man's presence was on Christmas Eve when she and her father shared a quiet moment together. A few weeks ago she wouldn't have dreamed something like this was possible ever again, and certainly not with T. J. Savage. But thanks to Aaron, she had come to know T.J. differently.

"I wonder who was more surprised tonight," she mused aloud, a soft smile curling her mouth. "You or me?"

T.J. sat stiffly in the chair. With all the adventures he'd had in his life, none of them had ever had him so ill at ease as he was just then. Smiling lamely when she glanced over at him, he raised his glass to his mouth and said nothing.

"You know, I like the name Thomas. It has a strong sound to it." She sighed dreamily, took a sip from her glass, and stared at the fire again. "My father never really cared for his name, either. Sterling Lloyd Chase," she recited, then laughed. "He said it always made him feel like a teapot."

The comment lessened some of T.J.'s anxiety. "I wish I could have met him."

"Oh, you'd have liked him," she guaranteed. "Most everyone did." Stretching out her legs, she wiggled the soreness from her toes. "I hate shoes."

T.J. smiled. "So I've noticed."

"I've never quite understood why we have to wear them . . . except when it's cold or rainy outside. But in the house . . ." She leaned back in her chair. "Papa never seemed to mind. But Mr. Trumble is always after me to put them on. I'm not sure why, really, except that perhaps he thinks it's more ladylike." She giggled, then added unexpectedly, "He'd die of apoplexy if he knew how unladylike I've been with you."

The statement seemed to rumble around inside her head for a while before she realized what she had said and to whom. With sudden clarity, she straightened in her chair, startled by her own audacity and the ease with which she had said it. Afraid to look at him, she sat stone-still and felt the hot blush rising in her cheeks. For four days she had avoided seeing T.J. simply because she had hoped never to have to discuss the topic with him, and here she was bringing it up herself as easily as if they were talking about the weather.

"Catherine."

The warmth of his deep voice tickled the flesh beneath her ear. Wishing she could take it back or better still just disappear, she raised the glass to her lips and ignored him.

"Catherine," he said again. "I know how that night has affected you, and that's why I wanted to talk to you before I went away."

No, you don't, she thought. *You haven't a clue as to how it's affected me. I can't sleep. I'm constantly thinking about you, and the idea of jumping off London Bridge has crossed my mind a time or two.* Suddenly the last of what he'd said registered in her brain.

"Where are you going?" she asked, turning her head to look at him. "For how long?"

"I have to leave London on business in the morning. I shouldn't be gone very long, but what I wanted to tell you can't wait another minute. I must know your answer before I leave."

His response calmed her a bit, but the reason he wanted to talk confused her. "My answer to what?"

Earlier while he had dressed for the party and calculated exactly how he would ask her, it had all seemed relatively simple. But now that the time was upon him, T.J. was having a difficult moment just opening his mouth and getting the words to come out. If only he could have spoken with Christian first . . .

"T.J.?"

He blinked, smiled crookedly, and set down his wineglass. He was on his own. "The other day . . . I tried to apologize for pushing you into doing something you wouldn't have done if you'd had the time to think about it," he began, finding it easier than he'd thought it would be once he got started. "But you denied me the chance. Instead of listening, you shut me off. In so many words you claimed that what happened between us wasn't all that important, that it had been a mistake, and that within a couple of days, you'd forget about it. A part of me was hoping that was true. Another part was afraid it would be, and if my pride hadn't gotten in the way that day, I would have stayed and had it out with you. But I didn't. I went home with the intention of not seeing you for any other reason than business."

Sighing, he stood and circled around behind his chair where he paused and laid one hand on its back. "And it worked . . . for about ten minutes. Suddenly the thought of being separated from you started eating away at me. I couldn't explain it at first. Nor could I explain why you had reacted the way you had." He remembered his talk with Denton while the valet helped him dress, and he smiled. "Then a friend helped me to understand. With or without shoes, Catherine, you're a lady. And what we did that night wasn't something a lady would do . . . not to your way of thinking, anyway. You were ashamed of what you'd done and you thought that by sending me away, you'd get over it. Have you?"

When she refused to answer or to even look at him, he smiled to himself. Her silence was all the answer he needed.

"I know we have some problems to solve between us, but I have every confidence that they will be. And maybe I should wait until they're resolved before asking, but . . ." Drawn by the desire to touch her, T.J. moved away from his chair to hers and gently took her hand. When she looked up, he pulled her to her feet and tenderly brushed back a tendril of pale hair from her brow. "What I'm trying to say, Catherine, is that I want you to be my wife."

The color that had darkened her cheeks faded. She took a breath to speak, but no words came. Her heart beat erratically, and the sensation of being warm and cold at the same time washed over her. She knew she'd had more wine than she normally would, but not enough to affect her hearing. Yet, she couldn't quite believe her ears. Was there a chance she had imagined this?

"Catherine?"

His voice penetrated her fog. Closing her mouth, she straightened her back and pulled her hand from his. No, she wasn't dreaming. T.J. had truly asked her to marry him. But why?

Does it really matter? her romantic side asked.

Yes, it does, answered the logical, suspicious part of her mind. *T. J. Savage is a thief. He might not be a murderer, but he's definitely a thief. And a man who steals is by nature a liar. It's their only defense in covering up their actions. So what is his motive? What does he hope to gain by marrying me?*

Trembling slightly, she raised her glass to her lips, saw that it was empty, and crossed the room to the wine decanter. She poured herself a liberal amount, took a swallow, then faced him.

"Why?" she challenged, doubting his answer would be an honest one.

Despite the satin dress, pearl necklace, and the flower in

her hair, T.J. wasn't fooled by her appearance. Catherine Chase, the investigator, had returned, and he silently battled the urge to tell her why he was keeping secrets from her. However, the one time he'd agreed with something Lewis Rhomberg had told him came to mind, and he surrendered to the man's better judgment.

"Why?" he tossed back at her. "I don't know, Catherine. Why does a man ask a woman to marry him?"

One shoulder bobbed. "There can be a host of reasons, but I'm only interested in yours."

T.J. hadn't honestly expected her to melt and become uncharacteristically feminine after he'd proposed, but her accusing attitude annoyed him. "You certainly don't like yourself very much, do you?"

"What's that supposed to mean?"

"Well, you make it sound as though a man has to have an ulterior motive for wanting to marry you."

Catherine's eyes narrowed. "If any other man had asked, I wouldn't think a thing of it. With you, I'm suspicious."

T.J. released an irritable sigh. "I don't believe this. Are you trying to tell me that you think I'd offer marriage as a way of getting you to forget about a few stolen paintings?"

One side of Catherine's mouth moved. "You brought it up."

"Damn it," he exploded, turning his back. "Damn it!" Tempted just to leave without an explanation—she really didn't deserve one—he glanced at the door, twisted slightly, and shifted his eyes on her, then spun back around. "You are the most infuriating woman I have ever come across in my entire life, and if I had any sense at all"—his hand shot out to indicate the door—"I'd walk out that door and never look back. I'd go about my business as though the past few weeks had never happened, that you and I had never happened! I'd forget about the obstinate little chit whose life I saved—not once, but twice!—and I'd find someone else willing to settle down with me, a woman who wouldn't question why I asked her to marry me." At the brink of losing his temper and sorely tempted to throw something, he gritted his teeth, knotted up his fists, and waited for the sensation to pass.

With her head cocked to one side, her arms crossed in front of her, and one toe tapping softly on the rug beneath her, Catherine replied, "You said a lot, Mr. Savage, but you really didn't say anything at all. You still haven't answered my question. Why do you want to marry me?"

T.J.'s nostrils flared a little. "Aren't you smart enough to figure that out?"

Catherine smiled cynically. "Yes. I'm just waiting for you to admit it."

"Oh?" He raised a brow. "All right, then. If that's what you want—a confession—then I'll give it to you. I'm not really sure why, now, but a few days ago I was strongly attracted to you, and I let my passion have free rein. I made love to you, and at the time I thoroughly enjoyed it. You, however, didn't." He glared at her for a second, then looked away as he returned to his chair and sat down. "Now, being the gentleman that I am, I soon realized my responsibility." He turned his head and stared at her. "And the sacrifice; my freedom for a lifetime of misery." He saw how the last insult sparked the kind of reaction he wanted, and his mouth twisted into a sneer. "But honor first, I always say."

She drew a quick breath to defend herself, only to clamp her mouth shut again when T.J. raised a finger and silently ordered her to keep quiet.

"I'm not finished," he snarled, leaving his chair and coming to stand very close. "I guessed you wouldn't be very receptive to the idea since you're so positive I'm a thief, and I see that I was right. And I suppose love hasn't a place in your logical little world. Of course it doesn't. If it did, you'd have said yes to my proposal even before I'd finished asking."

Her tawny brows dipped downward, and T.J. snorted.

"The word was 'love,' Catherine. Ask somebody if you're not sure what it means, but once you do, stand back and take a good hard look at me. Maybe then you'll understand my one and only reason for coming here tonight."

He stared at her for a moment longer, started to turn, changed his mind, and shot out an arm, roughly enveloping her around the waist. Crushing her against him, he glared down into her eyes, the hurt and frustration showing clearly in his own, before he lowered his head and kissed her.

The feel of his steely long length pressed against her, his muscular arm trapping her in an unyielding hold, and the warmth of his lips touching hers made her head spin and raised a trickle of worry that he would have his way with her . . . with or without her permission. Filled with a sudden panic, she brought up her hands, desperate to fight him off and to break the viselike grip he had on her, but to no avail. She was about to tear her lips from his and demand that he stop, when she felt the strong fingers of his other hand cup the back of her head. In the next instant, he twisted his mouth across hers and thrust his tongue inside, sending waves of scorching white heat through her entire body. Despite the tears of rage moistening her lashes, a budding surrender began to grow from somewhere deep within her, and while the logical part of her mind begged her not to fall prey to his trickery, her heart rejoiced at his insistence.

At some time during her struggles the pins in her hair had fallen free, sending a torrent of silky blond curls down her back and the flower she had placed above her ear tumbling to the floor. She could feel the thunderous beating of his heart against her thinly veiled breasts and the intoxicating scent of him dulled her sagging resistance. His warm breath upon her cheek felt cool against her burning flesh, and when his mouth moved hungrily over hers, then on to trace the delicate line of her jaw to her ear, she let her head fall back and a tiny sigh escaped her lips.

Silently damning the weakness he never failed to arouse in her, she gave in to the desire raging through her. She brought up her arms, locked them around him, and turned her head to accept his smoldering kiss once more. A bolt of searing heat charged through her and melted her bones when she felt his hand roam the length of her spine and come to rest on her buttocks. Her breathing grew labored.

Her passion ran high. But just as her fingers slipped beneath the edges of his coat, intending to slide it from his shoulders, T.J. released her with such abruptness that she staggered back a step or two before she could catch her balance.

Hot and breathless, confused by his sudden change of mood, Catherine cringed at the anger she saw in his dark brown eyes, and shame rose up to sting her cheeks and chase away the rapture of the moment. "T.J.?" she beckoned in a shaky voice, when he turned to leave. "T.J., where are you going?"

He seized the knob, twisted it, and yanked hard, swinging the door wide. Haloed in its framework, he paused and looked back at her, and when he spoke, his voice was cold and hard. "As far away from you as I can get, Catherine Chase. You're like a heady wine to me. The more I drink, the more I want. You intoxicate my mind and make me lose control. Well, before you think to have me crawling on my knees, let me warn you it won't happen. I'll put the topper back in the crystal decanter and set it on the shelf. I'll look at it, but I'll never taste its sweetness again." He leaned closer and said, "I promise you that." With one last dark scowl, he turned and stalked from the room.

CHAPTER 14

From the moment T.J. had left his house in London until the hired rig pulled up in front of a hotel in Paris, he had repeatedly questioned the need for such a long journey. Catherine had made it quite clear that although she was physically attracted to him, she in no way would marry him. So why was he risking his neck and spending his hard-earned money to track down a man who probably had nothing to do with her father's death?

"Because I don't want to see her get hurt," he muttered to himself as he stepped down to the sidewalk. "Well, that's not the only reason. I've always loved adventure."

"Pardon, monsieur?"

Realizing he had spoken aloud and that he'd been overheard, T.J. glanced down to find a young boy staring back at him. He smiled lamely at him and shook his head.

"May I help you with your bags, monsieur?" the youth offered, apparently used to the oddities of Englishmen.

"Yes," T.J. replied. "I mean, *oui*."

The boy gave him a fleeting look as if to say that he understood T.J.'s English better than his French, and moved to the back of the carriage, while T.J. paid the driver and headed into the hotel.

"Bonjour, monsieur," the clerk greeted once he spotted T.J. walking toward him.

"Bonjour," T.J. repeated as he lifted the top hat from his

head and took off his gloves. "Do you speak English? I'm afraid my French is very limited."

"Oui, monsieur," the clerk answered with a pleasant smile.

"I'd like a room," he advised, pulling at the strings on his cape. "I'm not sure for how long. I'm here on business, and it might only take a day or as long as a week to complete."

"Of course, monsieur. You are welcome for whatever ze length of your stay," the clerk guaranteed. He opened the registry book, and while T.J. signed it, he reached for one of the keys hanging in back of him. "I have chosen a room with plenty of sunshine, monsieur. I hope eet will be satisfactory."

"I'm sure it will," T.J. replied, slipping out of his cape, while the clerk handed the key to a valet.

"Lyle will help you settle in."

Glancing first at the one with the key, then at the young boy carrying his bags, T.J. nodded at the clerk. *"Merci."*

As promised the suite faced south and late morning sunlight flooded into the room through the triple set of tall, diamond-paned windows opposite T.J., though he truly didn't notice. He was tired, his head ached, and he longed to have a hot bath and to lie down for a while, neither of which he knew time would allow, since Catherine was sure to be making arrangements for *her* trip to Paris. Instead, he asked that his luggage be taken into the adjoining bedroom, while he carelessly tossed aside his cape, hat, and gloves on the settee and crossed to the small writing desk. Retrieving a folded piece of paper from his breast pocket, he sat down, took the quill from its well along with a fresh piece of paper and began to scribble down a note, while Lyle stood silently off to one side, waiting. A moment later, T.J. sealed his letter, stood, and handed it over to the man.

"I would appreciate it if you'd see this is delivered right away," he said.

"Oui, monsieur." Lyle nodded curtly.

"And please tell the gentleman that I'll be waiting in the hotel dining room for him," T.J. added.

He closed the door behind the two Frenchmen and turned

back for the bedroom. He'd wash his face, change his clothes, and then head downstairs to the dining room to wait and to have something to eat.

An hour later found T.J. sitting alone at one of the tables in the restaurant and having his third cup of tea, and although he hadn't expected Sorrell Duve to make an appearance much before now, he was nervous nonetheless. Lewis Rhomberg had told him that his friend was temperamental and that there was a chance the man wouldn't offer his help, but T.J. was willing to wait a while longer. After all, without Duve, T.J.'s search for the chemist would be that much more difficult . . . and risky.

A shadow passed across his line of vision as he sat idly watching the waiter serve another group of guests, and he blinked, glanced up, and saw a stranger staring back at him. Lewis had told him that Sorrell Duve was an odd-looking character, but it hadn't prepared T.J. for what he saw now . . . if indeed this was the man with whom T.J. had asked to meet. Tall, and much too skinny for his frame, he gave the appearance that he hadn't eaten in weeks. He had a pasty complexion, narrow-set dark brown eyes that seemed to look right through T.J., and his hawkish nose turned downward to such a degree that it nearly touched his thin lips. His cheeks were sunken, his chin pointed, and his pale brown hair was in dire need of a trimming.

"Monsieur Savage?" he inquired in a high-pitched, thickly accented voice.

T.J. quickly came to his feet. "Yes," he replied, holding out his hand. "And you must be Sorrell Duve."

The man stared at T.J. for a moment longer, glanced off to his left, and then pulled out a chair on which to sit, blatantly ignoring T.J.'s offer of a polite handshake. "I'm very busy, monsieur," he announced, staring off across the room. "Suppose you tell me what eet iz you want from me."

Wondering if he'd been wasting his time, T.J. lowered his arm, drew in a tired breath, and sat down. "I'm looking for someone, and a mutual friend said you might be willing to help."

Duve cocked a bushy eyebrow at him. *"Un ami commun,"* he repeated. "And who might that be?"

"Lewis Rhomberg. From London. London, England," T.J. supplied.

"I know where London iz, Monsieur Savage," Duve jeered. "And I know of Monsieur Rhomberg. I do not, however, know you. How can I be sure you are his friend?"

T.J.'s patience was running thin, something of which Christian had taught him never to lose control. If waiting was the only way to get what was needed, then a man had to wait. That didn't mean, however, that T.J. had to be polite at the same time. Gritting his teeth and inhaling through his nose, he lowered his chin and glared back at the man.

"I thought you said you were a busy man, Monsieur Duve. Well, so am I, and I haven't got time for games." He reached inside the breast pocket of his coat and withdrew the piece of paper on which Lewis had written Duve's address, and handed it to the Frenchman. "It's the only proof I have in assuring you that Lewis and I, at least, know each other. Our friendship is something you'll have to take for granted." He glared a moment longer, then added, "If you are who you say you are, then you'll recognize the handwriting."

Duve studied the poorly written words for several moments before a vague smile began to show on his thin face. When he looked up, his brown eyes were sparkling. "I haven't seen Lewis in close to ten years," he admitted, the thick French accent gone, "but we've kept in touch through letters. Yes, I recognize the handwriting, but only because I can hardly read it." He stretched out his hand toward T.J. "And the name's Adamson. John Adamson."

Numbed by the man's confession, T.J. was slow in exchanging the handshake Duve had earlier refused.

"I used to work for the CID," Adamson explained with a chuckle. "About twenty years ago . . . until I got myself into a little trouble and had to leave England. Anyway, the moment you mentioned Lewis's name, I knew you were a friend of his." The smile faded from his lips once he saw the spark of anger smoldering in T.J.'s eyes. "Lewis didn't tell you about me because of a promise he made," Adamson quickly went on to say. "He knew I'd been framed for something I hadn't done, but he couldn't prove it, and rather than see me go to jail, he helped me start a new life . . . here in Paris under a different name. He swore to me that he'd never tell anyone where I had gone, and he never has. And he's never asked anything of me until now. That's how I know the two of you are good friends. Whatever it is he feels I can help you with must be very important." He raised his brows at T.J., waiting for him to accept the excuse for Lewis's deception, and when T.J. seemed to relax, Adamson smiled. "So why don't you tell me who it is you're looking for?"

If this man had been talking about anyone else, T.J. probably wouldn't have believed his story. But he was talking about Lewis Rhomberg, a man who devoted his whole life to sorting out facts and bringing the guilty to justice. Catherine might not know it yet, but she was very fortunate to have Lewis on her side.

"His name is Gustaf Valdemar," T.J. revealed. "He's a chemist, and he's supposed to be working here in Paris. I have to talk to him, but he's not to know ahead of time. If he were to learn someone was asking questions about him, he might disappear."

"Gustaf Valdemar," Adamson repeated with a frown. "The name isn't familiar, but that doesn't mean much. I'm not familiar with chemistry." He was quiet for a moment longer, then added, "But I know someone who is. Give me an hour to check it out, and I'll meet you back here. Which room is yours?"

T.J. spent the time confined to his room anxiously pacing the floor. Whenever he heard someone walking down the hall outside his door, he would rush to it and put his hand on the knob, ready to free the latch the second Adamson knocked. He repeated the exercise five times before he finally gave up and forced himself to sit in the chair by the hearth. But when the hour stretched into two, his anxiety turned to irritation, and just when he had decided to do a little snooping on his own and he'd left the chair to fetch his cape and hat, a soft rap sounded on the door.

"It's about time—" he blurted out, flinging the portal wide and changing his mind about finishing the sentence once he saw one of the bellhops staring back at him.

"Pardon, monsieur," the young man apologized as he held out a folded piece of paper. "This message just arrived for you."

Frowning, T.J. took the note, fished in his pocket for a coin to give to the boy, and hurriedly closed the door again. As he walked to the window where the light was better, he unfolded the paper and glanced at the signature.

Meet me in the alleyway behind the hotel, Adamson wrote. *And be sure no one follows you.*

Reaching for his cape and hat, T.J. quickly donned them as he crossed to the fireplace and tossed the message into the flames. Once it caught fire, he turned for the door, lifted the key and his gloves from the table beside it, and hastily exited the room.

Late afternoon sunshine flooded across the opening into the alley, and before T.J. turned his full attention to finding the man who had asked to meet him there, he paused, glanced over his shoulder, then across the street, and up ahead of him to make sure no one was interested in the direction he took. The need for such secrecy bothered T.J., but it wasn't something he'd ignore, since it was quite possible that perhaps Adamson's spying had gone awry and the chemist had already fled or, worse, had sent someone chasing after T.J.'s contact. Knowing of no other way to find out besides asking, he slipped into the shaded recesses of the back street, his eyes alert and his heart racing in anticipation of what he was about to learn.

"Is something wrong?" he questioned, once Adamson had flagged him down and pulled him into the guarded alcove of a doorway.

"No, just a precaution," Adamson replied, leaning past T.J. to glance back down the alley. "We've already been seen together once."

"So, did you have any luck?"

Adamson nodded as he pulled a scrap of paper from his inside pocket. "I've drawn a map that will take you to Valdemar's laboratory, and if he's not there, you can try his room." He pointed to the address he'd written on the bottom of the page. "He wasn't as easy to find as I thought he would be," Adamson admitted with a shrug. "So I'd suggest you be careful. Whatever he's working on apparently isn't something he wants anyone to know about." He smiled, then added, "I assume he's not a friend of yours."

"Far from it," T.J. answered pointedly as he folded the paper and put it in his pocket.

"Then be doubly careful, T. J. Savage," he warned, reaching out to squeeze his companion's shoulder. "If something happened to you, Lewis would come looking for me."

"Maybe," T.J. challenged with a smile.

He was about to express his gratitude for Adamson's help when a wagon pulled into the alleyway and started toward them. Instead T.J. shook the man's hand and hurried off in the opposite direction of the intruder, never looking back and quickly turning the corner once he reached the end of the alley.

Finding Valdemar's laboratory was relatively simple for T.J. Adamson's map clearly marked each street and several establishments along the way, but the trip took him close to an hour, since he had decided to walk rather than hire a cab and leave a trail. Standing at the entrance into the two-story building, he wondered if he should just go inside or try to find a back way in. The idea was to surprise the chemist and ruin any chance he might have of sneaking off before T.J. could confront him, since locating him a second time probably wouldn't be as easy. Deciding that perhaps the second choice would be the wisest, he turned away from the front door and cut down the narrow gangway dividing the building from the one next door.

Even though the alley in back was deserted, T.J. proceeded with caution. He hadn't come this far just to make a mistake now. Spying a staircase attached to the outside of the building, he went to it and started up, hoping that the door at the top would lead him directly into the laboratory. At the landing, he paused and peered in through one of the windows located on either side of the entryway and soon discovered that he had not only arrived at the chemist's workshop, but that the man wasn't there. Cursing his untimeliness, T.J. half turned to leave and changed his mind. Why not check things out without the Swede's interference?

Twisting the knob, he was not at all surprised when it wouldn't budge and free the latch. Who would be stupid enough to leave his office door open to thieves? Leaning, he tried one of the windows and found that it was locked. So was the second one.

A minor deterrent, he thought with a smug grin as he plucked the diamond stickpin from his cravat. Locks had never stopped him when he was a boy living in the back streets of London.

In under a minute and after he'd bent the shaft of the pin to fit the keyhole a certain way, T.J. was inside and studying the interior of the place. In the center of the room stood a long table filled with vials and flasks and other paraphernalia a chemist might use. To his left was a bookcase crammed with an assortment of volumes. In the far corner was a rolltop desk with papers scattered across its surface, and it was in that direction T.J. moved. Sometimes a man wouldn't talk even when he was threatened, and when given the chance, the one doing the asking opted for the simpler way of getting the answers he wanted. It might not be the honorable thing to do, but T.J. was desperate and honor hadn't a place in the realm of things just then.

Most of what he read had to do with Valdemar's research, and although the notes were written clearly enough, T.J. didn't understand the majority of them. Not that it mattered. He was truly only interested in one specific experiment . . . nitroglycerin and whether or not the man had gone ahead with his work despite Professor Chase's refusal and subsequent death.

A noise in the alleyway below distracted T.J., and he looked up, wondering if Valdemar was about to make an appearance and if he should find himself a hiding place close to the door where he could jump the man once he stepped inside. But when several moments of silence passed and the sound of footsteps never came, he went back to examining what was left of the papers on Valdemar's desk. His task awarded nothing out of the ordinary and he was about to turn and exit the laboratory, when he noticed a half-filled wastebasket sitting on the floor near where he stood. Crouching down, he carefully sorted through the refuse.

The only scrap of paper that piqued his interest was a letter he found and the vague reference the author made to an experiment he was working on. What made him fold the message and tuck it in his pocket was the invitation the writer extended to the chemist to visit his laboratory in London next month when he was sure his project would be completed. T.J. knew it was possible the letter had nothing to do with Professor Chase, but since it was the only thing he had to go on so far, he decided to show it to Lewis and let him decide.

Rising, T.J. glanced around the room one more time just to make certain he hadn't overlooked something and moved toward the window. The street below was deserted and, without wasting any more time, he stepped out onto the landing and closed the door behind him before descending the stairs. His next stop would be the boardinghouse where Valdemar stayed, but this time he'd hire a rig to drive him there. Shivering when a cold breeze swept through the narrow alleyway and billowed the fullness of his cape, he raised the collar close against his neck, secured his hat more snugly on his head, and started for the corner of the building. At that same moment, a noise from in back of him spun him around.

"Catherine?" he questioned disbelievingly, once she had stepped out from behind the open staircase and into the fading sunlight. "Catherine, what are you doing here?"

Icy blue eyes stared back at him from within the shadow of the hood of her cape. "Acting on a hunch," she calmly replied.

T.J. absently glanced up at the doorway at the top of the

stairs. He knew firsthand how good she was at tracking people down, but he couldn't understand the speed with which she had found the chemist's laboratory. And when had she left for Paris? Before or after his ship had weighed anchor? Remembering her answer of a moment ago, his frown deepened as he looked back at her and repeated questioningly, "A hunch?"

Catherine nodded. "You see, a few nights ago a man asked me to marry him. At first I was flattered, even giddy, you might say. I actually thought he meant it. But then I started questioning why he wanted to marry me, and when I posed the question to him, he became sarcastic and accusing. He never once said he loved me. He just walked away from me claiming he never wanted to see me again." She glanced off to her left for a moment, then continued. "And that made me even more curious. Especially once I remembered something he had said earlier . . . that he had to go away on business." She looked at the ground in front of her and idly began to pace while she spoke. " 'What kind of business?' I asked myself. He was financially secure, so why would he have any business to take care of?" She paused, looked at him, and raised a finger in the air. "Then it struck me. He had some very important merchandise to dispose of and he didn't want me to know about it. Now, in order to do that, he had to distract me. And what better way to distract a woman than to ask for her hand in marriage one moment, then withdraw the proposal the next? That would surely set her head spinning."

She raised her tawny eyebrows at him and started pacing again, ignoring the heated flare to his nostrils. "Well, it didn't distract *me*. I simply packed a few things, hired a cab, and then sat across the street from his house waiting for him to leave."

"So you could follow me," he finished for her, his tone filled with resentment. "Then tell me, Detective Chase, what did you think once you discovered that I was headed for Paris?" He took an angry step toward her as he raised one hand and shook his head. "No, let me tell it. For a fleeting moment you wondered if you might be wrong about me, that perhaps I wasn't on my way to meet with someone interested in buying stolen artworks. After all, Mr. Trumble admitted to you that he'd told me about the letter you'd found in your father's diary and that the man who wrote it lived in Paris. There was a chance—a slim one—that hinted at the possibility I was going to Paris to find the chemist. Am I right?"

He could see that some of the fire had left her eyes and the determined lift of her chin had lowered a small measure, and he rushed on. "But that would mean you'd have to admit that the great detective Catherine Chase had made a mistake." He threw up his hands. "Lord forbid!" he mocked. "So rather than use that analytical mind of yours, you ignored the obvious and set out to catch me in the act." He narrowed his eyes and leaned toward her. "Well, I hate to disappoint you, Miss Chase, but the only thing you caught me doing was breaking into a man's laboratory."

He saw the surprised look on her face, and when she glanced up the staircase to the second-story entrance, he laughed sardonically. "That's right, Catherine. I wasn't meeting with a buyer. I came here to talk to Gustaf Valdemar, but unfortunately he's out at the moment."

Catherine shot him a doubtful look, and he wasn't sure if it meant she doubted the room belonged to Valdemar or that she thought T.J. was trying to keep her from talking to the man by claiming he wasn't there. Either way, he knew she'd have to see for herself . . . with or without his permission. In a sarcastic gesture, he swept out his arm toward the staircase, silently inviting her to satisfy her suspicions.

A slow smile parted her lips. "I don't think so," she said, reaching into the satin drawstring purse she carried.

T.J.'s eyes followed her movements, then widened in stunned disbelief when he saw her pull a gun and point it at him. "What in the—"

"Did you really expect me to just turn my back on you?" she challenged, motioning him toward the steps with the end of the pistol. "I'm sure that's what you wanted . . . so you could run off when I wasn't looking."

"Why would I run off?" he said angrily, refusing to

move. "I'm having such fun here with you." His temper flared even higher when he hear her cock the gun. "Catherine!"

"Don't argue with me, T.J.," she threatened with a tired sigh. "I might not kill you with this, but I certainly wouldn't hesitate to give you a permanent limp." She nodded toward the staircase again.

Positive she wouldn't even blink an eye when she pulled the trigger, he glared at her for a second longer, then started up the steps. "I hope you're planning to apologize once you see I was telling the truth," he said, moving to one side of the landing and out of her way. Leaning back against the railing, he crossed his arms and glowered at her while she peered in through the window. "Now before you humble yourself by saying you're sorry," he scoffed, "perhaps I should give you something to think about first. Maybe I'm only telling a half-truth."

Catherine looked over at him through lowered brows, the pistol still pointed at his midsection.

"Well, maybe I was lying when I said I wasn't meeting a buyer here. Maybe Gustaf Valdemar wants to buy the paintings." It was an absurd notion. He knew it, and he was sure Catherine knew it. He was merely trying to point out how stupid some of her ideas were. "I would also like to suggest that we take our argument elsewhere to finish. Breaking into someone's office is a crime, and I'm not anxious to wind up in jail because I stayed around here too long bantering with you."

He was making it easy for her not to feel ashamed of her accusations, and she guessed it was because he was so obviously enjoying how good it made him feel to have shown her that rational thinking wasn't always correct. That was probably it, yet there was something else about his complacent attitude that bothered her, and she concluded it had to do with whatever he had found in the chemist's laboratory . . . a bit of important information he wasn't planning to share with her. Slipping the pistol back into her purse, she nodded at the staircase.

"Then go," she told him as she reached for the doorknob.

T.J.'s temper exploded. If she left him no choice, he'd drag her kicking and screaming, but one way or the other, they were leaving. Jerking upright, he shot out a hand, seized her wrist, and started back down the stairs.

"Damn it, T.J.," she cried. "Let go of me. I'm not leaving until I've examined everything in that room!"

"There's nothing there," he barked, glancing all around. Someone was sure to have heard them and summoned the police by now.

"To the untrained eye perhaps," she argued, twisting and pulling against the restraint.

"To any eye," he insisted.

Stepping off the last tread, he jerked her ahead of him and exchanged his hold on her wrist for the tender spot just above the back of her elbow. He felt her wince when he got too rough, but he didn't care. She'd be damned lucky if a couple of bruises was all he gave her.

"Where are you taking me?" she demanded, half walking, half running to keep pace with his long, angry strides.

"I'm not sure," he muttered.

"Then why are we in such a hurry if we're not going anywhere in particular?"

"Because it keeps my mind off something I'd rather do."

"Are you threatening me?" she charged, stumbling and nearly falling only to have her captor yank up hard on her arm. "T.J., you're hurting me!"

"Would you rather be dead?" he challenged, hurrying her out of the alleyway and stopping long enough to look for a cab. "That's what you'll be if you stay around here much longer." He faced her. "Good God, Catherine, I thought you were smarter than that. If Valdemar knows anything about your father's murder, finding you looking through his things would make him panic. He'd kill you before he'd let you go."

He unknowingly relaxed his grip and Catherine instantly took advantage of it to twist free of him. "I thought of that. It's why I brought a gun."

T.J. rolled his eyes, then turned away to wave at an approaching cab. Did the little fool really think a gun was all she needed to protect herself? If he'd been of a mind to, it wouldn't have taken him a second to disarm her a moment ago. And Valdemar would have been just as successful. Only the result would have been different.

"T.J, I *have* to go back," she complained, once the cab had pulled up beside them and he leaned to open the door. "My father was murdered, and there might be something in that laboratory that would give me the proof I need. It might even tell me who was responsible."

Recognizing the stubborn determination in her eyes, T.J.'s dark mood lightened a bit. He understood her feelings, but he couldn't let her go back. It was just too risky. Besides, there was nothing there. "How much do you know about the chemist?" he quietly asked.

Catherine bobbed one shoulder. "Not much. I haven't had a whole lot of time to ask questions. I've been too busy following you."

Reaching in his pocket, T.J. withdrew the map Adamson had made for him and handed it over. "See the address at the bottom? That's the place where he's staying. Now if you'll swear to me that you won't interfere and that you'll do exactly as I say, you may come along. If he's not there, then we'll try his laboratory again." He raised a finger and jabbed it toward her nose. "But make one objection or cause me an ounce of trouble, and I'll tie you up, gag you, and lock you in my hotel room. Do we have an understanding?"

Ordinarily a threat such as that would have enraged Catherine. Instead she found herself smiling back at him and consenting without the slightest hesitation. And while they rode in silence to the place where T.J. had said they'd locate Gustaf Valdemar, she enjoyed the feel of her companion's body bumping against her own whenever the cab hit a rough spot in the road. She couldn't name exactly what it was she felt for this man or why the first sight of him there in the alleyway a short while ago had started her pulse racing, but she knew it wasn't even in the same category as the excitement she experienced chasing down a criminal. T. J. Savage wasn't a criminal. She knew that now. Everything he'd ever told her was the truth . . . right from the very beginning. And now here he was offering his help to her when there was no obligation. In fact, if there was a debt to be paid, she'd be the one reaching into her pocket.

"T.J.," she said suddenly and before she had made up her mind to speak. "T.J., I know it's probably too late, but I'm going to say it anyway." She swallowed, took a deep breath, and continued to stare at her hands lying folded in her lap. "I'm sorry."

An expression of surprise crossed his face before he turned his head to look at her. That had probably been the hardest thing she'd ever done in her life, and he respected her for it. "It's not too late," he replied, glancing away. "It's just not necessary."

"Not necessary?" she repeated with an abbreviated laugh as she twisted in the seat to face him. "I've accused you of being a thief, a murderer, and a liar, and you're telling me there's no need to apologize? T.J., I pulled a gun on you back there and I would have used it if you'd resisted. If anything, saying I'm sorry isn't enough!"

"It's not necessary, Catherine, because I don't deserve an apology," he answered. He drew another breath to continue and to tell her how he'd never been totally honest with her from the start, and changed his mind. What purpose would it serve except to make him feel better about himself? If she knew he'd been hiding something from her all this time, she'd pull away from him. She'd *never* be able to fully trust him, and without trust, there could be no love.

The only explanation Catherine could give for his remark wasn't that he didn't think he deserved an apology, but that he didn't want it. "You hate me, don't you?" she suggested earnestly.

"Hate you?" he laughed, tugging on his earlobe. "If I hated you, Catherine, why would I have asked you to marry me?"

Shamefaced, she sunk back in the seat and stared at her hands again. She *had* thought it was because he hoped to buy her silence. Then *he* had implied it was simply the honorable thing to do, considering how they'd spent the night together. Now, she truly didn't know why. "There are a lot of reasons why a man would marry a woman," she finally managed to answer, her voice low and weak.

Shocked by her response, he frowned and turned to look at her. "For other men, perhaps," he told her. "But not for me. There could be only one reason why I'd ask a woman to spend the rest of her life with me." He waited for her to supply the answer, and when he saw how she was struggling to find it, he answered for her. "Love, Catherine. I would have to love the woman I married."

She suddenly felt warm all over. Was he confessing he loved her? How could he, after all she'd done to him? And if he loved her when he proposed, did it mean he still loved her? She had just drawn up the courage to ask when the cab rolled to a stop. Realizing they had arrived at the chemist's boardinghouse, she decided to wait until later to discuss it. There wasn't enough time now, and it was too important not to insist on privacy.

"Just follow my lead," T.J. instructed as he knocked on the door of the two-story house nestled in among a row of others. "We don't want to scare him off."

A moment later, a short, rotund older lady answered his summons, and he quickly removed his top hat.

"Bonjour, madame. Parlez-vous anglais?" he asked, smiling warmly at her.

"Oui, un peu," she replied, her gaze slipping past him to Catherine.

"We're looking for Monsieur Gustaf Valdemar."

The old woman cocked an eyebrow at him.

"We're friends of his," T.J. quickly explained. "We haven't see him for quite some time and we'd like to surprise him, if we may. Is he at home?"

"Oui," she replied with a frown as she stepped aside and pulled the door open all the way. "His room ees upstairs. Ze second door on ze left."

"Merci." T.J. smiled, ushering Catherine in ahead of him. They had just started up the steps when the woman's offhand comment stopped their ascent.

"Monsieur Valdemar has lived here for a while now, and

he has never had so many visitors in one day. Strange, don't you think?"

T.J. and Catherine exchanged worried glances. "How many visitors?" he asked.

The old woman's rounded shoulders jutted upward. "Two, I think. Maybe three. My memory . . . eet iz not what eet used to be."

"Were they strangers?" When she frowned at him, obviously not understanding the word, he rephrased it. "Did you know any of them?"

"Non," she replied with a shake of her head.

T.J. couldn't explain why, but he had a terrible feeling that he and Catherine were already too late. He thanked the old woman for her honesty, then firmly took Catherine's elbow and escorted her up the remainder of the steps and down the hall to the chemist's room. Knocking once, he leaned an ear to the door, listening.

"T.J.," Catherine whispered. "T.J., I don't like this."

"Neither do I," he replied, turning the knob.

The door opened to his touch, but before he swung it open, he glanced at Catherine, silently asking if she wouldn't rather wait in the hall. The deep breath she took and the look on her face told him that wherever he went, she'd be close on his heels, and although he would have preferred she stay behind, he knew it was useless to argue. Hesitating only a moment more, he shoved the door inward.

The instant they had a clear view of the room, they knew their worst suspicions had been warranted, and it began with the trail of blood they saw on the floor and how it disappeared around to the side of the bed. Holding out his hand, T.J. motioned for Catherine not to come any farther inside while he moved to check it out.

"You'd better fetch the landlady," he said after a moment. "She's going to have to be the one to identify him . . . although I don't think we really need to hear it."

"Is he dead?"

T.J. nodded. "Someone slit his throat."

"How long ago?" she pressed.

Stooping down, he touched the man's ashen face. Although his flesh was cold, the skin was still pliable. "Maybe an hour," he advised, glancing around for a clue that might help them figure out who the killer was.

Immediately guessing what he was doing, Catherine asked, "Do you see something?"

T.J. shook his head and stood. "Not even a button, this time," he half murmured to himself. What struck him as odd, however, was the man's behavior just before he died. He hadn't tried to leave his room and summon help. Instead, he had dragged himself around the end of the bed to collapse. Why? Was something in that part of the room more important to him than his own life?

"What are you thinking?" Catherine asked, cutting into his thoughts.

"Nothing," he replied, waving her out of the room with a flip of his hand. "Go and get the landlady. Tell her what we've found so she won't be too shocked once she sees him."

"All right," she said, yielding a bit reluctantly. "But don't touch anything until I get back."

"Yes, madam." He grinned and gave a quick, mocking salute.

The second he heard her footsteps on the stairs, he turned and opened the drawer in the nightstand. Other than a Bible written in Swedish, a gold pocket watch, and the man's purse, he found nothing else of importance. He decided to look in the armoire that was situated very close to where Valdemar had fallen. Obviously not a very wealthy man, the chemist had only a few changes of clothes, one wool cape, one top hat, and three pairs of shoes. Yet his sparse wardrobe wasn't what interested T.J. once he noticed the leather satchel sitting on the floor of the armoire. Picking it up, he laid it on the bed and withdrew the papers he found inside.

Most were written in Valdemar's native language, but of the couple that weren't, only one drew T.J.'s attention. It appeared to be his notes on his most current experiment . . . nitroglycerin, and T.J. decided that if Valdemar thought it was important enough to die for, then T.J.

shouldn't leave it behind for the police. He quickly folded the paper, stuffed it in his pocket along with the letter he'd found in the wastebasket at the chemist's laboratory, and returned the satchel to the armoire. There was no way of knowing for sure if Valdemar's murder had anything to do with Professor Chase's death, but it seemed awfully suspicious to T.J., and just as soon as he had Catherine safely at home again, he intended to pay Lewis Rhomberg a visit.

"The inspector made it sound as though he believes Valdemar's murder was just another in a string of them happening around that area," Catherine commented as she and T.J. sat in the hotel dining room waiting to be served their dinner. "But I don't agree. Do you?"

They had spent the last two hours at police headquarters trying to explain how they could be friends of the dead man, when they had had to rely on the landlady's verification that it was indeed Gustaf Valdemar. Another lie had covered up the first one, but T.J. still wasn't sure the inspector believed he and Catherine were Valdemar's illegitimate children and that they had never seen him until then. As far as he was concerned, the sooner they left Paris, the better off they'd be. He'd heard too much about French prisons to want to risk finding out if it was true.

"I might if I didn't know about his connection to your father, and that your father died under some rather questionable circumstances," he replied, raising a hand to hide the yawn he couldn't suppress. He didn't know if he was more tired or hungry.

"So what should we do now? Just forget about it?" she mocked, truly not expecting him to respond. There was nothing more they could do. Valdemar's murder had left them at an impasse . . . at least in that direction. There was still Reginald Hastings, her father's assistant, and just as soon as they returned home, she planned to contact Phillip. He'd had enough time by now to locate the man.

Luckily for T.J., he was given a little time to consider his answer when the waiter returned with their meal. He was tempted to show Catherine the papers he had taken from the satchel in Valdemar's room and the one he'd found at the laboratory, since she would know as much about them as Lewis Rhomberg would. But it also meant she'd be tagging along if either of them were of any importance, and he didn't want that. There was a strong chance two men had been killed as a result of someone else's desperation, and just because Catherine was a woman didn't mean the killer would show her any mercy if she stood in his way.

"Well, we could stay here in Paris for a while and hope the police catch the man who killed Valdemar," he finally replied. "But I honestly doubt it would serve much purpose. It's my guess whoever killed him was hired to do it, and maybe he'd confess and give us a name, but—"

"But it wouldn't be a legitimate name," Catherine finished for him. "I know that, T.J. We're dealing with a very smart individual. He isn't about to leave a trail." She was quiet for a moment while she flipped out her napkin and laid it across her lap. "It's just so frustrating, that's all."

He could read the sadness in her lovely blue eyes, and a heaviness pulled at his heart. She wanted so desperately to catch the man responsible for her father's death that it was tearing her apart. Some of her unhappiness, he was sure, came from the knowledge that it had taken her so long to discover her father had been murdered, and she was accusing herself of being a neglectful child. None of that was true, of course, but she wouldn't be convinced of it until someone was in jail.

"I know it's frustrating, Catherine," he soothed as he reached for her hand. "But don't let it get the best of you. We'll find him. I swear we will."

It was just a few words and a promise T.J. might not be able to keep, but nonetheless, knowing he would try made her feel better. Until that very moment, she had thought she was all alone.

"Thank you," she whispered, smiling softly and enjoying the warm touch of his hand covering hers.

The topic of Gustaf Valdemar faded from their conversation while they ate, and once their dishes had been cleared away and they were enjoying a glass of port afterward,

Catherine finally started to relax. Leaning back in her chair, her fingers idly toying with the stem of her glass, she deliberately stared at T.J. until he sensed he was being watched and looked up. A smile instantly glowed in his dark eyes and brought a slight blush to Catherine's cheeks. Uncomfortable all of a sudden, she turned her head and took a sip of wine.

"I know we've already discussed this," she said after a moment or two, "but I can't let it rest . . . not until I hear you say you forgive me."

"For what, Catherine?" he replied. "For following your instincts? For doing your job?" He leaned and took her hand again. "I'm not angry with you anymore, if that's what you really need to hear. You took some terrible risks that I would have preferred you hadn't, but that's the nature of your work. If anyone needs to apologize, it's me. From the day we met, I've been in your way, and I've probably hampered some of your investigation. Instead of arguing with you, I should have offered my help. We could have gotten things done much sooner if I had."

Catherine smiled and shrugged a shoulder. "Maybe," she said. Her cheeks darkened again, and she couldn't bring herself to look at him while she added, "And if we hadn't argued, we might not have ended up in bed."

Chuckling, T.J. fell back in his chair. "Oh, I don't know. I think that would have happened no matter what. Destiny, as they say." Being reminded of it and remembering her claim that they had made a mistake, his mood turned serious. "Catherine," he began, "what was the real reason you ran off that night? Were you embarrassed to learn that you actually felt attracted to me?"

It had taken them a few minutes to arrive at the topic she really wanted to explore and now that they had, she found it hard to put into words. She chewed her lip, smiled nervously at him, and resettled herself in the chair before she took a breath to calm her jittery nerves. Where was her rational thinking when she needed it?

"I don't intend this as an insult," she finally managed to say, "but until you came into my life, I had never given romance a thought. That night . . . well, it caught me off guard. I hate to think that curiosity was all that allowed me to continue, and after it was over, I'm sure I realized it wasn't, that I truly was attracted to you. And that's what scared me. It had all happened so fast that I feared you would think ill of me." She glanced down at her hands in her lap. "I knew I wasn't the first woman you'd ever made love to, and I guess I was worried that after a period of time you'd have trouble distinguishing me from all the others."

A brief smile parted his lips as he shook his head. "You're making it sound as though I've bedded every woman I've ever met. Let me assure you I haven't." Leaning forward on his elbow braced against the tabletop, he reached and placed a knuckle under her chin, forcing her to look at him. "And I'd have no trouble distinguishing you from *hundreds* of other women, Catherine, because you're the woman I love."

Tears suddenly blurred her eyes. "Really?" she asked.

"Yes, really, you silly little goose. It's the reason I asked you to marry me. What did you think? That I meant it when I said it was the honorable thing to do?" He grinned devilishly. "Well, I guess maybe it would be, now that I think about it." He cocked an eyebrow at her. "Are you saying you've changed your mind?"

She honestly hadn't had much time to think about whether she would or not, but now that he was pressing her for an answer, a whirlwind of doubt swept through her. "I—I don't know," she replied. "I wouldn't make a very good wife, I'm afraid. I don't like doing the things a wife is supposed to do. You know that. I'd rather be investigating a crime or finding a lost child or a murderer. The thought of planning meals or entertaining guests doesn't appeal to me."

"So?" he challenged.

Catherine laughed. "So what good would I be?"

"What good?" he repeated, dumbfounded. "You'd be filling a void in my life, Catherine. You'd give me a reason to smile in the morning. And I'm rich enough that you wouldn't have to do the usual wifely chores. I don't have a wife now, and it all gets done, doesn't it?"

She laughed at how foolish she had sounded. "Yes, I suppose. But what about the things I'd rather do? I couldn't give up being a detective."

"Who said you'd have to?"

Although a smile still gleamed in her eyes, she gave him a skeptical look.

"We'd work together," he offered. "We make a good team, don't we? That way I'm there to protect you if you need me, and I can give you an objective opinion from time to time." He folded his arms and leaned them against the edge of the table. "So what do you say? Will you do me the honor of becoming my wife?"

Catherine had to fight the urge to nod her head. "There's one more problem," she said instead.

"Name it and we'll fix it," he answered confidently.

She stared at him for a moment, then confessed, "I'm not sure if what I feel for you is love, T.J."

It wasn't something he'd even considered, and now that she'd brought it up, he understood her reluctance. "Yes," he murmured, some of the sparkle in his eyes fading, "that could be a problem. I certainly wouldn't want to force you into something you'd later regret." He waved off the waiter who approached the table with the offer to refill their glasses with port. "And it was presumptuous of me not to even consider the possibility. I apologize."

Catherine hadn't meant to hurt him, which from the look on his face, she had, nor did she mean to laugh. But she couldn't help it. "First I'm apologizing, then you're apologizing. . . . Can't we ever talk to each other without having to say we're sorry for something?"

He snorted. "It seems that way, doesn't it?" He smiled warmly at her and stood, holding out his hand. "I don't know about you, but I'm tired. And since there's nothing here in Paris for us, I suggest we have ourselves a good night's rest and get an early start for home in the morning."

"All right," she agreed, taking his proffered hand and

coming to her feet. "We'll sleep, and maybe in the morning I'll have an answer for you."

T.J. wanted very badly in that moment to pull her into his arms and kiss her, but neither the time nor the place was right. "There's no rush, Catherine. Now that I've made my feelings known, I can wait." He brought the back of her hand to his lips. "I just want you to be absolutely sure."

As they walked arm in arm from the dining room, Catherine wondered how there could be any doubt. T. J. Savage was an exceptional man, and the only one who had ever made her heart flutter. But was that what love was all about? She wished now more than ever that her mother were still alive. Vivian would have had the answers Catherine needed to hear.

CHAPTER 15

The instant Catherine opened her eyes the next morning, an exuberant smile spread across her face. Bright sunshine filled the room and the noisy chatter of birds outside her window added to her cheerfulness. She'd hardly slept at all the night past, yet she felt rested and relaxed, and she knew it had to do with the reason why she hadn't been able to nod off. Her thoughts had centered around T.J. and the conversation they had had over dinner. He had said he loved her, that he wanted to marry her, and that he'd wait for however long it would take for her to decide if marriage was what she wanted, too. Catherine had never rushed into anything in her entire life. She had weighed the circumstances of any decision she had had to make, and had then chosen the most sensible. She had wanted to be judicious about this decision too, but she honestly couldn't come up with any issues to argue regarding her feelings for T.J. Either she loved him and wanted to spend the rest of her life with him or she didn't.

"But I do," she murmured, her eyes twinkling. "I really, really do love him. And I couldn't imagine my life without him." Giggling, she snuggled down further into the soft feather mattress and closed her eyes. "Won't Mr. Trumble be surprised? Well, actually he'll be pleased, I'm sure. He likes T.J. and he's been trying for years to get me to settle down." She laughed again and threw off the covers.

"The poor man. He'll have half of what he wanted for me. I'll be married, but I won't settle down."

Springing off the bed, she hurried to the washstand to splash cool water on her face. Now that she'd made her decision there was no sense in waiting to let T.J. know. Should she tell him over breakfast? Or should she suggest they go sight-seeing and then tell him while they stood in some romantic spot?

"I think we'll go sight-seeing," she announced, picking up her hairbrush. "I'm too excited to eat."

Twenty minutes later Catherine entered the hotel's dining room looking for T.J. The message at the desk had told her he was already there, and it took her only a moment to recognize his handsome profile among the many other guests seated at various tables. She had taken only a couple of steps toward him when he seemed to sense her presence and looked up, a loving smile instantly parting his lips as he stood to greet her.

"You look radiant this morning, Catherine," he complimented, taking her hand and pressing a light kiss to the back of it. "Sleep well?"

"Actually, no," she confessed, feeling a warmth rising in her cheeks. "I had too much on my mind." She glanced nervously around, saw that there were too many people close by, and asked, "May we go somewhere to talk?"

"Certainly," he quickly agreed, frowning slightly. What she had to say was obviously meant for his ears alone, and he worried that it would be something he'd rather not hear.

He suggested they stroll the hotel gardens, and once they had retrieved their cloaks from their rooms, they met again in the lobby. Taking her arm, he escorted her out onto the flagstone path that curled and wound its way through the seemingly endless rows of sculptured hedges. They walked for several minutes in silence while Catherine debated the best way to make her announcement, since there would be conditions to her acceptance of his proposal. T.J., on the other hand, feared the worst. Finally, when he could no longer stand the inevitable, he paused near a white wrought-iron settee and motioned for her to sit down while he stood off to one side.

"Has this to do with our conversation at dinner last night?" he asked even though he was sure he already knew the answer.

"Yes," she said, bracing herself for what she guessed would be a lengthy discussion. "Before I tell you of my final decision, there are a couple of things we need to talk over."

His hopes rose a notch. Had he heard her correctly? Did she mean . . . ? "Certainly, Catherine. Whatever you wish."

She glanced up at him, then stared straight ahead. She couldn't give in just yet. They had to agree on some very important issues first. "I want you to swear to me that in a month or two or even years from now you won't go back on your word."

"My word?" he echoed.

"Yes. I won't marry you unless you agree to my conditions and swear to stand by your decision."

T.J. frowned warily. "Conditions? Such as? That we sleep in separate bedrooms?"

Catherine laughed. "No, silly. Nothing like that. I just want to make sure you understand that I won't be tied down to some antiquated idea of how a married woman should behave."

"Oh, that." He moaned dismissingly.

"It's not just 'oh, that,' T.J.," she rebuked, looking up at him. "I have to be sure that we'll never argue over my work or that somewhere along the way you'll see it as an embarrassment to have your wife doing things most would think were meant for a man to do. If I'm to give it up, it must be *my* decision and not yours, and not because you pressured me into it. Do we have an understanding?"

"Catherine—" he began.

"Do we have an understanding?" she repeated more strongly than before.

"I thought we already did," he shot back, laughing when she frowned at him. "Don't you remember? We discussed this last night. I have no objection to your wanting to continue your work. In fact, I said we could work as a team. Oh, Catherine," he murmured, dropping on one knee and catching both of her hands in his. "If you're saying you're worried about our future together, let me assure you every married couple has their disagreements. But if they love each other, they can work through them and become stronger because of it. All you have to figure out is if you love me."

Pale blues eyes glanced away from him. "That's why I didn't sleep well last night."

T.J.'s heart sank.

"Most of the time I lay awake, I was wondering why I didn't just tell you then." She looked at him again and saw the hurt in his eyes. "I do, T.J.," she quickly told him. "I do love you." Once she'd said the words, the rest came easily. "And yes, I'll marry you. I *want* to spend the rest of my life with you. I can't imagine it any other way!"

It was what he had prayed to hear her say, yet now that he had, he wasn't sure he could believe his ears. "Are you positive? I mean I haven't forced you into saying it, have I?" He saw her nod then shake her head, and he laughed joyfully as he stood and pulled her to her feet. "Oh, Catherine," he said. "You won't be sorry . . . *ever*!" Filled suddenly with an excitement that made his heart pound, he placed his hands on her waist, lifted her up, and whirled her around until she had to beg him to stop.

"You're making me dizzy." She laughed, draping her arms around his neck as he slowly lowered her to the ground.

"And you've made me the happiest man in the world," he beamed. "You could make me even happier if you'd marry me right now, right here in Paris."

"What?" She giggled.

"Why not?" he rushed on. "It's probably one of the most romantic, beautiful cities on earth . . . a perfect place for us to stand before God and witnesses and vow our undying devotion. Say yes, Catherine."

"But—"

"But what?" he argued enthusiastically.

"But shouldn't we get married in London . . . where all our friends are?"

T.J. thought of Arnie, Edith, and Lewis Rhomberg, and of Christian and Alexandra. Other than those five, he had no one else. And his adopted family was too far away to be able to attend. Besides, he didn't want to wait. He was afraid she'd have second thoughts.

"We could, I suppose. I guess every bride deserves a big wedding."

Only Mr. Trumble's name came to mind when Catherine mentally made out her list of those most dear to her. "It wouldn't be that big. The only person who means anything to me is Mr. Trumble. Who would you invite?"

"I can think of five, but since two of those live in Australia, I have to agree . . . it wouldn't be that big a wedding." Hoping she would change her mind about waiting, he studied her face without saying anything else. It had to be her decision.

"Well . . ." she said after a moment. "It is a romantic city."

"Very," he encouraged.

"And since we don't really have any family close by . . ."

"None," he added.

"I suppose we could . . ."

"Yes?"

She had been teasing him and it surprised her that he hadn't realized it. "Well, if you really want to get married here . . ."

"I do!" he quickly assured her, then corrected, "but it's your decision."

A happy smile lit up her face. "Then let's get married, T. J. Savage . . . right now, right here. Let's celebrate our union drinking champagne and viewing Paris from our hotel window . . . anything, my love," she murmured, stretching up on tiptoes, "as long as you swear to me that we'll be together forever."

He answered her with a kiss, a long, passionate kiss that

left no doubt in her mind. This was the man God had placed on the earth to care for her, to love her, to share a life filled with joy and tenderness and commitment. She would be his wife and he would be her husband for all eternity and beyond.

The next three hours passed in a blur for Catherine. The first stop they made was at the dressmaker's where T.J. paid a handsome price to have her fitted for an ivory-colored satin gown with pearl buttons and lace trim and to have the wedding dress finished as quickly as possible. Catherine had protested, saying that she didn't need a special gown in which to get married, but T.J. wouldn't hear of it. The day was special, he had told her, and the dress should be, too.

Their next stop was at a jeweler's, and before Catherine could open her mouth to complain, T.J. told her not to argue. The ring she would wear on her left hand had to match the love he held for her in his heart, and he wanted to make sure that the moment someone looked at the ring, they would know no other woman in the world mattered as much to him as Catherine. She had never been one to care what other people thought, but since this obviously meant so much to him, she had stood back quietly, allowing him to make the selection. His choice was a cluster of diamonds and rubies surrounding a large pink pearl, and tears filled her eyes the second he looked at her for approval.

Their final destination was Notre Dame Cathedral where T.J. asked her to wait on the steps while he went inside. A few minutes later he reappeared, a broad smile on his handsome face and his dark brown eyes sparkling. When she questioned him about their reason for being there, he answered by saying she would learn soon enough.

From there they returned to the hotel and stood in the hallway outside the door to Catherine's room exchanging a warm kiss.

"I hate the thought of being away from you for even a moment," T.J. murmured against her cheek. "But I suppose I must." A devilish smile twisted his mouth as he leaned back to look her in the eyes. "Unless, of course, you'd like me to help you with your bath or to brush your hair or help you to dress?" he offered.

"I'm tempted," she grinned. "But no. I still haven't adjusted to the fact that within a few hours I'll be a married woman. And that you'll have every right to wash my back." Her face warmed at the thought, and she turned away to unlock the door and swing it inward. "You know," she said, facing him again, "if someone had told me that one day I'd be as happy as I am right now, I never would have believed them." She laughed. "I certainly wouldn't have believed them if they had told me *you* would be the reason." She reached up and gently ran her fingertips along his jaw, smiling when he caught her hand and kissed the palm. "Now go, before I wake up and find that this has all been a dream." She gave him a playful shove and stepped into her room, watching him blow her a kiss as she slowly closed the door on him.

"I pray it isn't a dream," she sighed, leaning heavily against the thick wooden barrier and listening to his footsteps fade down the hallway. "I pray nothing happens to ruin this wonderful feeling I have."

Catherine had hardly finished with her bath when a knock sounded on her door and a young female voice called out to her from the other side. Thinking she had come to deliver the dress T.J. had purchased for her, Catherine clumsily tied the sash on her robe as she rushed to let the girl in. To her surprise, however, she discovered a troupe of young women all hired, they said, by Catherine's fiancé to help prepare her for her wedding. Catherine couldn't see the need for so many, but since T.J. had gone to such an extreme to make everything perfect, she wasn't about to argue.

Sometime during the whirl of busy hands and cheerful chatter Catherine's wedding gown arrived along with several small packages T.J. had obviously ordered sent to her. While everyone looked on, she excitedly tore away the wrappings to find a pair of ivory stockings and lace garters, satin slippers, ribbons for her hair, and a string of pearls with matching earrings. He had spared no expense, and

Catherine couldn't remember ever having felt so pampered before in her life.

With the help of three of the girls, Catherine slipped into the gown and a moment later she stood before a full length mirror marveling at its beauty and perfect fit. A bride was supposed to be made to feel special, and T.J. had outdone himself. Her only hope now was that she would never disappoint him.

The last finishing touches were applied, and it was time for her to meet the man she would marry. Yet, as she allowed one of the girls to help her on with her cape, she was struck by a moment of sadness. This was going to be the most important day in her life, and her father wouldn't be there to share it with her.

"Is something wrong, mademoiselle?" the bright-eyed girl named Céleste inquired.

Brought out of her thoughts by the worry she heard in the maid's voice, Catherine smiled. "No. Everything's fine. I was just wishing my father could be here." She smiled again as she gave the group a sweeping glance. "Thank you all for your help. I don't think I could have done it without you."

"Eet was our pleasure, Mademoiselle Chase," one of them replied, followed by a rush of French as the others agreed.

"But we are not finished," Céleste promised. "We were instructed to escort you outside."

"Outside?" Catherine echoed. "Why?"

"You will see," the girl said, giggling. Crossing to the door, she opened it and motioned for Catherine to lead the way.

Catherine wondered if it was just her imagination or the simple fact she was being trailed by half a dozen excited females that made it seem as though everyone in the lobby was staring at her as she made her way to the front entrance. But whatever the reason, she was enjoying the attention, and she had to bite her tongue to keep herself from announcing that this was her wedding day to any and all who would listen.

Outside on the front steps she came to an abrupt halt once she saw the carriage and the footman waiting for her. Yards of white ribbons and an array of gigantic bows adorned the elegant landau, and the sight of it made her laugh. There was only one thing missing, however, and when she turned to Céleste to ask where T.J. was, the girl wiggled her fingers at her.

"You'll see," she said. "You'll see."

Feeling much like the Queen of England, Catherine sat regally in the seat, smiling and waving good-bye to the covey of giggling young women as the driver snapped the reins and set the carriage in motion. At the corner they turned, and when the girls were no longer in sight, Catherine settled herself in for the ride, studying the scenery and thinking of T.J. and how he had made all of this possible. What other surprises had he in store for her? she wondered.

They had traveled a fair distance before the pealing of church bells sounded in the clear, crisp afternoon air, and it was several more minutes before Catherine suspected T.J. had something to do with their ringing at such an odd hour. She was sure of it when the landau swung down the last avenue and she could see Notre Dame Cathedral just up ahead. And there on the steps stood T.J., a breeze rustling his dark hair and billowing his cape, his handsome face smiling, and his brown eyes glowing with his love for her. Then, as the carriage rolled to a stop at the end of the sidewalk, he descended the stairs, opened the door, and held out his hand for her.

"No regrets?" he asked, pulling her close and brushing a kiss against her temple.

Suddenly choked with tears, she swallowed hard and whispered, "Only that my father couldn't be here to give me away."

"Ah, but he is, Catherine," he murmured tenderly. "He'll always be with you. All you have to do is think about him." He smiled at her, softly kissed her mouth, then turned with her and started up the steps.

The moment they entered the cathedral a chorus of young

soprano voices began to sing from somewhere high above them. Catherine wanted to turn and look, to smile her appreciation to the children, but her attention fell instead upon the beauty and reverence of the sanctuary and the hundreds of candles glowing warmly all around her. Tall, magnificent stained-glass windows told the story of Christ and flooded the cathedral with an angelic light. White ribbons garnished every pew, and a white satin runner lay upon the marble floor from one end of the aisle all the way to the altar.

"T.J., it's beautiful," she murmured.

"And it pales in comparison to you, my sweet," he whispered, bringing her hands to his lips.

A movement to her left distracted her and she turned, a look of surprise on her face once she saw Célèste and the bridal bouquet she held out to her.

"For you, mademoiselle," the young girl explained, handing her the flowers and subtly removing Catherine's cape.

Fresh tears moistened Catherine's eyes as she held the flowers close and breathed in their scent. T.J. had thought of everything. She turned to thank him and frowned, confused, to find that he had left her. In that same moment the sweet music of a chamber orchestra began to play, and a whirlwind of happenings closed in around her. The footman, who had driven her there, appeared suddenly to take Célèste's arm, and together they started down the aisle, followed by a little girl dressed in white and sprinkling flower petals on the satin runner. The children's choir began to sing again, and once Catherine realized she was standing all alone at the back of the church, a nervous tingle ran through her. If she wanted to change her mind, now was the time to do it. She lifted the bouquet to her nose, smelled its sweet fragrance, and smiled.

"And miss being married to the most wonderful man in the world?" she whispered, looking up to see T.J. waiting for her at the altar. "I'd have to be a fool."

With tears streaming down her face, she started toward him, unaware of everything else around her. *Papa?* she called out in her thoughts. *Are you here, Papa? Do you approve? Are you happy for me? I love this man, you know. Just the way Mama loved you. From this day forward I will be Mrs. Thomas Jefferson Savage.*

She felt T.J.'s hand cover hers. She heard the seraphic voices of the choir, the orchestra, and the church bells. She saw the priest and the two young altar boys. She listened to T.J. repeat the words, to make his vow before God to be her loving and faithful husband so long as they both shall live. She heard her own voice make the same vow, and she felt the ring he slipped on her finger. It all passed as a dream until he turned her in her arms and kissed her, a warm, loving, lasting kiss that sealed their destiny.

Suddenly they were outside the cathedral and bright sunshine touched her face. The bells of the church chimed again, this time much louder it seemed. Laughing, they raced down the steps, where T.J. lifted her into the carriage and a moment later the footman was there to drive them through the streets of Paris. Strangers along the way stopped to cheer them, and Catherine wondered if there would ever be another day as glorious as this one.

They pulled to a stop outside the hotel and a crowd gathered to watch as the newlyweds descended the carriage and went inside. In the lobby another group of people shouted their congratulations to the couple, and instead of heading toward their room, T.J. turned her in another direction.

"One last surprise, my wife," he told her when she looked questioningly at him. "A wedding isn't complete without a toast."

Catherine didn't know whether to laugh or to cry once he'd escorted her into the grand ballroom and they stood before a host of smiling people, a glass of champagne in everyone's hand and a table filled to overflowing with a feast fit for a king. In the center of it all, she saw a ten-layer cake decorated with white frosting, pink flowers, and a miniature bride and groom on the top.

"Oh, T.J.," she teased with a shake of her head. "Have you saved enough money to buy our passage home?"

A waiter appeared before them with a silvered tray and two crystal glasses of wine.

"Catherine, I'm rich enough to buy you the world if you want," he promised, picking up the glasses and handing one to her. "And if you prefer, we could even live here in Paris. There's nothing stopping us."

She thought of the real reason why they had traveled so far, and some of the joy left her. "One day, perhaps. But not now."

T.J. instantly understood. "That was insensitive of me. Of course not now. Nothing comes before finding your father's killer. Forgive me for my selfishness."

Catherine laughed. "How can you say that?" She swept out her hand. "Does this look like the act of a selfish man?"

He grinned, raised his dark brows, and glanced fleetingly around the room. "Not really. Simply a man in love." He took her hand and guided her toward the center of the room. "A toast," he proclaimed, lifting his glass high and silencing the guests. "To Catherine, my wife, may our love for each other grow stronger every day."

His eyes warmed as he stared at her and just when he was about to touch the edge of his glass to hers, she raised the glass and declared, "To T.J., my husband, for now and always."

A vociferous shout of approval exploded in the room while everyone watched the couple drink their wine, then exchange a kiss. "*Vivat! Vivat!*" they chanted. "*Vive l'amour!*"

The waiter appeared again to refill their glasses, and while those T.J. had invited to share in the celebration moved toward the banquet table, he motioned for the string quartet to begin playing as he pulled Catherine into his arms.

"Have I told you how beautiful you are?" he asked, holding her close and breathing in the scent of her.

"I'm not sure," she murmured. "Maybe you should tell me again."

He nibbled on her ear while he swept her across the dance

floor. "You're only the most beautiful woman God ever created," he professed.

Catherine laughed. "I doubt that, my silly husband, but it's nice to hear you think so." She leaned back against his arm to look him squarely in the eye. "Will you still think so when I'm old and gray?"

He wrinkled up his brow as though he might be giving it some consideration, and when he heard her gasp, he gave her a squeeze. "Of course I will," he promised, grinning devilishly. "Do you think you'll still love me then?"

Now it was Catherine's turn to tease. "That depends, I suppose."

T.J. stopped dancing. "On what?" he asked seriously, failing to see the twinkle in her blue eyes.

"On whether or not you've been a faithful husband," she answered, rushing on when he opened his mouth to defend himself. "By your own admission you're a very wealthy man, and I'm sure in the past you've come across a woman or two who showed an interest in you merely for the sake of your money. And I'm sure there will come a time later on when I'm old and gray and you are too that a young thing will throw herself at you for that very same reason. That, dear husband, will be the ultimate test. Will your love for me hold true?"

The slight upward turn of her pretty mouth challenged the gravity of her question, and he decided to play along. "Then perhaps we should eliminate the temptation. Once we've returned to London, we'll buy a modest house and modest furnishings, and give away all the rest of my money. If I have none, no young thing will throw herself at me and I won't have to make a decision."

She knew he teased, and she laughed. "T.J.," she threatened playfully, "one day your lies will get you in a lot of trouble."

A smile spread across his face, but it failed to reflect in his eyes. She had unknowingly struck upon the truth he had purposely ignored, and being reminded of it gave life to a new kind of worry. He had married her without revealing all of his secrets to her, a mistake he feared would cost him her love once she learned of them.

When the song came to an end, a tall, distinguished-looking gentleman politely asked if he might dance with the bride. T.J. willingly consented since he felt he needed that moment to sort out his thoughts. Standing at the side of the room, he watched his beautiful wife laugh and dance and enjoy herself. Every so often she would glance his way with a smile, and when one partner left her, a new one took his place, an irony that troubled T.J. Would another man as easily take *his* place once Catherine learned the truth about her husband? And when should he confess to her? Tonight? Next week? Never?

He finished off his glass of champagne and took another from the waiter. Catherine would never believe him if he were to tell her that he hadn't said anything *before* they were married simply because he hadn't thought about it. But it was true. He'd thought of nothing but planning the perfect ceremony once she had agreed to be his wife. What man wouldn't? So where did that leave him?

The answer seemed plain enough. He'd take her back home to London, settle her in his home, then start all over again investigating the explosion in Professor Chase's laboratory until he found the missing clue that would lead him to the man's killer. Once that was done and the murderer was awaiting execution, he'd sit his wife down and tell her everything. Catherine would understand. She wasn't like most women. She never jumped to a conclusion. She always took the time to examine every angle before she made a decision, and once he explained why he had kept secrets from her, she'd forgive him. He was sure of it. So why ruin their wedding night?

"T.J.?"

He'd been so caught up in his guilt that he hadn't seen Catherine leave the dance floor and approach him. Masking his unrest with a warm smile and a kiss to her fingers curled around his hand, he asked if she would like a glass of champagne, which she declined.

"Are you all right?" she asked worriedly. "You have such a faraway look on your face."

"I'm fine," he guaranteed. "I was just thinking about Christian and Alexandra and wishing they could be here to see this." He placed his glass on the tray of a waiter passing by, then wrapped his arms around his wife's waist and pulled her close. "They're never going to believe the scruffy, foul-tempered boy they raised has come to such a marvelous end."

"How long has it been since you've seen them?" she asked, pushing a stray curl of dark hair off his brow.

"A little over two years." He sighed. "I've written to them every couple of months, but they obviously don't know about you."

"Then I guess we'll have to pay them a visit," she suggested. "I'd love to meet them, and I've heard Australia is a beautiful country."

"It is if you like kangaroos crocodiles, and solitude," he replied, sounding a bit disapproving. "Of course, Sydney isn't like that. In fact it reminds me a lot of London."

"With dirty little street urchins trying to pick your pocket?" she teased.

T.J. laughed. "I suppose there are a few. Maybe we can adopt one while we're there."

Catherine took a moment to look around them and to make sure no one was standing close by. "It's all right with me," she whispered suggestively. "But they'd have to learn to get along with the other children."

T.J. straightened. "What other children?"

Her mouth curled seductively. "The ones we're going to have."

"Oh?" He chuckled. "And how many are we going to have?"

Catherine shrugged playfully. "I always thought a nice round number was easier to remember. Would a dozen be all right with you?"

"A dozen?" he questioned, grinning broadly. "Good heavens, Catherine, if we're to have a dozen children, then we shouldn't waste any time talking about it." He took her hand and started for the exit, pausing only long enough to tell one of the waiters to see that everyone's glass was filled for as long as there was someone to drink it.

He pulled his laughing wife along with him through the lobby and up the wide staircase, nodding politely at everyone they met along the way, then down the hall to another corridor where he turned and hurried her toward the door at the far end. There he stopped and swept her up in his arms.

"I believe it's tradition for the groom to carry his bride across the threshold," he stated as he nudged the door open.

"It is, but it's supposed to be the threshold of their new home," she giggled, locking her arms around his neck.

"Well, then we'll just have to do it again later, won't we?" He smiled, stepping into the room and kicking the door shut behind them.

Earlier, while Catherine had dressed for the wedding, T.J. had talked to the desk clerk, instructing him to have their things taken to the largest suite the hotel had to offer once they left for the cathedral. He had tipped the man a little extra to see that a bottle of chilled champagne and two glasses were brought up and that the room was filled with flowers. Pleased to see that both requests had been carried out and that his idea delighted his wife, he gently set Catherine down, and while she moved to the closest bouquet to smell its aroma, he turned the key in the lock.

"Oh, T.J.," she murmured, when she felt his arms slip around her waist. "You're unbelievable. I doubt there's another man alive as romantic as you."

"Does that mean you approve?"

"Of course, silly," she assured him, laying her head back against his shoulder. "What bride wouldn't approve?" She closed her eyes and exhaled a long sigh. "Promise me every day from this day forward will be even better, that we'll never stop loving each other."

"I promise," he replied, turning her in his arms. "No matter what happens, I will never stop loving you."

The champagne she had drunk, the excitement of the wedding, and his pledge clouded her ability to hear the subtle implication in his words. Smiling, she draped her arms around his neck, raised up on tiptoes, and gently pressed her lips to his.

"Then let us consummate our vow," she suggested alluringly, slipping out of reach when he tried to pull her close.

The look in her eyes told him he would have to wait, that first she wanted a moment alone, and although it demanded a lot from him to yield, he remained where he stood while he watched her step into the adjoining bedchamber. Thinking to pass the time with an activity that would distract him, he unhooked the buttons on his coat, tossed the garment on the settee, and loosened his cravat as he crossed the room to where the bottle of champagne sat on a table.

Removing the cork, he poured two glasses, drank nearly all of one, and poured another before he decided to sit down to wait. Lounging uneasily in a chair by the crackling blaze in the hearth, he listened to his wife move about in the other room. The ticking of the mantel clock grew louder with each passing second, and after what seemed to him to be the hundredth time he'd looked at its shiny ivory face and brass hands, a movement in the doorway caught his eye. Awestruck by the sight of Catherine dressed in a white lace gown cut low over her bosom with its matching robe falling open in front, he was unable to move for several seconds. She had taken the ribbons from her hair and had brushed out the mass of thick curls. Long strands of strawberry-blond hair fell across one shoulder and breast, and T.J. found himself wanting to run his fingers through it, to feel its silky texture and to smell its sweet fragrance. Then he saw her smile.

"Does this mean you like what you see, my husband?" she teased, moving toward him.

Exhaling the breath he had unknowingly held all the while, he snapped his mouth shut and stood. "Oh, yes," he finally managed to reply. "I like it very much." He handed her a glass of champagne, clinked the rim of his goblet against hers, and then took a slip, his eyes locked on hers. She was the most beautiful woman he had ever seen in his entire lifetime, and what made him smile was knowing that she belonged to him. "I don't deserve you," he said after a moment as he took her empty glass and set it alongside his own on the table. "I don't think there's a man on this earth good enough for you, but I'll thank God every day that He allowed me to try."

Her bright blue eyes glowed. "That's odd. I was thinking very nearly the same thing, that I really don't deserve you. Do you suppose all newly married couples feel that way?"

He shrugged a shoulder, wrapped his arms around her, and pulled her close. "Perhaps," he said, kissing the tip of her nose. His blood warmed instantly at the feel of her scantily clad breasts touching his chest, and his time for waiting was over. Bending slightly, he caught her up in his arms, and carried her toward the bedchamber. "And perhaps we should stop talking and begin working if we're to have a dozen children," he teased, delighting at the sound of her giddy laughter.

Catherine had lit a single candle in the room while she changed, and its yellow glow flickered warmly all around them. Their playful mood turned to passion once they neared the bed, and before T.J. had slipped his arm out from under her knees and her feet had touched the floor, their lips had met and they were clinging to each other in a fierce embrace. Anxious fingers pulled the cravat from his neck, then moved to pop the buttons on his shirt free and send both garments floating to the floor. Hot kisses moved along his neck, while he stripped away the satiny fabric of her gown and robe and tossed them down to join his discarded clothes. Their lips met again, and this time there was an urgency in the union, as if both husband and wife feared an evil force would pull them apart.

With one arm around her waist, T.J. bent a knee upon the bed and caught their weight with his other hand as he lowered her down upon the sheets. Silky tresses of red-gold hair fanned out across the pillow and candlelight bathed her ivory skin. For one long moment, T.J.'s eyes devoured the sight of her smooth flesh, the curve of her long neck and rounded shoulders, the firm mound of her breasts, narrow waist, and supple legs, until his passion soared and his desire to have her raged beyond control.

Kicking off his shoes and shedding the rest of his attire, he came to her again, their legs entwined as he braced himself on his elbows above her. He kissed her brow, her temple, and nibbled on one earlobe while he whispered sweet desires against her cheek. He dotted a moist path with his tongue to the hollow in her neck, then further on to the full, ripe curve of her breast. He heard her moan and felt her move beneath him, her hands coming up to trace the hard muscles along his back to his buttocks, and he knew her time for waiting had reached an end as well.

Shifting his weight, he parted her thighs and slowly pressed the bold evidence of his ardor deep inside her, while he slid his hand under her hips and pulled her up. Breathless and hot, she responded, matching his sleek, sure thrusts with her own, and lifting them higher and higher beyond the simple pleasures of the mind and body to a plateau only their souls could reach. Within moments a wild, searing explosion of ecstasy burst upon them, stealing their strength and plummeting them back from whence they came, exhausted and weak, contented and at peace.

Neither of them spoke afterward, satisfied simply to enjoy the warmth of each other's body as they lay molded against each other. Lying on her side, Catherine snuggled close within her husband's encompassing embrace. A smile parted her lips as she listened to his gentle breathing against her ear and felt the steady rhythm of his heartbeat. Golden candlelight continued to flicker about the room, and when she crossed her arms over his, the precious stones on her ring finger caught the yellow glow and sparkled in her eyes. Who would have thought a month ago that she would be lying here in bed with her new husband and that that man would be T. J. Savage?

CHAPTER 16

"Are you sure you don't want me with you when you tell him?" T.J. asked as he and Catherine stood with their arms wrapped around each other on the front steps of her town house.

"Yes, I'm sure," she replied, smiling lovingly at him. "It's not as if I'm about to tell my father that I ran off and got married without his permission. Mr. Trumble is a friend, but he has no say in what I do." She brushed the backs of her fingertips along his jaw. "Besides, you said you've got business to take care of, and the sooner you're finished, the sooner we can sit down and make plans."

"Plans?"

She laughed and tapped her finger on the tip of his nose. "Such as where we're going to live, silly. Or did you have it in mind to live in separate houses?"

T.J. honestly hadn't given it much thought. He had just assumed she'd want to move into his home. It was much bigger and a little more elegant than the town house, but now that she'd mentioned it, he realized that the town house had belonged to her father and leaving it might not be something she'd want to do. Hoping to soften his blunder, he grinned devilishly at her. "I really don't care where we live just as long as we sleep in the same bed."

The notion made her laugh. "I can hear the gossip now. Who'd believe we were legally married if they saw us coming from one house one morning and another the next?

But I agree." She smiled provocatively. "We must sleep together . . . if sleep is really what you had in mind."

T.J.'s eyes darkened as he pulled her close. "I was being polite," he whispered.

"Then hurry on with your business, husband of mine," she urged scampishly. "The sooner we decide, the sooner we can go to bed."

He could feel his heartbeat quicken with anticipation, and the idea of postponing his visit with Lewis Rhomberg crossed his mind. "Why not test the beds first . . . to see which one is more to our liking?" He nudged her off the top step. "We'll start with mine."

"T.J.!" she exclaimed merrily. "You have things to do and so do I. We'll have the rest of our lives to lounge around in bed if we want, but not now." She wedged herself free of his embrace and turned him away from her. "Go. Finish your business and then meet me here later." He tried an about-face and she pushed him down the steps.

"All I wanted was a kiss," he pouted, stopping at the bottom and looking back up at her with round, sad eyes.

She touched her fingertips to her lips, then held them out and blew across them. "You'll have to survive on that," she said, laughing when he stuck out his lower lip even further.

"I'm not sure I can," he argued. "But if that's the way you want it . . ." He crossed the sidewalk and climbed into the cab. "Just remember whose fault it is when they find me lying weak and wasted in some alleyway," he called to her as the rig pulled away. He tried very hard not to smile, but the sight of her standing on the steps shaking her head and laughing undermined his resistance and he grinned. "I love you, Mrs. Savage," he shouted above the rumble of the wheels and horse's hooves against the cobblestone street.

"And I love you, Mr. Savage," he heard her call back.

The moment the rig rounded a corner and pulled out of view of her, the smile left his mouth. His talk with Lewis Rhomberg in the next few minutes would be very crucial in proving to his wife why he had been keeping secrets from her. As he was sure Lewis would agree, Catherine mustn't know about the papers he had taken from Valdemar's laboratory and bedroom for the simple reason that if they turned out to be as important as T.J. thought they were, Catherine would demand to be included in whatever he had planned. She'd already shown him how daring she could be, and her knowledge of how a criminal mind worked would probably be of great help to him, but he didn't want her tagging along. He loved her too much to put her in any kind of danger, and he was sure the trail he followed would lead him straight to it.

Time wouldn't allow him to take his usual route in contacting his friend. Instead, he asked the driver to pull up outside the front door of Scotland Yard and to wait for him while he went inside. If everything went as he hoped it would, he'd have need of the cab and its driver just as soon as he finished discussing his find with Lewis.

As always, the lobby was crowded with people. Glancing only briefly at the desk sergeant to find him arguing with an old woman, T.J. headed down the hall toward Lewis's office at the far end. He had traveled half the distance when a door to his right opened and a man stepped out, nearly colliding with him.

"Oh, I'm sorry," Ferris Hargrove, the assistant to the commissioner, apologized. "I suppose I should look where I'm going." He smiled at T.J., then asked, "May I help you?"

T.J. would have preferred not answering, but to do so would be rude and would probably raise the man's curiosity, something T.J. didn't need right then. "Perhaps," he said politely. "I'm looking for Lewis Rhomberg. I was told his office is this way."

Hargrove turned and pointed. "Yes, down there. The last door on the right. But he's not there."

T.J. waited for the man to instruct him as to where he might find Lewis, but when he merely stood there staring at him, he asked, "Do you know where he is?"

Hargrove nodded, but didn't offer any more.

"Where?" T.J. asked, trying very hard not to let his irritation show.

"He's downstairs interrogating a prisoner. Perhaps I could help you."

T.J. shook his head. "I don't think so, but thank you anyway." He pointed in the direction he thought he would find the staircase, waited for the man to nod, then started off again, silently concluding that it was no wonder Scotland Yard hadn't made an arrest in the museum robbery case if that imbecile was an example of the kind of men assigned to work on it.

Upon reaching the stairs, he hurried down them and made a quick turn to his right at the bottom, hoping to locate Lewis without any further delay. The first cell was empty. In the second one he saw an old man huddled on the cot, and before he reached the third, he heard Lewis's voice coming from the last cell at the end of the corridor. Rushing forward, he stopped in the open doorway and waited for his friend to notice him. Once he had, he motioned for Lewis to step into the hallway with him.

"Don't tell me. You weren't able to find Valdemar," Lewis guessed after he had locked the cell door and had moved to the opposite side of the corridor.

"Oh, I found him," T.J. advised as he dug into his pocket and withdrew the papers he wanted his friend to read. "But I was about an hour too late. He'd been murdered."

Lewis's brows lifted in surprise. "A rather odd coincidence, wouldn't you say?"

T.J. nodded. "I thought so. It was almost as if whoever killed him knew I was on my way there. And truthfully I think he did. I just don't know how he knew . . . yet." He unfolded the papers he held and handed them to Lewis.

"What's this?"

"I found that one in the chemist's satchel before the police came. I might not have any experience in the field, but I can read, and it appears to be his notes on nitroglycerin."

"You're partly correct," Lewis informed him. "It's about nitroglycerin, but they're not Valdemar's notes. Here, take a look," he instructed, holding out the paper. "See how the *i*'s are dotted with little circles? Unusual, hm? Well, I've only seen one person dot an *i* like that and that was on the day I spoke with Professor Chase. He was writing on the chalkboard when I walked into his office and those damned *i*'s nearly jumped off the board. So unless I'm horribly mistaken, this paper belongs to him."

Stunned, T.J. stood there for a moment, thinking. "But how would he have gotten them? According to Catherine, her father refused to work with the man." A new thought came to mind. "Unless . . ."

"Unless he was killed for them?" Lewis finished.

T.J. nodded. "And I'm willing to bet I know who killed him."

"Who?" Lewis asked anxiously.

"The man who wrote that letter," he said, pointing at the second paper he'd given to Lewis.

Not bothering to read what was written in it, Lewis skipped to the signature. "Where'd you get this?"

"In a wastebasket in Valdemar's laboratory. Why? Do you know this Reginald Hastings?"

"Not personally, but I've heard enough about him to doubt he'd have the courage to commit murder, and certainly not his longtime friend and coworker."

T.J. frowned. "What are you talking about?"

"Reginald Hastings was Professor Chase's laboratory assistant and had been for years. From everything I've been told, the man could hardly control his grief at the professor's funeral." Lewis shook his head. "I think you're looking in the wrong direction, T.J., but I'm not so close-minded as to tell you not to ask the man a few questions . . . for instance, how Valdemar happened to have a letter from him inviting him to come to London. That is, of course, if you can find him," he added, walking toward the staircase. "After the services, the man just seemed to disappear, and I never had the time to look for him."

"Have any suggestions as to where I should start?" T.J. asked, pausing at the bottom of the steps.

"I'd try the chancellor at the university. He might be able to help."

"I'll leave right away."

"T.J." Lewis beckoned, stopping the young man as he turned to ascend the stairs. "I don't have to tell you to be careful. Up until now, I was only suspicious." He wiggled the papers he held. "This says otherwise."

"Don't worry, friend. I'll be careful. I have a wife to think about now." He waited for his words to sink in, grinned playfully, and mounted one step before Lewis caught his arm and pulled him back.

"A wife? What are you talking about?"

"I got married while I was in Paris."

"To whom?" Lewis exclaimed.

"To Catherine."

"What?"

Full of the devil, T.J. reached over and tugged on his friend's ear. "Having a little trouble with your hearing, Lewis?"

"My hearing is fine," he said. "I'm just having trouble believing you. Was she unconscious at the time? Or were you holding a gun to her head?"

T.J. laughed. "Neither. I simply told her that I loved her and that I wanted to marry her, and she accepted."

Lewis cocked a doubtful brow. "Just like that."

"Yes."

"And she just happened to be in Paris, and you two just happened to run into each other."

"No, she followed me there. The last time we were together I told her I had some business to take care of, and she got it in her head that I was planning to meet a buyer for the stolen museum paintings." He could see and understand the skepticism in Lewis's eyes, and he chuckled. "It's a long story. I'll tell you all the details later. Right now I've got something more important to do."

"T.J., does she know about these?" He held up the papers.

"No. And she doesn't know about you and me yet, either." The humor disappeared from his tone. "I'd like to keep it that way for a while . . . until I've found the man who murdered her father. I've got a lot of explaining to do for her, and I want to ease the shock of it by handing her the killer's name first."

"I hope that will be enough, my young friend. If she ever thinks you tricked her . . ."

T.J. sighed heavily. "I know, Lewis," he admitted drearily. "I know."

Nothing more was said as the two men shook hands and the eavesdropper at the top of the stairs fled before he was discovered.

"Catherine Chase," Mr. Trumble scolded, "you've never done anything so spontaneous before in your life. What were you thinking?"

"How much I loved him and wanted to be with him," she shot back over her shoulder as she climbed the stairs to the study.

"But you hardly know the man," the servant complained, hurrying after her. "And the last time we talked about him you were sure he was a thief."

"And you were positive he wasn't!" she shouted, spinning on him. "Have you changed your mind? Or do you know something about him that I don't?"

Mr. Trumble struggled with his words. "N-no . . . it's just that—"

"That what? We should have announced our engagement and waited a proper amount of time to get married? Why? Because it's what society demands? To hell with social etiquette!"

"Miss Chase!" he murmured, shocked by her language.

"It's Mrs. Savage now, Mr. Trumble, Mrs. T.J. Savage, and nothing you have to say will make me regret it." Twirling, she mounted the rest of the stairs and dashed into the study, quite certain Mr. Trumble wasn't finished with her yet.

"Social etiquette has nothing to do with it, Miss Catherine," he called to her as he raced up the stairs and came to a halt in the doorway. "If your father had ever been worried about what others thought, he would have sent you to boarding school and seen you married years ago . . . to a man of *his* choosing." Realizing how he had lost his temper with her, he took a deep breath, let it out slowly, and squared his shoulders. "I know I didn't react the way you would have liked me to react, Miss Catherine, but you must understand that it came as a bit of a shock. After your father died . . . well, I felt your well-being was my responsibility. And before you correct me," he cut in, his right hand raised, "I'll admit that you're old enough to take care of yourself. I know that. It's just hard for me to accept, especially since I was there the day you were born. You're like my own daughter, Miss Catherine, and I don't want to see you get hurt."

Catherine hadn't meant to snap at him, and she wasn't really sure why she had. Picking up the stack of letters that had come for her while she'd been away, she rounded the desk and sat down. Several moments passed before she looked up.

"I don't act very grown-up sometimes, do I, Mr. Trumble?" she asked, smiling weakly. "And you're right. I've never done anything this crazy before in my life, and I guess that's why it feels so right. I do love him, Mr. Trumble. I can't imagine life without him. Maybe we should have waited, but I don't think it would have changed anything. We were meant to be married."

Mr. Trumble had very little doubt that what Catherine felt for T.J. Savage wasn't love. He could see it in her eyes. What worried him was whether the young man truly loved her. He was smitten with her—Mr. Trumble had recognized that the first time the two of them had talked in private about Catherine—but that didn't constitute everlasting commitment. And that was what he had been trying to tell her.

"I know you love him, Miss Catherine," he quietly confessed. "And please accept my apology for making it sound as though I didn't."

"There's no need to apologize, Mr. Trumble. In fact, I should thank you for speaking your mind. At least now I know you feel something for me other than responsibility." She grinned impishly at him. "You do, don't you?"

A warmth began to rise in Mr. Trumble's face. Never

before had he admitted his feelings to someone and his lack of practice made him uncomfortable. "Yes, madam," he finally managed to reply.

"Well, I'm glad because I care about you, too. So why don't you fix something to eat, and just as soon as I'm through looking at these"—she held up the letters in her hand—"we'll sit down and have a long talk. All right?"

He bowed politely, started to say something and changed his mind, then exited the room.

A soft smile graced her lips while she stared at the empty doorway. "I was wrong, T.J.," she murmured to herself. "It *was* like telling my father." She sighed and thought, *Maybe that's because his approval means as much to me as my father's would have*. With a dismissing shake of her head, she turned her concentration on the sealed papers she held.

The first was an invoice from the grocer that she laid aside. The second was a letter from Cherry Hammerand, and Catherine smiled as she read how the young girl had decided to visit relatives near Liverpool and that they had asked her to stay. The death of her two friends had made her think long and hard about continuing her line of work, and since she'd been offered the job of a seamstress, Cherry was contemplating giving it a try. That pleased Catherine. She liked Cherry and didn't want any harm to come to her. Cherry finished her letter by inviting Catherine to pay her a visit if she was ever in Liverpool and Catherine mentally agreed that she would.

The last note wasn't signed, which signaled a warning to Catherine, and she quickly scanned what was written. At first she thought it was a prank, some fiendish joke someone wished to play on her. Then she read it again, and the blood drained from her face. She didn't want to believe a word of it; in fact, she *wouldn't* believe it, and she considered throwing the note away, but her experience with following up on anonymous tips wouldn't let her. Too many times they'd helped her solve a case, and this particular case was one that continued to eat away at her confidence. If what she'd been told was true, she could put it to rest. However, in the process it would also destroy her life. With trembling hand, she refolded the paper and stuffed it in the pocket of her skirt as she rose and hurried from the room.

The sun was just beginning to set when T.J.'s livery cab entered the outskirts of London on his way home. His trip to Oxford University had been fruitless, even though Chancellor Wycliff and his staff had been extremely cooperative. The last time any of them had seen Reginald Hastings was at the professor's funeral and only the chancellor would speculate on where he thought the man might have taken up residence after leaving Oxford. T.J. appreciated Wycliff's help, but London was a large city, and if Hastings didn't want to be found, T.J. would have a difficult task in locating him.

One curious bit of information he had learned came from one of the students. T.J. had asked permission to look around the laboratory even though he doubted he would find anything, and a young man of eighteen was instructed to take him there. The walk across the campus to the chemistry building had provided the pair enough time to get acquainted, and the moment T.J. mentioned he was looking into the explosion that had killed Professor Chase, his companion offered up his opinion on the accident and how he didn't truly think it was an accident at all.

According to the young man, two days before the explosion, he had overheard Professor Chase arguing with his assistant. Although he couldn't actually hear what was being said through the closed door of the professor's office, he knew by the shouting that Professor Chase wasn't pleased with something Reginald Hastings had done. The student went on to admit that although he had no proof, he'd heard that the professor's office had been broken into the night before he had heard the two men arguing and that Professor Chase had refused to report the incident. He also acknowledged the possibility that the two events might not be connected in any way but that he couldn't help thinking Reginald Hastings had had something to do with the break-in, that the professor had fired his assistant because of it, and that out of some sort of revenge, Hastings had wanted to hurt the professor by destroying the laboratory. He knew it was a horrible accusation to make and he had softened his conclusion by saying that he didn't believe Hastings was aware Professor Chase had been in the laboratory at the time.

T.J. had thanked the young man for his honesty and openness and had asked him to contact T.J. should he happen to remember anything else that might help in the investigation. The young man had said he would, and after T.J. had made his examination of the laboratory, he had climbed into the cab and headed for home. He would have liked to ask Catherine about the argument her father had had with his assistant, to find out if she even knew about it, but to do so would mean he'd have to admit to how he had come by the knowledge, and he wasn't ready to do that just yet. He'd have to be content to discuss it with Lewis first. Then if all else failed, he'd confide in his wife.

A smile parted his lips when the vision of Catherine came to mind. Their trip home from Paris had been wonderful. They had spent an extra day there sight-seeing in the afternoon, having dinner in the hotel dining room, and making love well into the night. The next morning they had hired a coach to take them to the coast, where they booked passage on a clipper ship named *Angelica,* and the time it took for them to cross the English Channel had been spent below decks in their cabin . . . making love.

Their mood had still been light and happy when the *Angelica* docked at the wharf in London, and although T.J. hadn't wanted to be separated from his wife for even a second, the matter of her father's murder took priority. He would have felt better about leaving her if his trip had been a little more rewarding, but since he knew he couldn't change any of it, he decided to make up for it by planning a romantic evening. He'd heard there was a new opera opening at the theater, and after he'd stopped off at his house first to bath and to don fresh clothes, he'd go to Catherine's and suggest they attend. They'd have dinner in one of the finest restaurants, and afterward they'd spend the night at his house. Then in the morning they'd talk about where they would set up permanent residence, and while she was busy making arrangements, he'd visit Lewis again.

Feeling good about his plans for the next few hours, T.J. relaxed in the seat to watch the scenery pass by, tempted every time he saw someone on the street to call out and announce his marriage to Catherine. He checked the desire several times, certain the strangers would only think him mad rather than exuberant, and wound up chuckling to himself instead. The happiness left him, however, once the livery cab rounded the last corner and his house came into view, for there on the veranda stood Catherine and four uniformed bobbies.

The rig had barely come to a complete stop before he bounded from it and rushed up the steps toward his wife, confused by the angry, somewhat pained expression on her lovely face.

"Catherine?" he questioned softly. "Catherine, what is it?"

He jerked back when he started to reach for her and two of the officers stepped between them.

"What's going on?" he demanded, his gaze shifting from one policeman to the next, then finally to his wife.

"I'm having you placed under arrest, T.J.," she answered, her throat tight.

"Arrest?" he repeated. "For what?"

"For the robbery of the British Museum."

Her declaration was cold and filled with false bravado, and before he could deny the charge or demand proof, the front door to his house opened and two men emerged carrying a gold-framed painting covered haphazardly with a cloth.

"Catherine, no!" he exclaimed, stepping toward her again, only to have the bobbies grab his arms and pull him back. "Catherine, you're wrong. I had nothing to do with the robbery." Desperate to have a moment to plead his case, he struggled to free himself, his temper flaring when the hold on him tightened. "Damn it, let me explain!" he hissed through clenched teeth.

"You'll have your chance, Mr. Savage," she predicted, her chin quivering. "That's what our courts are for." She nodded for the policemen to take him away.

Enraged, T.J. managed to break the hold of one of the men, but before he could swing a fist, the other two bobbies attacked. With one arm twisted painfully behind him, T.J. yielded only a small measure, forcing the officers to half drag, half carry him to the awaiting prison van. The scene brought tears to Catherine's eyes and before they streamed down her face, she blinked them away.

"I can prove my innocence, Catherine," he shouted, his gaze locked on her as he strained against the hands pulling him backward down the sidewalk.

"Can you?" she challenged, the pain of betrayal stabbing at her heart. "How? By telling me another lie?"

"By telling you the truth!" he countered, struggling again. "Go to Scotland Yard. Ask for Lewis Rhomberg. He can tell you all about me."

The name stirred a vague memory, yet her pain forced it away. Her entire body shook, and while she watched her husband being roughly shoved into the barred wagon, she gritted her teeth and raised her chin high. Lies and foolishness had brought her to this end. She would not be so easily tricked a second time.

She started at the sound of the metal door slamming shut and the key turning in the lock. Tears burned her throat as she continued to watch and saw how her husband was unable to stand erect inside the van. Down on one knee, his hands gripped around the bars, his handsome face, flushed with anger, turned her way, and when their eyes met, his expression softened.

"I love you, Catherine," he stated simply. "And no matter what happens, I always will."

A single tear spoiled her indifference when it spilled over the rim of her lashes and fell down her cheek.

"Always, Catherine," he repeated just as the prison van jerked, then rolled along the cobblestone street away from her.

Paralyzed, Catherine remained on the veranda watching

until she could no longer see him, and once the impact of what she had done hit her, her knees buckled and she collapsed to the floor, sobbing uncontrollably.

Mr. Trumble had a disconcerted expression on his face as he stood at the bottom of the staircase listening to Catherine play the piccolo in the study. Ordinarily he would have thought some event had triggered the memories of her mother, but he knew differently this time. The instant she had walked back in the front door a few minutes ago, he had seen her red and swollen eyes, and even though he hadn't asked her about it, he was sure something had happened between her and her new husband. And it had to be something very grave to make Catherine Chase cry.

He hesitated a moment longer, wondering if a glass of warm milk would help and decided against it as he started up the steps. As far as he was concerned, he didn't need an excuse to talk to her, and whatever was troubling her was simply too important to postpone discussing while he waited for the milk to heat.

At the doorway he paused, his heart aching once he saw her. She was sitting in a chair by the fire, Satan curled up in her lap, the piccolo held to her lips, her eyes closed and tears running down her face. She hadn't heard his footsteps, and he wondered if he should make a noise to warn her or simply go inside and take his place in the chair next to hers. At that moment, a sob racked her body, and she dropped the silvered instrument on the carpeted floor at her feet.

"He lied to me, Mr. Trumble," she wept, scooping up the cat and hugging him to her.

It didn't surprise Mr. Trumble at all that she knew he was there. Nothing got past Catherine. At least that was what he had always thought.

"I assume you're talking about your husband," he said as he walked to the chair and sat down.

"My husband?" she laughed through her tears. "Oh yes, my husband. Do you know that he actually had the audacity to tell me he loved me while he was being driven away in the prison van?" She turned moisture-laden eyes upon him.

"He's a thief, Mr. Trumble, just as I suspected all along. But I let my heart cover up the truth. I let him woo me with words and promises. Oh, God," she sobbed, dropping the cat and hurriedly leaving her chair. "How could I have been so blind?"

"Tell me what happened, Catherine," Mr. Trumble tenderly instructed. "I need to hear it all if I'm to help you."

"Help me?" she echoed. "How can anyone help me? I've made a shambles of my life and now I'll have to live with it."

"Catherine Louise," he coaxed. "Stop being stubborn and let me help."

It took her a moment to realize he had used the same bidding her father had employed whenever she was being difficult, but once she had, she looked at him, awkwardly wiped her tears from her face, and forced a smile. Her father had always seemed to make things right whenever they had had a similar discussion. Perhaps Mr. Trumble could make everything right, too. Returning to her chair, she sat down and looked him squarely in the eye.

"I was told I'd find one of the stolen museum paintings in T.J.'s house." She took another breath to continue, but Mr. Trumble interrupted.

"Told by whom, miss?"

The question threw her off balance. She frowned, thought about it for a second, then replied, "I don't know who, Mr. Trumble. The note wasn't signed. I suppose it was someone—"

"A note? Someone sent you a note accusing your husband of stealing? A coward's way, wouldn't you agree?" Mr. Trumble didn't like what he was hearing nor would he believe it. "And I suppose that's the reason you left the house a while ago in such a hurry? You had to march right over there to see if it was true?"

"Mr. Trumble." Catherine rebuked him with a frown. "You're—"

"So what did you find?" he cut in. "Just one painting? Or all of them?"

"One," she quickly replied. "One was enough, don't you think?"

"To convince me?" he asked.

Catherine nodded.

"No. But it was enough to convince you. So what did you do? Summon the police?"

"Of course!" she snapped, bolting from her chair and nearly tripping over Satan as he lay on the floor at her feet. "What was I supposed to do? Bring it here and hide it in the attic?"

"I would have expected you to give him the benefit of the doubt. Did you? Did you allow him even a second to defend himself?"

"Ha!" Catherine exploded with a toss of her long strawberry-blond hair. "Why would I? Because I enjoy being lied to?"

Mr. Trumble's temper began to rise. "Because you've never been one to jump to a conclusion." Leaving his chair, he approached where she had stood glaring out the window. "I've seen you poring over your notes on a case just because the evidence against the accused wasn't conclusive enough to suit you, while everyone else had him tried, convicted, and sentenced to hang. Yet when your own husband is the accused, you bring the rope. I thought you told me you loved him."

"I do!" she shot back in a rage. "I mean I did." She threw up her hands. "Oh, I don't know anymore," she moaned, turning away to plop back down in the chair.

"You were right the first time," he charged. "And if you weren't so busy feeling sorry for yourself, you'd start asking questions."

"What kind of questions?" she pouted.

"Well, for one: who sent the note? And why? Where are the rest of the paintings? But most importantly, what has Mr. Savage to say about all this?"

Catherine mumbled something he couldn't hear.

"What?"

"I said he told me to talk to Lewis Rhomberg."

"Lewis Rhomberg? With Scotland Yard?"

"Yes," she answered, straightening in the chair. "Do you know him?"

Mr. Trumble shook his head. "Not personally. But I've heard of him. He's a very fine detective. Why would Mr. Savage tell you to talk to him?"

A twinge of shame nudged her conscience. "He said Lewis Rhomberg knew all about him."

Mr. Trumble's chin dropped. "And you did nothing about it? Good God, Catherine."

She opened her mouth to defend her actions, quickly realized they didn't deserve defending, and sighed dolefully instead. "You're right, Mr. Trumble," she announced, springing to her feet and making a grab for her cape hanging over the back of the settee. "Whatever you're thinking of me right now, you're absolutely right. And when I have time later, I'll ask properly for your forgiveness. But first, I have to go to Scotland Yard."

"What did you say?" Lewis Rhomberg asked, looking up from the report he'd been writing when Nathan Beecher burst into his office.

"I said Miss Chase caught the museum burglar. They have him in custody right now," the young man beamed.

"Who is it?"

Beecher shrugged. "I don't know. I didn't hear anyone mention a name. I can find out for you, if you want."

Lewis shook his head. "How many of the paintings were recovered?"

"Just one so far. Would you believe the fool actually had it on display in his house?" Beecher grunted. "The nerve of some men."

Lewis went back to his report as he commented, "That's why criminals always get caught sooner or later. They think they're infallible."

"That and because they don't stand a chance with Miss Chase on their trail. Of course, the commissioner wouldn't agree with me."

Lewis could hear the admiration in the young man's voice, and he smiled to himself as he wondered if Beecher's feelings for Catherine would change once he'd heard she'd gotten married.

"Well, I can see that you're busy, and I was just on my way home, so I'll leave you alone," Nathan promised, backing toward the door. He started to make an exit, paused, and added, "Would you like to stop off somewhere for a mug of ale, Mr. Rhomberg?"

The invitation sounded appealing, and even though his report could wait until morning, Lewis had been using it as an excuse to wait for T.J. "I appreciate the offer, Nathan," he answered, looking up, "but I'm supposed to meet someone here in a little while. Tomorrow night, perhaps?"

Nathan smiled. "All right. We'll do it tomorrow night." He turned, stepped into the hallway, and came to an abrupt halt. "Miss Chase?" he questioned, concern heavy in his voice. "Are you all right?"

Lewis immediately came to his feet even though she hadn't moved into his line of vision yet.

"I'm fine, Nathan," he heard her reply. "I'm looking for Mr. Rhomberg. Is he in?"

Lewis's mind raced. Why was she asking to see him? Had something happened to T.J.? Had he sent her? Or was T.J. even aware that she was there? He rounded the end of his desk and met her in the doorway.

"Miss Chase?" he said politely and extended his hand toward his office, noticing just as Beecher had that she'd been crying. "Won't you come in?"

"Yes, thank you," she replied, stepping past him.

Certain Nathan wanted to be included, yet knowing what they had to say to each other was meant to be private, he took the young man's elbow and moved a step further out into the hall. "Perhaps you'd better wait out here, Nathan. If I need you, I'll call. All right?"

"Yes, yes, of course," he agreed, his face wrinkled with worry. "I'll be right here."

"Thank you," Lewis replied, moving back into the office and quietly closing the door. His next tough assignment was how he should react to the young woman sitting in the chair beside his desk. He certainly didn't want to ruin anything for T.J. by letting something slip.

"May I get you a glass of water, Miss Chase?" he asked as he came to stand next to her.

"No, thank you," she answered. "I'm fine. At least I hope to be once you and I have talked."

Nervous, he forced a smile and returned to his chair. "How may I help you?"

Catherine didn't know where to begin. Taking a deep breath, she exhaled in a rush and loosened the strings on her cape. "I would suppose by now that you've heard T.J. Savage was arrested for the museum robbery."

"What?" he exploded. He started to say more but the words wouldn't come. Instead he just sat there with his mouth hanging open. Finally, once the shock had passed, he angrily shoved back his chair and stood. "Oh, this is ridiculous."

"Where are you going?" she asked when he rounded the desk and headed for the door.

"To see that he's released," he fumed. "He's no more a thief than I am."

"Then let him sit in a cell for a while," she suggested, her own temper flaring. "It will do him some good, don't you think?"

At first Lewis didn't understand. With his hand gripping the doorknob, he looked back at her, angry that she thought an innocent man should have to spend even a minute in jail. Then the image of his young friend locked up behind bars flashed before his eyes, and laughter rumbled deep in his chest.

"Yes, Miss Chase," he grinned. "I think it *will* do him some good. Lord knows I warned him often enough that that's just where he'd wind up if he didn't stop meddling in other people's business."

"So you do know him," she remarked, the tension leaving her body as she watched her companion sit down again.

"Since he was twelve years old. And he's just as reckless and stubborn today as he was then." Crossing his arms, he leaned forward and braced them against the desktop. "So how did you find out?"

"He begged me to come and see you while he was being taken off in the prison van."

"I'll bet he did." Lewis chuckled. He stared at her for a moment, then added, "He's a good man, Miss Chase. And everything he's done so far has been for your own good, even though it might not seem like it to you." He sighed and reached to toy with the pen lying near him. "And it's my fault he's in this mess."

"Your fault?" she repeated. "How could it be your fault?"

He smiled softly at her before he began the lengthy explanation. He started by telling her of his suspicions long ago about her father's accident and how he'd been unable to follow up on them until T.J. came along. He said his friend had decided on his own to track down the robbers in the museum case, only to have it blow up in his face when she got in the way. Chuckling, he opened the top drawer of his desk and handed her the gold button he'd taken from inside, saying that it was the one found at the murder scene and not the one she had thought had been torn from T.J.'s coat. He confessed to having forced his friend to promise not to let her know that they were investigating her father's death, and that that was where the trouble really began. By not being able to tell her the truth, T.J. had had no way of proving his innocence to her. Additionally, Lewis couldn't understand how one of the stolen paintings had gotten into T.J.'s house and how she'd come to learn about it.

"I'd say whoever put it there was the same person who sent me the anonymous tip," Catherine speculated.

"But why?"

"To get T.J. out of the way. Apparently he was getting too close."

Lewis shook his head. "If he was, he didn't know it. He'd given up looking for the robbers so that he could devote his time to finding your father's killer."

Catherine exhaled a long sigh. "There's little sense in doing that anymore."

"Why do you say that?"

"I'm assuming he told you about the letter I found in my father's diary." When Lewis nodded, she continued. "And you knew he was going to Paris?"

"We talked about it and agreed he should. Why?"

"Have you talked to him since his return?"

Again Lewis nodded.

"Then he must have told you that Gustaf Valdemar was murdered. Without him, we have no leads."

T.J. had told him that for obvious reasons he'd kept the papers he'd found a secret from Catherine, and Lewis agreed it was a good idea. But that was before all this. Pushing out of his chair, he crossed to a file cabinet and opened a drawer.

"T.J. found this in a wastebasket at the chemist's laboratory," he said, handing her the first paper and watching a frown form on her brow as she read it. When she looked up, he gave her the second one. "And this one he took from the man's satchel in his room. I believe that's your father's handwriting, isn't it?"

Catherine didn't like the feeling she was getting. "Yes," she answered weakly. "And I hate to think how Valdemar came to have it."

"Hastings," Lewis supplied. He saw her nod and added, "It's what T.J. and I suspected, and that was why he went to the university this morning."

"To see if anyone knew where to find Hastings?"

"Yes."

"He wasted a trip. I could have told him that. No one's seen him since my father's funeral." Suddenly she remembered whom she had nearly knocked down on the front steps when she had left her town house a short while earlier and whom she had asked to wait in the kitchen for her. "But I'll wager *I* know someone who can tell us where to find him."

"Who?"

"A young friend of mine by the name of Phillip Preston." Rising, she retied the strings on her cape as she headed for the door. Once she reached it, she paused and turned back. "I think T.J. deserves to sit a while, Mr. Rhomberg, after all the secrets he's kept from me. But since his heart was in the right place, maybe you should turn him loose. Tell him to meet me at the town house, and tell him I said he has a lot of apologizing to do."

Lewis smiled. "He already knows that . . . Mrs. Savage," he replied, coming to open the door for her. "And if I were you, I'd stretch it out for as long as I could. You owe him that much."

Catherine laughed. "Yes, Mr. Rhomberg, I certainly do."

A smile, then a frown alternately changed the expression on Catherine's face during her ride home. It felt wonderful to know her husband wasn't a thief or a murderer, and that very soon they could truly start their life together as man and wife. Then she'd think of her father and how he would miss out on her happiness and why that was so. She didn't want to believe that her father's longtime associate and friend had had anything to do with the explosion in the laboratory, but from the clues gathered so far, Reginald Hastings had to have known something.

The last of the evening's sun cast long shadows over the city, and for the first time that night Catherine noticed now beautiful the sunset was. The smile returned to her face as she wondered whether or not T.J. could see the splash of color from his jail cell, and just how grateful he'd be once he was standing outside in the fresh air again. She should have instructed Mr. Rhomberg to leave him there overnight just to prove a point, but if Phillip had the answer she wanted to hear, she'd need T.J.'s help.

As the cab turned the corner and the town house came into view, Catherine noticed the well-dressed shape of a man standing on the front steps. A moment later he turned, and she instantly recognized Aaron Courtland. Surprised to see him, she voiced the thought once the rig had rolled to a stop and he had helped her to the sidewalk.

"I heard about T.J.," he explained, "and I came to offer my sympathy. I know how much you cared for him. It must have been very hard for you to just stand back and watch him being taken off to jail. Is there anything I can do?"

Catherine thought it strange that T.J.'s childhood friend never once defended T.J.'s innocence. Granted the two of them had had to steal as young boys to keep from starving to death, but they were both grown men now, and they each had enough money to buy a bakery rather than steal a single loaf of bread. Perhaps their friendship hadn't survived.

"Yes, it was, Aaron," she replied, climbing the steps and opening the front door. "It was also a mistake." She motioned him inside.

"A mistake?" he questioned, waiting for her to close the door so that he could help her off with her cape. "But I heard one of the paintings was found in his house."

"It was," she admitted, watching him hang his cape and hat on the hall tree before she started down the hall to the kitchen, certain she'd find Phillip there. The boy liked the food Mr. Trumble gave him nearly as much as the money Catherine paid him. "Mr. Rhomberg and I believe someone schemed to have it look as though T.J. was the thief because he was getting too close to the man who really stole the paintings."

"Oh?" Aaron remarked, following closely behind her. "And was he? Close, I mean?"

"Perhaps, but that's not important now," she said, waving a hand dismissingly as she entered the kitchen and smiled at the young boy sitting at the table. "Hello, Phillip. I'm sorry I had to leave without talking to you first, but I had some very important business to take care of. So what did you find out?"

Wiping his mouth on the back of his sleeve as he shoved his empty plate away, Phillip's gaze shifted from Catherine to the man standing behind her.

"It's all right. Mr. Courtland is a friend. He can hear what you have to say. Did you find Mr. Hastings?"

Phillip's frown deepened when he noticed the surprised look on Courtland's face and how quickly the man forced himself to recover. He might be a friend of Miss Chase's, but there was something about him Phillip didn't like and he wasn't sure she should be calling him a friend.

"Please, Phillip. It's important. Were you able to locate Reginald Hastings?" Catherine repeated, excusing the boy's hesitancy to talk in front of Aaron simply because Phillip was always leery of strangers.

"Yes'm," he finally said. It wasn't his place to tell Miss Chase what she should and shouldn't do. "He's set up some kind of a workshop in a warehouse about a mile south of the city on Chelsea Bridge Road."

"Marvelous!" she beamed. "Now I need you to do something else for me."

"It'll cost ye," Phillip replied, reaching for his glass of milk.

"And you'll be well paid, Phillip, just as soon as I return."

He froze with the glass halfway to his lips. "Where ye goin'?"

"To talk to Mr. Hastings. But I want you to wait here. Just as soon as Lewis Rhomberg and Mr. Savage arrive, you're to tell them where I've gone and that I'm with Mr. Courtland. Will you do that for me?"

Phillip's eyes moved to look at Courtland. "Yeah, I suppose I could," he said. But first he planned to go to the stable out back and ask Mr. Trumble about this man Miss Chase called a friend.

Excited, Catherine stepped closer, grabbed Phillip's chin and gave him a hard kiss on the cheek. "Thank you, Phillip," she whispered, kissing him again before she turned on her heel and fled the room, leaving behind a very surprised and embarrassed young man.

"Catherine," Aaron implored as his driver headed the rig toward the south of town, "would you mind telling me what this is all about?"

"It's a long story, Aaron," she replied, "but the short of it is that I believe Mr. Hastings had something to do with my father's murder."

"Murder?" Aaron exclaimed. "Your father wasn't murdered. The CID investigated the explosion and couldn't find anything to suggest it was more than just an accident. What makes you think it was?"

"A series of things, Aaron," she said, twisting on the seat to look directly at him. "First of all, it happened at night. My father never worked after dark because he was having

probably belonged to Reginald Hastings and she mentally prepared herself for his feeble attempt at explaining why he had turned against her father. What she wasn't prepared for, however, once Aaron had shoved her through the doorway, was seeing Ferris Hargrove frantically helping Mr. Hastings stack and place items on a table. Nor was he prepared to see her once he caught a glimpse of someone standing in the doorway and he stopped to look up.

"What the hell is *she* doing here? Are you insane, Courtland?" he demanded. "Now she knows about me."

"It couldn't be helped," Aaron shot back, giving Catherine a shove that sent her tumbling to the floor. "Between her and Savage, they'd figured everything out." He waved the pistol at his cohorts, silently instructing them to continue their work, before giving Catherine an evil look. "Since she was coming here anyway, I decided she could be of some use to us just in case her *husband* makes an appearance before we've had the time to get away."

"He's in jail," Hargrove sneered. "You saw to that."

"He was," Courtland revealed, continuing to glare at his captive until he saw the surprised look on her face, and he grinned. "I'm not sure how she managed it, but she convinced Rhomberg to free him. They're probably on their way here now. So hurry!"

"You're the museum thief, aren't you?" Catherine hissed. "And you put that painting in T.J.'s house and sent me the note."

Courtland shrugged arrogantly. "A waste, as it turns out. I would have preferred selling it. I need the money." He turned his head to watch the progress of his men.

"And you're the one who killed the two men T.J. had gone to meet about buying the artworks."

"They got greedy," he replied without looking at her.

"My father wasn't greedy. Why did you kill him?"

"You father was a fool, Catherine," he snarled, spinning back and squatting down in front of her. "He had something I wanted and all he had to do was sell it to me. He could have been a very rich man, but his principles got in the way. He lost his temper, we struggled, and he wound up dead. What happened was his own doing, not mine."

"You bastard," she hissed, her blue eyes crackling with hatred.

Aaron chuckled, unaffected. "If you're trying to insult me, Catherine, you're not. Calling me a bastard is exactly what I am. And so is your husband." He reached out, grabbed her chin, and squeezed. "The difference between us is that it never really bothered T.J. He didn't care what people thought of him." He gave her a shove and stood. "I always envied him that." He stared at her for a moment, then turned to his two companions.

"Hastings," he ordered. "Find something to tie her up with."

Some of the papers Hastings held clutched against his chest slipped from his grasp. "What for?" he asked nervously. "What are you going to do with her? You're not going to hurt her, are you?"

"Just find a piece of rope, you old fool, and stop arguing with me."

Perhaps Mr. Hastings didn't have the foresight to know what Aaron had planned for her, but Catherine did, and she intended to be as uncooperative as possible. With Courtland's back to her, she saw her chance. Springing to her feet, she charged him, but Hastings's startled look unwittingly warned Courtland in time. Turning, he brought his fist around and smashed it against the side of her head, hurling her backward and knocking her unconscious before she hit the floor.

Reginald Hastings had cursed the day he let greed change his loyalty. Professor Chase had been his one and only real friend, and Hastings had traded that friendship for the promise of wealth and fame. He also cursed the cowardice that forced him to stand aside and watch while someone he cared about was murdered. He'd done it once, but he wasn't about to do it again. Dropping the books and papers he held, he let out a vicious roar that surprised not only himself but the other two men in the room, and during that split second Courtland stared disbelievingly at him, Hastings catapulted himself through the air. His noble effort ended with the earsplitting crack of a pistol being fired, the burning sensation of a bullet piercing his flesh, and an excruciating pain in his chest that crumpled him down to his knees. With his vision blurred, he became light-headed and his skin began to tingle. Every ounce of energy drained from him, he felt himself collapsing to the floor, a blissful kind of peace enveloping him and dissolving his pain.

Hargrove had watched in stunned horror, and without touching the stricken man's pulse, he knew Hastings was dead. Perhaps Courtland had only meant to defend himself against the attack and hadn't really meant to kill him, but Hargrove doubted it. He knew what kind of a man Aaron Courtland was, and he also knew that without Reginald Hastings, he was of no further use. Glancing a second time at the unmoving body on the floor, then at the unconscious woman, Hargrove lunged, certain his fate was in his own hands now.

Courtland expected Hargrove to make a stand. He actually wanted him to try something . . . anything that would give Courtland the excuse he needed. Flipping the empty gun in the air, he caught it by the barrel and brought it around just as Hargrove reached him, striking the butt of it against Hargrove's temple and plummeting him to floor in an unconscious heap.

"Now, why do you suppose you were never promoted beyond assistant commissioner, Hargrove, old boy?" Courtland jeered, a faint smile curling his mouth. "Do you suppose it was because you weren't smart enough to be anything *but* an assistant?"

He snorted derisively and turned to toss his empty gun in the box of papers and books Hastings had been collecting. He knew it was time for him to move on and that he could always find another chemist to finish the work, but he wasn't leaving without the research notes the man had accumulated. He'd also need a diversion that would keep T.J. and his friend busy while he returned home for his mother and any valuables he had time to pack.

Glancing around the room, he spotted a bottle of pure grain alcohol sitting on one of the tables, and he smiled as he hurriedly set about pouring the flammable liquid across the floor and on every piece of furniture. At the doorway with the box tucked under one arm, he studied the scene he had created for one long moment, before he struck a match and threw it down. A wall of fire exploded almost immediately, driving him backward. He hesitated a second longer, then turned and fled down the stairs.

The throbbing ache in Catherine's head grew more intense as she was roused into a semiconscious state by the thick smoke filling her nostrils. She coughed and rolled onto her stomach, bemusedly thinking that she could avoid inhaling it by burying her face in the crook of her elbow. It didn't help, and a moment later she came fully awake with the sudden memory of what had happened and the conclusion that Aaron Courtland intended she die in the fire he had obviously started.

Realizing she had only seconds to escape before the building collapsed around her, she began to crawl on her hands and knees toward the staircase, but a rush of hot, red flames cut her off. Jerking back, she raised a hand to shield her face while she looked for a second exit and spotted what she thought was a window. Dragging herself toward it and trying not to breath any more often than necessary, she had covered half the distance when she came upon a dark shape lying on the floor in front of her. She didn't allow herself the time to wonder who it was or why he had been left behind. Instead, she gave him a hard shake.

"Wake up!" she shouted. "We've got to get out of here!"

The man moaned, then coughed, and Catherine grabbed his arm, pulling him up.

"Where's Hastings?" she yelled above the roar of the fire, certain that Courtland had deserted them all once she saw the blood streaming down Hargrove's face.

"He's dead!" Ferris advised, struggling to rise. "Don't worry about him. Can we make it to the stairs?"

"No," she answered, holding him down. "Stay low. There's less smoke closer to the floor." She pointed to the window. "We'll have to climb out through there."

"But we're two stories up," Hargrove complained.

"I'd rather break a leg than die in here," she shouted, crawling past him.

The window was locked, and rather than waste any time trying to rectify the problem, Catherine reached for the microscope she saw lying on the floor beside her. Turning her face away, she swung the instrument above her head and shattered the glass, cringing when tiny shards rained down upon her. Her head still throbbed, and Hargrove appeared to be in as much agony as she was, but the heat of the fire urged them both onward. Pulling herself up to her feet, she peered outside.

"We're in luck," she called back over her shoulder. "There's a ledge under the window. We can crawl along it to a tree."

Without waiting for Hargrove's comment or approval, Catherine hiked herself up on the sill, swung her legs over it and stretched until her toes touched the six-inch shelf below. The instant she was safely outside, she sucked in a long breath of fresh air, coughed, then drew another breath. A moment or two later, Hargrove was standing beside her and together, with their backs pressed against the wall for balance, they crept along the ledge toward the huge oak tree only a few feet away.

"We're going to have to jump to reach it," Catherine informed her companion once she'd analyzed the situation. "Do you have the strength?"

"Do I have a choice?" he shouted back at her when an inferno of flames shot out the window.

For only a moment Catherine thought of T.J. and how very much she wanted him to hold her in his arms again, before she took a deep breath, steeled herself, and lunged. The thick branch swayed, creaked, then bent downward with her sudden weight clinging to it, and she held on with all her might, her eyes closed, and a fear she would slip tightening her fingers around the rough bark.

"Let go!" she heard someone call to her. "I'll catch you."

Catherine wondered if it was her imagination or if she had really heard T.J.'s voice, and she screamed his name.

"Yes, Catherine, it's me," he shouted back. "I'm here below you. Let go. I'll catch you."

As the branch swung downward again, she opened her eyes to look and saw her husband standing there with his arms outstretched. She waited one more full sway of the limb, then at its lowest point, she loosened her grip and fell. He caught her only an instant later, and together they tumbled to the ground unhurt.

"Oh, T.J., T.J." She sobbed against his shoulder as he pulled her across his lap and hugged her close. "I thought I'd never see you again. I thought I would never be able to apologize for not believing in you. Oh, T.J., I'm so sorry. Say you forgive me."

"Hush, Catherine," he soothed, stroking her hair. "It's over now. We'll never be separated again."

Giving way to all her grief and fears, Catherine wept, while her husband gently rocked her in his arms and Lewis and the group of men who had accompanied him helped Ferris Hargrove from the ledge of the burning building.

"I'd like to believe you were trying to rescue Mrs. Savage," Lewis charged, glaring at Hargrove as the man coughed and wheezed and trembled with fright, "but somehow I don't think so. Would you care to explain before I have your carcass hauled off to jail?"

In a halting voice, Hargrove managed to tell only a limited version of what had happened, that Aaron Courtland had been the mastermind behind it all, and that Courtland had killed Professor Chase, had Valdemar eliminated, and that by setting the warehouse on fire, he had hoped to silence those few who knew the whole story. Once he'd finished, he looked at Catherine and begged her forgiveness, claiming that it had never been his intention for anyone to get killed.

"Is this true, Catherine?" T.J. asked, not quite able to believe that his childhood friend had actually tried to kill her.

Gathering her composure, she nodded.

"Where is he now?" T.J. demanded.

"I don't know, T.J.," she replied, "but I would guess he's

collecting all he can carry and heading out of the city as quickly as he can go."

Rising, T.J. pulled her to her feet and motioned for Lewis to take her. "He can't run fast enough," T.J. snarled. "Or far enough to outrun me. He couldn't as a boy, and he certainly won't be able to now."

"Damn it, Mother, don't argue!" Courtland exploded as he stood behind his desk shoving papers into a satchel. "Just grab whatever's important to you and be ready to leave in five minutes."

"Not until I've had an explanation," the red-haired, hot-tempered woman demanded. "I've suspected all these years that you haven't been totally honest with me about how you acquired the money it takes to own a house like this, and from the look of things right now, I'd say my suspicions were right. You're running from someone. Who, Arnie? Who's after you?"

"Does it matter?" he barked, clutching the leather bag against his chest as he rounded the desk, came forward, and roughly took her elbow to usher her out into the hall.

"Yes, it matters!" she snapped, jerking free of his hold. "It matters because you're planning to drag me down into whatever mess you've gotten yourself into. I love you, Arnie, but I won't be a part—"

The explosive crack of the front door being swung open and slamming back against the wall cut their discussion short. Startled, both mother and son turned in that direction, but while Edith frowned at the angry young man standing haloed in the entryway, Aaron spun on his heels and raced off through the house, planning to make his exit out a back door.

"What the hell is going on?" Edith shrieked, nearly knocked off her feet as T.J. stormed past her. When neither her son nor T.J. would answer her, she lowered her chin, squinted her eyes, and chased after the two.

Courtland had enough of a head start that by the time T.J. had rushed through the open French doors in the dining room and out onto the spacious veranda circling around the back of the house, Courtland was down the steps and heading toward the stable. But in order to reach the horse barn, he had to run parallel with the porch railing, a mistake he didn't realize until he saw T.J. from out of the corner of his eye.

Timing it perfectly, T.J. sprinted across the porch, jumped onto the railing, then hurled himself through the air at just the precise moment his foe was passing by. With his arms widespread, he caught Courtland around the chest and crashed with him to the ground. They rolled, then broke apart as the satchel Courtland had been carrying flew up in the air, opened, and sent the contents floating all around in a shower of white parchment. Scrambling to his feet a second before T.J., Courtland bolted off again, only to come to an abrupt halt when T.J. entrapped the man's ankles and tumbled him to the ground. A fist slammed against Courtland's rib cage, one to his jaw, and another to the midsection, all equally painful and disarming as his opponent straddled his lower torso and grabbed his shirt-front to continue the attack. He heard the bones in his cheek crack and blood squirted from his nose while tiny silver stars dotted his vision. Still the unrelenting assault increased. Teetering on the brink of unconsciousness, Courtland tried to shield his face with his arms, certain one more blow would kill him. Then suddenly he heard the angelic voice of a woman begging for mercy.

"T.J., please!" she called. "Let the courts deal with him. Don't *you* be his judge and executioner."

T.J. heard the voice too, but it took a while longer for the words to penetrate his rage. When finally he succumbed to her wishes and dropped Courtland to the ground, he rolled onto one hip and laid his arm across a bent knee while he caught his breath and let his temper cool, his angry eyes staring at the cowering form of his childhood friend. Suddenly Catherine was kneeling beside him, and when he looked at her, he saw the tears streaming down her face, and he smiled.

EPILOGUE

The trial of Aaron Courtland ended as everyone thought it would. He was found guilty of theft, kidnapping, attempted murder, conspiracy to commit murder, and four counts of first-degree murder. Several witnesses had been called to the stand, including Catherine and T.J., but it was Ferris Hargrove's testimony that had sealed Courtland's fate, and no one had been surprised by what they heard.

It had all begun six months earlier, Hargrove had confessed, when Aaron Courtland needed to cut corners on the expenses incurred by his gold mine in Mexico, and he had hired a chemist named Gustaf Valdemar to come up with a cheaper form of dynamite. The chemist had told Courtland that he knew of a man, Catherine's father, who was experimenting with nitroglycerin and that he would contact the professor with an offer to buy the formula. But the professor had refused. Hastings, Hargrove's half-brother, had accidentally learned about the proposal when he intercepted one of Valdemar's letters to Professor Chase, and thinking he could finally get out from under the shadow of his mentor by stealing the professor's notes, Hastings wrote to Valdemar offering a deal. But it hadn't been that easy. Chase had caught Hastings rifling through his papers, and because he guessed what it was Hastings was planning, Chase fired him and told him never to come back to the university.

Hargrove further testified that after corresponding with

the chemist, Courtland decided to talk with Professor Chase personally, stating that when he still refused to sell out and Courtland threatened him, Chase became angry. They fought, and as a result of the scuffle, Chase was killed. To cover up the crime and because he blamed Reginald for the mess, Courtland forced the weak-willed assistant to blow up the laboratory with the professor's body in it. That's when Hargrove got involved.

Full of guilt over what had happened, Reginald had gone to his half-brother to confess to everything. But Hargrove, seeing a perfect opportunity for both of them to make a great deal of money—first by selling the formula, if Reginald could finish the experiment on his own, then by blackmailing Courtland once everything was finished—bade his half-brother to keep silent. Reluctantly agreeing, Reginald had accompanied Hargrove to the university where they helped themselves to the professor's notes before the CID could make an investigation.

Everything had gone along quite nicely after that until T. J. Savage had somehow gotten involved and planned a trip to Paris to confront Gustaf Valdemar. Left with no other alternative, Courtland hired a man to kill the chemist before Savage had the chance to talk to him. From there things started to fall apart, and in a panic, Courtland tried to frame Savage for the museum burglary just to get him out of the way. Then Miss Chase stepped in and Courtland knew he was about to get caught. Thinking to give himself enough time to flee the country, he set fire to the warehouse with Miss Chase, Reginald Hastings, and Hargrove inside.

Every person in the courtroom, including the judge, had been appalled to hear just how coldhearted Aaron Courtland was and to what extreme he would go for the sake of wealth. Only T.J. understood. Being the son of a prostitute with no father around to care for him, Aaron had had to fight off not only the pangs of hunger, but the insults as well. He'd gotten it in his head that by being rich he could change how people looked at him. And that was all Aaron cared about. Honor, pride, love all took second place to respect. But what Aaron never realized was that his new set of friends didn't respect him. All they wanted was to share in his wealth any way they could.

"You're thinking about Aaron, aren't you?" Catherine asked, as she stood beside her husband at the railing of the *Friendship* while the huge ship drifted out to sea.

T.J. exhaled a long sigh. "Yes. And I'm not sure if I should hate him or just feel sorry for him. He caused so much pain because of his greed." He frowned, then shook his head, falling silent again.

"That's not what's really bothering you, is it?" she challenged, smiling softly at him when he looked her way. "You're trying to take some of the blame for what happened. You're standing there telling yourself that you should have second-guessed him. There's no way you could have done that, T.J. The Arnie you knew was a youngster with little-boy ideas. Aaron was a grown man, and one you hadn't seen in twenty years. How could you have possibly known what was going on inside his head?"

His dark eyes warmed and he turned to pull her into his arms. "How did you get to be so wise?" he teased.

Catherine shrugged. "By growing up in a man's world, I suppose. I never had time to think about the things a girl was supposed to think about."

"Well, I'm glad," he admitted, kissing the tip of her nose. "If you had, you'd have probably been married by the time we met and I would have had to steal you away from your husband."

"Oh?" She laughed. "Rather sure of yourself, aren't you?"

His brown eyes glowed. "Yes."

The squawk of a sea gull overhead turned their attention to its winged flight and the cloudless blue sky that stretched for as far as they could see. Snuggling close, Catherine laid her head against T.J.'s chest.

"Will Australia be as beautiful as this?" she asked.

"It will be once *you're* there," he complimented, grinning when he heard her laugh.

"Do you think it's a good place to raise a child?"

He shrugged. "I don't know. I guess you'll have to ask

Alexandra." The question seemed odd of a sudden, and he leaned back to look at her. "Why?"

A twinkle of devilment sparkled in her blue eyes. "Because ours should be born about the time we arrive, and I thought that if I liked Australia and you agreed, we could stay—"

T.J. grabbed her elbows and held her at arm's length. "What?"

A broad smile spread across her face. "I said that our baby should be born about the time we arrive."

Stunned and not quite sure he'd heard her correctly, his gaze dropped to her flat belly, then back to her face. "*Our* baby? You mean you're . . ."

"Yes, T.J.," she laughed. "I'm carrying your child. Does that please you?"

"Please me?" he echoed exuberantly, pulling her close. "More than you know, Catherine. More than you know."

The sea gull squawked again, and while they turned to watch it soar across the sky, Catherine thought she felt the presence of someone standing close by. Glancing to her left and finding no one there, she assumed she had been wrong until she suddenly realized that she had been thinking of her father.

He'll always be with you, Catherine, T.J. had told her. *All you have to do is think of him.*

A happy smile curved her mouth, knowing T.J. had been right.